Muse
Unexpected

V.C. Birlidis

www.crescentmoonpress.com

Muse Unexpected
V.C. Birlidis

ISBN: 978-1-939173-74-4
E-ISBN: 978-1-939173-75-1

Cover Art: Taria Reed
Editor: Kerri Nelson
Layout/Typesetting: jimandzetta.com

Crescent Moon Press
1385 Highway 35
Box 269
Middletown, NJ 07748

Crescent Moon Press electronic publication/print publication: January 2014 www.crescentmoonpress.com quotations embodied in critical articles and reviews.

Dedication

For Mom, Nanny and Joel
You proved a life of laughter is a life well
lived

Chapter 1

Chios, Greece — 1950

Georgia sucked in a deep breath as she felt the nail of her right index finger tear.

"Ow. Ow. Ow." She pulled herself across the edge of the cliff, got to her feet and stuck the throbbing finger in her mouth, attempting to somehow lessen the pain. The nail was barely held in place by her cuticle and after a quick examination she used her teeth to tear it away and then spat it out.

"Damn it." She popped the finger back in her mouth.

A wave of physical exhaustion threatened to make her double over in dry heaves, but Georgia smiled, both relieved and surprised she had made it. She stood on the edge of the cliff looking at the starting point of her journey—the valley down below and its tiny cluster of houses. As a moment of contentment filled her mind, her left foot slipped over the edge and she stumbled backward. She steadied herself, closed her eyes and took several deep, calming breaths, trying to ignore the throbbing of the cuts and scrapes she had earned on her journey. The skirt of her favorite yellow sundress was filthy and torn. Her mother would be furious at her for ruining her only decent Sunday dress, but she pushed the thought out of her mind and grabbed for the bag slung over her shoulder.

"It's still there." She patted it closer to her hip. *So much depends on this bag.*

She swallowed the lump in her throat, afraid to turn around; afraid of being disappointed; afraid she'd risked everything just to find out she'd been a fool. She knew she was meant to take this journey. She had the chance to change her life, and she wasn't about to turn back. She would scream

~ ☾ ~

to hell with her mother, to hell with the beatings and screams of "no" "you can't" or "know your place". She would seize what was hers and once she had it, no one would ever take it away.

Georgia began humming the latest Billie Holiday song, "God Bless The Child". It reminded her of her beloved Yiayia and the countless afternoons they'd spent together. Remembering her Yiayia always made her feel better, stronger and more confident. Always dressed in the same heavy black polyester dress, Yiayia's deeply lined face would light up whenever she saw Georgia, and once they were both sure Georgia's mother wasn't around, Yiayia would pull out the old leather book she hid under her bed and tell Georgia of the endless stories of their long, amazing and magical family history and the greatness for which she was destined.

She stopped humming and turned around. She had always pictured the temple on the top of the mountain as being untouched by the elements, as if it could avoid the relentless winds and the brutal Chios winters full of massive downpours that whipped around with such force that they were sometimes mistaken for hail.

But now she realized this was just a fantasy. Her history books and numerous trips to Athens did not prepare her for the size of the structure in front of her. It was massive, with countless Ionic columns, each at least twenty-five feet thick and tall enough to make estimating their height impossible. The main temple was flanked by several connected chambers with their own separate entrances, each a smaller version of the temple itself. The exterior walls were made of what appeared to be stone of varying sizes and textures, but the wind, rain and salt air had eaten away at the façade, making it look like coral. It was hard to see where one stone ended and another began. Many gnarled mastic trees had sprouted alongside the temple, uprooting some of the foundation's massive stones. Major cracks worked their way up the walls, like a system of veins pumping life into its stone body.

Georgia scurried forward, entering what appeared to have been a courtyard at one time. The remains of several long marble benches were scattered throughout the area, almost completely hidden in the tangle of vines and grass. There

~ ☾ ~

were also countless statues with eroded and stained bodies. As she walked past the statues, she stopped for a moment. While she was certain she was alone, the journey to the remote, virtually unknown ruin being too difficult for most, she was sure she heard voices. Barely whispers, but they were there, floating in and out on the wind.

Don't look back, you idiot. Ignore it.

She glanced over her shoulder as a sudden gust of wind made the vines on the statues sway, unnerving her enough to make her turn and run blindly toward the temple's entrance. Her foot caught on a hidden root and she tripped, sending her flying into the portico, slamming into a set of massive iron doors. The impact created a cloud of dust and rust flakes, and one of the doors swung open with a horrible screech that echoed throughout the structure.

"Could this get any worse?" She lay there with her face on the cold, filthy floor, coughed and spit out a few rust flakes and a small bug. She slapped the floor, hard, and stood up. "Whoever is in charge of housekeeping needs to be fired." She glanced back at the door she came through. Something moved, just out of her line of vision, and she shivered and walked forward.

Her eyes took a moment to get used to the temple's pitch-black interior. It reminded her of so many Greek Orthodox cathedrals she had attended services in. She walked in-between two massive white columns and found herself in the center of the temple. Several birds, startled by her presence, took flight and flew out through the nonexistent roof. Appearing to be somewhat interested in her, a single white dove flew into a nook between pieces of rotten roof timbers.

She was a bit unnerved by the stillness attacking her confidence. She set down her bag, pulled out a large book, several tightly wrapped packages, a large flashlight and a lighter. Above, the dove cooed from its perch, flapping its wings before nestling deeper into its nook.

Her flashlight beam sliced through the dark, revealing the profile of a white statue. A burst of adrenaline surged into her heart.

It's not one of the rotting statues from the courtyard. Calm down.

~ ☾ ~

The statue was in perfect condition, the only exception being the jasmine vines and tree roots covering its base. It depicted a beautiful woman holding a grapevine. The vine entwined itself around her, all the way up to the woman's head. A golden crown glistened with several large, roughly cut stones embedded in it. Georgia cast her beam of light around the chamber, revealing other statues, all in different poses, holding different objects. Her Yiayia had been right all along. This temple had been created to worship the Muses, the nine daughters of the King of the Greek gods, Zeus. She was exactly where she needed to be.

She rushed back to her pile of items and picked up the large book, fumbling with its pages. Finding what she was looking for, she placed the book on the ground, angling the flashlight so she could read the text. She reviewed the diagram of the interior of the temple and thought she must have selected the wrong page because it was different from what she remembered reading earlier. Instead of being a diagram of the temple as it appeared during ancient times, the diagram now illustrated the temple as it appeared to her now, including the depiction of a girl holding a book in one hand and something she couldn't make out in the other. Georgia reminded herself, regardless of whether or not the map had changed, there was some sort of hidden trigger she needed to find.

She knelt and pushed on the tiles around her, but the floor felt solid. She stood up again and began biting her thumbnail, closing her eyes to think. She guessed the mosaic pattern was confusing her and assumed it was created to do just that. Forgoing her sense of sight, she knelt and ran her fingers across the tiles again. Finding nothing, she changed her tactics.

"If the tile won't give the secret away, maybe the filthy, disgusting grout will," she muttered, as she followed the rough pattern outlining the mosaic pieces. She winced as her fingers touched the centuries of filth. Directly underneath the spot where she stood, she felt a slight difference in the grout's texture. She pushed on it and the tile seemed to give a little, so she pushed harder. The tile popped up, held in place by a metal rod. She twisted it. The first turn brought nothing. The

~ ☾ ~

second and third caused the temple floor to shudder for a few
seconds. With a trembling hand she twisted the tile a fourth
time and braced herself. The pressure of her pounding heart
filled her ears. The dove cooed from above.

As she was beginning to calm, the temple floor shook
with such force she was sure the building was falling off of
its foundation and would slide off of the cliff. The room
filled with overwhelming sounds of crunching and growth.
The roots below the floor strained against their marble
prison, sending mosaic tiles, soil and rock shooting into the
air. Georgia fell backwards and covered her head against
the falling debris. Something squirmed across her foot and
she yelped, turning over to discover the tree roots and
jasmine vines crawling across the floors and engulfing the
columns they had been strangling for centuries. Enormous
trees grew and expanded, shattering what remained of the
roof.

Among the churned up roots and soil appeared a large
round formation of pure white marble, the raw stones
creating a circle around where Georgia crouched. Several
deeper roots grew, fusing together and growing leaves out of
the tips of their tendrils. A large slab of marble forced into the
air reached the end of its airborne journey and she scurried
back, expecting it to either crush her or slam into what she
assumed was a young mastic tree. The slab hit the tree with
such force she was sure it would shatter, but the roots caught
the stone and held it in place, forming a high altar.

The floor ceased shaking and she stood up, unsure what to
do next. The dove cooed above her and she scrambled to
gather her items, placing them on the newly formed altar. She
took a deep breath and reopened the book to the temple
diagram. Like before, the diagram of the room had changed
and she took a moment to glance around her new
surroundings. It was surreal, a fairyland, the trees creating a
natural canopy of branches and leaves, and the jasmine vines
covering the columns with their fragrant flowers. The statues
of the Muses remained unchanged, although the roots
surrounding their bases seemed thicker, as if they were
straining to keep the statues from flying away.

She opened the packages she'd brought. One contained a

~ ☾ ~

bundle of white sage, Greek oregano, lavender and aged cedar, which she placed on the altar to her left, along with a small lighter. With great care, she unwrapped the next package, which contained three pounds of raw sea salt. The next set of packages had nine candles, and after referring to the diagram, she placed them onto the marble slab.

Although she tried to, she couldn't shake the feeling she was being watched as she worked, and when the breeze gently working its way through the trees suddenly stopped, a chill ran down her spine. She wiped the sweat out of her eyes and decided it was time to act. Below the diagram was some handwritten text titled *The Awakening Invocation*. She read the spell she had been practicing for the past several weeks and feeling sure she had it correct, she chanted in ancient Greek.

"Oh, sweet inspirations, in eternal sleep,
I, the soul unworthy, call you from your keep,
Remove thy self to bestow Zeus' power
And deliver my birthright this golden hour
For what was stolen, be now restored
Or else feel my sorrow, forever more."

Several sparks of lights crackled and then extinguished themselves in the ancient rusted torches dangling from the stone walls. Both exterior iron doors slammed into the vestibule walls. She jumped, nearly dropping the book, as they banged open again and again with such force their rusted hinges snapped and the doors flew into the main worship space. Wincing, as the echoes off the temple's walls made her ears ring, she picked up the bunch of herbs and flicked the lighter open.

Click. Click. Click. "Shoot. After years of lighting Yiayia's nasty cigars, now you decide not to work." She shook the lighter, hoping it would help the flint to catch. Click. Click. Click.

The lighter sparked, producing a large flame and she lit the bundle of herbs. She breathed in the fragrant smoke and threw the smoking bouquet into the round tiled pit in front of the altar. The sense of being watched was almost suffocating

~ ☾ ~

and she glanced around the room. She saw nothing, but right as she was about to push the thought out of her mind she heard a low guttural growl. She fought every ounce of her instinct to turn around and began chanting again.

"Oh, sweet inspirations, in eternal sleep,
I, the soul unworthy, call you from your keep,
Remove thyself to bestow Zeus' power—"

The torches sputtered again, but remained dark. The deep growl came again, except it was louder now and coming from several places in the room. She continued her chanting and did her best to speak in clear and even tones.

"And deliver my birthright this golden hour
For what was stolen, be now restored
Or else feel my sorrow, forever more."

She whimpered, her hands shaking as she noticed the room becoming even darker, the remaining light coming from the candles and the burning herbs.

Georgia raised her eyes. Crouched in a large tree was one of the courtyard statues, except it was far from motionless. The thing glared at her, its mouth open in a silent scream. It moved from left to right and then stood on its perch. It leapt into the air and slammed onto the floor with such force the root-covered tiles shattered beneath it. It paused for a second and then moved toward her.

Frightened, she turned her head away and came face-to-face with an equally frightening statue, inches away from her, its face caught in the same silent scream. Spinning, she tried to find an escape route, but she was surrounded by numerous other courtyard statues either working their way towards her or jumping from higher points in the temple, their impact shaking the floor beneath her. Black, shiny, lifeless eyes stared at her with rage, their moss-covered mouths dripping with a rust-colored slime as the creatures gnashed their jagged teeth.

She froze, unable to take her eyes off them as they paced back and forth in front of her.

~ ☾ ~

"Guardians," she whispered. She had read something about them, but in her panic she couldn't recall –

Suddenly, she remembered something. Careful not to move too quickly, she reached over and grabbed a handful of salt and threw it at the creatures. They roared in pain, the salt sizzling on their skin, creating seeping wounds. After checking the book again, she saw a figure holding a round object, with light coming from the center of it. The guardians were also added to the drawing, appearing to crouch in fear and pain. Georgia grabbed the final package from the altar. She ripped off the wrapping and in her hand she gripped the only piece of jewelry Yiayia owned. It was a gold brooch, with a red stone. Its gold and jeweled surface shimmered in the candlelight.

One of the creatures caught a glimpse of the brooch and rushed at her. As it reached the stone circle, the statue's eroded face smacked against an invisible force and it crashed to the floor howling. This angered the others and they all rushed forward, but they encountered the same invisible wall. Ignoring their attempts, she searched the book for help. The book had once again changed, except now every ancient page was completely blank. Disgusted, she threw it down.

"The answer has to be obvious," she said. "Yiayia wouldn't have done this to me. She wouldn't send me on this journey to fail."

The guardians reacted violently to the brooch. Maybe it could help keep them away or help me read the book.

Georgia held it in front of her, making sure to catch the firelight and as she predicted, pinpoints of light shone around the room. The guardians screamed in pain, as the light caressed their rocky flesh.

This can't be it.

The guardians had moved towards the opposite end of the chamber for protection, but she knew it was just a matter of time before they would regain their confidence, and she didn't know how long the salt or the candles would last. She flipped through the still-blank book, testing the brooch's prism effect in case it might uncover the now hidden text, but nothing she tried seemed to work.

Tears welled in her eyes as she realized she had lost

~ ☾ ~

complete control of the situation. She closed the book and hugged it close to her heart.

"Please, Yiayia. Help me. Tell me what I need to do."

A breeze rustled through the trees and the scent of wild jasmine surrounded her. A single name burned its way through her confusion.

Athena. The goddess' name produced a spark in her mind, which blossomed into fireworks as all of the stories Yiayia had ever told her came flooding back.

"Athena, I beg you, help me. I know I'm not worthy to call you from the heavens. Athena, please grant me an audience. *Please*, Athena."

The guardians surrounded her on all sides; their grotesque mouths open as the rust-colored slime oozed down their torsos and dripped onto the floors, sizzling on impact. One legless guardian scraped its body toward the edge of the circle, its eyes in line with Georgia's and its once slackened mouth now even more grotesque as it grinned horribly back at her.

"Death, little one," it said with a gravelly, rock scraping against rock voice. It spoke in a strange dialect of Greek Georgia could follow with some difficulty.

"We shall tear you apart, piece by piece, and feed on you while you scream for mercy."

Without thinking, she grabbed another handful of salt and flung it at the talking statue.

"Oh, shut up," she shouted.

The guardian laughed, in spite of the sizzling sores the salt caused. It crawled closer, careful to avoid the circle of stones, then leaned in so the moss-ichor dripping from its wounds seeped onto them. The slime sparked and bit-by-bit ate away at the marble.

In frustration, she threw the remaining salt into its face and the guardian reeled back and fell over screaming.

"Athena, I call to you." She raised her arms upward. "I beg you to come to my aid."

She scrambled onto the altar, unhooked the brooch's sharp pin and, taking a deep breath, jammed it into her palm and scraped it toward her wrist.

"Athena, I give you my pain, my blood, even the most

~ ☾ ~

precious object I have, as an offering to you." She threw the brooch into the fire and raised her head towards the heavens. "Please Athena, hear my call. Come to me, now."

Georgia could feel the tears collect in the corners of her eyes. She blinked hard, attempting to keep them deep inside, but she was losing faith. One of the guardians kicked away a marble stone, breaching the protective circle and she waited for what she knew would be a painful death. Looking towards the heavens and kneeling down on the altar, she let her arms drop to her sides, with her palms facing forward. Following her mother's example, she began reciting the Lord's Prayer, over and over again.

As her voice echoed off the walls, she saw the white dove that had been watching her from its roost, take flight. It soared into the air, its body taking on a silvery tone and glowing with a shimmering light. The guardians froze. The bird circled the room twice and then made a spiraling dive as it grew in size. Within seconds, it was twice as tall as even the largest guardian; with a wing span double its height. The glow from the dove's feathered body filled the chamber and the guardians bowed down, moaning and screaming in frustration.

Feathers morphed into flesh, talons melted into legs and the creature's shape took on a more human female form covered by a long tunic and plates of silver, feathery armor. As the being's feet touched the ground her wings folded behind her and melted away. The feathers around her face grew into a long mane of dark brown hair. Her head was crowned with a shining silver headpiece.

She pulled out a long sword with a large red jewel at the bottom of the hilt.

"Enough." The goddess shouted at the guardians, her voice making the very trees tremble at the sound of it. With one enormous thrust, she plunged her sword into the ground and a blast of light shot from it, sweeping over Georgia and beyond the altar. It washed over the guardians, who moaned and shuddered as cracks formed on their exterior shell. The guardians began to glow and there was a moment of deadening silence before they exploded, sending shards of stone in every direction.

~ ☾ ~

Georgia cowered and covered her head, but when she didn't feel the impact or any pain, she opened her eyes. The room was filled with flower petals, floating in all directions, reminding her of the military parades she had once seen as a child. There was no trace of the guardians.

She faced the goddess, falling to her knees in gratitude. The goddess walked closer.

"Child," Athena began, with a calm and gentle tone. "Why have you summoned me? This modern world has lost its way and I grow weary of seeing its destruction by the hand of man caused by his hunger for war."

"Forgive me, wise goddess. Forgive a believer, who is not worthy," Georgia replied.

"Do not be coy with me child. I am no fool. You have taken a journey, fraught with risk. You summoned the guardians of this temple, which is a great feat of magic for someone who knows nothing of such things. I do not know what you are, but I can say with great certainty, you are not unworthy. I see your thoughts as clear as if they were my own. You come here for what was once yours, but was taken away. A birthright."

"Yes, Athena," Georgia began. "For as long as I can remember, I have been told of our family's history. I am told we are descendants of the Muses themselves and I have—"

"You are not the first to beseech me with such claims of glory," Athena interrupted, examining Georgia. "Why should I believe you, above all of the many who have claimed similar birthrights? Do you dare to believe you are any different from those who are more worthy?"

Knowing her time was limited, Georgia paused, wracking her brain for the right response. She knew Athena was known for her compassion, but she also knew even the compassionate Athena could be temperamental. She reached down and picked up Yiayia's book.

"In here is our family history," Georgia said, looking down at the restored pages of her book, which were now filled with the recently missing text and drawings.

Athena interrupted with a dismissive motion of her hand, tearing the book from Georgia's grip and sending it skidding across the temple floor.

"I know this book. It is full of mere words written on a

~ ☾ ~

page. Stories told to a grandchild do not a birthright make.
Careful, child, I have damned others for doing much less than
wasting my time with fairytales. I once blinded a man, who by
accident glanced at me while I bathed in a hidden lake."

Georgia's cheeks burned with embarrassment and tears
swelled in her eyes.

Athena stepped closer and took Georgia's bleeding hand
into her own. A tingling warmth washed over Georgia's
wounded hand and she lifted it and watched the wound close
up and heal.

"Thank you, Athena. I am who I claim to be, a descendent
of the—" Georgia began again.

The room darkened. "Do not waste my time, girl," the
goddess spoke the words through a hiss. "Although no
temples are built in my honor anymore, I am even more
significant and powerful today than ever."

Georgia searched the goddess' face, trying to understand
what Athena wanted, but then her gaze shifted toward what
remained of her smoldering herb bundle with the brooch in
the middle. Georgia reached for it, surprised to find it cold to
the touch. An idea shot through her mind, something Yiayia
had said to her about an answer to a question being found in
the question itself. She humbly placed the pin on the ground
in front of the goddess.

"You know I speak the truth," Georgia said and Athena
glared in response. The room darkened further.

"Forgive me," Georgia began. "You are wisest among the
gods. You said you have continued to receive the prayers of
others. That many have called upon you with similar claims
of birthrights linking them to the gods."

Athena's manner softened. "Yes, they call to me, begging
for help. These voices, throughout centuries, beseech me to
deliver them from their misery and unto the heavens. I even
hear those who walk in the Valley of the Shades."

Georgia looked into Athena's eyes. They were like dark
chocolate vats, flickering with flecks of starlight. Keeping her
voice steady and unemotional, she said, "I was once told that
sometimes the answers I seek can be found in the questions I
ask. I ask you, Athena, why me? Out of the thousands you
hear, why answer my call?"

~ ☾ ~

If I weren't speaking the truth, Georgia thought, *how would a goddess know of Yiayia's book? A book handed down for generations to be kept safe. A book containing magic so strong its pages change at will. Athena had to know it was the book giving me directions and spells to take on this journey.*

"I was meant to do this," Georgia continued. "And if I was meant to do this, clearly directed to do it by the gods, then how can you deny me?"

Although the goddess remained still, the room lightened and Georgia continued, "Restore what is rightfully mine. For too long I have wandered with a veil covering my eyes and I beg to have it removed. Forgive me for saying this, but the answer to your question is found in the mere fact that you stand before me, asking it."

Athena reached down and picked up Georgia's brooch. It seemed tiny in the goddess' hand, but glowed brightly, and Athena smiled.

"Clever girl. You are a very clever girl." With one blurred motion, Athena reached behind her and removed the sword from where it stood and threw the brooch into the air. As it fell back toward her, she swung her sword, shattering it, the sparkling pieces shooting all over the room.

Georgia stopped herself from protesting the destruction of Yiayia's broach as she noticed the roots gripping the Muses' statues begin to unfurl and retract. Athena walked to the closest statue and struck it at its base with her sword. The resulting crack worked its way to the top of the statue; the marble façade shattered and a woman in a flowing white gown flew out of the debris. The Muse surged into the air, arching her back and stretching her arms as if she had just woken from a nap. She fell backward at a ferocious speed, stopping a few inches from the ground, and placed her feet gently on the floor.

One by one, Muses emerged from their sleep, shattering their marble prisons and soaring into the air as if they had been shot out of a cannon, the space above Athena and Georgia looking like the billowing sails of an armada as each Muse joined the group gathering behind the goddess. Yiayia's jeweled pin reappeared with a crack of lightning and clattered

~ ☾ ~

into the tiled pit. Georgia rushed to retrieve it, holding it close to her heart.

Athena turned her back on Georgia and spoke with her fellow Olympians. The old book, which had been forgotten, shook violently and slid across the floor, stopping at Georgia's feet. It slammed itself open, hitting the ground with a loud thud and Georgia glanced down to see the words and diagrams begin to melt and swim on the page. The ink raised itself off the page, collecting into a large pool mid-air. It surged towards Georgia and she gasped as it took the form of a woman, wearing a heavy black gown and a long, flowing black veil. Both the gown and veil appeared to have no end. The stranger did not acknowledge either Georgia or the goddesses, but walked toward the tiled pit, where she chanted, swaying side to side, raising her arms towards the heavens. The room grew brighter and Athena and the Muses ceased their conversation to watch with apparent anticipation. One of the Muses whispered the name "Aletheria" and another murmured "the Oracle." Georgia wondered where she had heard those names before.

Aletheria made a horizontal movement with her hand and the ashes and remaining debris in the pit flew across the room and rested at the base of a column. She threw into the pit several pieces of what appeared to be small rocks and the pieces rose from the floor, assembling midair in the pattern in which they had landed. Georgia crossed herself, fearing the woman might be evil. But then she remembered Aletheria was an Oracle, a powerful witch, someone Yiayia's oldest stories had mentioned – a magic rooted in her own family tree.

But that was centuries ago. Aletheria, how could you possibly be here? I guess anything is possible in this temple.

Aletheria spoke, her English heavily accented, her voice deep and threatening.

"How dare you. How dare you begin this journey. You have drawn me back to my former prison. For what? To witness your foolish actions that could lead to the destruction of this world? You have disturbed and defiled this temple and awakened Athena and The Nine Daughters of Zeus by breaking through the veil separating the Olympians from this

~ ☾ ~

world. Do you know what risk you have taken? By calling them forth, you have risked setting others free. Others that were locked away for the sake of humankind."

Georgia stood seething, her face flushed with heat.

"You have corrupted the thread the Fates had for you, and now you have two paths to select from. This path is a curse never meant for my descendants. It will lead to great peril for your soul. There are others meant to carry this burden, and yet you come rushing forward to embrace it. My foolish child, my dearest foolish child, do you understand what you are asking from these Olympians?"

Georgia walked a little closer to Aletheria. "Yes, I do," she said.

The woman pointed at the girl, which sent the masonry pieces flying towards her. They hung in the air inches away. Georgia could see the pieces were polished stone etched with ancient Greek letters. As Aletheria walked toward Georgia, they orbited around the girl.

Aletheria opened her hand and the tiles stopped and fell into her palm. The Oracle glanced at them and shook her head, "Do you not see Athena is using you to enforce her will onto this world? Her actions are as selfish as your own. You see this choice, this path as a way to escape to something better. But it also is much more dangerous than your young mind can comprehend. You *must* understand. You must have the clarity to see this decision will change your life and the lives of your descendants."

Aletheria bent her head towards Georgia and let out an exasperated sigh. Again she threw the stones into the air to encircle Georgia. She repeated this seven times, faster and faster, until she pointed downward, making the stones fall to the ground in front of the girl.

"The casting stones do not lie. I see two choices. One choice is filled with happiness, love and family. It is a long and prosperous life." Aletheria crouched down to examine the tiles.

"I also see another choice, full of moments of incredible glory and excitement that are overshadowed by a journey filled with great sorrow, regret and risk. I look into your eyes and see the temptation and hunger growing inside of you.

~ ☾ ~

You will risk everything to satisfy this hunger for power and glory. Do not do this."

Georgia looked at Aletheria and shook her head. "I know who you are and I have heard your warnings, but no matter how powerful you are, I have free will and claim this as my destiny. Fate has placed me here. I will not be denied. Like so many others, you would have me grovel for whatever crumbs this miserable life would give to me. I refuse to live like my mother, made bitter by a husband who abandoned his family for another woman. I refuse to end my life as an old woman in a crumbling villa, in an old, black dress, with a face lined with many years of starvation and worry. You are a fool to think I would accept this, Aletheria. Now, go away."

Aletheria grabbed Georgia's arm, her touch strong and cold as her nails dug into Georgia's flesh.

"Georgia, you are damned by your own greed. One day, you will remember my warning and wish you had listened," the Oracle said, as the hand holding onto Georgia transformed into blacken ash. "Remember my words and understand that those you love will come to curse your name."

Horrified, Georgia tried to yank her arm free as she watched Aletheria's face collapsing into itself, exposing her skull underneath. The witch was disintegrating before her eyes. Georgia scrambled away from what remained of the Oracle.

The trees and jasmine vines swayed, as the room dimmed again. The nine women faced Georgia with hands joined, as a strong wind swept across the sanctuary. The wind gathered Aletheria's ashes and bones into the air and held the debris suspended, creating out of them a ceiling of dark clouds that cracked with lightning and thunder.

Georgia backed away as the nine women glided toward her, their gowns creating a billowing white cloud behind them. The storm grew stronger and lightning bolts struck throughout the room. Athena stood among them, smirked, then raised her arms and disappeared into an explosion of light.

The Muses, whose feet still did not touch the floor, surrounded Georgia. She was terrified. Some of the women

~ ☾ ~

chanted, others sang, as their voices joined into a single wall of sound. Their bodies floated around her.

"I'm ready," Georgia shouted above the roar of the wind.

The Muses circled faster and faster, seeming to merge into a single, blurry form. A Muse crowned with a wreath of grapevines broke away and moved closer.

In ancient Greek the Muse said, "Forgive me."

Before Georgia had time to ask what she needed to be forgiven for, the first of nine lightning bolts struck her.

~ ☾ ~

Chapter 2

Columbus, Ohio — Present Day

Callie could hear the buzz, buzz, buzz of her daughter's alarm clock through the bedroom wall. It had been going off for the past ten minutes. She assumed Sophie was too lazy to reach over and hit the snooze button.

Dear God. How does Sophie use that annoying alarm rhythm to lull herself back to sleep? Would it be too much to ask her to wake up and get ready for school without me having to pound on her door?

She sat up and glanced over at the temporary husband she'd made out of pillows.

"How I hate it when you travel," Callie mumbled to her pillow husband, as she climbed out of bed and ran fingers through her hair. It was time to shatter her daughter's dreams of another fifteen minutes of sleep.

She hoped the sound of her footsteps, the flip flop of her slippers muffled by the ancient gold shag carpeting, would serve as warning enough for Sophie.

"Sophie?"She knocked gently on the bedroom door. "It's time to get up, sweetie."

She leaned her sleepy head against the door.

"Honey, I don't hear you getting up."

Callie was more tired than she'd realized. Her Greek accent was heavier, a clear sign of exhaustion. She never slept well when Angelo was away.

Coffee. Momma needs her medicine. She heard Sophie groan and turn over in her bed.

"Turning over is not the kind of movement I'm talking about." She sighed.

Another game of morning chicken, Sophie? Lord, give me strength.

~ ☾ ~

"Sophia Maria! Up! Now!"

"I'm up. I'm practically out the door," Sophie shouted. The sound of a stuffed animal hitting the opposite side of the bedroom door was a clear sign Sophie was serious.

"That's better," Callie said, yawning again and making her way downstairs to the kitchen. As she began making her morning pot of Greek coffee, she thought of the argument she'd had last night with Sophie. On a scale of one to ten, the argument had been a fifteen. Sophie had managed to push the right buttons, which meant she was putting herself down—and that was something Callie couldn't tolerate. Hearing her daughter proclaim she was built like a stereotypical, heavy-set Greek waitress and then ask Callie if she wanted fries with her Gyro was enough to send her blood boiling. If only she could give Sophie a little push, a dash of inspiration, but using her powers wasn't allowed. *Wasn't inspiring others what Muses were expected to do?*

She wondered for the millionth time what the point was of possessing supernatural powers at her fingertips, if she wasn't able to use them.

But she knew the answer to her question. It was the deal she'd made. She was no longer a supernatural being in charge of inspiring mortals to reach their true potential and keeping them on the path Fate had meant them to be on. She had, in small quantities, used her powers, but not for herself or for Sophie. One of her talents was cooking and through her cooking she could change the course of a person's life. So when asked by the PTA to help raise funds through a silent auction, by offering to cook a meal for 10, not including the cost of food, she couldn't resist the opportunity. Sure, maybe she was showing off, but weren't the gods themselves guilty of letting their egos get the best of them? Sometimes she couldn't help it, and the $5,600 she'd raised purchased a lot of band uniforms. She was sure the ends justified the means. *A small, brief flicker surely couldn't attract anyone's attention.*

"Besides, a leopard never changes its spots, especially this leopard."

She heard Sophie walk into the kitchen and turned as the girl threw her things down into a vacant chair. Her daughter

~ ☾ ~

walked across the avocado and gold linoleum, opened the dark brown 1970's 'sun tan' refrigerator and pulled out the gallon of milk.

Pouring a cup of Greek coffee for herself, Callie grabbed the box of corn flakes and sat down next to Sophie.

"Your father will be back tonight. Plan on being home for dinner."

"Okay," Sophie replied, pouring milk over her cereal.

"Wow." She paused, mid-sip of her coffee. "No, 'do I have to?' No, 'but Bippy or Buffy is having a barbecue?' Not even a 'but it's a Friday, Mom.'"

"All right, I get it. Really subtle, Mom," Sophie said, stopping mid-bite and looking up. "There is a party, but I think I would prefer being home when Daddy gets here. This last trip has lasted way too long. I've missed him and, to be honest, I can't deal with the living hell you would make my life if I wasn't here."

Callie smiled, brushing off a few imaginary crumbs off the table. "And who says you can't teach a teenager new tricks? Well, I've missed him, too. I hate it when he travels. I can't protect..."

Sophie laughed. "Yeah, like your spaghetti sauce creates an impenetrable force field. Which is nothing compared to your exploding—"

"Stuffed grape leaves?" she said, throwing a napkin at Sophie.

She reached out to give her daughter's hand a squeeze, and Sophie slid her hand away.

Oops. Mustn't get too close to the teenager. Keep all hands and feet inside during the ride.

"Stop being a drama queen," Sophie said. "You make everything out to be some sort of Greek tragedy. Ohhhhhhhhh, the gods are angry at us. Booooooooooo."

Callie's smile dropped and Sophie winced.

"How many times must I tell you we don't joke about such things? Whether or not you believe in something doesn't mean it is open season on another person's belief systems. It isn't a smart thing to do, to mock Fate." She lifted her hand and pointed at her daughter. "The Fates..."

Sophie rolled her eyes. "Oh my, the Fates? The three old

~ ℂ ~

hags with one eye, stirring a caldron? Jesus, Mom, enough. Give it a rest. You're such a freak sometimes."

"That's *Clash of the Titans* and all I'm saying is that it isn't right to make fun of things you don't understand and even if you don't embrace it, it is still part of your heritage."

Sophie placed her spoon down and crossed her arms in front of her.

"Honey, I'm sorry," Callie said. "I guess I've been watching *My Big Fat Greek Wedding* again and I'm feeling a bit homesick for Greece."

"You're right. I shouldn't joke about *my heritage* and I'm gonna be late." Sophie jumped up, grabbing her book bag and giving her mother a quick kiss.

"Remember, home tonight," she called after her, as she watched Sophie shut the wooden gate. She noticed the gate's paint had begun to peel and made a mental note to stop by the hardware store later to pick up some paint.

Oh, what I would give to bring back days when everything I did wasn't an embarrassment to her.

Lately, everything from the way Sophie crumbled her clothes into her dresser, to the cluttered mess Sophie's room had become, drove Callie crazy. A few weeks ago, she found several dresses shoved to the back of Sophie's chest of drawers, dirty clothes mixed in with clean ones and a lost peanut butter and jelly sandwich squashed between the wall and Sophie's bed. It had been there so long she wasn't sure if the mold was jelly or the jelly was mold.

Callie reached down and retrieved her copy of the *Columbus Dispatch*. On the front page was a story about a murder, with the words 'Cult Killing' as the headline. Below the headline was a picture of several bodies draped in bloodied sheets and a close-up of one of the victim's arms showed a symbol branded onto it. The picture was blurry and Callie couldn't make out the symbol.

It looks like... Don't be ridiculous, Callie. It couldn't be.

She stared at the picture a little longer before letting go of a memory she had long since forgotten.

There is no way that Greek word is branded into that person's arm.

Callie remembered the stories of the senseless killing.

~ ☾ ~

When people were hunted because they were different.

But it was hundreds...no thousands of years ago. I refuse to let my imagination get the best of me.

Callie made up her mind to toss the paper away before Sophie got home, when something in the yard caught her eye. It was a shadowy figure and she turned her head to see who it was, but nothing was there.

Add to my daughter's long list of embarrassments that her mother is starting to see things.

She chuckled to herself, in spite of a sudden drop in temperature making her teeth chatter. It was strange, considering most of the spring had been surprisingly warm. She grabbed the frost-covered doorknob and stopped, her attention being drawn to a small section of garden to her right. A fragile-looking butterfly fluttered past her and landed on a tulip. She couldn't recall ever seeing one this early in the spring. The insect's wings, which had some of the most vivid colors she had ever seen, were dazzling in a shaft of sunlight that had broken through the morning cloud cover. She watched it continue to beat its wings, at first slowly and then faster and faster.

It knows I'm watching it. She was mesmerized by it, as the colors in its wings moved like a kaleidoscope, blinding at first and then hypnotic. She knew she had to be dreaming because the butterfly was quickly growing larger. It was now the size of a large crow.

She recalled reading somewhere that hallucinations were a warning sign of strokes and wondered if she were about to have one.

"That and the scent of buttered toast."

The butterfly liquefied into an oil-like red substance that dripped onto the creeping phlox and tulips. The colorful flowers faded, shriveled and sizzled, like someone had poured acid on them. Callie's mouth went dry as she watched everything coming into contact with the putrid liquid shrivel and melt, adding mass to the slime. As it seeped onto the front lawn, the liquid engulfed and devoured everything in its path, including the boxwoods lining the front walk, the weeping cherry tree Angelo had planted last fall and even the massive maple tree and river birch. All of them lost their

~ ☾ ~

color, shriveled and died, falling into an even larger pool of the red liquid that became brighter and seemed to throb in its hunger and intensity. It formed a small river on the opposite side of the front yard, gathering more mass as it churned, bubbled and fell back onto itself.

The once overcast and muted sky had become ominous and threatening. A crack of lightning followed by a burst of thunder exploded above, and the river of red liquid crashed against a huge rock in the front yard, causing it to change direction and form a semi-circular whirlpool. The wind picked up, feeding the rushing liquid with additional velocity, and it rose onto itself, creating a grotesque funnel cloud with the debris from the yard swimming inside of it. As the funnel was about to collide with the far corner of the house, it fell away as quickly as it had formed, revealing a shrouded, blood-drenched figure.

"Oh my God." Callie said. The figure moved towards her, not on legs, but on a wave of the red substance surging several feet behind it, forming a wall that continued to consume anything near it. Its robes were made of heavy black material shredded into long pieces. Each of the strips moved, independent of the others, stretching mid-air, hungrily searching for her, their razor sharp edges whipping outward and snapping back, slicing through the air.

The apparition reached up and pulled its hood away, exposing a disfigured face, the flesh burned and caked with blood, and two gold coins visible over its eyes. It opened what remained of its blistered lips and howled, lifting its arm and pointing a boney, burnt finger, beseeching her. It hovered several yards away before it rushed forward. Its movement broke Callie's paralysis and she scrambled back against the front door, slamming into it. She grabbed for the door's handle, but in her haste she jammed the lock. She clawed at the door, gasping for breath. In desperation, she threw all of her weight against the door, which gave way with a loud crack, and she flew through the opening as the specter's hand touched a strand of her hair.

She rushed back to the door and slammed it shut. A chorus of desperate screams and screeches exploded on the other side as the thing pounded the door with its fists. The

~ ☾ ~

impact of the blows threw her off balance, but she grabbed the umbrella stand and slid down the door, attempting to catch her breath and calm herself. The thing let out one final scream, this time calling her name in its hoarse voice, and she pressed her hands over her ears as each word brought a searing pain to her head. Then, the screams stopped. Her ears rang as the room filled with complete silence.

She shuddered and removed her hands away from her ears. She was drenched in sweat and her lungs demanded more air, but she held her breath as she tried to catch any sound of the thing outside. She heard nothing.

"Nearly twenty years," she yelled, as tears ran down her face.

"Nearly twenty years of normal. Twenty years of nothing but PTA meetings, garage sales, of complete and utter bliss, of keeping my past in the past, denying those miserable old Fate hags and the destiny they said was mine and now I'm back to square one."

Oh my God. The killings in Cleveland. It was the word, Nothos. Someone is hunting and sending me a message. Sophie! No, wait, she's safe... in school. Callie closed her eyes and rested her head on her knees.

She jumped when the doorbell rang. As a joke, Sophie and Angelo had purchased a novelty doorbell that could play hundreds of songs thanks to a memory stick. Today's selection was "La Cucaracha." Last week it had been the Greek standard "Never on a Sunday." She broke out into nervous, hysterical laughter.

She got to her knees and stood up, noticing she had bruised her thigh and with some hesitation reached over and turned the doorknob. The piece of wood that cracked when she forced the door open fell and clattered onto the cement stoop.

Standing in front of her was a deliveryman holding a bouquet of red roses.

"Mrs. Drago?" the man said, reading the delivery form. He didn't bother to hide his surprise at her appearance. The look in his eyes told her she looked as crazy as she felt.

"I'm sorry," she began, wiping the tears from her cheeks. "I had just closed the door, when you rang. It gave me quite a shock."

~ ☾ ~

"Oops, my bad. I have a delivery for you," the man said.

"Thank you," she said behind the large bouquet. "Let me get you a—"

As the words fell from her mouth, the deliveryman shoved the roses at her and rushed back to his truck. With some hesitation, she glanced at her front yard. It was perfect, not a single leaf out of place, and judging by the way her neighbor waved good morning to her, Callie's yard lacked any sort of hellish visions. She kicked the piece of broken woodwork into the house. Closing the door behind her, she reached over and slid the deadbolt into its locked position.

She walked into the kitchen, placing the flowers on the counter and then eased herself down into a chair at the kitchen table, rubbing her bruised thigh. All of a sudden she burst into laughter again, realizing the mere sight of her in the morning was enough to ward off even the most aggressive deliverymen.

Her mind couldn't let go of the newspaper and its horrible picture. She retrieved the paper and carried it into the kitchen.

She shook her head as she smoothed out the wrinkled paper and began reading.

"Those poor people. How horrible."

Several Cleveland teenagers had thrown a party at a fellow student's house. No adults were present. No explanation could be given for what happened to them. Police were called to the house when neighbors complained of screaming. They couldn't get the door open and had to break through one of the windows. The bodies were found throughout the wrecked house. Each teenager had a dog collar around his or her throat. The leather of the collar was embedded into the throat of each victim, demonstrating each had been tortured before his or her necks were crushed. Each had the same brand, written in Greek, on their right wrist.

"Nothos," Callie said, recalling the definition of the word. "Mutt, mongrel. That which is considered beneath the gods to see. Those deserving the wrath of Olympus by their mere existence. The living scourge."

I don't know what to do. The Omen. A black omen. By all that is holy, I will kill who ever…

~ ☾ ~

"But, my past is behind me. I drive carpool. I'm a member of the PTA. I recycle. I collect cans for Cat Welfare. I donate $18 each month to ASPCA. I have a damn gate to paint. I don't have time for this nonsense."

She paused. *Shoot...shoot...shoot. What was it trying to tell me? Those poor children. It all has to be connected. What am I going to do? What the hell. Who....*

"Stop it, Callie. You're babbling like a hysterical little girl. Nobody gives a damn about your carpool. People are being murdered. Maybe it isn't connected. Maybe it was just a mindless apparition."

Don't be stupid, mindless apparitions don't just appear out of nowhere. Something was coming.

Her instinct told her they were all in danger.

She breathed in and out slowly, hoping it would calm her heart. She wondered what Sophie would have thought of the Greek tragedy she had experienced a few seconds ago and a sinking feeling settled in her stomach. She had to figure out what it all meant.

She rested her chin in her left hand and drummed her fingers on the table, tossing around the image of the omen in her mind. She glanced at her cup, filled with the thick Greek coffee and wondered if she should do what she was thinking about doing. Her 'special abilities' weren't easily switched on and off. Powers like hers had an addictive and seductive quality.

But, this is different. Thanks to someone, I have no choice.

Reaching for her cup of coffee, she doubted she even remembered how to do a coffee grounds reading that would allow her to see into the future. She took the last sip and put the saucer on top of the small cup. Placing one hand on the bottom of the cup and one on top of the saucer, she closed her eyes to concentrate. After about a minute, she sighed. Nothing. She closed her eyes again and furrowed her brow, concentrating harder. Still, nothing had happened, and she opened her eyes again, feeling panicked. She wondered if her powers had been 'a use it or lose it' type of thing and then smirked at the thought. Could she have turned herself into a mortal?

"Bull. My mother must be laughing her tightly-wound

~ ☾ ~

head off. I was born a Muse and I remain a Muse."

She closed her eyes again, cleared her mind and focused. It started as a tingling sensation, as the familiar pinpricks of warmth started in her core and spread throughout her body. Her entire being was drawing energy from the room and conducting it towards her hands. She couldn't help but feel thrilled that her abilities were still intact and she opened her eyes and saw the familiar sparks of light shooting from her hands, flooding the entire kitchen.

"Hello, old friend," she said to the sparks and realized she'd better tone it down a bit or the neighbors would think the kitchen was on fire. With one quick action, she flipped over the cup and saucer and placed it on the table, careful not to break the seal between the two. As she waited for the coffee grounds to slide down the sides of the cup, she retrieved the flower arrangement card. She sat back down and glanced at the card tapping the unopened envelope in a random and mindless rhythm. She placed it in front of her. Angelo's gestures of love always took her by surprise.

He shouldn't have. The flowers were far too extravagant of a gift. She pushed the card away and turned her attention back to the coffee cup.

After three minutes had passed, she couldn't wait any longer and pulled the coffee cup away. As soon as the seal was broken, sparks shot free and bounced around the room before fizzling out. She saw the coffee grounds' sludge sitting in the center of the saucer and for a second she wished she hadn't started this reading and was half tempted to wash the cup out without even looking at its contents, but she knew she couldn't. *This is for Sophie.*

She held the cup and stared down into pattern the grounds made. She knew it would be simple. She would glance down and her answer would be there.

As Sophie would say, "easy peasy."

But it wasn't easy peasy. The magic sucked her in so quickly; she was freefalling into a sea of coffee sludge, her eyes rolling into the back of her head. She lost control and struggled to breathe, but managed to draw in some air as she coughed and choked, her body wracked with spasms. In the cup were ominous swirls that melted towards the bottom. A

~ ☾ ~

small red drop in the center drew her attention.

The drop exploded, engulfing her in the same red, festering liquid the black omen had used. Worse than the liquid were the sounds of screams echoing in her ears. She slammed the coffee cup down, breaking the spell. The liquid disappeared, the screams died away and she began to breathe normally again, her mind racing back to the omen. She had never experienced a reading so powerful and although her mother had never told her what the fortune of death looked like; she knew death was what the fortune was telling her. Frantic, her mind swimming, she tried to remember any small detail that could tell her the omen's message.

She remembered the grotesque, burnt face, with coins for eyes.

No, the coins weren't the eyes; the coins were over the eyes.

"Oh, God." She thought about the ancient Greek tradition of placing coins over the eyes for the dead to pay the ferryman.

"Why didn't I see it?" She tried to remember what the omen was wearing. "It was a red robe? No, it was covered in blood. I've seen it before. The material was striped. No, it was pinstriped, like..." She paused a moment. "Like...like...like... Angelo's business suit."

Tears pooled in the corners of her eyes, as images of the omen flooded her mind. She was drowning in them. The ghastly mouth, howling, calling her name—its hand pointing at her. It was wearing a ring. A thick gold band of intertwining vines, with small cabochon stones. They were rubies. It was the mate to the ring she wore, except hers had sapphires.

She pressed her lips together and her mouth began to twist, fighting the sobs swelling inside her. Her mouth burst open and she began to wail. She glanced at the small coffee cup and saucer and with a spark she didn't know she'd created, shattering the coffee cup, saucer and the vase holding the roses. She glanced down at the now drenched and stained white card and snatched it from the counter. Her hand began to bleed from the small cuts caused by the shards of glass covering the counter. She ripped the card open with

~ ☾ ~

such force it tore in two. Placing both pieces in front of her, she read the message.

You and me against the world.

Love, A.

Death was coming and she knew it was coming for Angelo.

~ ☾ ~

Chapter 3

A strong breeze blew across the island of Chios, Greece,
rustling Georgia's bedroom curtains. She sat up in bed,
immediately knowing something wasn't right and breathed
in, her nose wrinkling at the sour-sweet sent in the air she
knew meant no good. The clock on her fireplace mantle made
her moan at being awake at the ungodly hour of three a.m.

*Damn. Might as well get up and fix myself something to
eat.* She hesitated for a second, knowing the moment she
stepped into the kitchen, Winnie would appear, insisting she
make her a fried egg sandwich and a warm glass of milk.

"It's Callista."

An overpowering sinking feeling told her she was right.
She rushed out of her bedroom, not stopping to change, nor
caring to fix her frazzled appearance. Members of her own
Vasilikós, similar to the other eight houses of inspiration,
would be asleep, but she didn't care. She was the Head of this
Vasilikós and no one would dare criticize her about her
appearance. The folds of her nightgown gently shifted and
floated with every movement she made and she found
comfort in the touch of it against her skin. She ran from one
room to another, and rushed down the Grand Entry Hall's
staircase, almost stumbling on the last step.

Callista... Sophia... Her mind raced. She was frantic.

"The vines," she said. She knew she would learn all she
needed to know by seeing and touching the vines, maybe
even tasting some of the ripening fruit. She knew what she
had been waiting for was finally happening, but she needed to
be sure before she acted.

Flinging open the massive French doors in front of her,
she walked onto the terrace overlooking the countless acres of
vineyards. She drifted down the wide staircase leading to the
orchard, her feet barely touching the ground.

~ ☾ ~

She reached the entrance within seconds and stood in front of a large gate made of iron and wood. Massive, almost foreboding, the gate had an extensive design on it of grape vines shooting in all directions and in the center of the gate's peak, a figure of a woman could be seen tending and picking the grapevines around her. The vine's tendrils ended in razor-sharp spikes at the top of the gate. Above her, a golden Sun god smiled as he watched from Mount Olympus, its' worn, foreboding smile looking more like a sinister grimace.

Georgia placed her hand over her heart and grasped a golden key that always hung around her neck on a long chain. She closed her eyes for a moment and raised her hand towards the lock. The lock was ornate and had figures of a group of smiling mischievous nymphs and a somewhat leering Pan playing his flute. Heat began to build in her hand and light shot from her fingers, sending sparks towards the gate. The gate's lock came to life. The iron nymphs fluttered their wings and the sound from Pan's flute filled the air. One by one the nymphs flew through the lock, followed by Pan, who got stuck half way through. As the poor faun struggled in the lock, Georgia heard a loud click and pushed the gate open, rushing in.

The hundreds of fireflies that had been lulling about after an evening of mating sensed her presence and buzzed around her, lighting the walkway. She paused and took a sniff of the air. After reaching the farthest vine in the first row, she stopped in her tracks. As if drawn to it, all of the fireflies landed on a single vine where the grapes seemed to be ahead of schedule.

"How strange." The single bunch of grapes captivated her; they appeared to be bursting out of their skins. She hesitated.

Stop being a fool, old woman.

She stretched her fingers and reached for one of the grapes in the group and pulled it off of the vine. The grape she held wasn't even part of the genus planted there. The fruit was green rather than the rich purple the vine produced and the fruit appeared iridescent with an unnatural glow that rivaled the light created by the fireflies. She sniffed at it and caught a little of the sour smell from the taut skin of the grape.

"Well," she said to the vine. "This is why I'm here, so I

~ ☾ ~

better get this over with."

She popped the grape into her mouth and bit down onto it. As her teeth broke the tough, leather-like skin of the grape, she understood this wouldn't be a pleasant experience. An overpowering sour taste flooded her mouth. She gagged and fought every instinct in her body to spit the vile thing out. She fell forward, her hands breaking her fall on the gravel walk. Pictures filled her mind and she thrashed from side to side. She saw everything that had happened to Callie in several quick, blinding and painful bursts.

"Oh God." A gasp escaped her lips and tears streamed down her face. She shuddered and her mind went blank. She lay there for a few seconds, frozen, unable to move as saliva pooled and bubbled in her mouth. Deep in the recesses of her mind, she shouted, *Get up, get up, get up, you old fool.*

She shook off the paralysis, struggled to her feet and looked at the vine. As she had expected, the grape she had spat out into her hand and the cluster of grapes themselves had returned to their natural size and purple color. She placed the broken grape at the base of the vine and lost herself in thought as she walked back through the vineyard. The fireflies fell behind her, forming a funeral procession and the gate closed behind her with a loud clank.

She was drained and yearned to sit at her kitchen table and rest her head on its well-worn surface. She took several deep breaths until a wave of nausea passed, and addressed the vineyard, with its row after row of vines.

Sacrifice. I have sacrificed so much for this moment.

"Callista hates me and she won't make this easy," she said to the vines. "But now, everything is different and my daughter will have to respect and obey what she has forsaken. This time I will do everything in my power to get things the way they should be. Callista will return and Sophia...oh, Sophia, what plans I have for you."

She sensed members of the Vasilikós were stirring. The first few women sleepily made their way onto the veranda. She leaned against the balustrade, waiting for the rest to arrive and gather around her. Some of the women carried lanterns, while fireflies surrounded others.

"I will have to leave you for a short time. Suffering has

~ ☾ ~

fallen on the house of my daughter and I must go to her. I leave this Vasilikós alone, but will not return as such. I will bring them home."

A woman stepped forward and began singing an ancient song of mourning; the notes of her voice had a physical quality that hung midair and then, along with the fireflies, weaved themselves around the large group. The fog gathering around the vines drifted toward the veranda, floating around the gathered women. The singing woman glowed with a warm light as each note mingled with the mist, transforming the fog into hundreds of fluttering iridescent butterflies. She sang of a longing for loves lost, of want, need and regret.

The sound of her song, along with the butterflies, travelled across the vineyard, crossing the darkness for many miles. They seemed attracted to a small cottage sitting on a hill where nothing grew. The dusty hill was covered in a mass of withered vines intertwining onto themselves, choking whatever trees, grass and flowers that had once made the hill one of the most beautiful places on the island. Only a single olive tree seemed immune to the vines, seeming to thrive yet producing no fruit. The tree stood in defiance of the vines— stoic, waiting and wanting. It almost seemed to be looking up towards the heavens, beseeching anyone or no one, as the curtains in the cottage's upper bedroom window moved slightly.

***

The woman in the house saw the butterflies, which stopped at the tree and rested on its leaves, seeming to try and soothe it. She couldn't help but stare at the tree, which now glowed with hundreds of the butterflies, twinkling with their rustling.

"Hope always seems to spring eternal. Well, not if I have anything to do with it. Let the games begin," the woman said, as she let the curtain drop back into place. She paced her bedroom, exhausted, the weight of her burden heavy on her shoulders, but stopped. Depression, grief and rage surged through her and unable to keep her emotions in control, she rushed back to the window, ripping the curtains down and slamming the window open.

Gathering all of her strength, she screamed, "Nothos!"

~ ☾ ~

and slammed her fist down on the windowsill, the impact creating an echo of shattering pottery that rushed back towards the tree.

In the instance the sound touched the butterflies, the glowing creatures exploded into drips of light, lighting the twisted vines at the foot of the tree. And when the last fluttering bit of light died, she sat in the darkness, sobbing, her rage uncontrollable.

~ ☾ ~

Chapter 4

If anyone were to ask Sophie what happened during the
twenty-four hours after she arrived home from school, she
would have said it was a painful blur.

She'd arrived home from school two hours late and was
greeted by her mother rushing to meet her, grabbing her into
a hug.

"Mom?" she said, choking on a strand of her mother's hair.
"Mom, you're squeezing the breath out of me." She struggled
to loosen her mother's grip, but was unsuccessful.

"Sorry, honey. I..." Callie paused, her face darkening.
"Why didn't you tell me you were staying late at school? You
had me worried sick, thinking something had happened. You
can be so selfish. Damn, Sophie."

"Whatever, Mom. Once again you didn't look at the
schedule on the fridge. Today is my afternoon to help out at
the school newspaper. You know that." Sophie shouted back,
hurtling her book bag down and splitting open the zipper.
Her books fell out into a heap on the floor. Using it as an
excuse to turn her eyes away, she bent down and gathered her
books and the broken book bag into her arms. She was sick of
her mother's mood swings and right now she couldn't stand
the sight of her.

*Only have to last a few more years and I'm free. College
will take me away from this crazy woman.*

When she looked up, her mother had raised her hands to
touch her own flushed cheeks.

"I'm sorry. You're right." Callie reached for Sophie's arm,
but she pulled away. "I forgot all about it. It's been one of
those days."

She forced a small, pressed-lipped smile. "Whatever,
Mom, I've got some homework." Turning her back, Sophie
made her way upstairs, careful not to make any sound. She

~ ☾ ~

knew her mother would be listening and she didn't want to give her the satisfaction of knowing how angry she was. She had lied about having homework, but she knew it was the quickest way to get away from the big serving of crazy her mother was doling out in abundance. *Here's to hoping her level of freakiness isn't hereditary. Freak. Freak. Freak.*

Opening up her calculus book, in case her mother burst into her room to go for Round Two, Sophie lay back against the neatly arranged stuffed animals on her bed, sending some of them toppling over the edge.

She reached over and switched on the radio, snuggling deeper into the mound of soft plush toys and listened to the first strains of Vivaldi's *Winter* concerto. A wave of weariness hit her and what seemed like a moment of closing her eyes ended up being a long and welcome nap. The memory of the argument she'd had with her mother was replaced with a world of nothingness.

Several hours later, she opened her eyes and glanced at her alarm clock. It was nine p.m.

"Shoot." Her mind raced as she tried to remember her father's schedule. He should have arrived home around seven-thirty and she wondered why her mother hadn't woken her up.

She ran her fingers through her hair and pulled it back; securing it with a band she had around her wrist. She didn't bother to look at her reflection in the mirror and unlocked her door, opening it a crack. There were several voices downstairs, talking in hushed tones, and this puzzled her because she knew her mother never invited guests on the same night her father returned from a long overseas trip. The old wooden floors underneath the shag carpeting creaked and in response to the sound the voices downstairs stopped mid-conversation.

Once she reached the bottom of the stairs, she paused and glanced into the living room, surprised to see several of the neighbors sitting there, talking with each other in hushed tones. The gold faux-brushed velvet, made during the ice age, furniture set didn't have a single unoccupied spot.

This is so not okay. No one goes into the living room, unless it was a special occasion like Christmas or Easter, or

~ ☾ ~

maybe a dinner party.

She nervously smiled at the group, wondering whether her mother would make her vacuum and rake the shag carpeting. She entered the kitchen and walked into an even larger group of people. Seated at the table was her mother, who had a bottle of whiskey and a glass next to her. Next to her mother was an ashtray with one of her father's cigars in it. It was lit, filling the room with its scent.

She stared at her mother and panicked because her gorgeous, always put-together mother looked twice her age, with streaked make-up, messy hair and bloodshot eyes. She knew something was wrong.

"Mom?" Her voice squeaked. The sound didn't catch the attention of anyone in the kitchen. She licked her lips and cleared her throat.

"Mom, what's wrong?"

Callie stood up with a slight teeter and walked towards her. When she reached Sophie, she hugged her then pulled away to look Sophie in the eyes.

"Sweetheart," Callie said.

She caught the eye of her mother's good friend and their long-time neighbor, Stephanie, trying to get some sort of answer from her, and when she saw tears beginning to swell in her eyes she turned back to her mother.

"Callie," Stephanie interrupted, with a choking sound, "wait."

Standing up, Stephanie took her husband Gil's hand and they exited the kitchen, followed by the rest, leaving her alone with her mother.

"Okay, this isn't funny. What's wrong with you?" Sophie demanded.

"Honey, I need you to be strong. There was an accident and Daddy," Callie began to cry. "He died."

She couldn't remember what else her mother said because her legs lost all of their strength and she started to fall. She sensed her mother's arms wrapping around, stopping her from falling to the ground. .

At first, Sophie wished whoever was screaming would stop, but then she realized she was the one who was screaming—so out of control she could feel the strain in her

~ ☾ ~

throat, in-between sobs for breath. She tried to wrestle herself away from her mother, pushing her fists against her, but her mother held her tightly, saying what she assumed were Greek words of comfort.

Her screams had died away to silent crying and her mother kissed her on the forehead several times, continuing to hold her.

"Can you stand?" Callie said. "Because my legs are about to give way and the *very* last thing I want to do is sit on this filthy floor."

Sophie couldn't help but laugh. "Oh, Mom. When has this floor ever been filthy?" She stood on her own feet and grabbed her mom's hands, showing her she was okay.

Sophie managed a weak smile. "You look like crap, Mom."

Her mother rolled her eyes and ran her fingers through her hair, which made it look worse.

"Well, you'll have to excuse me for my appearance. I wasn't expecting guests."

Sophie sat down at the table.

"What happened?" she asked.

"There isn't much use going into the details. We can..."

Sophie nodded her head in agreement, but then changed her mind. "No. No, get it over with so I can deal with it all at once."

"Sophie, I don't think—"

"Damn it, Mom," she shouted hoarsely.

"I don't know. I don't know. The police don't know what happened and I sure as hell don't know. He's gone. Do you understand? He's gone and I don't know what to do. What to say. So shut the hell up!" Her mother's hand flew to her mouth and she began to cry. "I'm sorry, Sophie. Oh, God. I am so sorry. Forgive me."

She burst into tears and threw herself into her mother's arms. "Oh Mom..."

~ ☾ ~

Chapter 5

With a flash of light and crack of electricity, Georgia appeared outside of the small Cape Cod in Columbus, Ohio. She noted that her luck continued to hold up, as she glanced around and saw the street was empty. Knowing how and when to Shimmer unnoticed was a true talent and one she had mastered. She stood for a second, catching her breath. It had been a long time since she travelled so far. Shimmering from one room to another was one thing, but Shimmering thousands of miles was enough to make her feel like she was about to vomit. She almost did, but refused to allow herself to show any kind of weakness. When her head stopped spinning, she straightened and checked herself to make sure she was presentable. Her long, honey-colored, streaked-with-white hair was pulled into a modern French twist. She doubted herself a little, wondering if her outfit was overkill and would send the wrong message, but she pushed the concern out of her mind. She wore a sleek, tailored couture black suit, with a matching black trench coat, black gloves and a pair of black designer pumps accented with shiny, red-lacquered soles. Several strands of pearls, of varying sizes and lengths, rested against her skin inside her opened white shirt. Her gold brooch with the large red stone was fastened to her lapel.

She knew she didn't look like the stereotypical grandmother.

I refuse to show up wearing a granny dress, shawl and sneakers. My daughter, the rebellious one, wouldn't be fooled by such an outfit and if I'm going to win Callista and Sophia over, I need to be savvy and being savvy requires my incredible good luck and my exquisite sense of style and good taste.

She opened the small gate and shook her head in disappointment at its peeling paint.

~ ☾ ~

"I'm used to walking into a room and commanding attention without much effort and there was no reason why now should be any different." She tightened the belt of her trench coat to emphasize her point. However, the closer she got to the door, the more her nerve began to slip away again.

But it's always good to have a contingency plan.

She reached into the front pocket of her trench coat and pulled out a small vial. Taking care, she uncorked it and smeared some of the blue liquid onto her gloved right hand. She reminded herself she now had only a minute to touch Callie.

If she won't return to Greece willingly, a veil of obedience potion should remove any willful notions Callista may have. She raised her other hand to knock and the door swung open.

She forced herself not to sneer at her daughter's meager environment. *It was unacceptable. It was pathetic. Here's to hoping the time in this hovel will be short lived.*

"Callista?" she called, her heavy Greek accent hanging off of each syllable she spoke.

Callie's mouth flew open. "Oh, shit," Callie said. "Georgia?"

"Language, Callista. Georgia? Have I reached such a lowly place in your heart? Am I *now* to be referred to as Georgia and not Mother?" Stepping forward, Georgia embraced her daughter and kissed her on the cheek, making sure her right hand touched the back of Callie's head. She felt the shudder run through her daughter's body as the spell took hold and she stepped back.

Georgia stared at her daughter, waiting to see who would be the first to blink. Callie sighed and stepped aside to allow her to walk into the house.

I should have used the veil potion on her ages ago. Think of all the time I've wasted.

Her thoughts of triumph were short-lived as she saw the group of people standing behind her daughter. She glared at them, leaving little to the imagination as to what they should do.

"Well," she said, watching the group depart, "that is much, much, much better. Callista, you know people will sit around like spectators at the crucifixion, licking the tears and

~ ☾ ~

drinking in the sorrow of others like a fine wine. It's so distasteful."

"Georgia..." Callie said, in a low tone, almost a growl. "Now is not the time for you to throw your ego around. Please, be quiet. Sophie is in the next room and has just found out about Angelo."

Georgia removed her coat and laid it on the nearest chair.

"We've all made mistakes and I have been gracious enough to see beyond your shortcomings and forgive you. I am here to help you through your time of need and judging by what I'm seeing, I may have arrived too late."

Callie stared back at Georgia. "You know what, Georgia, I know I shouldn't let you bait me, but I'm too exhausted. I am standing here, having been told my husband is dead, and you have the nerve to travel thousands of miles to resume an argument that ended whatever limited amount of goodwill we had for each other. What the hell are you doing here? Are you serious?"

Georgia ripped off her gloves and threw them onto her coat as she prepared for battle.

"Oh please, Callista. Is this where we're at? You yelling at me and me yelling at you, each of us refusing to even give an inch?"

She stepped back and clasped her hands in front of her and turned at the sound of a middle-aged couple rising to their feet. "And I don't believe I've had the pleasure, who are the two of you? I would think the time for you to depart has long since passed."

It is beyond mortifying to have these mortals witness how disrespectful my daughter is being toward me. This will not do.

The woman moved forward, extending her hand. "I'm Callie's friend, Stephanie. We live in the neighborhood. We've known each other for years. Both of our daughters were born around the same time and go to the same school. I don't know why I'm rambling. This is my husband, Gil." Stephanie broke out into a loud and nervous laugh.

What a nervous bundle of nerves this one is. I don't have time to bother with this obnoxious woman. Is this the sort of person my daughter and granddaughter are exposed to?

~ ☾ ~

Georgia glanced at Stephanie's outstretched hand and shook it with her left hand, fearing at any moment the woman would begin to cry.

Gil pulled Stephanie away. "It's been a real pleasure meeting you," Gil said, reaching for the door. "Callie, we'll call you tomorrow morning to discuss arrangements." The door shut behind them with a soft click.

"Damn, damn, damn, Georgia." Callie yelled. "I can't do this with you. And as for those people you dismissed, Gil and Stephanie have been more of a family to me than you ever were. You gave away your right to offer your opinion in my life when you banished me."

"I didn't banish you," she said through gritted teeth. "That is a lie, Callista, and I won't be lied to. You waltz into my office one day, interrupt a staff meeting to proclaim your love for that, that... that man. What was I supposed to do? You were talking nonsense. Love...normal life, you kept on droning on and on about what you wanted. Your needs. You were such a sniffling little, ungrateful wretch."

"Why can't you ever listen to me? You...you...you never listened and you always treated me like an afterthought. Like I was a possession you could use as a bargaining chip to negotiate a more powerful position for yourself."

"Is that what you think? Do you believe I cared so little for you? Listen to me, you ignorant child. Everything I have done I have done for you. I have clawed my way to the top on my hands and knees for our family's benefit. You didn't mind the power and wealth when I bought you that little English convertible. As long as you had your way, you were content."

"It doesn't matter, Georgia," Callie said. "None of this matters. What's done is done. Now, if you'll kindly leave."

"I didn't banish you," she said. "You made your choice and from that very moment, you took control of your own life. Whether or not you will admit it, I have responsibilities requiring sacrifice. Sacrifice from not only me, but also from those I love. And now, you intend to throw your mother out of your home. The woman who gave you life, who raised you, who loved you even when you cursed my name and kept me out of my granddaughter's life."

"Georgia, I had hopes. I had hoped your icy heart would

~ ☾ ~

have melted with the birth of Sophie. But, after sixteen years,
I am forced to admit it hasn't."

Georgia clenched her hands. "You were promised to
another and you had gifts, which were meant for more
important things. This?" She motioned to reference the house.
"This isn't what you were meant for." She stood up, her face
inches from Callie's. "You spat in the face of our family's
tradition and the Fates, and said no thank you; I don't want
the blessings you have bestowed upon me. You had a calling,
the ability to do great things and what have you done with it?
Nothing. You are an embarrassment to the Demigod..."

"Mom?"

A voice came from the kitchen and a young girl walked
into the room. "What's going on?" the girl asked.

*Be smart. You get one second to make an impression on
this girl.*

"Sophia? I've always dreamed of this day. Darling, you're
lovely."

*I'm sure I sounded as bad as I think it did. Stupid. Stupid.
Stupid.*

Callie walked towards her daughter and protectively stood
in front of Sophie.

"Honey," Callie scratched her head. "I don't know how to
explain, but this is Georgia."

Georgia corrected her. "Sophia, I'm your Yiayia."

"You don't look like a person who would go by Yiayia. I'm
sorry, but this is too much," Sophie said.

Georgia took a step closer to her granddaughter, not sure
if she should embrace her or wait for Sophie to make the next
move. Sophie left the room, running up the stairs.

Callie dropped onto the nearest couch, her head cradled in
her hands. "Well, your first interaction with Sophie was sheer
perfection. Looks like your relationship with my daughter will
be as successful as our relationship. Why doesn't the house
just explode? I think an explosion would make this evening
complete."

Georgia gathered her items and slowly walked toward the
front door.

*Come, come Callista. Stop being stubborn. Give in to it.
Let your last little bit of will power leave you.*

~ ☾ ~

"Mom...I can't believe I'm saying this, but you've forced me into a corner."

Georgia smiled inwardly.

"You've shoved your way into my life and for Sophie's sake; you have to stay with us."

Callie walked towards the adjoining hallway, to the first floor bath and guest bedroom. She switched on the bedroom's overhead light. The simple room featured a wrought-iron bed, patchwork quilt, over-stuffed reading chair and antique wardrobe.

"Georgia, you can sleep in this room. Is your luggage outside?"

"No dear. It's in the guest room."

Sparks of light bounced around the room, revealing to Callie a matching set of luggage. Callie shoved Georgia into the room.

"Are you crazy? Someone is going to see you Shimmer and we'll spend the next few days trying to get them to sip your special clover tea to make them forget. Stop being cute."

Georgia walked past Callie and sat down in the reading chair, reaching over to turn on the reading lap. She grimaced at the glare caused by the overhead light and with a sudden glint in her eyes the light switch clicked off.

"There. That is so much better."

Callie frowned. "I'd offer to help you unpack, but I'm guessing it's—"

They both finished the sentence, "—already taken care of."

Callie walked out of the room and returned with a towel and washcloth set. She placed them on the bed.

"Georgia," Callie began.

She raised her right eyebrow.

"Okay," Callie paused. "Mother, enough with the tricks. While you're here, you have to promise me you will leave the Shimmering stuff back in Greece."

Georgia got up and walked to the bed, reaching for the towels. She folded them again, avoiding her daughter's gaze.

"Mother, promise me. Sophie isn't part of this. You know it and I know it. She isn't like us and I would like to keep it that way. She's been through enough." Tears welled up in Callie's eyes.

~ ☾ ~

Georgia sighed as she stood up and walked over to Callie. "I will do my best."

Turning away from her, Callie walked out of the room, shutting the door behind her.

Georgia sat back down in the overstuffed chair. The one thought burning a hole in her mind was whether or not she would ever get her relationship with Callie right.

"You know what you did and she doesn't even know all of it," she said to herself. "You can pretend all you want, but you know why things are the way they are and if you aren't careful, all of your plans will be ruined."

She glanced down at her right wrist, removed the bracelet and rubbed it. Although it had healed decades ago, the scar was easy to read. The shame caused by the word Nothos branded on her still burned white hot in Georgia's heart.

~ ☾ ~

Chapter 6

Wearily Callie made it up to Sophie's bedroom and knocked at the door. She heard Sophie's muffled voice. "Come in".

"I can't begin to offer you an explanation as to why after twenty-two years Georgia has decided to walk back into our lives," Callie said.

Considering the timing, I can't even say if it's a curse or a blessing.

Callie stood watching her daughter, waiting for some sort of reaction and her heart broke when Sophie began to cry. Her daughter looked down at her messy bed and the stuffed animals on the floor and attempted to straighten-up her room.

Have I been so horrible to this poor child she feels it is more important to have a clean room?

"Sophie, don't worry about the stuffed animals. It's not important. Listen, I know the only thing you have invested in your relationship with your grandmother is the occasional thank you card for the money she sends you during the holidays. But, I don't want the history I have with my mother to interfere with you being able to forge some sort of bond with her. Although she and I may not be on the best of terms, her being here says something."

Sophie grabbed a pillow and hugged it to her chest. "Mom, I am so tired I don't know what to think. All I know is ... all I know is I love you, Mom. I know we haven't been... I know I've... I...I...I... don't know what I'd do if..."

Callie moved closer to her and cradled her in her arms.

"Shush, I know sweetie. I know."

Sophie rubbed her eyes. "Do you think you could sleep here tonight?"

"You read my mind, baby." Callie chuckled and after

~ ☾ ~

changing into sweat pants and a T-shirt she climbed into bed, letting out a sigh of exhausted relief. "You always had the best pillows. How did that work out? I think I'm going to have to steal a few from you."

"Mom, what are we going to do without him?"

"Go on, baby. We remember and keep him in our hearts, but we go on. It's what he would have wanted."

***

The next day, Callie woke up and noticed Sophie wasn't there. Someone was banging around the kitchen and she sighed. Between Sophie crying in her sleep and her own tossing and turning, Callie was sure she'd gotten maybe two hours of sleep. She got up and walked down the hall into her own bathroom, closing the door behind her.

"I look like hell." She glanced at her swollen eyes and the dark circles and bags under them. Her head was pounding and she swallowed three ibuprofen. She took a shower, brushed her teeth and walked down the stairs. At the bottom of the staircase, she paused on the last step. The house was spotless.

Following the sound of glasses and dishes being shoved into the dishwasher, Callie found Georgia standing in the middle of the kitchen, and Sophie and Stephanie sitting at the table glancing at several photo albums Callie recognized.

The counter nearest the stove had been made into a coffee station, with Callie's ancient, party-sized percolator chugging along as it brewed a batch of coffee.

Sophie should have said something to Georgia. She knows the large coffeemaker was only used for special occasions... Your husband just died. I think this qualifies as a "special occasion," stupid.

Wanting to watch the interaction, Callie took a few steps back and hid herself away from the doorway.

"Well," Georgia said. "I'm truly sorry you had to see your mother and me arguing. But I hope you know that although I haven't been a huge part of yours or your mother's life, I do care for both of you. But enough of old arguments and healed over wounds. I bet you would enjoy hearing about when your mother was young and about Greece?"

"I would love to hear embarrassing stories about my

~ ☾ ~

mom," Sophie replied.

"I'm not going to argue about hearing them," Stephanie said. "Do you have any really mortifying stories? I would love to hear those."

Georgia laughed.

Hidden from view, Callie listened to one story after another; shocked her mother even remembered any of them. *This was a woman who had no time to say hello to me. I can't even remember the last time she said she loved me or was proud or happy for me, and now she sits there like the doting mother, reminiscing about the daughter she barely acknowledged.*

A strange buzzing cut through whatever effect the painkiller was having and Callie decided to let the whole thing go.

"This is Callista, as a little girl," Georgia said, pointing to an old photograph in one of the leather-bound albums. "Such a beautiful child. Here she is during the grape harvesting festival. I have an orchard I tend to. Now, this is a good one." Georgia pointed to another picture. "This is Callista, with her first boyfriend. Little Gus. Oh my, was that boy in love with your mother." Sophie and Stephanie squealed. "He followed her around like a lost lamb. I made her dress myself. They're both dressed in traditional outfits from our village," Georgia proclaimed.

Enough is enough. Callie walked into the kitchen and after she poured herself a cup of coffee, she cleared her throat. Georgia sighed. "Okay, maybe I didn't make it. I believe my friend Euryale, who is well known for her couture and needlepoint work made it. I hope you like your coffee strong. Cream and sugar are already set out."

Callie sat next to Sophie.

"I can see you've been busy, Mother. The house is scrubbed from top to bottom, coffee is made and you've laid out quite the spread on the counter."

Georgia rested her hand on the tabletop. "I can't take complete credit for all of this. Stephanie was a great help and we managed to get things situated. You should eat something, Callista. The bagels are wonderful."

"I'm not hungry. I'll eat later," Callie said, noticing the pad

~ ℂ ~

of paper sitting next to Stephanie. On the top page was a long list of items.

"It's a few things to go over," Stephanie said. "You know, for the arrangements."

"Yes," Callie said. "There is so much to discuss."

"Excuse me for a moment," Georgia said. "I need to powder my nose." Georgia exited the kitchen.

"Powder my nose?" Sophie said, with a smirk. "My grandmother does cocaine?"

Callie burst out laughing. "Oh baby, I needed that. It's an old saying. It means she needs to use the bathroom."

"Oh. She could have just said I need to take a dump."

"Sophie. That's disgusting," Callie said, laughing. Stephanie snorted.

***

The following week made Callie thankful she had Stephanie to lean on. This included middle of the night crying sessions over countless bottles of wine as they flipped through the pages of too many photo albums. She was reliving her life with Angelo. There were pictures from the first moment they saw each other, continuing through their short-lived but passionate courtship. Pictures of their wedding told a story of two people alone in the world. In the wedding photographs, which she wept over, two people stood on the deck of a ship sailing to the United States, while the ship's captain presided over the ceremony. Guests for the happy occasion included a ship steward and a maid, both of which had conveniently been on their smoke breaks, and upon fulfilling their duties as witnesses, accepted twenty-dollar bills for the unexpected interruption.

The next album showed the young couple, struggling but happy. In their first, second, and third apartments located in their first, second and third states. Old ticket stubs to every movie, concert or play they attended, were pressed throughout this album.

She lovingly touched a few of the ticket stubs.

"A little secret about Angelo was he was so sentimental and kept each and every stub in a little silver box." Laughing through her tears, she continued, "After the box wouldn't close, I began transferring them into our photo albums. It

~ ☾ ~

was so silly and I would pick on him about it, but he kept on
keeping them, right through my eye rolling." She closed the
album.

She paused for a moment and shut the book. "Okay,
enough of this today. Now pick up your wine glass and let's go
see what my mother is up to."

As she walked down the stairs with Stephanie, Callie was
thankful Georgia was here and begrudgingly admitted she
was glad some sort of bond had developed between Georgia
and Sophie.

She reluctantly concluded it didn't look like Georgia would
be disappearing into the night and she had somehow worked
her way back into her daughter's and granddaughter's life.

Her thoughts were interrupted by laughter coming from
an open front door, as Georgia and Sophie walked in carrying
fresh cut flowers from the garden. Stephanie gave her a quick
hug, whispering she would see her at the service and would
be over to help before the guests arrived. Callie frowned as
she noted Georgia ignoring her friend.

"Sophia, get some vases for the flowers and we can put
them around," Georgia said.
Sophie rushed into the kitchen and placed her flowers on the
table.

She took the flower bunches out of Georgia's hands.
"Sophie, look in the lower right hand cupboard, near the
phone. There should be some vases there. Mother, these are
beautiful. Thanks for picking them."

"Glad to help, dear," Georgia said, as she reached for a
sharp kitchen knife to cut the stems. "I'll take care of the
flower arrangements, while you and Sophia go upstairs and
get ready for the service. I'll be ready to go to the church with
you by the time you get back downstairs."

Callie placed the flowers in the sink. Sophie gave Georgia a
quick peck on the cheek and dashed up the stairs. Callie
reluctantly went over to Georgia and gave her mother's hand
a squeeze, followed by a tired smile.

*Ten points for an awkward moment. A is for awkward.
We don't know how to act around each other and I'm not
sure I want to invest the effort in learning how to. Callie, I
think you're being a bitch.*

~ ☾ ~

Weary, Callie walked up the stairs.

I need to shake off this buzz. One more bottle of wine with Stephanie and I would have been useless to everyone.

The air shifted and goose pimples broke out across her neck. Out of the corner of her eye she saw the kitchen fill with pinpoints of light. She could have said something, protested at Georgia breaking her rules, but she turned a blind eye.

What harm could come from a little Shimmering. Considering the situation, she was grateful she and Sophie would be greeted by a room filled with perfect flower arrangements and a perfectly dressed Georgia, ready to support them through the rest of the day.

~ ☾ ~

Chapter 7

Sophie wasn't surprised at how nonexistent her father's service ended up being. Held in the tiny chapel located in the middle of the cemetery, she thought the ornate stone structure with its clay-tiled roof belonged in the Southwest and not in its green and lush environment. There was something about the stone façade, discolored with mildew and moss she found comforting. She took in a deep breath and her head swam with the scent of flowering tulips, lily of the valley and early blooming peonies.

There hadn't been a priest presiding over the service. An old, creepy monk, whom her mom and dad had known for years, said a few words and prayers, after which he'd invited her mom to speak.

Sophie watched as her mother stood up and felt sorry for her. She could tell this was the last thing her mother wanted to do. Callie's steps sounded loud, echoing off the stone walls and a hush fell over the gathered group of people.

"Angelo wasn't one for grand services, for priests sprinkling holy water over a casket or chanting for the dead. Nor was he one for filling a church with fragrant incense in honor of his memory. Those were his exact words; minus the seasoning of the four letter words he sprinkled throughout this topic. He had such a flair for words. He was a simple man. A man who found great joy in each and every person he met on his journey through life. He always had time to talk about even the most mundane of topics and added new meaning to giving the shirt off his back to someone who needed it more. He also was a humble man, whose greatest joy was found in our daughter, Sophia. Sophie had his heart the first moment he saw her and I can truthfully say I've never seen a more doting father."

Sophie hadn't expected it, but listening to her mother

~ ☾ ~

speak about her father was too much, and the emotions she
had kept in check surged forward and broke free. She burst
into tears, shaking with silent sobs. Georgia's arm pulled her
closer, while she whispered "I'm sorry" and "I know" over and
over again.

"As for me, he was my heart and my soul." Callie's voice
cracked. "He was the embodiment of everything I felt was
incredible in this world. We walked hand-in-hand through
the best and worst of times. He always used to say, "What
doesn't kill us may take a few fingers and toes, but I've always
believed toes and fingers were overrated anyway." Angelo
requested those who were comfortable doing so, come up and
share a memory or two of him. He believed the best way to
measure a person's life is by the memories they've created.
And if the sweet outweighed the bitter, then no matter how
long he lived, his time on earth would have been worthwhile
and filled with purpose."

Rejoined by her mother, Sophie attempted to hear what each
person said, but couldn't. It was too painful. She continued to
look down at her hands, which she held clasped in her lap.
Forty-five minutes later, her thoughts were interrupted by
Georgia, who whispered it was time to go to the grave- site.

"Okay. I'll be there shortly. Give me a sec," she replied.

"Okay," Georgia said, patting her shoulder. Her
grandmother made the sign of the cross and exited the
church with a loud click as the doors shut behind her.

She was glad to be left alone in the quiet, the stillness
bringing a small measure of relief to her raw nerves. Although
it had been a little comforting to hear how her father meant
the world to a lot of people, each story was like a dagger in
her heart, reminding her that those stories were the last ones
to be shared about him. She hated everything about the day.
The service, the grave, it was all so final. All she wanted to do
was rip off her outfit and soak in a hot bathtub until the
stench of those horrible funeral lilies and suffocating
carnations were forever erased from her skin.

She didn't understand why the whole mourning process
had to be so endless.

*I want my life to be the way it was. It's just so stupid,
stupid, stupid.*

~ ☾ ~

She couldn't help blaming her father for ripping her life apart. Had her father been like normal dads, who worked closer to home, he wouldn't have taken that trip, he wouldn't have gotten into an accident on his way back from the airport and her life would be as it had been... Normal.

Stop it. You're being horrible and selfish. Dad would just laugh at you and say, "That's the way it goes, baby."

She sighed and stood to smooth her dress, before going out and facing her new reality.

She was reaching for the iron handle of the chapel's heavy wooden door when she heard a noise on the opposite side of the room. A woman dressed in a black suit and large black hat with a veil was sitting in the front of the chapel.

"Excuse me," she said. "The graveside service is about to start." The woman ignored her. Sophie frowned.

Maybe she's here for another service. She pushed the door open to join her mother and the rest of the group.

It took everyone two minutes to reach the marker serving as a makeshift tombstone.

She stood there, feeling helpless, frustrated and conflicted. Somewhere deep inside, she still held on to the hope that her father wasn't gone.

The monk stood in front of the group, droning on and on to the point she wanted to put her hands over her ears and scream for him to shut up.

She turned away from the group, her head bowed down in thought, shoving hands into her sweater. Nestled into the front pocket among the clean tissues was a small folded item. Pulling it out, she glanced at it for a second until she recognized her father's stationary, with his strange gold family crest at the top. She held it, unsure what to do.

What the heck is this? She glanced at her mother and frowned, thinking her mother had put in some sort of note of support. *She shouldn't be using Daddy's stationary.*

But she knew she was being a brat because her father was dead. He no longer had any use for stationary.

She unfolded the paper. At first, her tired eyes were not able to focus on the ink blotches she assumed were words and for the briefest of seconds she thought she saw the ink on the paper swim across it, which she knew was complete nonsense.

~ ☾ ~

Do not mourn for me, my love. For I am not here.

She recognized her father's handwriting and her mind spun.

This isn't funny. Her hands shook. Her heart pounded, as she attempted to understand the meaning of the note. She crumbled the paper and was about to throw away what she was sure was a stupid joke, but stopped as a fresh crop of tears swelled in her eyes. She gripped the note in her fist, the paper feeling cold to her touch. Feverish and sick to her stomach, she accepted the last shred of hope she had been searching for.

My father is alive. I knew it. That's what the note meant. He's alive. He's alive, in hiding. Maybe he was a spy of some sort and had to go into hiding or a witness in a major trial and had to go into the witness protection program. They had to fake his death. That had to be it. He's alive. My father is alive.

The note slipped through her fingers and her eyes followed it, as it drifted to the ground. It landed with a loud thud and exploded into a million points of light that shot in all directions.

Everything appeared to melt away and she collapsed, unable to fill her lungs with air. She recognized she was having a panic attack and closed her eyes, concentrating on breathing in a slow, controlled pattern. After a few panic-filled minutes of wheezing gasps it had passed, and she lifted her head and looked around. She was alone.

Even though the wind whooshed past her, sending her hair and clothes rustling wildly about her, she didn't feel the cold of the Ohio spring anymore. Everything around her that had been so lush and vibrant now appeared to be muted and fuzzy. She walked forward, not seeing where she was going, but growing angrier as she wondered how her mother and grandmother could have left without her. She paused a moment as a distant spark of light caught her eye. It came from the far edge of the cemetery, which was bordered by a huge, dense wood on three of its four sides. Not sure why she was doing it, she changed direction and began walking towards the bright object, which

~ ☾ ~

she realized was a figure of a man motioning for her to come to him. She knew the man, she was sure of it, but couldn't make him out because he was too far away.

She wondered if it was Stephanie's husband or the creepy monk.

Who would want to be a stupid monk? Why not become a priest? Isn't that like being a paralegal versus a lawyer?

The clouds parted, sending some unexpected rays of late day sunshine into the clearing and as the man became bathed in the warm light, she gasped.

"Daddy? God! Daddy!" She broke into a blind run. The figure waved for her to follow as he walked into the woods.

"Daddy." She started panicking she would lose him. "Don't leave, Daddy. Take me with you. Please wait." She yelped the words as she stumbled over a low, broken tombstone, but jumped to her feet in a heartbeat, not wanting to lose sight of her father.

Sophie began to run again, getting closer and closer to the spot where her father had appeared, and the moment she reached it the clouds closed up and the light was gone. She was desperate, deciding whether or not to face the darkness of the woods and shivered a bit.

Don't go in there.

She took a few steps backward; convincing herself venturing into the dark woods was not an option her mother would approve of. Almost appearing to sense her hesitation, she watched the clouds part again, shedding light on a far off clearing. Like before, her father stood in the warm light, except this time he called to her.

"Sophie. We haven't much time. Come on, honey."

She strained to see him. He sounded a million miles away, his voice crackling like he was on a cell phone with a bad connection.

"Sophie." He called again and for a brief second she could make him out, as if he was a few yards away from her. Without even thinking, she silenced her voice of reason and rushed into the woods.

Her eyes adjusted to her darker surroundings and she could make out a well-worn path of pine needles, fallen leaves and dirt.

~ ☾ ~

Although her muscles and lungs were burning, she kept on running. Her father appeared to be even farther away. She tripped over fallen limbs and struggled through branches and vines that lashed at her skin. The wind picked up again; pressing on her so hard she stumbled.

Suddenly the act of running became easier and she realized she wasn't running anymore. Her feet had stopped moving and her body hung limp, the wind carrying her forward at a terrifying rate. Her father's body began to tremor as he rushed towards her with an inhuman speed. She cried out and closed her eyes, throwing her arms in front of her face, bracing herself for the painful collision.

Her eyes flew open right as her father's face loomed mere inches away. He laughed and dissolved into a cloud of smoke and ash as she passed right through him.

Sophie fell with a thud onto the ground, the impact making her teeth chatter. She thrashed her arms and legs, trying to get the remains of her father's ashes off of her. She lay still, terrified out of her mind, not sure what just happened.

There has to be a logical explanation for this. Don't know what it could possibly be, but I'm sure I will look back on all of this and... probably go bat poop crazy.

She calmed down; almost laughing at how horrific it was that she was brushing her dead father's ashes off of her clothes, face and hair.

"This has to be a dream," she said, glancing around. She was in some sort of large clearing in the middle of the woods.

She got to her feet and attempted to walk back the way she came, when she discovered she must have gotten turned around because there didn't appear to be an opening out of the clearing. She glanced to her right and then to her left to find the opening wasn't there either.

"Which means, stupid, the way home is behind you," she said under her breath.

She began walking, keeping her eyes towards the ground, watching for anything she might trip over and somehow stumbled into a woman. She was sure she hadn't seen anyone else in the clearing. It was the woman from the chapel, wearing the same black hat and veil. She tried

~ ☾ ~

to avoid falling into her and fell backwards instead.

"Oh great, you came just at the right time. I was just saying I need yet another person to throw me to the ground and here you are. Just what I needed, thank you very much." Sophie said, not caring who heard her. Although she couldn't make out the woman's face behind her thick veil, she sensed the woman was frowning.

"I'm sorry, that was rude of me." Sophie said, attempting to get back on her feet.

Without hesitation, the woman grabbed her arm, helping her to stand.

"Thank you, so much," She tried politely to release herself, but the woman didn't move. "I said I was sorry. Please let my arm go."

The woman stood there in silence. Sophie panicked, trying to get away, when a rumbling in the sky made her look up. She was surprised at how dark it had gotten.

The stranger moved closer, bringing her face within inches of Sophie's face.

"My name is Aletheria. I am the Oracle serving your grandmother," the woman said.

"The what?" Sophie asked, attempting to scream over the wind.

"I serve the Vasilikós of Greece and Italy."

Crazy. This woman has bought major property in crazy town.

"Why am I not surprised Georgia has failed to prepare you for any of this? I'm sorry, dearest. I hope one day you will forgive me."

"What are you talking about?" Sophie croaked, her voice trapped in her throat.

Aletheria raised her arms towards the sky as the wind rushed from behind her and whooshed upward, sounding like a freight train at full speed. Sophie lost her footing, stumbled and fell.

Cowering on the ground, fearing she had somehow managed to end up in the path of a spring tornado, Sophie began crawling on her stomach. She made it a few feet before being stopped by Aletheria, who didn't seem to move but rather materialize out of the gathering darkness and wind.

~ ☾ ~

The woman took a few steps closer to her, ignoring Sophie's attempts to scramble away. Aletheria reached down and lifted Sophie's chin with one hand, and with the other lifted her own veil, revealing a face of ash and waste with blue-hot coals for eyes, which seemed to burn the flesh in the woman's eye sockets.

Sophie yelped, slapping Aletheria's hand and pushing herself away. Aletheria straightened and tore at her clothes, which appeared to grow in length the more she ripped, the veil now reaching the ground as it billowed in the wind. Loose ash flew up into the sky, feeding into what was forming into a tornado. A rolling curtain of black clouds that crackled and sparked with lightning joined the funnel cloud. Sophie glanced back to where Aletheria had stood and only found the dress and the veil, which remained standing for a few seconds before the tornado sucked it up. The forest, which had seemed so far away, had shifted and moved in closer to her, as trees were twisted and uprooted by the funnel cloud, and slammed down closer to her. Several massive trees fused together in groups, forming what appeared to be the four corners of a rectangular space, the center of it being where she lay.

Terrified to the point of almost blacking out, Sophie struggled to her feet. She ran in the opposite direction of the first line of tree columns, but was stopped by several other trees slamming down in front of her, missing her by only a few feet. She reversed herself and ran toward another opening. Like the previous one, several other tree columns blocked it. She attempted to run between the trees and was violently shoved back by several branches. They reached for the neighboring branches, intertwining themselves and creating a natural barrier. What holes remained were filled with the forest debris being gathered by the storm, as vines, leaves and bits of rock wedged themselves to form solid walls. There were now four sides to the structure, which was the size of a football field. Unsure what to do, Sophie wandered towards the center of the space, as the funnel cloud disappeared into the clouds.

What am I going to do?

Feeling helpless, she cried out, "Mom..."

~ ☾ ~

Chapter 8

Callie stood in front of the grave, her eyes closed in silent prayer. A shiver ran up her spine as she heard a whisper on the wind that sounded like, "Mom."

She jumped, like someone had thrown cold water in her face. She grabbed Georgia's hand, who stood next to her, her head also bowed, eyes closed, reciting the Lord's Prayer.

"Mother," she said, touching Georgia's arm. Callie glanced around and then panicked. "Mother, where's Sophie?"

"Callista, she's right—" Georgia paused as she scanned the group, who stood motionless, frozen to the ground. "Well, she was right over—" Georgia pushed her way to the back of the group. "Has anyone seen Sophia?"

Each of the guests remained motionless and unresponsive, as if suspended in time. She saw an expression of dread appear on Georgia's face.

The vile word came back into her mind.

"Nothos. Filthy Nothos. A good Nothos is a dead Nothos." It's what they used to say. The Olympians killed people like us. They enjoyed it. They killed girls like Sophie for sport.

"Oh please, God, not Sophie. Please, anybody but Sophie," Callie prayed, hoping Sophie had gone back to the chapel. She rushed towards it. Understanding the funeral party was oblivious to everything around them, Callie disappeared in an explosion of light, reappearing in the chapel with a loud crack. Georgia appeared in a split second at her side. The chapel was empty, except for a single woman dressed in black who sat in the front pew.

She rushed forward, but Georgia held her back with a violent jerk. "Be smart, Callista. We aren't dealing with something from this world," Georgia said.

"Who are you?" Georgia shouted. "What have you done with Sophia?"

~ ☾ ~

The woman stirred, as she shook with the laughter spilling out of her.

"Done with?" the woman said in a heavy Greek accent. "I haven't done anything. I am just the catalyst, not the creator."

Callie ripped her arm away from Georgia.

"Enough of this. Are you the one who killed those poor children? Tell me where my daughter..." Callie shouted, rushing towards the woman. She stopped when she recognized her. "Aletheria? What are you doing here?"

Staring back at her was the ancient Oracle, someone Callie didn't expect to see and then it hit her, like a hundred-pound weight. She glared back at Georgia.

"What have you done?" Callie demanded, her voice shaking with rage. "What have you set in motion, Georgia? Tell me."

Georgia walked towards her daughter. "Come away from Aletheria. I haven't done anything. I don't know what—"

The Oracle laughed. "Careful Georgia, you'll catch yourself in the web you've been spinning for years. You wouldn't want to lie in church."

The color drained from Georgia's face.

Callie could see her mother was hiding something.

I could kill you right now, old woman. Electricity crackled around Callie as her hands channeled the energy around her. The irritating buzzing in her head she had been feeling grew stronger, bordering on being painful, urging her to get control of herself. She closed her palms, snuffing out the energy surge.

"We don't need your gift of sight. Go away, Aletheria. You aren't wanted here," Georgia said.

The Oracle raised her left eyebrow. "I believe your daughter thinks differently." Aletheria reached into the pocket of her suit and produced a handful of casting stones, which fell to the ground with a tinkling clatter.

"What would you like to know? I'll give you this knowledge for free," the Oracle said.

"What is to become of my daughter?"

The Oracle glared at Georgia, saying "The question should be, what *is* Sophia about *to* become."

Callie knew what the Oracle spoke of.

~ ☾ ~

"Ascension?" Callie said. "But, Sophie knows nothing of us, of the responsibility that comes with the power. She has the right to choose. It is written we are given the right to choose. You can't decide one day you want to change my daughter into a Muse. I demand you follow our laws." She looked at the Oracle and then back at Georgia.

She closed her eyes and raised her right hand to her forehead as she realized she couldn't run from it anymore. After years of trying to forget, trying to be normal, she admitted the truth. She was a Muse.

"I'm a Muse who has forsaken her gift, and now my daughter is going to pay for it. But this is my sin, not Sophie's and I can't let this happen," Callie said, backing away from the two women, the buzzing in her head returning. She ran down the aisle with the sound of the word Nothos ringing in her ears.

"I have to stop it." She hit the door and disappeared with an explosion of light. The doors were thrown open and slammed into the walls.

***

In the same clearing where Sophie had entered the woods, two bursts of light shot into the glen as Callie and Georgia appeared.

Callie took in her surroundings and saw Georgia standing in her way, staring back at her.

"Get away from me," she said. Her words more of a slap than a statement. She attempted to push her mother out of her way, but Georgia held strong to her spot and put her hands on her shoulders.

"Callista." Georgia shouted, but she couldn't hear her. Callie was running on pure protective mother instinct. Georgia grabbed her head and made her look into her eyes.

She couldn't make out what she was saying. Her mother's hands were burning into the side of Callie's head and her entire body shook as a jolt of electricity from Georgia's hands almost made her fall over.

Georgia held firm. "Nothing can be done. We have no control of this. This has been written by the Fates ever since Sophia was born. This is her destiny."

She pushed her mother away and began to pace as she

~ ☾ ~

ignored the torrential downpour soaking both of them to the skin.

"Bullshit, Georgia. Not true, not true, not true. This is all you and your hunger for power. Sophie isn't a part of this. There are people out there murdering children, branding *Nothos* onto them. Your desire for power will not put Sophie in jeopardy. It's your job to catch whatever vile creature from Olympus is running lose. It isn't my job anymore and it certainly isn't Sophie's. "

Hysterical, she rushed to her mother and threw herself on her knees, pleading. "I turned my back on the power. I wanted a normal life, to have a husband who loved me, and a child. A child not damned to this existence. Please Mama, please, not her. I'll go back and do whatever was destined for me, but please, not Sophie. She's just a girl. She can live with Stephanie. I can give her up to live like a normal, average girl. She deserves happiness. Please. Please." Callie groveled, as she touched her mother's shoes in total submission.

"I can't," Georgia said. "This isn't my doing."

Callie cried out in agony. "But she's not like us. She doesn't have the power within her. I would have seen it. Why is this happening?"

The disgust in her mother's face was all too apparent.

"Get up. Get up, Callista." Georgia demanded. "And stop your sobbing. You have always been a selfish, weak woman, never grateful for what was given to you."

"What? Given? What are you talking about?"

Georgia reached down and grabbed Callie by the arm, pulling her up by force.

"Do you think the time you had with Angelo wasn't a gift? Do you believe you had the power to turn away from them, the Elders, the gods, like handing in your two weeks' notice at some job? Is your ignorance so great? They allowed you to leave, to bring Sophia into this world. It was their plan, not yours."

Callie stared at the ground, still sobbing. Georgia reached over and smacked her across her face.

"You need to snap out of your sorrow because you have little to be sorry about. You don't think for one minute I would have loved to have the life you had with Angelo.

~ ☾ ~

To...to...to have simple moments not associated with my duties to the gods. There are moments when my body is so tired and my mind wishes I would tear it out of my head so I could have a moment or two of peace. And you stand there crying, not because of what is happening now, but because you want more, because it wasn't enough. Well, my little girl, there isn't any more. What you got came at great sacrifice and now the Sisters have returned for payment. So it is better to embrace what the Fates have given us and be thankful for the gift Sophia is about to become."

"But she has a choice. They have to ask."

Georgia took a step closer. "Not this time. You were right when you said Sophia wasn't like us. It is frightening how she's so beyond what you and I are. It is as if Zeus's hand has reached down to bless your child. Be happy, Callista."

The annoying buzzing sensation in her head made it difficult, but she ignored her mother and walked past her.

"Callista, where are you going?" Georgia asked.

"All you're trying to do is delay me with all of this grandstanding. I'm sick of it. Screw the blessing. No one is going to kill my daughter and brand her a Nothos. No one is going to force her into the dangerous life I was forced into. I will take her so far away from you; even the all powerful Georgia will never be able to find her." Callie continued to walk, expecting the warm sensation to build inside her, as it always did when she used her powers. She felt nothing. She tried again to concentrate and realized she wouldn't be able to call upon her powers. It wasn't going to be that easy. *Georgia bound my powers.*

"I don't need it," she said under her breath and ran into the woods, leaving Georgia alone.

~ ☾ ~

Chapter 9

Sophie didn't know what to do, so she stood there, waiting for something to happen. Everything seemed to be on edge. The air was electric. The grass and trees seemed to be suspended in time.

The clouds above shifted, creating nine twisting whirlpools. The clear night sky and stars were visible in the center of each vortex's eye. A rumble of thunder and a crack of lightning shot through one of the holes, striking the field a few yards from where Sophie stood and rupturing the ground. An intense light glowed from the crevice. A woman dressed in white appeared, standing in the center of the rupture. Sophie blinked to make sure she wasn't imagining things.

"This isn't good," she said, running in the opposite direction of the woman. She didn't get far as another lightning bolt shot out of another hole in the clouds, striking a few feet away from her. Nearly falling into the newly formed crater, she stumbled back and hit the ground again.

"You've got to be kidding. Wake up, wake up, wake up." Scrambling to her feet, Sophie could see from the corner of her eye another woman in white, standing on the far edge of the crater. She ran, not caring where she was going, ignoring the fact that there wasn't anywhere to run. All she knew was that she needed to keep dodging lightning bolts.

It is a shame the people at the Guinness World Records weren't around to record this. Jesus, I must be breaking some sort of freaky record.

The ninth bolt hit close, missing her by inches. She couldn't feel her toes and a massive shock shot up her legs, right before they gave way. She fell face first, onto the ground with enough force that her mind swam near total darkness.

She whimpered as she turned over. Her head was

~ ☾ ~

throbbing. She tasted copper in her mouth and reached up to find a small trickle of blood coming from her right nostril. Every muscle in her body ached, screaming for her to stop whatever it was that she was making them do. Sophie got to her feet and cried out. The pain in her right ankle told her she twisted it.

The entire field was dark except for the occasional wave of lightning shooting inside the mass of clouds. Sophie let out another whimper as she saw the nine women in white had gathered around her in a large circle. She had no way to escape them now. They all seemed to glow, but she realized the glowing was the least of her worries because the women's feet didn't touch the ground at all. They weren't merely floating; they flew.

From the corner of her eye, she saw one of the women now stood next to her. She cringed, thinking the women had to be some sort of vampire bride, hungry for blood.

The woman said something that sounded Greek, but Sophie didn't understand. The woman grew even brighter and began again, speaking in perfect English. "Don't be afraid, Sophia. We won't harm you."

She glanced into the woman's face, which she thought had to be the most beautiful face she had ever seen. Long blonde hair crowned delicately built features and a pair of deep-set eyes of a startling shade of dark blue with star-like specks of light watched Sophie. The woman offered a soothing smile, but Sophie was still afraid.

She attempted to ignore the pain in her ankle and limped for two steps before backing into another woman. She looked into the woman's eyes, and Sophie's fear and anxiety lessoned. The woman moved closer and Sophie didn't bother moving. She sensed she wouldn't be able to, even if she tried. A wave of warmth radiated from the group and she was comforted by it.

As a woman with hair the color of dark cinnamon sticks stepped forward, her fear melted away.

The woman said, "Once in a millennium comes a soul that possesses such power that its very existence has the ability to tilt the world back to its correct balance. Until now, we have suffered the slow death of inspiration in this world, as one

~ ☾ ~

war after another tore at the flesh of our very souls. For so long, we have hoped and prayed such a soul would restore the balance of good to this world, allowing us to once again walk the path of light."

"But I don't understand," Sophie said.

The redheaded woman stood up and gave her a single kiss on the forehead, and her mind spun. Sophie's body slowly drifted to the ground. She was conscious, but couldn't move.

"It is time. Her mother approaches and we must be quick," the women said, as they surrounded Sophie and reached down to gather her into their arms. A wind rushed forward, lifting the group upward towards an opening in the clouds and the glowing beams of the moon bathed the women as they disappeared into the sky, the clouds closing behind them.

~ ☾ ~

Chapter 10

Callie rushed through the woods as roots and branches tore at her. A leafless branch slapped across her face, drawing blood. Tripping, she cursed under her breath as her shin scraped across a fallen tree. The wind had picked up to compete with Callie's fury, and a violent downpour of rain made it difficult for her to keep her footing. Georgia caught up to her and helped her to her feet.

"This is crazy," Georgia shouted over the rain and claps of thunder.

A lightning bolt struck a nearby tree, shattering it and sending shards of smoldering wood in all directions. Georgia tackled Callie, sending both women sprawling to the ground as a large shard of wood landed behind them, missing them by inches.

Callie shouted in frustration.

"Callista, they won't let us out of this wood until it's over. It must be done. Stop fighting it."

"Stop fighting?" Callie yelled. "Never, Georgia. Not when it comes to Sophie. I have to stop it. I have to."

She pushed her mother away and scrambled to get up. She could barely see the clearing, but still fought her way through the underbrush. A faraway crash of lightning, followed by eight similar crashes, shook the ground beneath them. The shaking stopped and the forest fell into a deep hush as the now gentle rain died away.

Callie had heard the nine lightning strikes and knew what they meant. Defeated, she walked out of the woods, not surprised to discover she had been only a few yards from its edge. She told Georgia to stay back and ran toward the makeshift temple.

Sickened by how much it resembled the temple where her mother had taken her to receive her gifts, Callie dashed

~ ☾ ~

around, trying to find a way in–but there wasn't one. An intense interior light shot from every crack in the structure's exterior and she cried out in anguish, the anger building in her heart. She saw Georgia fling an energy blast that struck the temple and sent shards of wood into the air. She rushed into the hole Georgia created, ignoring the splinters of wood tearing at her feet. Callie stopped and dropped to her knees as she saw her daughter suspended by the arms in a cruciform pose, supported by invisible hands.

Oh, no. You aren't getting off that easy.

"Show yourselves. I know you're there, the cause of all of this. You were never cowards. Do not hide from the mother whose heart you have broken."

Blinding light appeared around Sophie and then died away as the Muses materialized. The group drifted to the ground. Sophie, still sleeping, didn't stir as she was laid onto an uprooted pile of moss. Without a word, a redheaded Muse stretched out to the heavens and shot into the air, followed by the other Muses.

Callie stood up and walked to her daughter. Sophie lay sleeping. She was a living and breathing piece of sculpture by some Old Master. Her once unruly hair now cascaded into reddish brown pools. Her face, which she had always believed to be beautiful, was so breathtaking Callie couldn't help but feel a pang of jealousy. Sophie's skin was smooth with a touch of summer tan and Callie noticed the slightest dusting of freckles on her nose and cheeks.

Georgia walked up from behind. "She's breathtaking. I expected incredible, but this is..."

"Yes, you're right, except she was always beautiful. She didn't need this."

Georgia became silent and reached out to hold her daughter's hand, but Callie rejected the gesture. The strange buzzing moved through her head again.

"She can't live here in this world anymore, at least not until she can learn to control her powers," Callie said. "We'll have to leave before anyone sees her. How could I possibly explain the way she looks to anyone who has seen her before? We have to return to Greece and set up residence at the Vasilikós."

~ ☾ ~

Sophie stirred and opened her eyes, which now twinkled with starlight. Callie knew Sophie hadn't become the same as she or Georgia. Sophie wasn't a run-of-the-mill-Muse.

"So much more," Georgia said under her breath, and Callie cringed at the greed in her mother's voice.

~ ☾ ~

Chapter 11

Sophie's cries echoed in the large room and she thrashed her arms with such force she threw herself off the bed. She was dreaming of attending her own funeral. As she stood in front of the open grave she turned to see a perfect version of herself staring back at her. The clone's perfection was like a slap across her face and she wanted to cry. She tried to call out to her mother and tell her she wasn't dead, but a flash of energy was thrown at her and she fell into the grave, crashing through the coffin. She landed on something cold and damp. It smelled like the frogs she had dissected in biology class. Dead arms wrapped around her and a mouth with a foul smelling breath whispered 'die, filthy Nothos' in her ear. She tried to yell for help but the coffin gave way and she started falling towards a fiery pit she knew was Hell.

The fall from her bed brought her fully awake. Sophie shuddered at the thought of her dream. She sat on the floor, not sure what to do.

Where the heck am I? This isn't my room. She shuddered again as her feverish skin dropped in temperature.

The room was vast; the bed she rested her head against was huge and ornate, it belonged in a museum and not a bed she would choose to sleep in.

Sophie examined the rest of the room. Two large stone fireplaces flanked it and without doing so she knew she could easily stand in the mouth of each of them. She walked toward one of the ceiling-to-floor windows and touched the heavy embroidered drapes hanging from iron rods. Taking a deep breath, she closed her eyes and couldn't help but smile because the scent of the sea brought back fond memories of family vacations she had long since forgotten. The breeze blew a thick strand of her hair across her face, and once her eyes focused on it she panicked.

~ ☾ ~

"My hair...oh my God, my hair. What is wrong with my hair?" Sophie said, grabbing and examining a clump of it.

"Nothing's wrong with it. It's beautiful," Callie said, closing the door behind her. She stood for a moment, staring at her daughter and then walked toward her.

Sophie looked at her mother. "Where are we?" Her hand drifted to her stomach and she looked down when she didn't encounter the amount of stomach she expected.

"Mom?" she wailed and started to sob. "Have I been sick? What's happened to me?"

Callie walked toward Sophie and embraced her. "Oh honey, no, you haven't been sick. It's, well—sweetie, come sit down over here." Callie motioned for her to sit on an overstuffed couch. "I know you have a lot of questions, so let me start with an easy one. We're not in Ohio. We've come to stay with Georgia, in Greece."

"Greece? Mom, I don't even have a passport. How can we be in Greece?"

"Well... Let's not worry about how we got here and deal with *why* we're here."

"Mom, did you do something illegal and we had to leave? Were you selling drugs? Oh my God, you're like that mother on *Weeds*."

"Oh God, no, that's not it at all," Callie laughed. "Honey, do you remember anything about Daddy's funeral? Do you remember what happened after we left the church?"

Sophie didn't know what her mother was talking about. She shook her head.

"Okay... here goes...I need you to suspend your disbelief," Callie said, "because I'm about to tell you myths, fairytales and things that go bump in the night are real."

"What?" Sophie said, starting to get frustrated. She glanced over her mother's shoulder and noticed a floor length mirror. The mirror's massive frame, with gold gilded swans, mythical creatures and reclining cherubs almost took up the entire wall. Callie's eyes drifted toward the mirror and she threw up her hands, sending a burst of light towards the heavy curtains on each side of the mirror. The curtains abruptly closed by themselves.

Sophie's mouth flew open. "Mom, how did you do that?

~ ☾ ~

Did you just do what I think you did?"

Callie stood up and walked towards the mirror, and turned back to face Sophie, gripping the curtains behind her.

"Honey, I have so much to explain and I'm not doing a good job of it. I never thought I would have to have this conversation with you. Think of your soul as a small room with millions of tiny doors. For most, the majority of those doors are shut."

"Mom, step away from the mirror. Let me see what has happened to me."

"But I need to explain first. It's like this, some people may have a few additional doors open and because of those open doors, they have some extra abilities like being able to tell the future or being able to speak with the dead. Now, beings like us have the majority of our doors opened and our soul is expanded to allow us to do the things we can do. Otherwise, our soul would be ripped to shreds."

Sophie's arms shook; a searing heat building inside her as crackling electricity filled the air. "What has happened to me, Mom? I need to see." She lifted her head; her eye's meeting her mother's. The heat was almost unbearable, burning in her eyes and moving toward her clenched fists. Her hands tingled and burned. She was sure they were going to explode.

Callie held firm. "Honey, calm down. You don't have control of your emotions. It's always difficult at first, but—"

Sophie was furious and she let whatever control she had slip away. Her eyes were burning through her mother, in an attempt to reach the covered mirror.

With a steady voice, Sophie said, "Let me see." She shook her hands, in an attempt to shake off the heat pooling in them. Instead of feeling relief, the energy surged from her.

Callie threw herself out of the way, falling forward onto the floor as the energy burst hit the mirror, ripping the heavy curtains and massive iron rods off the wall and cracking the mirror from top to bottom. Sharp pieces of mirror rained down, as both women crashed to the floor.

"Ow!" The slivers of mirror glass sliced her palms. She grew silent watching the mirror-shards pushing themselves out of her skin. The cuts bled a little then stopped bleeding and healed before her eyes. She stood, afraid to move, trying

~ ☾ ~

to get her mind around what she was seeing.

"What the heck is wrong with me?" Sophie said, as she burst into tears.

Although a good portion of the mirror was destroyed, Sophie could still make out most of her reflection. She lifted her right hand and touched her face, realizing she was staring back at the girl from her nightmare. It was the girl who had pushed her into the grave.

This is more than just a little liposuction or a hair straightening. Am I a victim of an alien attack? Was this the work of body snatchers?

The voice coming from Sophie's mouth was sorrowful and lost. "Was I so hideous you couldn't stand another moment of looking at me and you had to change me into this?" She gestured at herself, feeling years of fear and inadequacy bubble up inside her. "What did you do to me, Mom? Knock me out and put me through some sort of *Princess Diaries* program from hell? Did you look at me and wonder how something so ugly could be created from you and Daddy? Do you finally have the daughter you've always wanted? I always knew I was a big disappointment, but this is...are you happy?"

Callie stood there, eyes downturned.

"No, Sophia, she's not happy. If there is someone to blame, blame me." Sophie was surprised to see Georgia standing in the doorway.

Georgia walked deeper into the room and noticed the shattered mirror.

"Now, I know my daughter didn't do this because she knows how much this mirror means to me." Georgia stooped to pick up a few pieces of mirror before throwing them onto the floor. "Sophia, was breaking the mirror necessary? You are going to have to get control of your powers because I can't have you tearing this Vasilikós apart. Not to mention I find such wasteful demonstrations of your powers vulgar and tasteless." Georgia flicked the tips of her fingers away, as if brushing a piece of lint off her dress and the motion swept the pieces of shattered mirror into a neat pile. Again, she flicked her hand in dismissal—sending the fallen curtains, brackets and bar back to their rightful place. "That mirror has

~ ☾ ~

been in our family for longer than I can remember. It was given to this Vasilikós by Athena herself. I believe it was forged from late evening mist, Hades gold and starlight."

Sophie snorted in response, unable to stop the laughter from bubbling out from her. "Evening mist and starlight? Don't forget pixie dust and cotton candy."

Georgia grimaced. "Callista, you will teach your daughter to hold her tongue and to give a Demigod of my status the respect I deserve or I will bind her tongue until she learns her lesson."

Georgia clapped her hands, which sent the pieces of mirror into the air. They hung like miniature prisms, filling the room with a light.

"Assemble," Georgia said, a spark shooting from her right hand. The pieces zoomed around each other, each acting like they possessed a mind of their own, as they located their original starting place.

"With all due respect, Georgia," Callie spat out, fighting the buzzing in her head urging her to remain quiet, "stop showing off."

Callie stood and walked over to the floating pieces of mirror and placed her hand flat against the mirror's surface. Her hand began to spark and glow with heat, and with a slight push the floating wall of glass slammed into the mirror's frame with a loud crash.

Sophie walked past her mother and stared at the mirror, while dripping bits of light slid over the cracks, fusing them together and restoring the mirror back to perfection.

"Are we witches? Vampires?" Sophie asked.

Georgia snorted. "Goodness, no. How silly to even suggest such an idea. In addition to requiring a natural ability to cast, witches require spells, potions and other nonsense. I'd go out of my mind having to remember the correct pattern of words or carry a wand. Don't misunderstand me; some of my good friends are witches. As for the vampire thing, we are a far cry from those horrible creatures. Vampires aren't the tortured, brooding creatures that possess a strong jaw-line, piercing eyes and six-pack abs. Such rubbish, but I digress," Georgia said, as she walked toward the hallway.

"Callista, why you have such difficulty doing a simple task

~ ☾ ~

like this, I'll never know." Georgia stopped and straightened a tilted lampshade. "We're Muses," she said, glancing at Sophie, and walked out the door, calling behind her. "Hopefully your mother can explain the rest without my help."

Without anyone touching it, the door slammed closed behind Georgia.

~ ☾ ~

Chapter 12

Sophie snorted. "We're insane. That's got to be it. Either I'm nuts or this is a dream. And I'm leaning towards crazy. I mean I've always *known* you lived on the border of Crazytown, but not me."

"Sophie," Callie started, but Sophie motioned for her mother to not say a word.

"Muses?" she said, twisting a piece of her hair as if the action could help yank out a better understanding of what her grandmother said. "Muses don't exist. They're not real. They don't even make decent movies about them. The only Muses I know are from that sucky movie you made me watch where they were on roller skates and wore peasant blouses and leg warmers. So if you think I'm about to throw on a pair of skates and feather my hair, you're crazier than I thought. Out of all of the supernatural secrets my family had to sprout from, I get to be part of the losers of Greek mythology. Muses are so lame. Please just tell me you guys are kidding."

Callie shrugged. "You don't understand how much I wish it were so. There were moments in Ohio when I began to believe the lie I told myself. That Muses were left in mythology, as mere explanations to what was unexplainable for the ancient Greeks. But that's the thing. They—I mean—we...exist. We're Muses. We're not vampires or fairies. We're not werewolves, nor witches, and trust me, there were moments I wished we were, but we're not insane. We're Muses." Callie sat down on the couch, motioning for her daughter to join her.

Sophie walked toward the couch and sat with her back to her mother on the farthest possible edge.

"I've always known what we were," Callie said. "It's not like Georgia would ever let me think about anything else." Callie sighed out a deep breath. "Sophie, I didn't have a

~ ☾ ~

normal childhood like you. I grew up always knowing I had a role to fulfill and each day Georgia took great pains to make sure I walked the path she thought I should walk. I knew I was expected to live a certain way and dedicate myself to..." she paused and smirked, "to the family business. I was raised to be obedient and being a Muse required great sacrifice. When I, like you, went through the change, the pressure to live up to Georgia's expectations was like being crushed."

Sophie looked at her mother. "Why is she so horrible? She wasn't like this back in Ohio. She was nice. A bit strange, but nice, and what the heck is a Demigod?"

"Well, I wish I knew why she is so strict, but I've never known her not to be." Callie laughed nervously. "I believe she is that way because she has to be. Georgia has a lot of responsibility. I'm not making excuses for her, but the responsibility takes its toll on her. Everything in our world has its cost. Unfortunately, with Georgia the cost comes across in being cruel and controlling. But, she always means well. And since we are now living under her roof, we're going to have to walk on eggshells a bit until we figure out what we're going to do."

"So what happened that made you a not-so-obedient daughter?"

"Your father happened. Being a Muse requires a woman to give up so much. She serves as a vessel for inspiration."

"A vessel? I don't..."

"A topic for another time, but let's just say falling in love isn't part of the deal, or at least not with someone who isn't part of our world." Callie, paused and mumbled, "They had to be part of Olympus."

Sophie shook her head in confusion. "So you're telling me the whole Mount Olympus, gods and goddesses, Centaurs, Gorgons with snakes for hair is all true? Please tell me some of it is made up."

"It's very real," Callie began. "This world, *our* world, isn't simple. It's not good or bad. It all depends on many factors. There was a time things were black and white, but things have changed. We've evolved as a community. So, picture me as a young woman, dedicated to her work and always listening to whatever her mother said and doing with

~ ☾ ~

complete perfection what she was told to do. She had
accepted that she would be told what she should think, what
she should wear, how she should act and even whom she
should talk to. An arranged marriage to an Olympian was in
her future. And as you will come to know or maybe you
already do from the many myths I've read to you, Olympians
do not make great husbands. This woman would be told
whether or not she would have children – and if it was so
deemed she would have children, she'd be told how they
would be raised. One controlled day after another would pass
by until the day she died. Imagine what that life would be
like."

"It would be a sucky arranged marriage kind of life."
Sophie said and leaned back into the depth of the couch.

"And it did suck. I hated my mother, hated this Vasilikós,
and hated living in a world that existed behind the scenes,
injecting myself into the lives of others for the briefest of
moments, but never truly living a life of my own. But then,
one night I met your father and everything changed. We fell
in love and for a Muse love isn't part of the deal. People fall in
love with us, not the other way around. Georgia and I got into
such fights about it, but I wouldn't budge.

Your father and I came up with a plan and we eloped in
the middle of the night. I had planned for all sorts of
Georgia's tricks, but there were no surprises. The Vasilikós
was quiet and off we went, thanking God it had been so easy.
We thought we were lucky." Callie's voice trailed off and
Sophie reached over and held her mother's hand.

"Mom, you have to know all of this is so unbelievable.
What am I supposed to think? Just a few moments ago, I was
living in Columbus, Ohio, wondering whether or not I would
pass my next Advanced Placement statistics class. And now
I'm physically changed, which I guess could be explained
away, but for you to suggest the myths are real. I don't know.
Did dad know what you were?"

Callie shook her head. "No. I was very careful. But being
careful meant I couldn't use my powers and perhaps we
struggled more than the average couple, due to my forsaking
my gifts. If I had a dime for every time I cursed Georgia, so
sure in my mind that she did everything she could to make

~ ☾ ~

our life hard, but I knew she had nothing to do with it. Once we were married, Georgia left us alone."

Sophie wiped tears from her eyes.

"Oh sweetie, we were so happy. Your father and I had each other and that was enough and when you came, well, it was complete bliss. But, I was kidding myself and it kills me to say this, but once again I was doing what Georgia expected me to do."

Sophie nodded. "You had me."

"Yes," Callie said. "And now, you're—"

Sophie faced her mother. She thought for the first time in her life she saw her. Yes, her mother was still the same beautiful, loving, pain-in-her-butt, complete and utter nag she'd always been. But Sophie now saw that, like everyone else, her mother wasn't perfect. In fact she was *far* from perfect. Her mother had made mistakes. In this moment, Sophie felt the closest she ever had to Callie.

"I'm like you," Sophie said, putting her hands into her mother's, giving them a hard squeeze. She leaned into Callie, wrapping her mother's arms around her and laying her head below the woman's chin. In response, Callie held her daughter, kissing the top of the girl's head several times.

"So this is what it feels to be a size two," Sophie joked. "Nice perk."

Callie laughed. "You know, Sophie, I am so tired. I'm tired of crying and I'm tired of running."

"Well, then, stop," Sophie said, sitting up. "Why don't you start at the beginning and work your way back."

***

Sophie followed her mother into a large gallery that opened into a reading room with stone floors, overstuffed couches and chairs, and huge oriental rugs. Her eyes were drawn to a painting of a young Georgia dressed in a goddess gown, draped over a Grecian fainting couch. She was caught mid-laugh, one arm lay across the highest point of the couch.

Callie motioned for Sophie to sit down at an ornately carved library table.

In front of them sat a large glass box with heavy iron hinges. Detailed grapevines and a single Greek word were etched into the center of the glass lid.

~ ☾ ~

ευλογημένος

"It means blessed," Callie stated.

Inside the case was a book with cracked leather bindings. Sophie was sure the book would crumble at the slightest touch. Callie removed the book from its case, causing a puff of dust to drift into the air, making Sophie wrinkle her nose.

Callie began, "Many years ago, my mother and I sat in these same chairs and began the journey you and I are about to begin. You are expected to learn and adopt the teachings of our people. For example, Muses are part of the Demigod society, and as part of this community we do not judge on appearances or preconceived notions because both can be deceiving. Demigod means half mortal, half Olympian."

Callie rested her palm on the old book in front of them, and Sophie watched as her mother's hand began to glow. The light seemed to penetrate the book itself, seeping over its top, soaking into its worn leather and crumbling pages, appearing to restore it back to new.

"This is one of the prized possessions of our family," Callie said.

Sophie couldn't help but smirk. "Muses are supposed to be these powerful creatures and one of our most prized possessions is a book?"

"This isn't just a book. It's a living portal to our people's past and a source of incredible power. It can also provide glimpses into your future, if it desires to do so."

Sophie took a deep breath; getting bored with the lead-up to what she was sure would be a big disappointment. "You make it sound like it's alive? So, does it have pictures that move, like in *Harry Potter*?"

Callie placed the book in front of Sophie, "It depends on the person holding it. For every person, it tends to react differently. "

For a good ten seconds, Sophie sat there, staring at the book, not wanting to touch the thing.

"Sophie, it's just a book," Callie said, opening it and turning it to face her daughter. The book's pages were filled with a beautiful script and a hand-drawn boarder, accented

~ ☾ ~

by numerous jewel-toned inks. Callie placed her hand on the
center of the page and sang a Grecian chant, rocking back and
forth with her eyes closed. Sophie was puzzled.

Almost snakelike, the script on the book's open pages
began to move, unraveling itself. Sophie was fascinated yet
unnerved. The slithering ink seemed trapped by the page's
boarder, but much to Sophie's horror, the ink caressed her
mother's pinky and curled back onto itself before springing
like a viper, wrapping itself around Callie's hand, wrist and
arm. It created a moving tattoo on her mother's arm and
Sophie yelped as she attempted to scramble from her seat.
Callie abruptly stopped chanting and grabbed hold of
Sophie's arm, holding her in place.

Callie opened her eyes and Sophie cringed. Her mother's
eyes were now coated with a thick white film and all of her
exposed skin was now covered in the moving ink. Callie's eyes
filled with the ink. She grinned and the ink seeped out of her
teeth and gums, both of which were stained black.

"This is a first," Callie laughed, the ink continuing to seep
out of her mouth and before Sophie could react, the tendrils
rushed forward from Callie, arching high into the air and
slamming on top of the two women, submerging them in an
ocean of black.

Sophie opened her eyes to find herself in a place so dark
she couldn't see the floor, walls or ceiling. A breeze rustled
her hair and the ink's darkness swept away like fallen leaves.
With the ink gone, what was left was a white void. Her
mother stood next to her.

Callie smiled at her daughter. "We're in the Oracle's realm.
She must be drawn to you."

"Great. Lucky me. What's next, some coffee and pastry?
Can't wait to see what happens next," Sophie said.

The space seemed endless, lacking any boundaries.

"You'll have to excuse me." A woman's voice came forth
from the void in front of them. It spoke in velvety richness
and sounded musical. "Forgive me for saying, but isn't it
proper etiquette to call first before dropping in. I believe I
read it somewhere in a book." The voice burst into laughter.
"Oh my, you see, even after numerous millenniums of
existence, I still have a brilliant sense of humor."

~ ☾ ~

Sophie glanced at her mother and slipped her shaking hand into Callie's, giving it a squeeze. Although it had not been there a few seconds ago, a large white dressing table with a huge mirror appeared out of nowhere in front of them.

Mom, I swear, don't you dare walk me towards that thing. I don't want to go near it, whatever it is.

Callie led them towards the object. Sophie realized it wasn't real, but was a detailed hand drawing of a dressing table. Or rather an invisible artist was drawing it right before them. The mirror didn't face them and the faint sounds of movement came from behind it, while multiple lines continued to appear out of nowhere. Once the dressing table was finished, the unseen artist began working on the surroundings. A pale white hand reached for a drawn silver hairbrush.

"There are so many problems with surprise guests." The white hand gestured towards Sophie. "If not given enough time to dry, my artwork can smear."

The white hand set down the hairbrush and displayed its open palm, which was now dirty with ink.

"Why, I haven't even had time to put on my face." The voice laughed again, a thick European accent dripping off each syllable. With one quick motion the dressing table flew out of the way, exposing the woman behind it. She was dressed in a glittering, floor-length velvet dressing gown with a high collar. The woman had straight, thick black hair and true to what she'd said, she lacked a face. Three gaping holes appeared where the woman's mouth and eyes should have been. Seeing the shock in Sophie's face, the figure laughed, the larger hole twisting in what would have been a smile, had the thing possessed lips.

"That's enough of the games, Aletheria. You're scaring my daughter," Callie said.

The pale woman turned her head toward Callie, its mouth wide open in shock. "It has been a long time since you came for a visit, child." The thing advanced, gliding above the floor. It brought its blank face right up to Callie's.

"So I'll let your rudeness go unnoticed," Aletheria said, with an audible growl. She smiled shyly as black lines dripped onto the white surface of its face. Within seconds, as if drawn

~ ☾ ~

by Michelangelo himself, a two-dimensional face appeared. Aletheria took a deep breath, filling her cheeks with air and, grabbing her newly drawn nose, blew hard as if trying to stifle a sneeze. With a pop, the face's features shot out. Sophie jumped back, and Aletheria laughed heartily, each gasp of air filling the pale figure with color.

Sophie glanced away and noticed the surrounding room had taken shape, as the final scribbles to the temple's chamber filled in, the scratching sounds of an unseen pen dying away.

"There was a time when your mother would spend endless hours with me," the Oracle said to Sophie. "Asking me question after question after question. Oh, how I have longed for those times. Although you think otherwise, I am not your enemy, Callista, and you would do well not to become mine."

The Oracle's large brown eyes, accented by thick, dark mascara and long lashes, looked deep into Callie's face. "But, I forgive you. I forgive you, my love, for out of all of the Muses I have served, and there have been many, you are my most beloved. At least for now." Aletheria warmly placed both her hands on Callie's shoulders. "Now, if you'll excuse us, I think I'd like to talk to Sophia. Alone."

Aletheria waved her right hand and dismissed Callie, who disappeared with a loud crack.

~ ☾ ~

Chapter 13

Sophie jumped back in reaction, having brief recollections of how the Oracle had treated her back in Ohio. *Aletheria is the last person I want to be alone with.*

Aletheria threw off her dressing gown, exposing a knee-length sundress. In mid-air, the dressing gown's black lines unraveled and it disappeared. Turning on a pair of extremely high and what Sophie considered to be fashionable wedges, Aletheria walked toward two large, heavy doors and threw them open as if they were made of air. She placed the large hat on her head, pulling the brim forward.

"Come. Let's go grab a bite to eat. You must be famished." Without waiting for an answer, Aletheria walked out the door, waving her scarf at Sophie.

Aletheria walked in slow, measured steps, but her stride was long enough that the much shorter Sophie struggled to keep up with her. The Oracle emphasized her words with her expressive hands and arms.

"Are we still in the book?" Sophie asked, wondering how any of this could be real.

The Oracle laughed, clapping her hands.

They were walking down a sunny cobblestone street Sophie didn't recognize, and for a moment she was overwhelmed. She couldn't help wonder what was expected of her.

What the heck was an Oracle anyway? Can everyone see her or is she like a ghost?

A few men whistled after Aletheria and she waved at them. She shouted something in Greek, which she told Sophie meant "they would do better to whistle at their own wives." The sun was bright and Aletheria winked as a pair of tortoise shell horned-rimmed sunglasses sketched themselves onto the bridge of her nose.

~ ☾ ~

"Are we still in the book? One of these days you Muses will ask me an original question. We can't be in the book, my dear. It's physically impossible, because I *am* the book."

They sat down in a café, one door down from a bakery. The air was heavy with the scent of frosted cakes, breads and baklava.

Aletheria took a sip of the bottled water the waiter had brought and glanced at the menu. Sophie's water sat untouched as she watched the Oracle.

Aletheria sighed and put her menu down.

"You aren't going to let me enjoy lunch until I let you ask me a million questions."

The waiter walked over and Sophie watched as Aletheria ordered one of everything on the menu.

Oracles must burn off more calories than Muses.

"What?" she remarked to Sophie. "I am famished and I've waited a long time for you to come along."

"To have lunch?" Sophie said, handing back her menu to the waiter.

"Oh, dearest, I can tell we're going to become great friends."

Sophie frowned and unscrewed the top to her water, taking a gulp. "Um," she began. "My memory is kind of fuzzy about the last few weeks, but I do remember you and you weren't *besties* with me."

Aletheria took off her hat and hung it on the empty chair next to her. "I'm sure your mother has spoken of the new world you now live in and things aren't—"

Sophie interrupted, "Black and white. Okay, I get it. So, after scaring the heck out of me with your whole nasty, ashy skin condition and verbally beating me up with your screams of doom and gloom, I'm now expected to believe you're someone I can trust?" Sophie's voice grew shrill and loud. "You want me to forget our past and pretend we're old friends. Like we comb each other's hair, eat grilled cheeses and talk about hot guys during sleepovers? I am not going to pretend I'm interested in your thoughts on the latest boy band."

Sophie winced as the strange burning sensation of energy began to build inside her. Like she has swallowed a sparkler.

~ ☾ ~

Okay, this sucks. Nobody said anything about heartburn being part of the deal. Remembering what had happened to the mirror, she took a few deep, calming breathes. The burning sensations under her skin lessened with each exhale.

I am in control. I will not lose control. Get your crap together, Sophie.

"All right, my dear, we'll take this slowly," Aletheria said. "I know you have been through more than the average person could take, especially one of your age. If I can help you understand a small part of this whole wonderful journey you have begun, then maybe I can prove to you what a true friend I am." She slapped Sophie's hand in a playful gesture and sat back in her chair, crossing her legs and arranging her skirt.

It took every ounce of control for Sophie not to roll her eyes as she noticed Aletheria was making sure she showed her legs in the most positive light. The Oracle purred like a cat, stretching herself in a sunbeam the moment she noticed a man walking by their table. Even the waiter wasn't excluded from Aletheria's attentions.

"I'm guessing your mother and Georgia haven't explained much to you. You know, your mother was always such a frustrating girl, especially when it came to dealing with difficult situations. That one was always stumbling over herself, saying she was sorry about this, sorry about that, moaning about wanting to be free of the ties binding her to this world. I used to pray that she would grow more of a backbone."

Sophie couldn't help but feel insulted. "You don't know her the way I know her, because if you did, you wouldn't say those things."

The Oracle continued, "And Georgia, well forgive me for saying so, but Georgia is what you Americans refer to as 'control freak.' Her hunger for power is constant, so driven and always planning. You just want to take whatever stick is shoved up her rump and pull it out."

The thought of a stick being removed from her grandmother's 'rump' was enough to make Sophie put her hurt feelings aside and smile.

It's more like a large branch or a small oak tree.

"There you go. I knew I would get a nice smile out of you.

~ ☾ ~

Now, I am going to give you an incredible gift. During this lunch, I am going to answer any question you ask. Go ahead. Ask anything you like, as long as it isn't about the future. Sharing future knowledge is for me to give and not to be requested."

The waiter interrupted the two women as he sat down the first set of dishes full of food. Aletheria inhaled deeply, taking in the food's aroma.

"What the heck are you?" Sophie said.

"I adore roasted chicken. This restaurant makes a chicken so tender the meat falls off the bone and melts in your mouth. You know the Greeks make the best chicken, with a hint of lemon they— but, there I go again, branching off into another topic, my sincerest apologies. I said to you that I am the book. Some say when a writer creates the written word a piece of their soul is given to his or her creation. Well, I took it to a higher level. Once, too long ago to even admit—so don't bother asking—I was a very powerful Oracle. An Oracle is a sort of witch. I was known worldwide, as one temple after another was erected to please me. It is quite easy to lose oneself in the adoration of others, and once you begin to see yourself through the eyes of the adoring masses you tend to lose your grasp on reality. You really should try this rice. It is simply heaven."

Aletheria reached for a serving spoon and piled a large amount of rice and several pieces of chicken onto Sophie's empty plate.

"Think of me as an ancient Greek talk show host. With fame, comes great power and responsibility." She emphasized each word with the swinging of a chicken wing.

"Now you're just quoting the movie, *Spiderman*."

"Oh. *Spiderman*. Wearing his tight little costume. They always get such handsome boys to play that role and that upside-down kiss. Oh, and they always have the tightest little...you really need to stop leading me off topic, Sophia. And with great power can also come great jealousy. Not from my followers and not even from the non-believers, because at the time there were so many gods to worship nobody cared who worshipped what and whom. Today, of course, is a different story. However, my ever-growing popularity did not go unnoticed by the gods."

~ ☾ ~

Sophie interrupted, with a quiet whisper, "So, they *are* real?"

"Goodness, me." Aletheria exclaimed. "Yes, they are real and incredibly dangerous. Take my word when I say the gods despised anyone whose popularity surpassed their own."

Great, so the Greek gods are the popular girls in school, multiplied by infinity. This keeps getting better and better. I wonder if Muses have to take yearbook pictures.

"At a party given by a king who is long since dead, I ran into Aphrodite, who was always a temperamental hag."

"I thought she was supposed to be the most beautiful woman in the world." Sophie said, between bites.

Aletheria rolled her eyes. "Everyone used to go on and on about her beauty. She's so beautiful. Well, let me say…her hair was a bit on the limp side and she didn't have much of a chin to speak of, not that you could tell because she tended to have two of them. And if it weren't for her ability to use glamour, everyone would have noticed she had a bit of a mustache and blemish problem. And her feet, oh my, the sharpest cheese grater couldn't help those cracking heels of hers. They smelled too."

"What's glamour?" Sophie asked.

"It's a sort of magic. It gives a person the ability to change and adjust their appearance in a way that makes them irresistible."

Finally, something I can look forward to. Why worry about makeup, when you can glamour? I knew there had to be an upside to being a Muse. Can't find time to shave your legs, no problem. A wink of my eye and poof, I've got glamour.

Aletheria took a sip of her water. "So, there I was, conversing with an attractive young man from Crete who had arms I couldn't keep my hands off of and a stomach I wanted to…well, he was the most beautiful man I had ever seen. It wasn't until later, after numerous drinks of the most amazing wine, I found out he was an Olympian. And as fate would have it, he was also the latest love interest of Aphrodite. Like that little tramp didn't already have at least six or seven other men she was…. Sorry, there I go again. Well, considering what happened to poor Medusa, a girl I had grown up with, I

~ ☾ ~

left the party, hoping I had neither caught Aphrodite's attention nor made her angry. One thing you need to understand is that Olympians will not accept any sort of rejection, and regardless of the consequences the young god chased after me. Aphrodite couldn't punish *him*, so what did he care?"

They don't sound much different from the guys I know.

"So, I'm guessing he found you, begged you to change your mind and you melted?" Sophie asked.

"Well, I'd like to think I put up some fight," Aletheria replied. "Remember, I was *The* Oracle, after all. But then he came up with an idea, a way that I would never die or could ever be hurt by Aphrodite, nor any god's wrath. After some discussion, among other things," Aletheria winked, "He created a diary of sorts. Except this was no ordinary book. By writing my thoughts into it, I not only gave the book my written word but also my soul, piece by little piece, until everything I was, everything I could ever be, was now tucked safely away in the book. A book that none of the elements, nor god nor human, could hurt. I was transformed into a different sort of being."

This is getting good. "Something tells me there's a catch to it. It's never that easy."

"There was a catch. The book was both my salvation and my damnation. It was a trap ensuring no other man could have me but this young selfish god and, as with all Olympians, his attentions soon wavered. Before I knew it, I was nothing more than an old book left on a shelf. Several centuries passed of me feeling sorry for myself, thinking I was the biggest fool there ever was, unsure how an Oracle of my standing and power was now someone's forgotten love, trapped forever and put away."

"It must have been horrible," Sophie said, taking a sip of her water.

The Oracle set her fork down. "It was cruel. But, then, one day a young Muse found me. I had been left in a remote ruin to rot. The Muse's name was Zoe. I believe she was a Muse of life, a generalist in regards to inspiration—life covers so much—but she tended to focus on second chances, giving those who have fallen from grace a shot at redemption. She

~ ☽ ~

found me and we struck a deal. I would no longer be bound to the young god's keep, nor controlled by him any longer. In addition to having the safety of the book to protect me against Aphrodite, because that old hag never forgets anything, I would also receive protection from the Muses, a group of goddesses even Aphrodite wouldn't trifle with. You have to remember, love without inspiration is not love, it's lust. I also received other 'benefits' from being under the Muses' care. I got back all of my lost Oracle abilities and I also could move between the worlds: the world the book represented, this world and other Olympian realms you will soon have access to. It was like being a god and all I had to do was be bound to a life of servitude to the Muses. "

"Considering the situation you were in, I think you got a great deal," Sophie said.

Aletheria put down the desert menu and called the waiter over. "We'll take two sundaes and I'll also have a slice of that delicious lemon cake your grandmother makes." The waiter left and returned quickly, placing two large sundaes in front of the women, along with a large, heavily frosted slice of lemon cake. The slice sat on a plate coated with powdered sugar.

"That is my story. I serve the Vasilikós of Greece and Italy, of which your grandmother Georgia is head of."

"Silli what?"

"Good God. Hasn't your mother even explained about the Vasilikós? There are nine of them? The original Nine Daughters established the Nine Vasilikós?"

Sophie shook her head.

The Oracle put her spoon down. "Why do I even bother to think that simple tasks like Muses 101 would have been the first thing they covered with you. Have they even explained the gods and how they fit into all of this?"

"Cut them some slack." Sophie spat back, not meaning for it to come out as rudely as it sounded. "I'm sorry, but you have to stop tearing my family down."

Aletheria eyed the girl. "May I?" the Oracle asked, pointing to the seat next to the girl. Sophie shrugged a 'help yourself'.

Aletheria moved next to Sophie. "I'd like to gather some information, but it requires me to touch your hand." Sophie

~ ☾ ~

offered her hand to the woman and Aletheria took it in her own and turned it palm side up and began tracing the lines on the girl's palm. The Oracle's brow furrowed. She brought her face closer to Sophie's and looked into the girl's eyes.

The surface to Aletheria's eyes became blank and shone like a mirror, reflecting Sophie's eyes back at her. Sophie's mind was freefalling into the infinite depth of the reflection as she watched her eyes change colors and glowed with an inner light.

"The light you see now is normal for a Muse, but there is something more to you," Aletheria remarked.

Sophie was beginning to feel uncomfortable, as she saw stars twinkle from the reflection of her own eyes.

"I see the stars, like the elders," Aletheria said. "I see the heavens. How is this possible?"

Sophie ripped her hand away from Aletheria, breaking the connection, but the Oracle remained in her trance. "You are no ordinary girl," she said. "You are no mere Muse."

Aletheria sat back in her chair, her eyes now rolling back into her head. She threw her hands up, cradling her head, moaning in pain. "Someone is trying to stop me from knowing. Someone is trying to hold something in place to blind my sight. Who would dare?" Aletheria asked as she brought her other hand back to her head. "It's a spell, a veil of obedience. If I can focus..."

Sweat began to bead on Aletheria's brow, causing her drawn face to smudge and slide off in long black drips. She dragged her hands down to her throat and Sophie grimaced as Aletheria's entire body seemed to smear and become even more grotesque, resembling the blood and guts Halloween masks that terrified Sophie as a kid. Globs of black ink dripped like mud, exposing the pure white canvas of Aletheria's face. She no longer had a mouth or eyes, each of these holes dripped thick, tar-like ink, reminding Sophie of poor animals caught in an oil spill. Aletheria grabbed the tablecloth and ripped it away from the table, somehow managing not to send the numerous dishes flying in all directions. Taking the cloth, Aletheria covered her face as even more ink seemed to surge and bubble from within her.

Sophie didn't know whether to applaud or get some help.

~ ☾ ~

Aletheria moaned one final time then slumped back in her chair, breathing heavily.

"Please excuse me while I fix my face." Within a blink she was gone and before Sophie could react Aletheria appeared again, restored to her original state.

"I know everything and I need to have a talk with Georgia," Aletheria said, throwing several large Euros onto the table and standing up to leave. "On the way, we can cover the gods."

They walked out of the café onto an uneven sidewalk made of huge slabs of marble. Sophie watched as Aletheria's flowing skirt whipped around and changed itself into a pair of English riding pants and the bodice became a crisp, white, long sleeved cotton shirt. The sleeves rolled themselves up and the once-stylish heels became a pair of riding boots. The Oracle shook her head, causing her long tresses to fall away, leaving a crisp pageboy haircut. "When it came to hair, the 1920's was my favorite decade. It was such liberation from the Victorian era."

"You said we would talk about the gods?" Sophie said.

"Yes..." Aletheria answered. "First, they aren't gods at all. I want you to try and picture the world during its infancy. Humans needed something to help guide their lives. Now, I'm not going to get into a theological discussion, since I have limited time today. So, when I say God, take it at face value. So, up in the heavens, God decides maybe a single god option is too complicated for his beloved children to grasp. And I'm guessing if God could be tired after creating the world, he was at a point of needing a vacation. He created the Heavens and the Earth and although I've never had the blessing of children myself, I am told raising children is an exhausting adventure."

"God gets exhausted?" Sophie asked.

"Well, not the way you're thinking. So in his infinite wisdom, God calls some of his most trusted associates to his side. They go by many names, but we'll call them Angels. He said, 'I'm going to take a few days off, and while I'm gone I want you select few to watch the children.' The Angels agree and God and the Angels come up with this idea of creating what is termed as a polytheistic society, meaning a society with more than one god. So, instead of saying the world and

~ ☾ ~

life are based from a single supreme being, we'll let the children believe there is one god responsible for making the crops grow and another god responsible for love and another god for the seas. Are you following me?" Aletheria turns to look at Sophie.

"It seems like a lot of work so God can take a vacation. Are you sure this is the way it happened?"

Aletheria nodded. "Use whatever title you want. God needed a break. Don't you sometimes have to take a break when you're working on a long assignment from your school?"

"Yeah, but...I'm not God. Can we sit for a second? I feel like I'm going to pass out," Sophie replied.

Aletheria walked over to a small park and Sophie sighed in relief, as they both sit down on a bench where the Oracle handed Sophie a bottle of water that drew itself into Aletheria's hand.

"Thank you," Sophie said. "So a god for each item to explain why things are the way they are."

"Exactly. So with God's help, the Angels establish themselves as these minor and major deities and God goes off on his vacation. Doing what, I have no idea, although Greece does have some of the most magnificent beaches. Now I know a lot of people believe Angels are these perfect beings who only do good, and for the most part that is what they were, at least until they started taking their role as gods a bit too seriously."

"I bet I can guess what happens. In the drama club, there was this one girl who always got the big parts and I always got stuck as stage or prop manager. Last spring she broke her leg during rehearsals for *Hello Dolly* and I was the understudy, so they gave it to me."

"And how did that make you feel?"

"Fantastic. At least until she convinced the drama teacher it would be so incredibly "forward thinking" if we had a Dolly Levy in a wheelchair."

"It must have been a horrible production. So glad I missed it. So, like you, the Angels find out they like the adoration, being worshipped, having temples and statues created to honor them and the roar of the crowds. In response to this

~ ☽ ~

newfound power, they created a whole world hovering between Heaven and Earth, called Mount Olympus. Olympus is where these new gods ruled and sat in judgment of mortals and themselves."

"And let me guess," Sophie interrupted. "Like *Clash of the Titans*, they were total divas. Always walking around, saying this is my hairbrush and don't use my pancake makeup. Like that girl in my drama class."

"You *do* have a way with words. Yes, there were constant battles between the gods, which are bound to happen with continual power struggles. More importantly, they discovered mortal love, and not only love but also sex with mortals, was like a drug to them. And it changed them. The more mortal love and adoration they had, they more they desired. A god could and would go from one mortal obsession to another, not concerned about what it left in its wake. Every loathing trait in the human race had been taken up and multiplied by ten in these powerful beings."

"Okay, so you're telling me the gods, these Angels, were complete and utter sluts, sleeping with anything that had a pulse. Ew, now it's getting kinda gross," Sophie said.

"The result of the mating between gods and humans was the creation of a type of beings caught between two worlds. They had one foot in Olympus and one foot on Earth. They were labeled the Demigods and forced to remain on Earth. These poor beings did everything within their power to hide their Olympian heritage."

"Why?" Sophie asked. "I would think having ties to Olympus would be beneficial. I mean…if I had this sort of 'get out of jail free' card, it would be pretty hard not to use it. Wouldn't it be like instant VIP status?"

"During the early years that may have been true, but as the reign of the Olympians went on, the Demigods were considered expendable. Remember, the Olympians had enough problems dealing with their own kind. Adding another layer of superior beings meant having to share the love of mortals, and that wasn't something they were willing to do. As the Olympians' addiction to mortal love grew, the adoration of mortals wavered because Olympian cruelty became unbearable. The line between love and hate is easily

~ ☾ ~

crossed and the gods discovered a similar rush could be derived from terror and fear.

So, as you can imagine, the Olympians fell out of favor. Temples, statues, anything created to show respect for these gods were destroyed and, like addicts who've been deprived of their drug of choice, the Olympians became enraged and inflicted even more harm and pain. Unable to fight the gods, the mortals attacked those less powerful, the Demigods, who from no fault of their own were guilty by association."

"Georgia referred to herself as a Demigod," Sophie said, half to herself, half to the Oracle. *Oh my God. Is that what I am? Some sort of freak of nature?*

"Yes, she is and so are you."

Aletheria took a sip of her water, replacing the cap back onto the bottle. "The Demigods were hunted down and killed by both those from Olympus and those from the mortal world. Some didn't even have a chance, not understanding the power they had or choosing not to use it, in complete defiance of their Olympian heritage. Some would rather die than toss a single lightning bolt or do anything that proved their Olympian father or mother gave them anything of value. Their Olympian family had turned their backs on them. The Demigods, in turn, rejected anything having to do with Olympus and died for it."

"It's so sad," Sophie said as Aletheria peeled away the label of her water bottle.

"Bodies of mortal and Demigod alike were strewn across the land, each marked in a way that their souls could not pass through the underworld and were damned to an eternity of misery in the river Styx. Eventually, the cries of his children, both human and Demigod, reached God's ears and in a fury, he tore the Olympians off their false thrones and demanded their immediate return to him."

"Well, it was about time. I mean... a vacation is one thing. Abandonment is another. Makes you wish they had some sort of children's services or something like it on the god level?"

"Some of the Olympians returned to God, but others remained. Some, like the Muses, stayed to serve a sort of self-inflicted penance. Although not guilty of the cruelty inflicted by their fellow gods, for the Muses, not doing anything made

~ ☾ ~

them guiltier. They had the blood of so many on their hands. Some gods managed to escape God's wrath and remained for other, darker reasons. Because they did not return as instructed, those Angels are the Fallen Ones, damned to an eternity of living among those they both despised and desired, but not as gods. They are powerless, shadows of their former selves, waiting for their opportunity to rise up and rule the earth and the human race. As for the remaining Demigods, they scattered to the ends of the Earth in an attempt to find the peace and security they searched for. The Muses and their Demigod descendants are the last defense from the Fallen Ones. Never be fooled into believing the Fallen Ones aren't a threat. They are immortal and time is on their side. There are also rumors that some are regaining their powers, which is a terrifying thought."

Sophie sat for a moment, completely numb and then spoke. "I'm sixteen years old. Do you know what most girls worry about when they're sixteen? Getting a pimple the day of school pictures, wondering if she will be asked to go to the spring fling, worried they didn't study enough for the next trigonometry exam or not getting their reading done for English lit, because who the heck wants to read *The Great Gatsby* when all you need to do is watch the movie?"

Aletheria faced Sophie. "That was another world, another life."

Sophie's face burned as a surge of anger rip through her. "I know this is another world," she said through gritted teeth. "How can I not know? I wake up earlier today to find I've changed physically. I don't recognize myself and I've got things shooting out of my hands and to make matters worse, I'm guessing I have no clothes to wear because my old ones are too big on me. I mean, whose clothes am I wearing? And now, on top of all of this, I have to believe in Greek gods or gods that aren't gods. No sir, they're angels, demi-angels..."

"Demigods," Aletheria corrected.

"I want to speak to my mother." Sophie stood up and began walking.

"You're going the wrong way." Aletheria shouted.

Sophie swiveled and headed back, walking past a stone wall with the word "Nothos" painted on it.

~ ☾ ~

Chapter 14

An old woman named Penny stood hidden behind a large bush, holding her breadth, gripping her cane with such force she thought her fingers would shatter into a million pieces. The can of red spray paint she held fell from her hand.

Damn arthritis. She decided the pain of retrieving the can of paint wasn't worth the effort. She had plenty other cans in her oversized purse and at home.

She didn't move until she knew for sure the Oracle had left. She saw the witch rush in the direction of what she assumed had to be the young Muse her visions had foretold. She heard the entire conversation and couldn't help but grin to herself. The young Muse was ignorant of her situation. Even if Aletheria would tell her everything, it wouldn't help the girl avoid her fate. She smacked her lips in delight, licking her upper lip, savoring the salty taste of her sweat. When Penny knew it was safe, she stepped from behind the bush and walked towards the lane leading her to the desolate house she had lived in for more years than she cared to remember. The heavy burden she carried for these many millennia seemed heavier today. Her legs and back groaned as she followed the long, winding street, and for a moment she thought her aches and pains would cause her to not make it.

It is the heat. It always made her feel worse. The mere thought that she would soon seek revenge for her hellish existence made her almost feel young and hopeful. She could picture in her mind the terrors awaiting the girl and Callie, and Georgia's screams of agony would be music to her ears.

Not a single day had gone by when Penny didn't think of ways to torture Georgia, of ways to prolong the pain she wished to inflict on the woman. She thought it ironic that Georgia was thinking she was preparing herself for such

~ ☾ ~

greatness, when in fact she was digging her own grave.

On her walk, Penny stopped every so often and pulled out another can of red spray paint. Glancing around and making sure no one would see her, she marked several walls and doors with the word, "Nothos." She thought her artwork was excellent.

How many millennia ago had God instructed Moses and the Jews to mark their doors with lamb's blood?

She thought it was fitting for her to mark the villager's doors the same way, except instead of sparing the life of the first son born in the household, she would murder everyone in the house and brand them "Nothos."

They all pitied old Penny. They all came around with their gifts of food and support because poor old Penny had no one. Their pity and casseroles were disgusting reminders of what was and should have been for the old goddess and she would make them pay. Spray-painting doors was only the beginning. Her powers and strength were returning to her and as they did, she knew she would become bored with continuing her simple vandalism.

But I need to be careful. If I become too greedy and exhaust my powers, I'll have to wait another unbearable nine cycles of the moon before they replenish again. Sending the Black Omen to that Nothos, Callista, and killing a group of filthy mortals in Ohio nearly left me helpless for months.

Thinking of the horrors she could unleash made Penny feel young again.

"Well, youngish," she muttered.

~ ☾ ~

Chapter 15

Sophie kept walking, wanting to leave the Oracle and her stories behind her. She heard Aletheria shouting for her to wait, but she didn't care.

"Look, I know this is a lot to take in, but you don't know enough about the island to go wandering off. Sophia, please stop."

Sophie stopped and stared at the Oracle.

"I know we just met, but I want you to know I feel a true maternal instinct for you."

Sophie smirked. "My mother didn't raise me to be an idiot. You don't know me, so you'll have to forgive me if I say you're full of crap."

"Okay, so you don't trust me. I understand and I accept I'll have to earn your trust, but please, let me take you back to the Vasilikós."

Sophie knew Aletheria was right. "Okay," Sophie said, waiting for the Oracle to show her the way at home.

"It will take us forever to walk to Georgia's. We'll ride this." Aletheria pointed to the empty space in front of them, as black scribbles drew a scooter.

Sophie couldn't help but think all of this was insane. *But maybe it's time to put such thoughts away.*

Aletheria handed to Sophie a freshly sketched helmet and Sophie slid it on her head, as she hopped onto the back of the new scooter. Her hands were sticky from the still wet ink.

"Hold on." Aletheria shouted, as the scooter roared to life. "This is going to be a fast trip and with a little luck, we won't kill anyone."

Sophie laughed, but wasted no time gripping Aletheria's waist right as the Oracle sent the scooter flying into the street.

"This is so thrilling." Aletheria shouted. "I've always wanted to do this. Look out." She yelled at a teenager, who

~ ☾ ~

wasn't watching where he was going and almost stepped in front of the scooter. They zoomed in and out of alleys and lanes, barely missing several small, elderly nuns shrouded in black from head to toe.

"Sorry." Sophie called after them.

A group of young men sat in a café near the water, and upon seeing Aletheria stood up, proclaiming their love for her. Aletheria laughed and brought the scooter to an abrupt halt. The Oracle flirted, baiting the young men to come closer. The men straightened their T-shirts, which were tight and showed off their well-toned torsos. As the men were close enough to almost touch, Aletheria sped off, screaming with laughter, shouting Greek taunts. "Poor boys," she shouted to Sophie. "They still have mother's milk on their chins."

They continued their ride for another twenty minutes until Aletheria pulled up to a small stone house on a desolate section of road. The Oracle got off, placed her helmet on the vacated seat and walked towards the house.

"Ummm, Aletheria?" Sophie said. "This can't be right. The bathroom I took a shower in was easily the size of this whole house."

Sophie watched Aletheria open the door, walk inside and slam it shut with an echoing bang. The wind picked up, clearly pushing Sophie towards the door.

"All right, I get the point," Sophie said to the wind.

The front door to the little stone cottage didn't open up into the room Sophie expected. She didn't expect to walk into her bedroom in Ohio, but it's what she found behind the door.

The shock of seeing the life she knew before was too much for her. Her mind had been aching for something familiar, for any kind of normality she could grasp onto and, as if she had rubbed some sort of magical lamp, it found her.

She went to her most prized possession. Sitting in a faded and paint-chipped wooden frame was a family picture. It was Sophie's favorite picture of the three of them. Callie lovingly gazing at Angelo and Angelo was looking up at a three-year-old Sophie who sat on his shoulders laughing and clapping.

Her lips trembled as the picture began to fade into a blurry puddle of colors, shapes and shadows. She blinked as the

~ ☾ ~

tears fell onto her cheeks, and she lifted a hand to wipe them away. With all of the talk of Muses, gods and Oracles, she had forgotten about her father, and the guilt of it slammed on top of her heart like a ten-ton weight and she found it hard to breathe. She remembered crying for her father before the change, but the wave of emotion wracking her body was so intense she thought her heart would burst.

She was doubled over in agony and fell onto her bed, crawling into a tight ball. Exhausted and mentally drained, she cried herself to sleep.

~ ☾ ~

Chapter 16

Georgia stood lost in her thoughts, clipping a few wayward tendrils away from one of the oldest vines in the entire vineyard. After saying a prayer in Greek, she placed the clippings into a basket. A slight breeze caressed her cheek and frowned.

"You know I don't like to be disturbed when I am tending to my vines," Georgia said over her shoulder as she removed her garden gloves.

"Well," the Oracle began, "I have learned we live in a world where rules are made to be broken."

An interrogation was not on my schedule for today.

"Aletheria, I don't have time for idle chatter. Now, if you'll excuse me, I've got a lot of work to do. Having my granddaughter here has taken up a lot of my time and these vines are in horrible condition."

Aletheria grabbed Georgia's wrist. "Did you think I wouldn't find out? Manipulation of the Oracle to this Vasilikós is not part of the deal I struck with Zoe, who I might remind you is a higher authority than you. Do you take me for a fool?"

"How dare you touch me, you rotten, festering book." Georgia shouted as she attempted to yank her wrist away, but the Oracle held fast.

"How *dare* I?" Aletheria screeched, dragging Georgia towards the main gates of the vineyards. "Let me remind you of who you are dealing with," the Oracle said as she ripped Georgia away from the vineyard in a blast of black ink.

Before Georgia could blink, she stood inside the ancient chapel attached to the main Vasilikós. The Orthodox Church was small, with eight rows of seating. Looking down from a domed ceiling was a massive mosaic of the Madonna holding the Christ child. Callie knelt in the front pew. With all the

~ ☾ ~

commotion, she swung around to face the interruption, as Aletheria materialized behind Georgia.

"So, tell me Georgia, shall I begin or will you? Who will be the first to tell your daughter what you have done?" Aletheria demanded.

Callie put down her prayer book and lifted her head. "Can't I have a few moments to mourn my husband?"

"Aletheria. This is neither the time nor the place for this kind of discussion. Can't you see my daughter is still in mourning?" Georgia demanded.

Aletheria laughed. "Thank goodness I know you, Georgia, or else I'd believe you were a concerned mother."

"Georgia. What is she talking about?" Callie asked.

"Honey, I don't know. She's lost her mind. Maybe it's a bad case of bookworms or binding rot. Let's go back to the Vasilikós—"

"All right," Aletheria said. "We'll do it the hard way. But first, allow me to give Callista a gift."

The Oracle reached over and placed her hand on the top of Callie's head. Callie began to scream as ink seeped from Aletheria's hand and the Oracle ripped away the invisible veil Georgia had placed over Callie's mind. Aletheria stepped back as Callie fell back into the pew.

"Callista," the Oracle began, "it would appear your mother has either been dabbling in the craft or had one of her many witch friends make you into the dutiful daughter she's always wanted. What was it, Georgia? A veil of obedience created with nightshade, lavender and mint-flavored Harpy tears?"

Georgia turned away as both women glared back at her.

"You see, Callista, it isn't any of my business what Georgia does. I don't care, as long as the integrity of this Vasilikós remains intact. However, when she decides to do something to *me*, well, my dear, I have to take action."

Callie gripped the back of the pew in front of her. "Is what she says true?"

Georgia sighed and sat down in the pew nearest to her.

"Yes," Georgia said wearily. "I didn't want to do it, anyway, but I had to get both of you back here. I had to and I'm sorry."

"I have to admit I'm completely disgusted with you, Georgia. I wish I could say I'm surprised. I went crazy

~ ☾ ~

wondering what the buzzing was in my head and, now that I think about it, it came back each time I tried to stand up to you. I always knew you were a bit of a control freak, but this goes beyond— why? Just tell me why?"

Georgia clasped her hands. "If I told you it was for your and Sophia's safety that I needed you to return and do what you were born to do, I'm guessing you wouldn't believe me and you'd shut me out forever. I knew if I told you the truth about Sophia you would have done everything within your power to keep her away from me and her destiny."

"You're insane. There is and was no destiny for Sophie, beyond living a normal life in Ohio. You created this mess and for what? Another Muse the world didn't need? "

"A ruler," Aletheria said with a smile. "Georgia wants to elevate this Vasilikós above all others."

Callie laughed. "Ruler? Do you know how ridiculous this sounds?"

Georgia ignored the comment.

"What have you done, Georgia?" Callie asked.

"I didn't do anything. How powerful do you think I am? This whole thing goes far beyond my capabilities. You need to come to terms with the idea that Sophie is something special and she will take her place as Queen over all of the Vasilikós."

"Another one of your power plays, Georgia?" said Callie. "Isn't it enough you have control of one of the oldest and most powerful Vasilikós?"

Georgia pressed her lips into a frown. "Callista, listen to me, now, because I am being upfront with you now. No lies, no agendas, just the truth."

Callie snorted. "Georgia, you wouldn't know the truth if it bit you on your as—"

"The Fallen Ones are trying to rise again, Callista. They are trying to take their place as gods to rule over this Earth and the Heavens. They're trying to reestablish Olympus. The hunting will begin again. You can't deny the signs."

The color drained from Callie's face, as she walked towards Georgia, stopping a few inches from the woman. "So, let me get this straight. You're telling me the Fallen Ones are back, trying to take things over and instead of protecting your family; you...you...you shove us right into the middle of a

~ ☾ ~

potential Olympian war? This is why you're back in my life?"

"Do you think I wanted this?" Georgia spat back. "I always knew you were a bit vapid, but *this is rich.* This whole situation was created way before you and I were even born. What would you have had me do? Pretend they would have left you alone? For the past two decades I have done exactly what you asked of me. I stayed away. Do you know how hard it was for me? I know what you think of me. The disgust you feel. Even though all I ever wanted was your and Sophia's happiness."

"Don't try the guilt card on me, Georgia. You've played that hand before and it never worked on me." Callie spat back.

Georgia smirked. "You're right and I deserve that. And before you think it, I'm not trying to be a martyr. I did everything to keep both of you hidden from their eyes, but you didn't behave. You didn't forsake your powers like you said you would."

"What are you talking about?" Callie said.

Georgia couldn't help but laugh. "Oh, Callista, now look who is being deceitful. You are too much. All of those cupcakes, all of those meals prepared for charities. Why, every meal you created had a little inspiration sprinkled in, even if you didn't know you were doing it. It was one twinkling light after another, pointing directly to the wretched Ohio hut you called home."

"Are you serious? A few cupcakes and my cooking at home is not an expansive use of my power. It shouldn't have even attracted a flea, let alone the Fallen Ones."

Georgia scoffed. "And I won't even begin to list the many other people you touched. A chance meeting between you and a young girl wanting to be a celebrity chef and poof, Suzy Sunbeam. Another chance meeting with a struggling Savannah mother and poof, Stella Dubois for some down-home southern cooking? Dare I even go into the little shots of inspiration that created *Top Cook, King of Cake*s and *The Meal Network*?"

"I don't know what you're talking about," Callie said.

Georgia took a step closer to Callie, and Callie diverted her eyes.

~ ☾ ~

"You wear your guilt wonderfully, my deceitful child."

"It was nothing."

"Who's the liar now, Callista?" Georgia remarked. "You at least have to lay claim to Ingrid Malworth. You picked a woman as distant as your own mother to thumb your nose in my face."

Callie turned away from Georgia.

"Well my dear, if I noticed, I can assure you *they* noticed and *they* took action to try to ensure Sophia's destiny was not realized. We wouldn't be having this conversation at all had you decided to meet Angelo at the airport."

"Angelo. They killed Angelo and I'm to blame." Callie whispered the words, as she covered her mouth. Fresh tears slid down her face.

"And they would have killed both of you had they had the chance. That's all it takes to undo everything—a chance."

"This is too much," Callie said to herself. "Too much to digest."

"So what would you have me do? Sit back and watch them kill my daughter and granddaughter? There was one way to protect you. I had to have you and Sophia here and I had to have Sophia come into her birthright. It was the only way. If she didn't, she would have been branded a Nothos and slaughtered. We had to fulfill what the Fates predicted. We all have roles to play in this war, Callista, and I won't deny it gives me great satisfaction to know both of you are back where I've always thought you belonged. I won't even attempt to hide my jubilation in knowing my granddaughter will raise our family to new heights of power because I can no longer deny the obvious. We are destined for greatness."

"She's a run-of-the-mill Muse. What greatness are you talking about?"

"Sophia will lead the Vasilikós and usher in a new renaissance, another Golden Era. She is the final defense from the rise of the Fallen Ones. She is our only hope of defeating the utter evil and darkness the Fallen Ones represent. That is her true destiny. She is our warrior."

Callie turned into the direction of the Oracle.

Aletheria lowered her head. "What she has told you is the truth. Your daughter carries a heavy burden."

~ ☾ ~

"So, Georgia," Callie began, "I'm sure you've got it all figured out. What do we do now?"

"We prepare Sophia. We protect her and we all get ready for the battle to come," Georgia said.

Callie gathered her tissues and shoved them into the right pocket of her jeans.

"One thing, Georgia, while I will never understand why you did the things you did, and as hard as it is for me to get beyond our past, I assume I still have to thank you. However, let me give you one small warning. If you ever attempt to hide anything from me, attempt to cast or have any spells put on Sophie or me in order to fulfill your ambitions, I will make it my own personal crusade to make sure you never have anything to do with Sophie ever again. Do you understand me?"

Georgia knew she was surrounded on all sides. Her hand had been forced and she'd been forced to tell things she wasn't ready to tell. Every secret revealed meant the potential for failure and failure wasn't something she could accept. Not to mention the very idea of her daughter thinking it was appropriate to speak to her mother in such a threatening tone didn't sit well with her. She didn't like it.

Not at all. So, do I put my daughter in her proper place? Tell her to keep her opinions and empty threats to herself? Show her what I am truly capable of? She swallowed down her anger.

"Finally, the backbone I always knew you had," Georgia said.

"In the mean time, how do you plan to protect Sophie?" Callie said.

Georgia stood up. "I've already put things in motion about that."

~ ☾ ~

Chapter 17

Clink...clink...clink.

Sophie clenched her eyes tighter in an attempt to ignore the annoying sound, wondering what was making it.

Clink...clank...clank.

She assumed it must be a strange Greek alarm clock and threw her arm towards her nightstand, knocking several items onto the floor.

"You know, Sophie, I'm sure I can think of *at least* a million things I could be doing, but nothing would be as fulfilling as watching you sleep. I'm having a wicked time."

Sophie's opened her eyes and winced at the morning sunlight streaming into the bedroom. She heard the owner of the voice take a sip of something and then set an object down with another clank.

Who the hell is in my room?

"We've got a busy day ahead of us and it doesn't include you sleeping in and a late wake-up call."

A throb to the center of her forehead made her cringe.

I am going to kill whoever is the owner of that crisp and tight New England accent. The room temperature is dropping five degrees with each syllable coming from it.

She sat up and yelled out in pain as her sore body asked her to stop moving.

"As you will learn, Muses tend to be on the emotional side. Emotions can be a trigger for your powers, but if you're not careful they can overwhelm you, leaving you helpless."

Seated at Sophie's desk was a beautiful girl in cut-off shorts, white shirt and well-worn leather sandals. She guessed she must be around her own age. Her skin was dark brown and her hair was a mass of arranged dreadlocks, each strand thick with golden threads weaved in.

The girl sat with her legs crossed and reached over to the

~ ☾ ~

mug sitting on the desk next to her, briskly stirred the drink and dropped the spoon onto the saucer with a loud clank.

"Who the heck are you? What are you doing in my room? And for the love of God, stop banging." Sophie groaned as she scratched the side of her head and scooted to the edge of her bed. "I'd say I'm surprised to find a complete stranger in my bedroom, but I'm sure this is all part of the wonderful world of Muse."

"Well, that is a step in the right direction. My name is Angela," the girl said, uncrossing her legs to face Sophie. "You know, I'm quite excited to have the opportunity to help a Muse develop her sea legs. You see, I've always found Muses to be curious creatures."

Angela stood up and approached Sophie, holding up her hand in front of her palm faced out. "You haven't been a Muse for very long. I can tell because newer Muses tend to radiate the energy they attract. It's one of the reasons why younger Muses are isolated from the general public. I can feel the energy radiating off of you. Can you feel the energy in the room being drawn to you?"

Sophie shrugged. "I don't know if I do or don't? I've felt different since I first woke up in Greece."

"The reason why you radiate energy is because you have the ability to attract and harness the energy around you. Originally, it was an escape trigger. Muses can harness the energy around them to dissipate into the air and reappear at a safe location. This power has evolved into a powerful defense mechanism through which they can concentrate gathered energy into a single compact mass and fling it at an enemy. Some of the more powerful Muses have the ability to throw bolts of energy, although I've never seen it done. They also have developed the ability to use the same energy to move and manipulate items."

"Wonderful. Thanks for Muse 101. I now have a long list of things I either don't know how to do or have no control of and won't remember. Because in a period of a few days, I've had the kitchen sink thrown at me." Her neck was stiff and the last thing she wanted was a lecture from someone she didn't know.

"Things could always be worse, although looking the way

~ ☾ ~

you do right now, I'd be hard-pressed to think of a way they could." Angela sniffed. "You are about as far from being *yawl* as a person could get."

"Okay, maybe I'm not at my *yawl* best, whatever *yawl* means, but your '*tude*' is a bit much for me to take right at this moment. I'd be a bit more spoon full of sugar if you could dial it back."

There was a recognizable knock at the door and Sophie called for her mother to come in.

Callie walked in carrying a tray with several covered dishes, two glasses of orange juice and a carafe of what smelled like coffee. "Good morning, honey. I see you've met Angela." Callie set the tray on Sophie's bed.

"Yes," Angela said dryly. "Sophia was finally waking up."

Callie gave Sophie an all too familiar "is that so" look. She removed the covers to the plate to reveal an overflowing pile of eggs, French toast, sausage, bacon and buttered toast. "I wasn't sure what you would want, so I made a little bit of everything. Angela, I made enough so you two could get to know each other over breakfast. There's an extra plate underneath this one."

"Thank you," Angela said.

Sophie groaned as she scooted closer to the plates of food to grab a piece of maple bacon, which she popped into her mouth, savoring its salty sweetness. Her head pounded a little less and the throbbing ache in her back and limbs was almost gone. Feeling better, she grabbed another piece of bacon. In response, Callie motioned for Sophie to invite Angela to eat something.

"Please, help yourself." Sophie grumbled. But in response the girl fixed her dark brown eyes on Sophie. A slight movement below Angela's ear caught Sophie's attention and for a split second she could have sworn she saw a lock of the girl's hair move. Angela reached over and plucked a single piece of sausage from a serving plate while her other hand pushed the loose dread back into place.

Callie got up to leave.

"Mom, where are you going? I have a million—"

"Sweetie, I know you have a million questions, but I don't have time to answer them right now. Georgia expects me to

~ ☾ ~

resume my work and I already have several assignments I
have to begin working on."

"Well, what a surprise. Who knew there was a huge
backlog in the inspiration business. So, just like that? You go
back to work, doing whatever a Muse does and I'm expected
to sit here and wait until someone decides to give me the
whole story? Why do I have the feeling I'm being kept in the
dark? It's driving me crazy." Sophie whined.

"Honey, look, I know you are struggling with all of this."
Callie sat down on the edge of the bed. She placed her hand
on her daughter's and gave it a squeeze. "That's why Angela is
here. She'll begin your education. It's summer and we'll begin
your real education in the fall, but for now, you're going to
have to let Angela help bring you up to speed. We have an
endless list of preparations to work on."

"Preparations, for what?" Sophie asked.

"At the end of the season, there is going to be a gathering
of the Vasilikós. Angela will go over this with you. I swear I
will spend some time and answer all the questions Angela
hasn't covered. I'm sorry, sweetie, but I have to dash."

With her last word, the air around Callie began to spark,
and with a large crack she was gone.

Sophie sat staring at the empty space.

"You'll get used to people Shimmering in and out of here,
especially when you start doing it yourself."

"Shimmering?" Sophie said, glancing over at Angela. "Is
that what they call it?"

"There are several names for it, including a difficult Greek
word, but I prefer Shimmering. Let's move our breakfast to
the Morning Room and I can take you on a short tour of some
of the more significant sections of the Vasilikós."

Angela recovered the plates and reached over to pick up
the cordless phone beside Sophie's bed. A voice immediately
responded.

"Anna? Could you please have our breakfast moved into
the East Wing's Morning Room? Yes, that's right. You might
want to reheat the items. Yes, fresh coffee please. Thank you."
Angela reached over and uncovered the plate of breakfast
meats and both girls took one last slice of bacon before
venturing into the hallway. The door to Sophie's bedroom

~ ☾ ~

hadn't even closed shut before a young girl appeared with a trolley.

"Thank you, Anna," Angela said, walking past the girl and down the hallway.

"How is it my bedroom now looks like my old one?" Sophie asked.

"It's Eupheme."

Sophie gave a puzzled look. "Who?"

"Eupheme is our resident Passiosensi Water Nymph."

"Yeah, wow," Sophie said. "You need to take it a bit slower."

"Sorry about that. Like many who live and work in this Vasilikós, Eupheme is a bit of a rare creature. She is a Water Nymph Empath who can draw her powers from water and from raw emotions. She also fancies herself a bit of an interior designer and don't bother asking why. I believe that was a bit of misplaced inspiration after a group of Muses had a few too many glasses of wine. Knowing she can learn a lot about a person from a single touch makes her a bit touchy-feely for my taste. But you can never change a Salem girl. We are frightfully private."

"But I've never met her."

"Well, I'm guessing you, being a new Muse, can create an emotional imprint everywhere you go. Your emotions are so strong right now even I could read them and I'm not gifted or sensitive in that way."

"So, the room isn't real?"

"It's not an illusion. Water Nymphs are well known for their ability to mesmerize, so I'm sure Glamour has something to do with it. I, for one, don't find the room attractive, but then it wasn't meant for me. However, what makes Euphe special is her ability to alter inanimate objects on the molecular level. So, what appears to be your room is in fact a duplicate based on your memories and emotions."

"Are you joking about this?"

"I come from Massachusetts. Our winters are about as bitter as we are. We don't joke."

~ ☾ ~

Chapter 18

This place is nuts.

Hallways seemed to go in all directions, attaching one large room to another. Numerous staircases made of different materials, styles, and varying sizes went up and down to different floors in the Vasilikós with no apparent direction or pattern. Every inch of the stone walls lining the many hallways were covered with paintings of gods, goddesses, mythical creatures, battle scenes and the occasional landscapes or freshly polished pieces of armor, swords, and other items of war. Certain precious pieces were in display cases and Sophie stopped to read the small brass plaque on the glass case to the right of her.

SWORD OF PERSEUS

Underneath the plaque was a warning about handling the sword.

"Danger! Gorgon Blood! POISON! Do not handle sword. Side effects can include dry mouth, constipation, blindness, shortness of breath, turning into stone and death."

"Gorgon's blood," Angela said. "The sword itself was a gift from Zeus to Perseus, and it was the actual sword Perseus used to slay the Gorgon Medusa. She was the mortal among the three sisters. They say she was an incredible beauty until Aphrodite changed her," Angela said with apparent sadness in her voice as she touched a marble bust of Medusa next to the display case. After removing a thin layer of dust from its pedestal, Angela continued the tour.

"This room, English and French in style, is the main Entry Hall and also serves as an Evanescia room," Angela explained.

"Evanes...what?" Sophie asked.

"Evanescia room. The mirrors found throughout the room serve as a form of transportation. While Muses can Shimmer

~ ☾ ~

here and there, most Demigods cannot. In certain cases, Shimmering is not permitted and protected against. I'll show you how the mirrors work later. The staircase in the entry hall is one of the largest ever created. I'm told it was chiseled from ten large pieces of marble, hence the lack of visible seams. These stairs are not original to this Vasilikós but were a gift from the Roman Vasilikós, which is now known as the Italy Vasilikós. Now, the next room is famous for its tall hand-carved oak paneling."

Angela's voice seemed to drift away as Sophie's attention was taken by an unusual mirror at the opposite end of the hall. It ran floor to ceiling along a stone wall, its frame gilded and embedded with semi-precious stones. The frame seemed to expand back into the stone behind it, like a vine gripping the wall itself. The surface of the mirror glowed a bit, and Sophie couldn't take her eyes away from it. The mirror was calling to her.

"What's up with the mirror?" Sophie said, over her shoulder.

"Nothing. It's nothing more than a mirror," Angela said.

"You're not telling me the truth," Sophie said, staring intently and walking towards it. She would have reached it had it not been for Angela, who rushed to Sophie's side and pulled her away.

"Okay. It goes somewhere, but it's not for me to take you on that journey," Angela replied, leading her away, letting Sophie know the mirror conversation was over. They walked into a large room off the entry hall and then into another long corridor leading to a hexagon room that had several other corridors connected to it, forming a starburst pattern.

"How big is this place?" Sophie asked as she stopped by yet another staircase and walked around it into a vast ballroom. The room's expansive wood floors gleamed as if it were recently polished. Several crystal chandeliers were wrapped in gauzy drop cloths and their heavy-lead crystal prisms twinkled and made a soft tinkling sound. Angela walked past Sophie to open up a few of the French doors, letting in a fresh breeze. Outside Sophie could see a large stone veranda with an impressive stone railing covered with crape myrtle blossoms. Intricate benches with overstuffed

~ ☾ ~

pale blue-seated cushions lined the walls and a balcony, hidden behind some wooden scrollwork, was where Sophie assumed the orchestra would play.

"This is the imperial ballroom," Angela stated. "It is used for formal balls, royal events of state, which is why it's normally closed up with the windows shuttered."

"But the floors are polished," Sophie said, recalling what her mother had told her. "What happens when they gather all of the Vasilikós? Does this happen every time a new Muse is born?"

"No, they don't usually open this room for the introduction of a new Muse into a Vasilikós. However, it is my understanding your introduction into this Vasilikós is very different."

"Different?" Sophie said, concerned about what was going to happen during this introduction. *What have I gotten myself into?*

"Your grandmother is head of this Vasilikós and very powerful. I'm guessing the introduction of her granddaughter into our world is a big event. That's all."

As they exited the room, several very short men and women walked in, carrying numerous boxes.

"Hurry up, Julia." The older woman at the front bellowed, her Irish accent about as thick as her tumbled, faded cinnamon curls. "We haven't got all dae and Georgia will be expectin us to be a lot farther along than we are. Malcolm. Will you stop dawdling or you'll be put back to catacombs duty and ya know how ya hate spiders. Oh. Hallo, Angela." The woman walked toward the two girls while she removed a dishtowel to wipe her hands. A small pipe was tucked into a snugly tied headscarf.

"Hi, Winnie," Angela responded.

At first Sophie thought her eyes must be playing tricks on her, but when the woman came closer she realized she couldn't be any taller than four feet. Winnie had a ruddy complexion with so many freckles it would have been impossible to count them, a bulbous nose and golden eyes. One ear poked out from underneath her kerchief and the top of it came to a point. Her smile and attitude were both intoxicating and infectious, and Sophie couldn't help but

~ ☾ ~

smile almost to the point of laughing.

"Glory be to God in the highest. You must be Sophia, Callie's girl." She beamed at Sophie and then frowned. "Alistair. How many times must I tell you you'll be needin' the tall ladder to get those drop cloths down?"

The young boy she was yelling at, who was even shorter then she was, carried a small step stool and dropped it in the doorway with a loud clatter. He left.

"Sometimes I wonder if he even has a brain in his head. If he weren't my sister Mary's son..." her voice trailed off, then quicker than a blink, changed her attitude. "Ah, Sophie, look at you. The spitting image of your mother, although I suspect we've got a wee bit of your father in you. Yes, the smile. Your smile is like your father's. I remember when I first saw him; it was about a fortnight before your parents met for the first time. So handsome. Had your mother not run away with him, I would have had him for myself." Winnie winked and burst into a roaring wave of laughter.

Sophie was surprised how loud such a little person could be.

"So sorry to hear of his passin'. I know both you and your mum loved him very much. He was always such a kind soul, granted I only ever saw him for the briefest of moments. He would come and meet with Georgia at least once a season."

Sophie's eyes widened. "Once a season? I thought Georgia hated my father."

Winnie paused. "Oh, but there I go, running on and on. Forgive me, dear heart. Are you enjoyin' your new home? I run the household for Georgia. My name is Winifred, but you can call me Winnie. If there is anythin—" Winnie stopped a moment to turn her attention to the returning Alistair, who wasn't alone. A tall, dark-haired boy followed him into the room; the heavy wooden ladder slung over the boy's left shoulder. He carried it with little effort then removed it off his shoulder and placed it down.

"Bennett. There you are," Winnie said. "You're such a luv. Thank you so much for bringing the ladder. Alistair, how could you bother Bennett, considerin' the work he has in the garden and on the grounds?"

Sophie knew she shouldn't stare, but she couldn't help

~ ☾ ~

herself. Her heart thumped in her chest and she thought she would have to remind herself to breathe.

Bennett wore a T-shirt that clung to his body like a second skin, its faded and cracked message about drinking some sort of Greek brand orange soda.

Oh my God. He's gorgeous. He needs a haircut. No, it curls so cute in the back and around his ears. It's perfect.

He stood well over six and a half feet tall and had the type of body that never had seen the inside of a gym but was naturally muscular. Well-defined muscles formed broad shoulders connected to an equally muscular back, forming the v-shape she knew many movie stars had paid ridiculous amounts of money to achieve.

Bennett stretched his back, the movement lifting his shirt to expose a defined six-pack. Apparently embarrassed by the exposure, he pulled his shirt down. He wore torn grass and dirt-stained cargo shorts that were a size too big. They balanced on his hipbones and showed the waistband of his white boxers. Sophie knew any Ohioan would say he possessed the classic corn-fed farmer build.

His mannerisms told Sophie that Bennett was the kind of person who didn't know he was good-looking and his humility made him even more irresistible to her. He had a shy smile and as he listened to some additional instructions from Winnie, his eyes showed a seriousness that wasn't brooding but very intense.

When Winnie asked him a question, the boy responded with his head held tilted down, another sign of humility, and he knelt so that Winnie could give him a peck on his cheek.

God, what I would give for a single kiss.

Bennett glanced toward Sophie and Angela, and gave both girls a quirky, crooked smile. Angela raised her hand to wave him over.

Her heart banged against her ribcage and she was sure it would burst out of her body. She wanted to die because she was sure she was a mess and pushed some hair away from her face. With a quick but sincere prayer she hoped she didn't have a piece of bacon in her teeth or, even worse, morning breath.

Bennett raised his large hand in an absent-minded wave.

~ ☾ ~

"Well." Winnie shouted beside him, pushing him toward the girls. "Don't just stand there. Let me introduce you to Sophie, Callie's daughter."

Bennett had started to walk over but stopped dead in his tracks the moment the words 'Callie's daughter' left Winnie's mouth, and Sophie watched his laidback demeanor change.

"If you'll excuse me, I have some tasks I need to address," Bennett said, his voice deep and monotone, betraying the slightest Scottish lilt. Without another word, Bennett exited the room, leaving an awkward silence.

A feverish blush rose in Sophie's cheeks.

Move. You're standing here, grinning like an idiot. I have never been so attracted to someone and he blew me off. What the hell?

"Don't take it to heart, darlin'. Bennett is a bit shy." Winnie said. "If you'll excuse me, I've got to be gettin' back to the cleaning. I've got so much to do and so little time to get it done," Winnie said, with an obvious forced cheeriness. She resumed her work, calling back over her shoulder. "Remember dear, if you need anythin', you let me know. Pick up the phone and ask for me. Abigail. Will you ever stop dawdling around? Take those cushions out to the veranda and give them a good shake and beating. Oh, for the love of Jesus, Joseph and Mary. If you drop a single crystal from that chandelier, Alistair, Georgia will have your hide and that's after I get through with you."

Two of Winnie's assistants escorted them from the room, closing the doors to the ballroom with a soft click. Winnie's voice, although muffled, boomed orders as the sound of tiny feet ran in different directions.

"Is she a hobbit?" Sophie asked. She was hoping to ask about Bennett first, but didn't want to sound too obvious and she didn't know if Angela and Bennett were more than friends.

"You've been reading too much J.R.R. Tolkien. However, she is a Hob, which is a sort of Hobgoblin. Winnie is from a clan of Hobs found on the Coasts of Ireland. They dwell in grand houses like this one, concerning themselves with the inner workings of it. To them, there is great honor given to the Hob who serves a household, no matter how small or

~ ☾ ~

large. Some Hobs are content being invisible and remain invisible in the outside world. Something broken one day and fixed another, without explanation, is the work of a hidden Hob. For Winnie, serving a Vasilikós, well, it's a life-long dream. Although, you should know having a Hob can be either a blessing or curse. A happy Hob means a happy house. However, those who insult and abuse a Hob often find them to be a curse because an ill-tempered Hob will not rest until complete misery befalls the owner and several generations after them."

"What about Bennett—" Sophie broached the subject, as the two girls took another turn and walked up a flight of stairs, only to immediately take another staircase down, but somehow ending up on a different floor.

"Bennett is a whole other story. He's not fond of Muses."

"Oh. Why?" she said, biting her lower lip.

"Sophie, it's not for me to say. If you want to know, you'll have to ask him yourself. We'll stop in here for a second. This is one of Georgia's crowning glories. The Muse Library has a copy of each and every book ever written, including items written before books were even invented. The scroll wing is off to your left and there is a whole attached building dedicated to hieroglyphics beyond it. It makes the Vatican's archives look like a local library branch."

To Sophie, the room was breathtaking. Domed ceilings soared high and made her memories of the Library of Congress pale in size and opulence. The room they stood in was circular with numerous alcoves and hallways attached to equally large or even larger rooms, offices and meeting rooms. Ornate plasterwork over the alcoves showcased reclining maidens reading scrolls and cherubs in midflight. If walls existed, Sophie couldn't see them because every inch of wall was covered with books. In a puzzle-like movement, bookshelves folded into other bookshelves, then slid over even more bookcases, which then slid to the next lower or higher floor. Iron, marble and wood balconies attached to walkways crisscrossed throughout the height of the room, creating a lattice pattern and forming a focal point for the gold-leafed dome, which had a center mural of the stars, sun and moon.

~ ☾ ~

Sophie's thoughts were interrupted as a woman on one of the higher balconies stopped shelving books and slammed one onto the railing in front of her. She made a loud shushing sound that drifted down to the two girls.

"Is she for real?" Sophie laughed, turning to look at Angela and not concerned at the volume of her voice. "Who is tha—?"

Another loud shush interrupted Sophie, followed by the sound of the woman leaping onto the railing of the balcony, which seemed strange to Sophie. How the woman could keep her balance and not get sick from looking down from such a height, seemed impossible to Sophie, not to mention the woman was still holding several books Sophie assumed she had meant to shelve.

Before Sophie could ask Angela what the woman was doing, the woman threw the books down and hurled herself away from the balcony and into the air. She dived straight down, her hair flowing behind her and the material of her long, heavy gown flapping in all directions. The woman's loose sleeves slid backward, exposing dark, bluish skin. Sophie realized the woman had feathers as wings erupted from her forearms and formed along the back of her arms, connecting to the mid-section of her back. Sophie winced, thinking she was about to witness the woman's guts splattering all over the place, when, the woman changed the direction of her body midair by moving her arms and flapped her wings as she descended to the ground.

Sophie's mouth hung open. The woman glared at the two girls as she reconstructed her makeshift beehive hairdo, securing it with two black lacquered chopsticks. The feathers that had appeared as she took flight smoothed back into place. The woman towered over the two girls.

Sophie glanced down and noticed the woman's dress had gathered in places, exposing her legs. Once again, she found herself staring, but couldn't help herself because the woman's legs were covered in the same bluish feathers and instead of feet the woman had razor sharp talons.

The nametag on the woman's dress had a symbol, which Sophie assumed must be associated with the Vasilikós, and below the symbol was the woman's name, 'Tammy.'

"This is a library, ladies. *The* library of the Greek and

~ ☾ ~

Italian Vasilikós," Tammy said with a rich Louisiana accent.

Tammy had amber eyes with specks of shimmering deep red. She was clearly agitated, drumming her talons on the floor much the same way a person would absentmindedly drum their fingers.

"We have rules in the library and ladies, those rules include complete silence. The only sounds I should be hearing are the occasional turning of pages, a polite but extremely muffled cough and the respectful yet hesitant steps of someone getting up to remove or replace a book on the *correct* shelf. Now Angela, did I mention anywhere in this description a casual conversation taking place in rude, loud tones?" Tammy took two steps closer to Angela, her talons clicking on the floor.

"No, ma'am," Angela answered back, her clipped New England accent showing both her embarrassment laced with a quiet fury.

"Very good. And who, may I ask, are you?" Tammy asked Sophie, with a superior smirk. "Clearly you are not of this Vasilikós. Everyone who visits or resides here is given The Book of Vasilikós Rules and Regulations on a personal eTablet. Chapter 8 provides clear and concise library guidelines, including library etiquette."

"Tammy, allow me the pleasure of introducing you to Sophia Drago. Daughter of Callie, Muse to this Vasilikós, Granddaughter to Georgia, Grand Duchess and Leader of The Greek and Italian Vasilikós of Muse," Angela said.

"Yes...." Tammy said, straightening her back to reach her full height. "Georgia was kind enough to let everyone in the Vasilikós know of Sophia's arrival." Tammy scrutinized Sophie. "Understand, young Muse, who you are will warrant no special treatment in this Vasilikós."

Without pausing, Tammy grabbed several books off the table closest to her and sprang into the air.

Sophie stood for a second and then exited the library, walking back in the direction they'd been going.

"Well," Sophie said as soon as Angela had caught up with her. "Excellent first impression. I'm assuming she is not a Hob, although if she were, several generations of my family and I would be in big trouble."

~ ☾ ~

"Tammy's the head librarian," Angela said. "Sorry, I mean she is a North American Harpy. I believe she is part of the Dupre Clan. They lived deep in the wetlands of Louisiana."

"We have a Harpy as a librarian?"

"Well, if you want the best to organize your library, you would be hard pressed not to select a Harpy. That is, if you can ever find one."

Sophie wondered where Georgia had found a Harpy, but then guessed a person didn't become a Grand Poobah or whatever she was by not being resourceful.

They continued their walking tour; eventually reaching the morning room and, much to Sophie's relief, breakfast.

***

Life continued similarly for the following two weeks, Angela continuing to discuss the next element of the Vasilikós and Sophie continuing to wonder if she would ever run into Bennett.

"Totally MIA," Sophie said to herself several times.

Her mother continued to be self-absorbed in whatever she was doing and always kept their interactions to simple topics—nothing requiring any thought or, for the most part, any real involvement. A distance was growing between them, and although she knew her mother could be annoying, nagging and sometimes embarrassing, she also had thought she could always count on feeling a mother/daughter closeness with Callie. It had never failed to be comforting to her. Now, everything was different, which was a fact Sophie often repeated to herself. When she asked her mother about the graffiti painted on the exterior Vasilikós' garden walls -- it was the word "Nothos"—her mother became irritated and flustered, and left the room. Whatever the word meant, the topic of "Nothos" was off limits.

It was the same with Angela. They had discussions about the Vasilikós, discussions about the catacombs, discussions about the attic, and they had discussions about the gardens, although once again, to Sophie's disappointment, Bennett was always kept off the topic list, along with the topic of the word "Nothos."

The impact of her first Bennett interaction faded and he became an afterthought. The only good thing from the

~ ☾ ~

painfully polite situation she was experiencing was the fact her demanding and, for the most part, horrible grandmother had kept her distance.

Now that's a distance I can embrace. Until the loneliness became unbearable and she found herself wishing her grandmother would at least nag or yell at her. The silence, the avoidance and the isolation were bad enough, but the thought piercing her mind over and over again was she was being kept in the dark.

~ ☾ ~

Chapter 19

Penny was frustrated. Her feet and back hurt, and she had fallen numerous times. She had stopped to rest and closed her eyes for a moment, enjoying the feeling of the cool wind against her face. She stretched her back and stood up again, looking around. She stood on the edge of a rocky cliff, eyeing the sturdy rope bridge that lay in front of her.

I trust that bridge about as far as I could throw Hades himself. She focused her eyes on the bridge and concentrated. Nothing happened and she put both hands on her hips and tapped her right foot.

I am out of practice. I know the bridge is enchanted and I can't seem to remove the spell.

She continued to concentrate, as a dull throbbing began in the center of her forehead. Sweat poured down her face.

"This is ludicrous," she said in frustration, turning her back on the bridge. Taking a few deep breaths she cleared her mind. She began twirling in place, allowing her arms to swing in the air. The energy was building inside her again. When she knew the time was right, she thrust her arms upward, sending the energy burst towards the sky. The wind died away as a rumble exploded in the sky. A sudden gust of wind came from the north and swept across the bridge, blowing away the covering enchantment. What had appeared to be a sturdy bridge was now rotten, with one side almost completely broken away and walking planks that she was sure they would have trouble holding the weight of a bird.

"Tricky, tricky," she said in a sing-song voice and laughed. "Dear old Haddie, always one for a good practical joke, not that I was ever ignorant enough to fall for any of them."

She searched for another means to reach the canyon below. A thick and foul-looking fog hung in the air a few

~ ☾ ~

hundred feet below and she couldn't make out a single detail of what she would find down there. The fog crackled and gurgled, making her wrinkle her nose.

"Such nonsense." she said, picking up her walking staff.

She examined the ground and found the flat stepping stone she was looking for. Covered in dirt, wild grass and rotted wood, the worn face of the stone was carved with the image of a skull. Stepping in front of it, Penny knelt, and removed some of the debris. When she was satisfied, she raised her staff and thrust the point of it into the skull's gaping mouth.

She waited, but nothing happened.

"I am so very rusty."

She lifted and slammed her staff three more times, the third time causing a bright spark to ignite, lighting up the skull's eyes before flickering out. She struck the stone so hard her teeth chattered in her head. In an instant, the stone shifted and the ground creaked and shook under her feet. She could hear earth shake off the side of the cliff, as stone slabs slid out and locked into place. When the ground was still, she walked to the edge and saw her way down to the canyon: a set of stairs disappearing into the thick fog.

"Well, that's helpful, but enough of these tricks. I mean, really Haddie, how childish of you." After she'd exposed the rope bridge for the fraud it was, Penny conjured another gust of air and swept away the fog, revealing what she guessed were more than a thousand steps. Her legs and back ached, telling her to go back home.

"You are a dead god, Haddie," she muttered.

After two hours of maneuvering down the steps, some were so crumbled they stretched the definition of 'step' to its breaking point; she reached the bottom and sat down on an outcrop of rocks.

"Maybe," she said to herself, between huffs of breath. "I'll maim him. Rip an arm off or maybe just a finger."

When she had caught her breath, she stood up. Even though the watch pinned to her blouse said two p.m., the canyon was deep enough it only allowed enough light to make a person think it was early twilight. Tall rocks with carvings on them were scattered throughout the canyon floor,

~ ☾ ~

reminding her of Stonehenge. She once again encountered the same thick fog, making it difficult for her to see where she needed to go. Using her staff, she tapped her way forward, keeping a wary eye for any surprises she might encounter. There were places where the fog seemed thicker and as she passed through them, she saw a figure, which vanished with an audible swoosh.

"Turn back," a harsh whisper said.

If sandpaper had a voice, this is what it would sound like.

"You are not welcome, Olympian. Turn back."

She rolled her eyes. "How annoying," she replied. "Go away, spirit. I have no need for you."

"Doom," the voice said. "Continue at your own peril."

The air gathered around her as another swoosh passed by. This time, it grazed her cheek and she raised her hand to her face and saw her fingertips were red with blood.

She now saw several places where the fog had gathered. The thing had brought reinforcements. Before she had time to react, she was surrounded.

"Not welcome," one of the entities said.

"Foul abomination." another voice said, screeching louder than the others.

"Fallen One." the first voice said as it took another swipe at her other cheek.

The group of creatures surged onto Penny and attacked.

She screamed as they tore into her arms, her legs, their teeth biting into her shoulder and neck.

A rage built inside her and Penny sensed her powers building. Bolts of energy shot from her hands and with one quick moment she threw them all off, forcing the creatures to retreat into the fog to gather their strength once again.

Not being one to come unprepared, she reached into her pocket and clutched a small white stone.

"How dare you touch me." she shouted at the creatures. "I, born from Olympus."

The creatures had gathered their strength again and pounced.

Blood from her cuts coated the stone and it began to glow, brighter and brighter.

"Foul abomination? Look at what a festering bunch of

~ ☾ ~

bones you are. How dare you even glance at me," she shouted.

The creatures fell backward as if stuck with great force, screaming in agony, as the stone's bright light attacked them and chunks of their bodies evaporated with a sizzling sound. She watched with glee as the guardians cowered. Penny knew they were dying and their ability to hide behind the fog was gone, exposing their skeletal bodies covered in strips of rotting flesh and wrapped in ragged, hooded death shrouds. They had shark-like teeth and their hands were more like claws with large black fingernails. Feeling light-headed and energized, Penny ran toward what was left of the creatures and watched them reach up with one final scream and disappear.

Her wounds were already healing and she wiped the blood from her face. She frowned as she noticed her skirt and blouse were ruined.

Bloodstains left untreated will ruin clothes. I should have brought my stain stick.

She continued to tap her way forward and after a few moments ran into what she was looking for—two large, crumbling stones, easily fifty feet in height.

An ancient, lifeless looking grapevine coiled itself around the tall entry stones and across the wide space between them. The trunk of the vine, created from the fusion of thousands of independent ones, was twisted and gnarled, and its tendrils gripped and girdled the stones with such strength the stones appeared to cave inward. What fruit grew from the vines was black and shriveled and dripped with a putrid-smelling sap-like substance. She walked between the two large rocks and heard the moans of the souls trapped within the vines' eternal embrace. Several arms shot-out from within the vines, attempting to grab her, but she chuckled as she stepped out of reach of the beseeching dead.

She stumbled a little and steadied herself, staring in awe at what was in front of her— the entrance to the Underworld. It was as she remembered. Truly a loathsome place, with dead, petrified trees surrounding it. Their trunks were stripped of bark and bleached white so they seemed to glow in the darkness. The entrance, a vast opening in the side of the

~ ☾ ~

mountain, resembled a screaming giant's mouth filled with row after row of razor-sharp teeth that jutted out in all different directions. The path leading to the cave and the cave's entrance was littered with the bones of both humans and animals. She walked forward quickly, but with cautious steps, to make sure she didn't trip and fall onto the sharp point of a ribcage or the shard of a shin bone.

The crunching sounds her footfalls made bounced off the walls and became almost deafening. With great relief, she could make out the rocky shoreline where the four rivers of the Underworld converged into a marsh, and she picked up her pace, reaching the edge where an old wooden pier stood, half submerged in the water and covered in moss and slime.

Several dead souls attempted to crawl onto the pier. Their bodies were pale white and had eyes resembling pools of shiny black ink. But the pier's slippery support logs and rotted edges sent them tumbling back into the putrid water, landing on top of dozens of other souls who were also attempting to climb out. She knew those were the souls who had no money to pay the ferryman. They were damned to stay in the river for hundreds of years before they had paid enough penance to earn their journey into the afterlife. Some of them had the word "Nothos" branded on them, the brand glowing bright red on their white skin. Those souls would never be allowed passage onto the afterlife. They were permanently damned, never to know relief from their suffering.

She eyed the pier and knew in its current state it wouldn't hold her weight and could cause her to fall in, allowing the dead to drag her down. She put the tip of her shoe on the pier and the soft, spongy wood creaked and broke away, proving her opinion correct. Penny reached into her pocket and pulled out a small vial full of an emerald green liquid.

She raised her arm and threw the vial down onto the pier. Even though the surface was soft, the glass vial shattered, and the green liquid sizzled and bubbled. The vial held a small amount of the substance, but it grew in mass as it worked its way across the surface of the pier's planks and dripped onto its support logs. The dead, attracted by the glow and sensing a change in the pier, became frenzied and rushed it, only to

~ ☾ ~

howl and scream as the liquid burned their tender, milky skin. A few drops dripped into the water and the dead rushed away in fear.

Penny watched as the green liquid both restored the pier and kept the dead away. She tested the restored pier with a toe and once assured it could hold her weight, she stepped out onto it.

Penny looked down into the black, murky water and was surprised to recognize a dead woman with long blond hair who had once been her neighbor. Penny had attended the woman's funeral and with great enjoyment removed the gold coins from the woman's eyes and branded the woman with the word "Nothos"; thereby forever damning the woman to her present situation. The woman had dared to complain about Penny's desolate yard to village officials and Penny had thus made sure she was paid back in spades.

Still holding her staff, Penny reached the end of the pier and ignored the stares of the dead, who grew silent. She slammed the end of her staff three times, the sound echoing off the walls and bouncing off the surface of the water. She waited and listened. She knocked her staff again three times, and after a few moments of silence heard a low, deep horn call back to her. She tapped her staff again and the horn called back again, but this time it was accompanied by the sound of splashes.

The ferryman is coming. She gathered the small coin purse she carried. Her coins were ancient and she knew Charon would be pleased to receive such treasures. A mist appeared on the water, which grew into a great fog.

"By Zeus, enough with the fog. You would think they would come up with something more original than fog. I shall deduct two points for lack of imagination." she said, noticing the dead had gathered in even greater numbers in their attempt to gain passage. The boat approaching the pier was old, although anything but decrepit. It was common knowledge among Olympians that Charon took great pride in the maintenance of his ship, and the mere suggestion it was rotted and miserable looking was enough to send the ferryman into a rage.

The truth about the state of Charon's boat was different.

~ ☾ ~

The lower part of the ship was black with a bottom stripe of red that could be seen depending on the tide. In contrast to the dark hull, the main deck was made of seasoned oak, with accents of cherry wood here and there. And there were several masts lacking sails but did have several pale blue banners flying at different heights with gold lettering. Each of the banners had the single letter, Omega, embroidered onto the fabric. Without the use of sails, the current of the dead and the golden oars jutting out of the hull's side caused the ship's main movement. Few had ever seen the creatures that worked the oars, although legend tells of beings with glowing green eyes living an eternity of the damned.

The boat reached the edge of the pier with a muffled bump and the dead remained silent, hoping to hear their names called to journey on. The only sound coming from the large ship's flapping banners.

"Charon..." Penny shouted. She waited a second and grew impatient. She thought at least one part of her journey should be easy.

"Charon." she shouted again. "I know you hear me."

"How can I not? Your voice is most disrespectful to me and the dead," said a voice. It was deep and casual but had a lofty air about it, as if it were greeting an undesirable on the street.

She faced the ferryman. Charon on many levels was quite pleasing to look at, with his white skin, straight black hair and jet black eyes. Similar to the dead, Charon's eyes were pools of shimmering black ink. They were hypnotic to mortals and could not be resisted. He was tall and was fashionably dressed in a black suit tailored to fit his strong stature. A black, French-cuffed shirt with golden coin cufflinks and black wingtips completed the look.

She wondered if being the ferryman afforded him time to work out and smirked at the ridiculous idea.

"Yoga and push-ups," was Charon's response, providing Penny a gentle reminder that in this realm he knows everything and can read the thoughts of anyone who ventures into his territory. She clouded her mind and allowed only the thoughts she wanted the ferryman to know.

"You know who I am and why I've come?" Penny said.

~ ☾ ~

"I do not serve those from Olympus, goddess. You have no right to be on this sacred ground and bother me with your travel requests," Charon said, matter-of-factly.

"You serve all who call you," Penny spat back. "And the reason for my journey is of no concern to you. Let me on your ship."

"Hiding your thoughts will not help your case," he said.

"Well," she said, changing her strategy. "If you feel that way, I'll take my gold coins with me, which would be such a shame, for they are special coins."

Charon lifted his eyes to meet Penny's and moved closer, appearing to grow several feet in height his complexion becoming paler.

"You forget who you are speaking with, Fallen One. You, who above all have caused great misery to those I travel with, have little ground to stand on right now. I hear their cries of anguish at your hands and take great satisfaction knowing I undo so much of what you have done," he said, allowing the last words to echo. "Maybe a dip in the river Acheron would silence your tongue and teach you humility. You are no more to me than a piece of filth I wipe off the bottom of my shoe." The last word came out like a curse and Penny took a step back, unaware of how close she was to the pier's edge.

Charon continued to curse at Penny as he took yet another step closer. Penny stood on the edge of the pier, her heels within reach of the dead. Suddenly, her former and very dead neighbor launched herself out of the water and grabbed hold of Penny's right ankle.

Taken by surprise, Penny hit the dead woman with her staff. The bag of coins dropped to the ground and the leather drawstring loosened enough to allow a single coin to pop out. The animated face of Medusa gleamed on one side of it, the snakes of her hair writhing and her sharp teeth gnashing. The coin flipped and the face of Aphrodite appeared on the other side. She smiled and winked. The dead woman ripped away Penny's staff and crawled up her back, her nails tearing through the old woman's blouse and sinking deep into her flesh.

Penny beseeched Charon, who stood laughing at her. Right as the old woman toppled towards the bog, she and the

~ ☾ ~

ferryman disappeared, leaving the dead neighbor to scream in fury as she fell backward into the water clutching a clump of Penny's hair. The green liquid evaporated and the pier crumbled into the bog. Within a few seconds the water bubbled and a new, ever-more rotted pier rose from its depths.

Penny fell face forward onto the deck of Charon's ship, her staff and the purse of golden coins clattering onto its surface. The purse was now fully open and more than twenty-five of the magical coins of Aphrodite glowed back at Charon. Penny thrashed around for a few more seconds and, after realizing she hadn't fallen into the bog, got to her feet.

"Where did you find these coins? Do you know what these coins are and what they do?" Charon asked.

Penny reached down and collected them, placing all but five back into the purse. Using a slight of hand trick learned years ago, she concealed the five coins until she was able to drop them into the front pocket of her skirt.

"Of course I do. Do you take me for a fool? Give me passage to Hades and the coins are yours to do with what you will. Refuse and I take them back and you can continue on your cruise up this lovely waterway," she said, not caring if Charon could hear the mocking tone in her voice.

The ferryman licked his lips. "You have a deal, but it's for only one way."

Penny smiled sweetly and handed over the purse of gold. "One way was exactly what I was looking for."

~ ☾ ~

Chapter 20

Sophie entered the dining hall, followed by Angela, after being 'summoned' by Georgia. Seated at the head of the long, dark mahogany dining table was her grandmother, engaged in conversation with her mother and Aletheria. A small male Hob, whom Sophie remembered her mother calling him Gavin, was standing in the mouth of the fireplace, sweeping ash and soot into a dustbin. A grunt turned Sophie's attention away from the dining table as Bennett walked in carrying several large white ash logs. She was determined to play it cool, but knew she was failing miserably as she grinned like an idiot... again.

It wasn't until she got about ten feet away from the table that Sophie realized there was something else in the room.

It was a rather fat cherub fluttering around the ceiling, an irritating giggle exploding from it the moment it saw Sophie. A small swath of cloth covered the bare essentials of its pinkish bloated body and the flapping sound its wings made was anything but angelic. Clutched in its chubby hands was a single white envelope with gold trim.

"What the heck is that? Sophie asked.

Georgia threw her hands up in exasperation. "Well, it's a page of some sort with a message, possibly an invitation."

"From whom?" Sophie asked.

Aletheria smiled. "If we could catch the blasted thing, we would be able to answer your question."

"Let me see if I can get it," said Callie, standing up. The page fluttered within grabbing distance and she reached over, but in a flash the cherub slapped her hand out of the way and zoomed to the highest point in the room, its giggles echoing off the ceiling and walls.

"Ouch!" yelled Callie, as she rubbed the back of her hand. "That little beast has a wicked slap."

~ ☾ ~

Aletheria laughed. "Don't be too forceful with it. It bites," the Oracle said as she lifted up Georgia's hand.

Sophie turned her attention to a new app she had been trying out on her Vasilikós-issued eTablet. The app used the built-in camera to scan and determine if the animal or human had supernatural or Olympian heredity. A full description of the entity was provided if it tested positive for either. It was called "Whatsit."

Sophie tried to capture the flying thing with her camera, but it was too fast. So she pointed it at Gavin, clicked the onscreen button.

Angela leaned towards Sophie and whispered, "In our society, it is considered impolite to inquire about a person's supernatural status without asking permission or being offered the information."

"Sorry, Gavin," Sophie offered. Gavin shrugged and went back to his work.

The cherub giggled and zoomed past Sophie, taking her by surprise. She lost her grip on the eTablet. As she tried to save it from crashing onto the stone floor, Sophie's foot became tangled in the cherub's wrapping-cloth and both fell crashing to the ground. The cherub's laugh turned into a high-pitched squeak as Sophie fell face forward on top of the creature with a disgusting splat. The tablet safely caught in her hands, Sophie lay there for a moment, not sure what to do.

"Oh, God." Sophie lowered the eTablet onto the floor. "Is it dead? Oh, God." She squealed. "Someone please look, because I think I'm going to throw-up."

A booming laugh from the mouth of the fireplace roared through the room, as Bennett finished positioning the logs. Within a few seconds, he stood above Sophie and offered his hand.

Sophie didn't need to look up to realize who's hand she was about to take and the agony over yet another embarrassing situation was enough to make her wish she were underneath the cherub and not the other way around.

I could just die. Please let me die.

"Please," Sophie said. "I'm afraid I've killed the little thing."

Bennett responded by crouching down to meet Sophie's

~ ☾ ~

eyes. His voice came in calm, rich tones.

"Well, I supposed you could just lie there for the rest of your life, with the remains of a dead fairy stuck to your chest, or you might want to let me help you up and see if the little guy is tougher then he looks."

Sophie raised her eyebrows and turned her head so one of her eyes could look up at Bennett. His large brown eyes were kind, reminding Sophie of a cow.

She smiled nervously and reached over to give Bennett her hand, but the squishing sound coming from underneath made her breakfast want to evacuate her stomach.

"Oh, God. I can't do it. I can't. Isn't there some sort of special Muse magic remover for gross gunk?" *I may be covered in cherub guts, but the last thing I'm going to do is vomit in front of a hot guy. All that's left for me to embarrass myself more would be to fart.*

Without warning, Bennett grabbed Sophie's hand and yanked her up into his arms before she could protest.

Sophie took a quick breath in surprise as she realized his strength. She felt as if she weighed next to nothing in his arms. Her head fell against his neck and she noticed he smelled of earth, grass and sport body wash. She knew she didn't know him, didn't even know if he liked her, but there was something about him making her feel safe and incredibly special.

The sound of Georgia's heels on the stone floor broke Sophie away from her long-awaited 'Bennett' moment and Bennett put Sophie down.

"Well, I will give you credit. That was one way to catch the little rat," Georgia said, as she nudged the flattened cherub with her shoe.

It was sprawled out on the floor, its buttocks exposed and raised. Had the poor, squashed thing not looked so pathetic, its expression would have been funny, as its tongue lay limply on the floor and one eye on the verge of popping out. A few seconds later, the eye did pop out, and Sophie gasped. The envelope was still clutched in its hand.

"Oh my God. Eww, eww, eww. That is so gross. I wish we could film this. Imagine the hits we'd get if we posted it online." Sophie commented.

~ ☾ ~

Georgia reached for the letter and much to everyone's surprise the thing extended a flattened hand to smacked Georgia's hand away. By this time, Aletheria and Callie had gathered near the group and even Gavin had stopped his work on the fireplace to see what would happen next.

Everyone stood watching as the cherub's mouth twisted and it let out a screech, which turned into a giggle, and it used its remaining functional limb to slap the floor as it tried to peel itself off.

Everyone grimaced but couldn't help staring until Winnie's voice entered the dining hall, long before the elder Hob did herself.

"Gavin, you had better be done with that fireplace." She walked into the room and took in the situation. "For the love of Mary and woodland goddess Ardwinna. You would think no one has ever dealt with a sprite page before." She stopped mid-sentence when she saw the state of the creature. "Tsk...tsk...tsk..." She clucked, pushing the eyeball back into the flattened creature's socket with a squish. "Who smashed the wee little thing? Look at it. Such a pathetic little tyke."

Everyone gestured towards Sophie and she couldn't stop her tears from welling up in her eyes.

"Oh, now Sophie, don't be working yourself up into a fit over this little tot." Without any consideration of the pain she might be causing it, Winnie reached down and yanked the flattened sprite up. She shook it roughly and everyone gasped as the sickening sound of tearing flesh and bone filled the room.

"What is everyone goin' on about? 'Tis the way me mum taught me how to handle a situation like this and her mum told her and so on," Winnie said, the flattened cherub filling out with each breath of air it took in. Winnie snapped the little cherub's body around as if she was shaking out a kitchen rug and Sophie winced with each yank.

The color had come back into the creature's face and Winnie gave it a quick rub with her dust rag.

"Sophie, remember for goodness sake, it's not a baby. It's a sprite. It takes a lot to kill one of these blasted things. The rest of you should know better. There," Winnie said, seeing the cherub smiling and giggling. "Good as new and probably

~ ☾ ~

even better than new. Oh, look, it's got a letter. I wonder who
it's for."

Still in a bit of shock and not wanting to risk flying, the
cherub reached out to Sophie and she took the sprite's lead
and approached it. With as much flourish as it could manage,
it handed the envelope to her.

"Well," Winnie said. "With that done, if nobody minds, I'll
take the poor thing in the kitchen for a cup of butter cream.
Would you like that, little one?" Winnie asked the cherub,
tickling one of the rolls in its neck. It responded by clapping
its hands and giggling. "Bennett, if you're done in here, come
along to the kitchen and I'll fix you a plate of cold, roasted
chicken and some bread and cheese. Can't have you wasting
away to nothing. I swear the boy eats like a horse."

Bennett nodded but hesitated a moment. Sophie enjoyed
having him so close and in her heart she hoped his hesitation
was because he felt the same. Callie caught Sophie's eyes and
smiled, nodding in approval, and Sophie couldn't help but
roll her eyes at how embarrassing her mother was being.
Sophie caught Georgia's eye and her grandmother's glare
made her quickly take a few steps away as Bennett excused
himself. He walked past Sophie, followed by Gavin, and her
skin tingled and broke out in goose pimples as his arm
brushed against hers. She could feel her skin flush and she
glanced after him, as he tried to hide the blush spreading
across the back of his neck. She would have high-fived herself
had Georgia not been staring at her with daggers in her eyes.

"Well, I guess I should open it," Sophie said. Everyone
held their breath as Sophie broke the wax seal and slipped the
heavy calling card out of the envelope. "Who are Cleo, Agatha
and Rose?" Sophie asked.

"No," Callie said to Georgia. "I won't permit it."

Georgia chuckled. "You say that, my dear, as if you know
who had a choice in you know what."

"Okay. I'm done," Sophie said, getting up from the table. "I
am sick and tired of being kept in the dark, while each of you
discusses my future behind my back. Aren't any of you the
least bit concerned I may have an opinion on the subject?"

"Opinion?" Georgia laughed. "I am amazed by the
ridiculous things falling out of her head and onto her tongue."

~ ☾ ~

Sophie stood there—face burning with rage. Then, she turned and walked towards the door, unconcerned about what Georgia or her mother wanted.

A spark and a crack exploded in front of her and the massive wooden doors slammed shut.

Sophie remained standing, even though she knew the doors were locked and she was stuck there.

"Come back to the table and we'll tell you everything," Callie said to her. "No lies, no half-truths. Anything you want to know." The touch of her mother's hand on her back made her cringed. She didn't turn around.

"What does Nothos mean?" Sophie asked.

The room fell quiet.

"It means," Callie began, "it means mongrel. It's what the gods called us Demigods. They would refer to us as Nothos as they hunted us down and rounded us up. After torturing a Demigod, they would brand it on their body, so they would be damned for an eternity in the Underworld. No matter what they do in their life, anyone branded with Nothos will suffer in the afterlife."

"It means this," Georgia said, walking over to Sophie and removing her bracelet to show the brand.

"Mama." Callie wailed, rushing towards her. "But you... never told me you bore the mark. Oh God, Mama."

"It also means this," Georgia said, unbuttoning her blouse to show several brands across her torso and back. "Each one of these brands represents a battle against an escaped Olympian."

Georgia pointed to the brand on her wrist. "This one was my first, given to me by Zeus' wife, Hera. She was a jealous goddess and didn't care for the idea of remaining in her prison, especially in the hands of a lowly Nothos like myself. When I gave birth to Callie, Hera came out of hiding and plotted to kill my infant daughter for revenge. I defeated her, but not until after she gave me this little parting gift. Aphrodite gave me three, including one you can't see. She plunged her hand into my back and burned Nothos onto one of my vertebra, just in case we had figured out a way to remove the brands from our skin. They damned me to a future of misery in the Underworld and with my last breath, I

~ ☾ ~

will make sure they are damned to an equally miserable existence." Georgia put her shirt back on and sat back down. "It's the very least I could do."

"Mama. Why didn't you ever tell me?" Callie demanded.

"How does a mother tell her daughter about something like this? It isn't something you bring up at the dinner table. And when your daughter decides to elope, you certainly can't bring it up then. When should I have told you? When you were a baby, in your crib, singing a lullaby to you? Hush little baby, don't say a word, Mama's damned to hell seven times over, now go to sleep?"

"Had you told me...had you trusted me...," Callie said.

"Things would have been different? My dearest, *dearest* girl, things were the way they needed to be. You found your happiness in the arms of Angelo. I found it here. I've had this wondrous journey full of excitement, sadness, regret and incredible moments of happiness and glory and there isn't a single thing that would make me want to have it any other way. How could I, when you have given me this incredible granddaughter?"

Callie wiped her tears away.

"But enough of this," Georgia said. "Aletheria, why don't you explain the need for us, since you were there when all of this came to be."

"You see, Sophia, you can't rip away a faith system like one would rip off a bandage," Aletheria began. "Free will must be given a chance to thrive. Without free will, there can be no system of faith. A choice must be given to believe or not, otherwise faith wouldn't truly exist. So, certain gods had to remain, but they do so with restrictions to their powers, and most importantly, restrictions on their interactions with mortals. So God let Olympians, like Hades, The Fates and others remain because they maintained a balance necessary to keep things moving in the right direction. The Muses were the exception. They were tasked with creating an extended family of Demigods to continue their work. You've heard the saying "kissed by a Muse"? Well, they did more than kiss. Eventually, after this family was created and thrived in its own right, the original Nine Sisters were called back. Now, this extended group of Muses serves many purposes."

~ ☾ ~

Callie jumped in. "Muses are more than Xanadu or the Grecian ideal of womanhood and femininity. We float in and out of the lives of mortals, ensuring they continue down the path they were meant to go down. We're the reset button to make sure those destined for greatness have another chance to reach their potential, whether it is to become the President of the United States or to give birth to a scientist destined to find the cure for cancer. Unfortunately, this is where it gets tricky. We can suggest, inspire, lead the horse to water, but we cannot make it drink. This ties back to free will because mortals must make the choice to get back on their destined path or to continue down the road they selected for themselves. This doesn't always mean that if they choose a different path they are destined for doom. But they won't be living to the plan."

"It's like dominos. Remember how you used to arrange them into all different designs on the kitchen floor and then knock them over? This is the same thing. Take one domino off the pattern and it impacts the dominos after it. So we spend a lot of time making sure the dominos continue to fall the way they should, and if one is taken out by free will we do everything possible to make sure the next domino falls as scheduled to maintain and continue the path."

"But...," Sophie interrupted, "wouldn't it take a lot of Muses to maintain the balance?"

"Thousands," Georgia said. "It's a very large extended family comprising the Nine Vasilikós. There's a reason why this Vasilikós is so big."

"Thousands?" Sophie furrowed her forehead. "But if there are thousands, why haven't I seen any of them? The only people I've seen are you guys, a few Hobs and Tammy, the librarian."

"I run a very tight ship," Georgia offered. "They are all incredibly busy, and because you were so new to being a Muse I thought it best they avoid the main areas of the Vasilikós until further notice. Also, most tend to live outside of the Vasilikós, either in the cottages located on the slope of the mountain or in certain cases in their own homes out in the real world. Sometimes it is better to have some stationed in the field, as part of our grassroots efforts."

~ ☾ ~

"So, we try and keep people on the path," Sophie said.

"But," Aletheria offered. "That's not all Muses do. You see, there was the issue of the gods who did not wish to leave. These vile Olympians enjoyed inflicting agony on mortals and wanted to continue laying waste to the Earth. So they resisted the call to leave Earth and ran to Olympus with a plan to start a war against God."

She waved her hand in the air, as she continued, "In reaction to this, several Olympians, with God's help, created a way to tear Olympus away from this world and create a prison existing in its own dimension. Unfortunately, the Olympians have not only found ways to have sight into our world, but they also have begun to find ways of escaping their prisons, which is why the Nine Vasilikós are so important."

"The Nine Vasilikós form the barrier keeping Olympus at bay," Georgia said proudly. "All of the Vasilikós would have to fall in order for Olympus to resurrect itself. It is our job to make sure the resurrection doesn't happen and to return any Olympians who find a way out of their prison."

"What has all of this got to do with me?" Sophie asked.

"My dearest granddaughter, you are our last hope. The Vasilikós is a dysfunctional mess. The Olympians are plotting to return to power and enslave this world. You are the one who will unite the Vasilikós. You will be the beacon calling all Demigods to join forces and fight. You are our savior."

The color drained from Sophie's face as she sat back in her chair, trying to take it all in. She glanced at Angela, who offered a sympathetic look. Even though the girl's hair was pulled up into a high ponytail with its ends tucked under, several loose strands fell against her long neck and those strands, without a doubt, were moving.

Sophie asked Angela the question burning in her mind. "What are you?"

"I'm a bit of a mutt," Angela said, tapping her fingers on the table. "One part witch, one part Gorgonian."

"Oh," Sophie said and understood why some say ignorance is bliss. Not wanting to let any of her questions go unanswered, Sophie peppered those at the table with question after question after question. Once she started, she knew she couldn't stop.

~ ☾ ~

Chapter 21

They reached the smooth, black sand covered shores of Hades sooner than Penny expected. Once she exited, the ship disappeared into the fog that heralded its approach. Before it vanished, she saw Charon on the ship's deck staring back at her, clutching the coin purse in his hand. She couldn't wait to see what chaos would take place because of those gold coins.

"So incredibly delicious," she said under her breath and made her way off the beach.

She stopped as a flicker of light caught her attention and was surprised to see in the distance a small fire near a quaint beach house with a wrap-around porch and large shutters propped open by a secured piece of wood.

This is new. Where is the foreboding castle? Have I landed on the wrong side of the island?

Near the fire sat a man who wore jeans and a fitted, Harvard sweatshirt. He wiggled his bare toes in the sand. She straightened her blouse, brushed some sand off her skirt and approached the fire.

The man looked up. "You shouldn't have come, Penny. After centuries of hostility, Saphie and I have reached a decent level of civility," Hades said.

"Saphie?" she said, sitting down on the log nearest to her. She was close enough to talk with Hades, yet far enough away to demonstrate respect for his status.

"Persephone became too tiresome to say," he said, with unhidden sadness, then smirked. "Besides, thanks to the others who created the "Haddie" nickname for me, she decided she wanted me to come up with a 'pet' name for her. So, I call her Saphie. She started getting a subscription to *Coastal Living* and now we live in a beach house. At first, I thought it was ridiculous, but I have to say it has grown on me."

~ ☾ ~

"Oh," was all Penny could say. She was embarrassed to witness the King of the Underworld reduced to a hen-pecked husband.

"What do you want, Penny?" Hades said. "You are interrupting one of the few moments of leisure time I get, and knowing how difficult it was for you to get here I know you want something."

"Revenge." She sighed. "If you must know, I want revenge against the Muses."

Hades poked the fire with a stick once more before throwing it into the fire. He waved his hands over the fire, putting it out. Stalactites twinkled like stars above, creating a false sense of sky and a realistic painted moon glowed down on them.

Penny guessed the moon was the work of Persephone. *She certainly is talented.*

"Go home, Penny," Hades said, getting up and walking towards the house. "I am no longer in the business of revenge or whatever your plan is. I am in the business of souls. That's it. It is my job to send them on their final journey and I do my job very well. What you are talking about is war and I have no patience for it."

She watched as Hades walked toward the porch of the house. The door opened and out rushed Persephone with a Pottery Farm catalog.

"Oh, Haddie," she called. "I think these outdoor tables would be perfect for alfresco dining." Her nose was buried in the catalog as she flipped to several dog-eared pages. "And look at these paper lanterns. They are so adorable. We could string them along the walkway and above the table. Did you see this wonderful beverage holder? It's like one of those old aluminum washing tubs, but it's painted the loveliest shade of blue." She looked up at Hades and smiled. Hades smiled back. She then noticed Penny and gasped.

"Penny? Oh. Dear, dear, Penny." The girl threw her catalogs down and rushed towards the elderly woman. Her hair was cut in a cute pixie cut and she wore shorts, a tank top and sunglasses perched on her head. The sunglasses tumbled off and clattered onto the steps of the house.

Like her mother, Persephone was a beautiful woman. She

~ ☾ ~

had an almost ethereal figure. She was in complete opposition to her husband Hades who was robust with his mop of unruly dirty-blonde hair. Penny thought he would fit in at any ivy-league school. The kind of person who liked to visit the Hamptons during the summer and loved both recreational and professional rowing and sailing.

"Persephone." Penny cried out, surprising herself at how happy she was to see the woman. They embraced.

"Darling Penny, you've let yourself go. Why do you look so—"

"Old?" Penny said, laughing at Persephone's grasp of the obvious. She had forgotten how vapid Persephone was. "I have lived in the mortal world for a long time. It tends to take its toll on a goddess, even if they have retained their immortality."

"Oh, Penny," Persephone responded. "Come on in and let's have some iced tea. I just brewed it. Haddie, I am sure, will be a dear and find something to throw on the grill, so you'll have to stay for lunch."

Penny turned her head to see Hades standing there, watching her. He shook his head from side to side, and she knew she would have to be very careful.

The two women sat in a great room with slip-covered furniture, a large braided rug, and a stucco and brick fireplace. The walls were a stylish mix of natural-colored stucco and bluish-gray knotty pine. Persephone turned-on several lamps throughout the room, including one near Penny's elbow. It was made of hand-blown glass and had the shell of a large crab inside it. To Penny's disgust, the crab had a miniature mustache and a tiny sombrero.

"Isn't he darling? I call him Senior Chi-Chi," said Persephone, before leaving the room and returning with a tray arranged with two tall glasses, a pitcher of iced tea, a saucer of sliced lemons and a painted bowl full of sugar cubes. "Help yourself to sugar," Persephone said, kicking off her flip-flops and tucking her feet underneath her. She greedily sipped her iced tea, which now contained five sugar cubes.

"What the heck are you doing here, Pen?" Persephone asked. "Haddie and I rarely get guests. I mean, with the

~ ☾ ~

guardians and the ferryman, and all of Haddie's little traps, we've grown accustomed to our exclusive little cul-de-sac."

Penny took a sip of her tea. It was delicious.

Delicious considering the ton of alcohol in it. Oh dear, dear Persephone, under the veneer of fancy-free beach life, I'm so glad you are the same old lush I knew from years past.

"Well, Persephone."

"Pen, please call me Saphie."

"Well, Saphie, it's a long story and I wouldn't want to bore you," she said, setting down her drink. She was exhausted from the journey and the drink was going straight to her head.

"Oh, come on. Who are you planning on killing, or is it straight torture you're thinking of?" Saphie said, running her fingers through her hair.

Penny knew she had been right. *This bird may be in a gilded Pottery Farm, Malibu Barbie cage, but she is no songbird. She's a predator, struggling to escape its prison.*

"Well," Penny said. "Since you insist."

She revealed her plan and Persephone listened intently. As she talked, Penny found it almost comical that the pretty little goddess was so interested in the potential death and carnage she was planning.

"It does sound like you have a somewhat aggressive timeline, Pen. But I wouldn't be a friend unless I pointed out some obvious flaws in your plan. You were always good at figuring out high-level strategic items like who you want to maim or kill, but to achieve your goal you need someone who is more detailed oriented for the day-to-day plotting."

Penny knew Persephone had made up her mind to offer help, as long as she was willing to ask for it. That was the unwritten code between gods. Ask and you shall receive, but there always was an extensive price to pay. Almost giddy at the thought, she knew all she needed to do was reel in the fish and, much to her delight, Persephone cut to the chase.

"You know Pen, I consider you to be a sister, with similar taste for, shall we say, eccentric hobbies."

"I couldn't agree more," Penny said, taking a gulp of her iced tea.

~ ☾ ~

"And all you would need to do is ask for my help," Persephone said as she fluttered her eyelashes.

Penny smiled. "Well, Saphie, you would be the very first goddess I would come to for help, but, what's your price? We all know nothing is for free in our world."

"Well, maybe we should start our negotiations with what I bring to the table," Have you seen my artist's studio? You'll love it."

~ ☾ ~

Chapter 22

Tears ran down Sophie's cheeks, as sobs escaped her lips. She sat at her desk, staring down at her shaking hands. She didn't bother to look up when she heard Angela enter her room.

"Please, Angela," Sophie said, "I need a second to be alone. For one second, I just want everyone to leave me alone."

"I can't. Friends don't leave when they are needed the most."

Sophie lifted up her hands and held her head between them. She heard the click of her bedroom door and before she could think she was alone, Angela's hand was touching her hair, as she brushed it.

"You might not think so, but you are incredibly lucky," Angela said.

"I'm a lot of things, but lucky isn't one of them. I'm an Ohioan. I'm an American. I'm a teenager. Hmmm, what else am I? Oh, yes, I'm a freak. I'm a Muse and now I'm some sort of savior. Now that I think about it, you're right. I'm so lucky."

"That's one way to look at it."

"Let me guess, you're going to begin listing all of the amazing things I should feel grateful for. It should only take you a few seconds."

"You have a mother who loves you very much. From everything I've heard about your father, he adored you. You could do no wrong in his eyes. Compared to my childhood, I'd say you have a lot to be thankful for."

"I'm sorry, I didn't mean..."

"You also have a grandmother who also cares a lot for you, in spite of her horrible way of showing it."

"Is this where I'm supposed to realize my life isn't so bad?" Sophie said, slumping into her chair.

~ ☾ ~

"Then there is Bennett—"

"Who runs in the opposite direction whenever I enter the room."

"I don't recall him running when he held you a few hours ago and I'm taking a bit of a leap here, but I think his running says more about how much he may be feeling for you. Not that he has said anything to me, but you would have to be blind not to see that he is feeling something."

"Well, clearly I must be blind because I don't see—"

"And then you have me, although I will admit your current attitude is making it pretty hard to admit how much your friendship means to me. It's pathetic for me to say this, but...here goes... you are the closest thing to a friend I've ever had. Go ahead and laugh, but it's true. I'm not saying this to make you feel sorry for me. I'm simply stating the facts. Growing up, my father considered things like friendship as a waste of time and completely unnecessary. I was created for a single purpose."

"You make it sound like you were nothing more than a project to your Dad. I'm sure he loved you."

"In his own way, I think he did, but the love he felt for me paled in comparison to his love for power and he never lost sight of the fact that I was expected to bring him the glory he believed he deserved. He was a powerful witch, but like many, there was always a growing and constant desire for more power. It was an unfortunate situation because the more I tried to make him proud, the more I pushed him away. The harder I practiced my spells, the more I achieved, the greater his jealously grew. I wish I could say that it is painful for me to admit this, but my father was a selfish ass. I did everything he wanted me to do and more, thinking it would make him happy. I was a fool to think if I could master one more difficult spell or create three more difficult potions, he would finally turn to me and—"

"And tell you he loved you," Sophie said.

"I don't ever remember my father ever saying those words to me. Can you say the same? Remember to not forget the many blessings you have in your life, no matter how hard the road in front of you becomes." Angela put the brush down and exited the room.

~ ☾ ~

Sophie sat there for a few seconds, not really sure how to react.

What the heck? Why is it, every time I turn around, I'm feeling like a complete ass? Everything I do is wrong. Everything I say is wrong and I'm supposed to save the world? Lead the battle? Be everyone's champion?

"I couldn't even save my father."

She realized she was being selfish, had always been selfish. She never had made things easier for her parents and now with her father was gone; she would never be able to make it up to him. He was lost.

But, I still have my mother and whatever relationship I have with Georgia. And Angela is my friend. She's my only friend, except for Bennett.

She began to feel a little bit better, until a sinking feeling hit her.

My dad would have liked them...my dad was murdered. He loved me and they killed him. They'll always be there, waiting for the right moment to strike. They will always hunt down what I love, until they destroy any happiness in my life. They need to learn that just because you have these super powers, doesn't mean you can kill whoever stands in your way. I want them to pay. I am lucky and it's about time I find out what a little luck can get me.

Sophie left her room and before she knew it, she was standing at the door of her mother's private rooms. She knocked and waited a few moments. She didn't hear anything except for the muffled sounds of the sea and knew her mother must be on her terrace. She tried the doorknob and found it unlocked. Her mother lay on a chaise lounge, asleep.

"Mom?"

Callie opened her eyes and smiled at her daughter. "Sweetie. I'm sorry, I was sitting here thinking and I must have fallen asleep."

"You know why I'm here. I have to go see them."

Her mother bit her bottom lip. "Look," Callie began. "You don't just go and visit the most powerful beings on this earth as if you were going to visit some kindly old aunts."

"I know, Mom."

"No you don't. We need to tread very carefully here. Once

~ ☾ ~

you start down that road, there isn't a way to turn back. It won't be like me. You won't ever have a chance for normal."

"Mom, normal doesn't exist for me anymore. It's not an option. Look, I know I don't understand everything one hundred percent, but what I do know is that I have my path and I've accepted it, or maybe I've decided not to fight Fate. I still have moments where I seriously can't believe I'm tossing around words like Fate, Gorgon and gods and goddesses, but I have to accept that this is my reality. So this world has all sorts of crazy creatures and danger lurks around every corner. It is what it is, but even here I know I won't let my father's sacrifice go unpunished. These Fallen Ones want a fight? Well, I'm going to give them one."

"You're talking like a child. Talk of revenge is childish. These are creatures who eat revenge like an appetizer and their main course is mortal suffering. Your fight with them isn't about your father." Callie stood up and grabbed Sophie, shoving her to the edge of the balcony. The energy around Sophie was tingling and sparking and with a loud crack Sophie's world went black.

Every part of Sophie's body tingled and her head spun. Wind came from all directions, cooling Sophie's skin and drying the perspiration on the back of her neck. She shuddered a little and opened her eyes, watching as they passed through rock, pipes and wood. She realized they weren't traveling outside the Vasilikós, but through it. Materializing on the roof, Sophie fell to the ground, her legs like rubber from her first Shimmering experience.

Callie reached down and forced her to stand. "Get up, Sophie. For once, you foolish girl, you must truly understand what all of this means. Do you see down there, in the village and beyond, into the mountains and beyond that? Look over here and see the sea, and see the lands beyond the sea, and the land and seas beyond even that. Do you see the millions upon millions upon millions of people going about their daily lives without a clue as to what is happening here? It is for those lives, for those souls you would be doing this. Those lives are in your hands. Each birth will be due to your successes and each unplanned death to your failures. So don't talk to me about revenge, as if that is even important. It pains

~ ☾ ~

me to say, but thoughts of your father are just a waste of your time."

Sophie winced at her mother's abrupt words.

How could she be so cruel about daddy?

She looked beyond the Vasilikós and begrudgingly understood what her mother was saying.

"And it isn't just one Fallen One. It's hundreds, but no one knows what was locked away in Olympus and what has managed to hide. That doesn't even take into consideration the Olympians who have escaped from their realm. All of them have one mission and that is to destroy or possess you. They don't care which, because it's all the same to them. Now do you understand?"

Sophie stood silently and continued to look beyond the seas. She imagined all of the other countries full of cities that were full of towns and full of souls. She imagined everyone she knew back in Ohio then doubled, tripled and quadrupled them in her mind. She then multiplied the group by infinity and saw an unending sea of people she was now responsible for, and the reality of her situation struck her like a double shot of adrenaline. Her heart began to beat in her chest faster and faster, and she thought of her father, as she closed her eyes, her head swimming.

"Come on, kid," said her father's voice. "Stop your bellyaching and jump in." His voice was so clear, as if he was standing right next to her. When faced with what she thought was impossible, her father always say the same thing.

"I'm counting on you. You'll do what's right," he said. The double-barrel shotgun of her father's words hit her, along with the boost in confidence it always gave her, and the darkness melted away.

He always believed in me, even when I didn't give him any real reason to do so.

She opened her eyes and looked at her mother.

She felt different. She knew now was the time to put childish things away, because she wasn't a child anymore.

"And so, the veil has been removed," Callie said. "You see our world as it truly is and I am saddened to see your childhood vanish."

"I'll still play with dolls if it makes you happy," Sophie

~ ☾ ~

said. "Tell me about the Fates and what I should expect."

Callie smiled and nodded. "In a moment, sweetie, let's enjoy the quiet for a few seconds more."

Two hours passed and the sun set. She lay there with her mother on the rooftop of the Vasilikós and watched the millions of stars appear. They held hands and talked about nothing important.

~ ☾ ~

Chapter 23

A week later, Sophie and Angela stood in front of the small stone cottage that hid the Vasilikós from the mortal world, waiting for Aletheria, who pulled up in a red, clearly vintage convertible.

"This is a beautiful car," Angela said, opening the door and stepping into the tiny back seat. Aletheria reminded the girls to tie their scarves around their heads to keep their hair from getting messed up, but when the girls couldn't quite get the scarves right Aletheria grew frustrated and sketched two scarves onto them. She laughed and proclaimed that they were perfect examples of 1950's chic in their summer dresses.

"Only answer what they ask and do not ask for *anything,*" Aletheria explained. "They never give anything away for free, but are more than willing to offer everything they know for a price."

The roads twisted and turned along a valley and sloped up a mountain, then gradually descended into another valley. Below them they saw a long winding road connected to theirs, which led them to a picturesque villa. A tall faded pink stucco wall surrounded the grounds, making it into a compound of sorts. At a brick and stone archway with an imposing gate, Aletheria brought the car to an abrupt stop.

Through the iron gates, Sophie saw a large cobble-stoned courtyard covered in climbing roses and wild jasmine. The fragrance of the flowers mingled with boxwood bushes, tall Italian cypresses, baking bread and brewed spice tea.

"This is where I leave you," Aletheria said, as the scarves erased themselves off the girls' heads. "Neither I, nor anyone else, can cross into their villa without being invited. The ladies and I haven't always been on the best of terms. My very existence is an exception to their rules and they hate any exceptions. However, I will be here promptly at three to pick

~ ☾ ~

you up. Remember what we've told you and you'll be okay. Unfortunately, when it comes to those three, our hands are tied."

Aletheria started her car again and with a squeal of her wheels drove away, taunting some young men working in the garden.

Sophie eyed Angela and thought that this was a situation where having a Gorgonian best friend was a good thing. She offered Angela a nervous, but optimistic thumbs-up.

"Let's do it," she said as she reached over to pull the bell string. A villa door located at the back of the garden opened and three women stepped out. She wasn't sure what to expect from three of the most powerful gods in history, but these three were a pleasant surprise.

"Sophie, honey." The tallest of the three called out to her in a heavy, gravelly Brooklyn accent. She wore a navy and white polyester pantsuit and her wrinkled face bore a lot of powder and blush, along with blood red lipstick. She threw open the gates. "So glad to meet you. My name is Rose."

The second woman was shorter and slighter, and had the appearance of being a grandmother out of the English countryside. She wore a comfortable flower print dress with a garden smock over it. She fumbled with the ties of her coveralls. Reading glasses were perched on the bridge of her button nose and Sophie found her comforting. Everything about the woman said Granny.

"Don't be rude," the woman chastised Rose with an upper-crust English accent. "Acknowledge both of our guests." She smiled at Angela. "Hello, my name is Agatha. So glad you could make it out for the afternoon." She shook Angela's hand and led her into the garden. "You'll be surprised to hear that I know your mother. She is such a charming woman. I even have a piece of needlepoint she gave me one Christmas many years ago. I'll have to show it to you. Such an attention to detail."

The third woman was the shortest of the three, albeit the largest in girth. Her skin was brown and she was dressed in what appeared to be her Sunday best. The navy suit was tailored to fit her wide frame and showcase what appeared to be her best physical assets—an almost comically large bosom

~ ☾ ~

and a robust rear end. She hit Sophie on the top of her head with her shiny white leather purse, which swung out of control as she shut the gates behind her.

"Sorry, Sophie. Did I hit you, child? By the way, my name is Cleo. It is going to be hotter than Hades today, so we'll be taking tea indoors," Cleo said, hooking her arm into Sophie's and directing the girl indoors.

"It's called alfresco, Cleo," Rose corrected.

"I don't care what you call it, Rose, 'cause I am *not* sweating in my good dress. You know how I get when I'm overheated," Cleo said. "It's my blood sugar, honey. All over the place and I can become very testy."

"Well," Sophie said with a nervous smile. "We wouldn't want that."

"No need to whisper, Cleo. Everyone knows about your blood sugar." Rose shouted over her shoulder. "It's all you ever talk about."

Sophie and Angela were ushered into a large comfortable room with tufted couches and chairs. Worn floral prints of all different types clashed with each other and Sophie thought it resembled the mismatched furniture her high school used in all of their theater productions. The couch in the *Diary of Anne Frank* had also made an appearance in the production of *Barefoot in the Park*.

Rose gestured for the two girls to sit down in a loveseat with a cabbage-rose pattern and a ruffled dust skirt. Several dust bunnies lingered in the corners of the room and Agatha apologized, acknowledging today was the cleaning lady's day off. Sophie noted the elaborate silver tea service hadn't suffered from a lack of polishing and hot steam poured out of the largest pot.

Agatha positioned herself as hostess and began asking preferences regarding tea. After everyone was served, the group of women settled down for a quiet afternoon chat.

Rose sat in an armchair next to a small end-table, where she had her *I Love New York* ashtray and unfiltered cigarettes. She opened a small drawer and pulled out an airplane-sized bottle of brandy and poured a swig into her cup. Agatha grimaced in disapproval and turned her attention back to her guests, but not before Rose had taken a

~ ☾ ~

sip of her freshened-up tea and smacked her lips in delight.

"I am so glad you could make the time for a visit," Agatha said as she began working on a piece of needlework. "We three are often so engrossed in our work that we hardly have enough time to interact with each other, let alone others outside of our villa. Isn't that right, Cleo?"

Cleo looked up, a large slice of bread in one hand and her teacup in the other. She put down her items and lifted her napkin to her lips to wipe jam from her upper lip and swallow the large piece of bread still in her mouth. "You have testified to the complete and utter truth, Aggie," she said. "Honey, if you only knew the requirements placed on goddesses like us. It's exhausting." Cleo glanced at the grandfather clock at the far end of the room, and opened her large white purse. She pulled out an empty spindle and began spooling golden thread onto it. The Fate reached over and took a sip of tea and grimaced. "Please pass the sugar bowl, darling," she said to Angela. "Agatha always makes her tea so strong and I have to watch my blood sugar. It's all over the place."

"Now, I'm not saying we don't have our slow periods," Cleo continued, "but vacations are often cancelled if there is a war going on. Without us creating the threads of life, measuring them to the precise length the Divine has allotted for each and then cutting threads from the fabric," she said, while removing her hat at the same time, "life as we know it would stop. It can run an old lady down. Of course you two young people don't have to worry about such things, *at least for right now*."

Sophie shifted in her seat as Cleo's emphasis on 'worry' and 'right now' made her feel uncomfortable.

"Confidentially, I don't like to think about the last part." Cleo said. "The cutting, I mean. It's so final and serious. But then, I don't have to worry about the cutting since I am responsible for the making of a life's thread."

"And I'm responsible for the measuring of a life's thread. Rose, please, my eyes are so tired today," said Agatha, sticking her needle into her needlepoint border. She handed it over to Rose who took out a small pair of golden scissors and cut the thread connecting the needle to the cloth. Sophie winced as the sharp scissors snapped the thread. In that

~ ☾ ~

moment, she was sure she had heard a soft, high-pitched wail. She hoped the scissors just needed oiling. Sophie didn't bother to ask what role Rose played in the life process.

"So—" Angela offered, attempting to change the subject. "As you mentioned, you are very busy and we wouldn't want to take up too much of your time. You wanted to see Sophie."

"Yes," Sophie offered. "What is it I can do for you?"

As soon as the words left her mouth, Sophie knew she had made a grave mistake.

Rose turned her head and blew a big puff of smoke into the air. She offered Sophie a somewhat grotesque mockery of a smile, the woman's blood red lips parting, revealing her tobacco- stained teeth.

"Well, since you were so kind and generous to ask," Rose said, taking no pains to hide her desire to come to the point as she brushed the wayward ashes off the top of the side table. "We have heard Georgia is having a major event to introduce you to the other Eight Vasilikós. We would like to be included in the celebration. We would like an invitation to the event."

Sophie watched as the three women stared at her on the edge of their seats, waiting for her answer. *Rose must think I am so stupid to not pick up on the fact that the Fates are up to something.*

"I was told by my mother the Fates tend to shun Vasilikós events," Sophie began. "Except for the Mid-Summer Wine Ceremony, of course, when we present you with the special wine created from Georgia's vines. It's my understanding this wine restores your powers for another year. Why would you be interested in something as insignificant as a ball?"

Rose's smiled changed as she gritted her teeth. "You know, little one, there are two things I don't like to be reminded of. One has to do with my spaghetti sauce and how some people in this house, who will remain nameless, think that because I start with Mrs. Angelino's spaghetti sauce as a base I shouldn't refer to my sauce as homemade. This argument never fails to put me in a foul mood. The other thing that pisses me off is the slightest mention of my dependence on the Muses. However, you are correct. The idea of wasting an evening with Georgia is something I usually won't entertain. I

~ ☾ ~

would strongly suggest that whomever gave you those little tidbits about us should stress to you it is impolite to discuss it openly."

"Rose." Agatha warned. "Put your shears away."

Sophie noticed Rose absentmindedly opening and closing the golden scissors.

"Before you do something we will all regret," Agatha said.

Rose froze and deposited her shears into her side table. "My apologies, girls," Rose said. "I've been foolish. I guess today is one of those days where I live up to my reputation of being a real witch."

There were a few beats of silence and then Cleo, Agatha and Rose laughed heartily.

Sophie didn't feel like laughing, but did her best to fake it and nudged Angela to do the same.

"In all seriousness," Agatha said. "We have to be at that party. When we say it's written in the stars, it *is* written in the stars. I won't explain, because as I'm sure you were told, information comes at a price when it comes from us."

"Oh Aggie, you aren't any fun." Cleo said. "Give her a little something, for old time's sake."

"No." Sophie said, jumping up and signaling Angela it was time to go. "We'll wait outside in the garden until our ride arrives, in another two hours."

"You're mistaken," Rose said, lighting up another cigarette. "You've been here for over four hours. Your ride, the book worm, has been waiting for the last hour."

Sophie stared at her watch and stared at it. She was sure they had just arrived. She took a sip of her tea to prove herself right, expecting it to still be hot, but it wasn't. It was stone cold.

Sophie panicked, wanting to leave even more than before. "We've taken up way too much of your time. My sincerest apologies."

"No need to apologize, Sophie," Rose said. "We're always so glad to have visitors and you must come again real soon."

"Of course," Angela said, as Sophie pulled her out of the room.

"I'll have Georgia send you the invitations," Sophie explained. "She was planning on a late summer, early fall event."

~ ☾ ~

"Well, my dear," Rose said, stopping them in their tracks as she flicked a piece of tobacco from her tongue. "You'll have to tell Georgia her plans have changed. Tell her you've invited us to the event and agreed to change the date."

Sophie whipped around and stared open-mouthed at the three women who stood smiling back at her. *Those aren't sweet grannies. They're sharks and I'm a bleeding swimmer.*

"What date are you suggesting?" Sophie said.

"Don't you remember, dear?" Rose said, her placid face frozen in a wide grin. Her red lips were bordering on grotesque and her face was more harsh than pleasant. "During our wonderful discussion about the Mid-Summer Wine Ceremony, we all agreed we should combine the events."

The slight tan Sophie had acquired over the summer drained from her face. She saw a few of Angela's dreads hiss and retreat behind her neck.

"But...I didn't..." Sophie sputtered.

"We'll see you in a month," Rose said. "If Georgia has a problem, you have her give me call."

The three Fates moved away, leaving Sophie standing next to Angela. They turned their backs on the girls, sat back down in the same chairs and returned to their work. Cleo made the thread and Agatha measured it. Before Sophie had the chance to hear the awful little high-pitched sound when Rose cut the thread, she grabbed Angela and rushed out of the villa. Angela jumped into the backseat as Sophie shut the door on her skirt. Aletheria floored the gas, sending a large dust cloud into the Fates' courtyard. They drove past several workmen, who were repairing a section of wall with a blackened and charred hole in it. The words *filthy Nothos* were painted in red beside the hole.

~ ☾ ~

Chapter 24

Georgia knew something was wrong. She could feel it deep in her bones. She suspected the Fates were up to something and it frustrated her not knowing. For the last few hours she'd sat at the large farmhouse kitchen table fretting. She loved the centuries-old table with its huge hand-carved legs. She even loved how worn and gouged the top was. She often came into the kitchen to help Winnie and her team of Hobs shell peas or cut vegetables. It was her way of taking a few moments to escape her daily life and its never-ending demands on her.

Winnie was buzzing around beginning dinner preparation. She announced to Georgia they would be eating roasted chicken with rosemary potatoes, buttered green beans with garlic, a garden salad and chocolate layer cake for desert. The cake had been baking for about an hour and Georgia was enjoying the delicious aroma.

"You're frettin', Georgia," Winnie said as she pulled open a big sack of potatoes and threw them, one by one, into the sink. "Frettin' will get you nowhere."

"I know," Georgia said and frowned. "Do you need help with those potatoes?"

Winnie rolled her eyes as she stood on the step stool in front of the sink. "Grab a knife."

Winnie eyed Georgia. "You know, I've never been a Hob to meddle in anyone's family situations."

Georgia laughed. "That's all you do, Winnie. You order me around like you are head of this Vasilikós."

"Well..." Winnie said. "Sometimes even the likes of needs a swift kick in the tush."

"I suppose you're right, although, don't ever tell anyone I said that. I'll deny it."

Winnie threw a few potatoes into the water and started on

~ ☾ ~

another. "Cut the pieces thicker, Georgia. Otherwise, they won't brown correctly," Winnie corrected and Georgia nodded.

"I know what you're about to say, Winnie. You've been fretting about it for the past few weeks."

Winnie frowned. "I was just going to say how lovely Sophie looked. That's all. You were smart in procurin' Angela as part of your Vasilikós."

"Angela is a good girl," Georgia said. "And I knew Sophia would need a friend."

"I'm sure it doesn't hurt that the girl is part Gorgon, with a huge dash of powerful witch. Few would dare challenge her. Even a Fallen One knows not to push one of those too far."

"You didn't expect me to allow my granddaughter to wander around helpless, did you? Two birds, one stone." Georgia scrubbed a large potato. "Come out with it, Winnie. You're holding back."

"You're bein' too hard on the girl and you're being terrible to Callie. Poor woman just lost her husband and the child is now faced with all of this Fallen One nonsense. Let me also remind you the girl just lost her father and has gone through a major change. She didn't expect to be mortal one day and a Demigod the next. Push. That's all you ever do to that poor girl."

"The child's lack of preparation was her mother's fault," Georgia said. "If I don't push the girl, who will? She must rise to meet my expectations."

"Oh, you're expectations, is it. Well...well, I guess we all better get our arses in line with your expectations. Don't you be takin' any sort of mighty tone with me, Georgia. I've known you long enough to know you're steppin into the marsh and not on dry ground. You'll sink if you're not careful."

Georgia didn't respond. She sighed and plopped another potato into the water.

"All I am saying is that you can't plan for everythin' and you're foolin' yourself if you believe you can control that young girl," said Winnie. "I think you've forgotten what it was like to be a mother and you have no idea how to be a grandmother. She's just a child. Don't forget when dealing

~ ☾ ~

with a child you have to be patient." Winnie took a sniff and glanced over at the oven. "Be a love and take the cake out of the oven."

Georgia stabbed her knife into the potato she was working on and placed it down on the cutting board. "What would you do without me to help you, Winnie?"

"Oh yes," Winnie said with an air of sarcasm as she threw down another finished potato. "Thank goodness you're around. I wouldn't know when I needed to wipe me bum without you to remind me to do it."

Georgia heard someone enter the kitchen and turned to see Sophie and Angela walking in, followed by Callie. As she listened to the details of their visit, Georgia flew into a fury.

"What do you mean a change of date? That event isn't some barbecue we can move at a moment's notice. Why did you promise anything to those women?" Georgia said through gritted teeth.

I am so disgusted with you, I could just scream. You stand there, girl, cowering like a wounded animal. How could such a weak woman come from my bloodline?

"She technically didn't agree to anything," Angela said.

"What, may I ask, does technically mean?" Georgia said, turning her attention to the Gorgonian.

"Well, I...I mean," Angela said as she winced. "We didn't agree to anything. We were told."

"You were told?" Georgia's voice went into a higher octave. "I'll tell you what happened. You allowed them to trick you. You two allowed them to charm you right into this mess. You were given specific instructions. You were to have tea, maybe eat a pastry, even get a tour of the villa, and then you were supposed to leave. Not ask questions. Not engage in tit for tat. And, most importantly, not agree to change this Vasilikós' society calendar. The invitations for the Wine Ceremony have already gone out with a save the date card for your presentation to the supernatural community. We will now have to completely regroup. To think of the extra work you have given to Winnie and the rest of the household."

"Don't be throwin' me into the middle of this, Georgia," Winnie yelled, as she threw the now-seasoned potatoes into the oven and slammed the oven door shut. She grabbed her

~ ☾ ~

dishtowel and rubbed an invisible smudge off of the big table. "It doesn't matter when these parties take place. They're *all* the same to me. And if I might be so bold as to say, gettin' both of those parties done at once is a dream come true. Two birds, one stone."

"You knew we were taking a risk by sending the girls," Callie said. "And if this is the worst to happen from the visit, well, we should count ourselves lucky."

"I won't have any of it! The nerve of that witch, Rose, thinking she can push me around. I just know it was all her idea. Those three women are nothing without our help. Nobody pushes this Vasilikós around. Not even the Fates." As her fury grew, red splotches broke out all over Georgia's face.

"Well, Georgia," Callie said. "I suggest we get to work, because sitting around, bitching isn't helping us prepare."

If I don't leave this kitchen, I will either kill each of them or burst a blood vessel and I'm afraid I'm leaning more towards the first choice.

Through gritted teeth she attempted a smile, and with a burst of energy she made every kitchen cabinet fly open sending pots, pans and utensils clattering to the floor. She walked towards the back door as Winnie's final words reached her ears.

"Oh, that's just fine, Georgia. Make a big, fancy exit and leave the rest of us to clean up the mess! Well, you better get it out of you or you'll have me to deal with. And you burned the cake!"

~ ☾ ~

Chapter 25

After Winnie insisted the mess be left for her to clean up, Sophie made a point to steer clear of the orchard and stood with Angela under a tall almond tree. In the far distance ominous dark clouds were gathering and Sophie shivered. She watched Angela close her eyes for a few seconds, as she extended her hands towards the clouds and mumbled what Sophie guessed was a spell. A whoosh of wind caught Sophie off guard and nearly lifted her off the ground as it swept upward and dispersed the clouds.

"Why did you do that?" Sophie asked. "Do those clouds mean something?"

Angela didn't bother to look into the sky. "No... not everything has to do with you and the Olympians. I've already torn my dress's strap. I'd prefer not to ruin it by getting caught in a rain storm."

And I'm supposed to believe you? She's worried about getting her dress wet? It has something to do with the Olympians. I know it.

"Georgia was pissed," Sophie said. She didn't know why, but she laughed and Angela joined her.

"Yes, I'm guessing you're right about that one," Angela said. "I've lived here for almost a year and thanks to you I have witnessed the first time Georgia blew her top like that."

Sophie was about to ask Angela how she ended up at the Vasilikós, but she lost all thought when she saw Bennett walking towards them carrying a blanket.

"Hi," he said, smiling at Sophie.

"Hi," Sophie said, smiling back.

"Winnie sent me out to bring this to you. She thought you might need it. She was concerned you would get some dirt on your dresses."

"If you'll excuse me, I really should fix my dress strap,"

~ ☾ ~

Angela said, showcasing her strap was indeed broken. "See you later, Soph."

Sophie liked her new nickname. She also made a mental note to thank her friend for a speedy exit. She turned back to Bennett, who had already spread the blanket on the ground and was getting up to leave.

"Don't go," she said.

Wow, that's really smooth. Could I sound a little more desperate?

"I should," he said, then took a few steps and turned to leave.

"Why do you do that?" she asked.

He stopped. "Do what?"

"Run away. Every time I run into you, you literally trip over yourself to run away."

"No, I don't," he said. "Look, I don't know what they've told you, and I don't think I should have to defend my actions to someone I barely know."

"Nothing. Nobody has told me anything," Sophie said, growing frustrated.

This is so not going the way I wanted it to. "Oh, why don't you go run away and leave me alone? At least it will be the one thing consistent in my life." She sat down so suddenly part of her skirt flew up into her face and she had to smack it down or risk displaying more leg than she cared to.

Bennett chuckled.

"What?" Sophie said looking up and fighting a smile. She lost the battle and Bennett sat down while Sophie tucked her legs underneath her skirt.

"Miranda," Bennett said picking up a fallen almond and flinging it away.

"Miranda?"

"She was a Muse, out of your grandmother's Vasilikós. We were an item for about a year."

"Oh," Sophie said picking at a blade of grass.

"One day she up and left, transferred to the Vasilikós in Italy. Not a word to me, except a Facespace posting that said, 'Sorry.'"

"Wait," Sophie said. "She broke-up with you on Facespace? That...is...ouch. Wow... that really sucks for you."

~ ☾ ~

She laughed a bit at the ridiculous nature of the situation. "Breaking up on a public Facespace posting is so not right."

"Tell me about it," Bennett said, flinging another almond into the yard. "And to make matters worse, she "liked" her own posting, along with fifteen more of my friends who later said they were sorry for not reading the post more carefully. They quickly 'unliked' it."

"I'm sorry for laughing, but you have to admit—"

"It hurt? Yes, it did. It hurt like hell."

"Well," Sophie said. "It's apparent she wasn't the right girl." She thought for a second. "So, let me guess, you've sworn off dating Muses?"

"Yep," he said, cracking open an almond and handing the shelled nut to Sophie who popped it into her mouth. "I was warned that Muses can be somewhat…"

"Somewhat what?" Sophie said, the color rising in her cheeks.

"Fickle."

"Well," Sophie said getting to her feet. "That's good to know."

"I'm sorry. I didn't mean to…I shouldn't have said that. It was so incredibly stupid and mean of me."

Sophie stood for a moment and glanced away to hide her hurt feelings. She knew her rollercoaster emotions weren't Bennett's fault, but she couldn't help the way she felt. She was pissed.

She noticed a man standing in the distance. He wore all black and his skin, devoid of any sort of color, had a grayish glow to it.

He looks a lot like my father.

A chill ran down her spine, as goose bumps broke out all over her skin. *That is my father.*

The vision stood there, looking at her. It raised its right hand and placed it over its heart and then reached towards her.

He's crying. Oh daddy, I miss you so much.

She wanted to run to him, call out, scream for him not to go, but something stopped her. The memory of the vision in the woods back home made her wary.

If only it were really you, daddy. I would do anything for

~ ☾ ~

it to be you. Just another freaky example of my 'normal' life.

Bennett said something and Sophie began to respond to him, but stopped when she saw her father was gone.

Flustered, Sophie shook herself mentally and realized Bennett was looking concerned. "No...," she said. "It's fine. I'm sorry. I shouldn't have laughed and you certainly have your reasons for lumping Muses into a single, fickle category." She brushed her skirt and glanced again to see if her father had come back. He hadn't, and she was both disappointed and confused.

"It must have been my mind playing tricks on me," she said to herself. "He was never there. My father is dead." Much to her relief and dread, her mother called from the Vasilikós. "Excuse me." Sophie walked away.

Sophie found her mother in the Entry Hall, leaning against the large library table with the registry book.

"Hi," Callie said. "Georgia asked me to show you something. She's a bit preoccupied right at the moment."

"She's a bit pissed," Sophie said. "Mom, it wasn't my fault."

"Language, Sophie," Callie warned. "She knows it wasn't your fault and doesn't blame you. Georgia may have anger management issues, but she isn't naïve. A good portion of her anger wasn't even directed at you. She and Rose have a difficult history. Suffice to say they aren't the kind of women who chat on the phone and exchange recipes. So, let's forget about it, because the next month of preparation is going to be one long experience in hell. All right?"

"Okay, Mom," Sophie replied and her mother gave her a hug, kissed her on top of her head and patted her shoulder.

"Come with me," Callie said as she led Sophie towards the large, ornate mirror Sophie remembered Angela had avoided during one of their endless tours.

"Remember how we told you the mirrors were used as a form of transportation?" Callie asked. Sophie nodded. "Well, they are also used to hide or protect things. Give me your hand, take a deep breath, and follow me."

"Through the looking glass?" Sophie said.

"Yes, Alice, like I've never heard that one before," Callie said with a smirk. "Follow me."

~ ☾ ~

Sophie watched her mother take a deep breath and walk into the mirror. The mirror's surface took on a liquid form, rippling as if a stone had been skipped across it. Her mother gave a tug at Sophie's arm and she fell into the mirror's watery surface with a yelp. It was much colder than she'd expected. Her mother gave her arm a stronger yank as she pulled her through to the other side. The mirror she stepped out of was a duplicate of the one found in the Great Entry Hall, except this mirror's frame design was reversed.

"It's a mirror image of the other one?" Sophie said, touching the frame.

"They are sister mirrors. There always have to be two. Any more than two and they become extremely temperamental and hard to control. This mirror and its sister were created by an Elf clan Georgia has on retainer."

"Elf?" Sophie said.

"Who else would you choose to make your transference mirrors? Granted, it's a complicated process. They subcontract with a group of water nymphs that gather and trap the mirror's surface off of a hidden lake in the Elfin highlands. I once got a tour of their factory when I was in grade school. It was fascinating."

"Yeah," Sophie said. "I got a trip to Lollipop Farm."

Callie laughed. "Hey, I liked Lollipop Farm."

Sophie glanced around, realizing she didn't recognize the room they were in.

Even the catacombs were more welcoming than this place.

The room was cold, dank, and, except for the light coming from a few torches, very dark. The chamber had stone walls, stone floors and ceiling, no windows at all and a prevailing stench of mold. It had a fireplace with a roaring fire in it, but the flames gave off little warmth. Although not feeling chilled, Sophie still continued to shiver and Callie told her she would get used to the temperature in a few moments.

"The cold feeling is an illusion, a defense mechanism," Callie explained. "Had you broken into this room, the cold would have continued until you became incapacitated. Stay close to me. There are many other traps found throughout these rooms."

~ ☾ ~

The room they stood in was a maze of spiral staircases connecting upper and lower floors. Each staircase was stranger than the first. Sophie took a step toward one of them and it disappeared through the ceiling as if it had been shot out of a cannon. She did the same to another, but this one fell through the floor only to reappear in the spot vacated by the first.

"These aren't right. A person could spend an eternity chasing after them."

"Sophie, get away from those! The last thing I need is for you to end up in another country."

A sort of gnawing feeling in the back of Sophie's mind drew her towards a different section of the room.

She went with her gut and stood in front of the fireplace. She reached down to warm her hands by the flames and realized they gave off no heat at all.

"It's not real?" Sophie said.

Callie's footsteps echoed in the room as she approached Sophie and the fireplace. She knelt down and without hesitation Callie thrust her hand into the fire beneath the wood and exposed an iron ring hidden in a trap underneath. She gave the ring a yank and something clicked.

"All-consuming fire created from the Sun Chariot. Yet another trap, created by a Norwegian witch friend of your grandmother. The same witch created the spiral staircase trick. A person who does not know how to bypass this spell is burned to a cinder."

A few other clicks followed the first and the stones around the fireplace shook a little as they retracted out of sight. The fireplace slid upward about ten feet, exposing a hidden downward staircase.

"Stay close to the wall and grab onto the railing," Callie continued. "The stairs get very slippery this time of year."

"Is that another trap?" Sophie asked.

"No, smarty, it's just common sense. But when you get ready to step off of the last step, skip it. Step on it and the entire floor collapses into a deep pit. I won't tell you what's down there. Let's just say it isn't pleasant."

Sophie followed her mother's direction, gripped the handrail and descended deeper into the Vasilikós. As they made their way down the stairs, other torches sparked,

~ ☾ ~

sputtered and lit themselves. Five minutes later, they reached the bottom of the stairs and, as her mother told her, Sophie avoided the last step.

The room they entered was about the size of several large auto-manufacturing plants combined and it was full of mirrors of different sizes and shapes.

Callie stopped short and Sophie, who was looking around, bumped into her.

"All right, now we come to the tough part," Callie said.

"The tough part?" Sophie winced. "You mean the other stuff was easy?"

"*Do not*, I repeat, *do not* touch any of the mirrors. Do not bump up against them. If they are covered, do not remove any of their covers. Do not stand for any length of time admiring yourself in them. Do you understand?"

"Yes."

"And," Callie continued. "If a mirror speaks to you, do not answer it back. I cannot stress how critical it is for you to follow my instructions."

"Okay, I get it. Don't look at them. Don't talk to them. Don't touch the mirrors." When her mother's back was turned, Sophie rolled her eyes.

Sophie kept her hands close to her side as they walked around the room. There were mirrors hanging on walls. There were mirrors leaning against walls. There were mirrors stacked against other mirrors that leaned against walls with mirrors hanging on them. There were even mirrors nailed to the ceiling, mirrors suspended from the ceiling and mirrors that seemed to float in mid-air with no form of suspension.

Floor-to-ceiling industrial metal shelving created a maze that made it difficult for Callie and Sophie to maneuver through. The only things that broke up the rows were other rows that created an intersection or a huge pile of mirrors stacked precariously.

One wrong move and those things are coming down on top of us.

She didn't know why, but her mother's voice was annoying her as she droned on and on about this rule and that trap, and why these mirrors were stored here. Sophie slowed her pace and ceased paying attention to what her mother was

~ ☾ ~

saying. Before Sophie knew it, she was alone. She dashed forward to catch up, but her mother wasn't there. She retraced her steps and took a few turns, but Callie was nowhere to be found. She panicked and rushed forward, her hand briefly touching one of the shelves. She stopped.

Please... I hope I didn't touch anything.

Right as she was about to call out to her, Sophie heard a woman's voice.

"Hello. Please, over here," the woman's voice said. Sophie tried to ignore it, but there was something so incredibly desperate and sad about the voice, she stopped for a moment and searched for its source.

"Over here, on the second shelf," the voice said. "Look for the delicate hand mirror with the red jewel at its center."

She saw the mirror, its surface glowing brightly, and she paused for a second, remembering what her mother had said.

If I touch it quickly, nothing could possibly happen. She reached her pinky and touched the tapered handle, quickly jumping back and nearly falling into a stack of mirrors so poorly stacked Sophie was sure the slightest movement would send it toppling over. The stack remained steady and the hand mirror didn't react. She touched the mirror again, this time for a little longer. Still nothing. Guessing that the mirror was harmless, she picked it up. A beautiful woman with curly blond hair stared back at her, looking relieved.

"Oh." the woman exclaimed as she clapped, tears in her face. "Thank you so much for picking me up. I've been trapped in this mirror for so many years and I know my husband and children must be worried sick about me. I have a little baby named Isabel and I miss her so."

This poor woman. Maybe she isn't telling the truth. But who would make up such a horrible lie? Living in a mirror can't be pleasant.

"Will you help me?" the woman pled.

Sophie shrugged. "But, I don't know—"

"All you have to do is grasp the mirror with both hands, making sure to touch the red stone at the center. It's that simple. Make sure to touch the red stone and wish me out of the mirror."

"That's it?"

~ ☾ ~

"Yes," the woman said, nodding her head.

"I'm not sure. Maybe I should ask my mother," Sophie said. She wondered if the woman was imprisoned in the mirror by mistake, remembering that part of her job as a Muse was to put people back on the right path.

Wasn't letting this poor woman free part of that? Maybe this was a test. Maybe Mom wanted me to find this poor woman and set her free; showing her I really did know what was expected of her. That had to be it.

The woman in the mirror became frantic. "Please," the woman begged. "Once you've picked me up, we only have moments to undo this horrible spell. If time elapses, I'll be stuck in here forever. If you won't do it for me and my suffering, then think of my poor baby girl growing up without her mother to love her, to read her bedtime stories and kiss her good night. Please, do it for my baby girl, for little Izzie!"

Sophie's hesitation melted away with each of the woman's pleas and she nodded her head. She thought she saw the woman's eyes briefly flash red, but dismissed it as her own eyes playing tricks on her due to the dim light. She put both hands on the handle, making sure to touch the stone.

"I wish you to be..." Sophie wondered what the woman's name was. "What is your name?" she whispered.

"Martha. My name is Martha," the woman replied.

"I wish you to be free, Martha," Sophie said with authority, her hands producing a burst of energy that shoved Martha out of the mirror.

For a second, Martha twinkled a bit. She was tiny, only about five feet tall, but as cute as a doll. The twinkling lights faded, and as they melted away so did Martha's beauty. Before Sophie could react, Martha had changed from a beautiful blond woman in a flowing gown into a horrific slimy troll with sharp teeth and long nails.

"You are just the sweetest thing," the troll said. "I bet you taste like sugar and spice." It leapt at Sophie, taking her by surprise.

Aletheria appeared out of nowhere and grabbed the hand mirror. Using it as a weapon, she stabbed its handle straight into the troll's eye with a disgusting squish. The creature's eye ruptured and blood poured out of its socket.

~ ☾ ~

"You vile creature. How dare you even think of harming this child," Aletheria shouted. Ink rushed from Aletheria's hands and wrapped around the troll, who screeched as the ink's tendrils tightly closed around her and shoved her towards the mirror's surface. The mirror glowed brightly again and Aletheria slammed it on top of the troll's head. A blinding light shot forth from the mirror, devouring the troll who was once again sucked into the mirror. The creature screamed profanities at Aletheria and the Oracle deposited the mirror back on the shelf. Out of breath, Callie rushed in around the corner.

"What could have possessed you to make this journey without at least two people to watch such a young Muse? Are you mad?" Aletheria shouted at Callie. She picked up the mirror again, showing the troll to Callie and Sophie. "I should have let old Martha take a bite or two out of you both."

"She said she had a husband," Sophie said.

"She did," Aletheria replied.

"And a child," Sophie added.

"Yes, Isabel. She ate them. Bashed the little troll's head in and roasted it on an open pit and slashed her husband's throat for not being aggressive enough with his night pilfering activities. He was baked into a pie."

"She lied to me," Sophie said.

"Well, what a surprise," Callie said. "It's hard to imagine a troll like poor Martha, who not only killed her own husband and baby, but also was responsible for the drowning deaths of at least six hundred children *and* was sentenced to spend an eternity in a cursed mirror would actually lie to you. I'm sure she feels horrible about it and will most probably send you a small gift and a greeting card with an apology."

"Mom, why are you being this way?" Sophie asked. "You're acting like Georgia. Okay, I made a mistake. I get it."

"Let me explain why I am acting like this," Callie said, her voice shaking with fury.

Aletheria took a few steps back.

"This isn't a game. What you just encountered, your simple mistake could have killed you and me both, had it not been for Aletheria. Georgia and I are only looking out for your welfare and although you think that I, or Georgia or

~ ☾ ~

Aletheria, will be around to save you—"

"Technically, I will always be around, as part of my agreement with—" the Oracle offered, but then took a few more steps back when Callie glared at her.

"So," Callie continued. "You will forgive us if we get a little bit upset when you *don't listen."*

Sophie burst into tears as Martha howled, causing the other mirrors to scream filthy curses at the three women.

"These prisoners are part of the trap. Weren't you listening to me? They are damned for the rest of their lives for the horrible crimes they have committed. Unfortunately, killing them isn't an option because their evil souls would be recycled over and over again. So it's better to leave them alive in these mirrors than to deal with the next version of them. Even if they get loose, they wouldn't have gone far, but not before they took care of anyone they encountered. Aletheria, please join us for the rest of this journey by walking behind Sophie." Callie shouted, attempting to talk over the voices. She reached over and gave Martha one final look before smacking the looking glass down with such force it cracked.

"With a cracked mirror, there is no way Martha would ever be roasting any children or tricking another young Muse, ever again," Callie said.

They continued through the maze of mirrors. Sophie kept her eyes straight ahead and didn't say a word. She was seething from her mother's lecture. She knew her mom was right, and the longer she thought about her recent encounter with Martha the more scared she became.

This isn't a game. I know she told me this, but everything poses a threat. I can't even trust the mirrors.

"I'm sorry," Sophie said.

"I know," Callie replied, not turning around. "We're here."

In the deep recesses of the warehouse was a dark corner where a large mirror stood, its reflective surface faded and discolored. There was a small tiny crack in the right corner of the glassy surface. The walnut frame was black with age and chipped in several places. It was large enough for all three women to easily step into it at the same time.

"Is it supposed to look like that?" Sophie asked. "It doesn't look safe."

~ ☾ ~

"Someone has tried to get access to the portal. Something very powerful. Powerful enough to crack the surface. But the crack doesn't scare me as much as this does," Callie said, holding out her hand as it lit up with a bright light in its center. Written on the surface of the mirror was the word, 'Nothos'.

"How dare they!" Aletheria said. "Those foul..."

Callie held out her hand. "I don't know how they did it—" A burst of energy shot from her hand and struck the surface of the mirror. The crack on the mirror's face fused and disappeared, but the word remained.

"Ignore it and hold my hand," Callie said to Sophie.

They stepped into the mirror and entered a large room lacking any furniture. An ornate mosaic tiled floor depicting Olympus took up the center of the space. Several crumbling Grecian columns made a perfect circle around the rectangular perimeter of the room. The ceiling to the room was made of arched glass.

"It's a temple," Sophie said.

"No," said Aletheria. "It's more than that. It's one of the Nine Portals keeping Olympus torn from this world."

"This is what is stopping the Olympians from taking over the world? This ruin?" Sophie walked forward and Callie stepped in front of her.

"Wait. You can't just start walking around this gate like a tourist at the Parthenon."

"It's the Olympians," Aletheria said. "They are growing stronger and as their strength grows, this portal feels the impact, hence the crumbling."

"How does it work?"

"It's rather complex," Callie said. "I'm only privy to so much, but these stones and the stones in the other Vasilikós are taken from an ancient temple destroyed during the Olympus wars. There were many Olympians who were killed during that battle."

"Wait, I thought they were all immortal," Sophie said.

"Well, yes and no," Callie said. "An immortal is only immortal on Mount Olympus. Put them on the mortal plane and it's a different story. Granted, they are extremely hard to kill, but they can be wounded and if wounded by another

~ ☾ ~

supernatural critically they can die. In the case of the Olympus wars, it was gods killing gods on mortal soil. So, when an Olympian dies their power has to go somewhere. For whatever reason, and we suspect divine intervention, those powers were sent into the stones you see here and they are what this and the other eight gateways are made from. They act radioactive. If the Olympians get anywhere near them they start to feel sick and their powers are drained. And if they touch them or attempt to destroy them, it's like a sun being sucked into a black hole. They die. That's the bedtime story version."

"So why doesn't it affect us? Aren't we part Olympian?"

"I don't know," Callie said, turning to the Oracle. "Aletheria?

Aletheria stepped forward and touched one of the stones. "It's not impossible for these stones to be intelligently designed to know the difference between a Demigod and an Olympian. But, I think the point of this trip is not to discuss how the stones work. This knowledge is given to the Leader of each Vasilikós and passed on to the incoming Leader. Your mother is introducing you to one of the many responsibilities you will have as a Muse. Each Muse has pledged, or, in your case will pledge, to defend this Portal until their last breath. As a Muse, you serve your Vasilikós, you serve your Leader and you serve this gateway. It requires a dedication starting the moment you become a Muse until the day you die. To serve this Vasilikós is to serve Humanity. It's to serve the Divine." A cloud of ink engulfed the Oracle and she was gone.

Sophie reached out and touched the stone nearest to her. It hummed under her fingertips. A small piece of marble fell from one of the columns and Sophie wished she was far away from the portal. She picked up the fallen piece of marble and placed it back to where it fell. The broken piece fused back in place. "Did you see that, mom?"

"See what, honey?"

Sophie shrugged. "Never mind, it was nothing. Do we have to go back through the mirror room?" she asked, groaning.

"No, it's a lot easier to leave this room." Callie grabbed Sophie and with a rush of energy they were gone.

~ ☾ ~

Chapter 26

The next few weeks were a whirlwind of planning and activities, all driven by a crazed Georgia. Due to the urgency of the situation, Georgia had called a videoconference with the other Vasilikós to discuss the newly adjusted timeline. Much to everyone's surprise, they all agreed the best way to deal with the crisis was to combine the events and make the best of it.

As part of the planning, the Muses from the Greek and Italian Vasilikós, who weren't on assignment, were called back from their remote locations to help with preparations. The Vasilikós, which had previously been deserted, was full to the brim with Muses and they all were excited to meet Sophie.

"It's like I've been plopped right in the middle of a sorority movie from hell," Sophie admitted to Angela. Her room was no longer a place for privacy because each time Sophie lay down on her bed for a moment of silence there was another knock at her door and yet another Muse who "just had to stop by to introduce herself to Georgia's granddaughter." To get some rest, Sophie ended up spending more time in Angela's room.

Sophie thought Angela's room was beautiful. It was done in a creamy white, with accents of yellow, red and black throughout. Her bed was a huge four-poster and there were several beautifully made quilts on the bed and stacked in piles throughout the room. The quilts were gifts from her full-blooded Gorgon mother, who was famous for her sewing. Some of the more intricate pieces were displayed on her suite of room's walls.

"How many quilts do you own?" Sophie asked as she jumped onto Angela's bed and sunk deep into its feathery comfort.

~ ☾ ~

"Well, do you want me to count the quilts in storage, the quilts on display throughout the Vasilikós and the quilts currently touring Europe in an exhibit under the guise of American Folk art?"

Sophie laughed and threw a pillow at the other girl. "Why yes, I wouldn't have it any other way."

"About four hundred and twenty-nine."

"You know, I'm planning on having them redo my room. I think I'm ready to move on from my childhood bedroom."

"Really?" Angela said, getting up from the bed and rummaging through a big cedar chest. "This was given to me by Winnie. No matter how much I throw into it, it never seems to fill up. You have to love the purity of Hob magic. It would take quite a feat of magic for me to create the exact trick."

"What are you looking for?" Sophie asked, rolling over to look at the ceiling. Her hand touched the gauzy material of Angela's bed curtains. She considered whether or not she would like something along those lines and then decided against it.

"A gift," Angela said, walking towards the closet to her right and flinging it open. "Damn. Wrong closet."

Laughter burst from Sophie as macramé plant holders, doilies and little southern belle toilet paper doll covers fell out in the hundreds.

"Damn it! I'll never get them all back into the closet."

"What the heck is this stuff?" Sophie said, getting off the bed and standing in front of the huge pile.

Angela grabbed a toilet paper doll and threw it at Sophie. "I didn't mention my mother has a sister and she likes to make—"

"Church bazaar crap?" Sophie said, laughing as she gathered a plant holder done in the shape of an owl and a toilet paper doll. "I think I'm set for gifts right now."

"No, stop laughing. She means well. I don't have the heart to throw this stuff out. I have a whole chamber in the catacombs dedicated to storing gifts from her. She was never the same after Medusa was killed. Kind of made her a few ingredients short of a potion. She loved her sister."

"Well, I think it's sweet that she makes this stuff for you."

~ ☾ ~

"You're making fun," Angela said. Palms facing front, Angela made a forward sweeping motion, magically shoveling some of the items back into her closet.

"No, I'm serious."

Angela stepped out of the pile, walked over to the other closet and opened the door. "I love the smell of cedar," Angela said as she took a deep breath. She sorted through a tall stack of quilts and found the one she was looking for.

"I think this will look great in your room," Angela said and shook the quilt open. The quilt depicted the four seasons, with a tree as the main focal point in each of its four squares.

Sophie was touched, and for reasons she didn't understand, she began to cry.

"Well, it wasn't supposed to make you cry," Angela said sitting on the edge of her bed.

"No, it's beautiful and so sweet. You are so kind...and generous... I...I...I think it must be the stress of the whole situation. I mean, I'm only sixteen for God's sake. I'm sixteen and somehow I'm responsible for saving the world. What the heck is that? How is that right? I have these powers and I don't know how to control them. I came close to killing myself and my mother by releasing some ugly troll named Martha. Have you ever seen a troll? They're disgusting and they eat human flesh...and have really bad skin...and smell. Dear lord did she smell. I should have better control of my powers so I can protect people—"

"But," Angela interrupted. "You're not supposed to, at least not yet. It's only been a few months. It takes time."

"And what the heck does a Muse do? No one has told me how I am supposed to 'inspire' anyone. How does that work? How do you know who the heck to inspire? And then all of these people are coming to gawk at me. What if I disappoint them? What if I'm nothing more than an awkward girl from Ohio?" Sophie said, hiding her face in her hands. "Name a sixteen year old who had such responsibilities."

"Well, history is filled with people who have been asked to make great sacrifice. Joan of Arc was much younger than you."

"And it worked out so well for her," Sophie said.

"Good point, but I bet that was some good barbecue."

~ ☾ ~

Sophie knew she shouldn't, but she couldn't stop herself from laughing.

"Sophie, let me give you some advice my Nanny gave me. She said, 'Listen to me little girl…' Whenever she got serious, she called me little girl. She said, 'Listen to me little girl. At the end of the day, no matter what happened, no matter who did what to whom, you have to laugh because, next to love, laughter is the most powerful magic.'"

"Laugh? Her advice was to laugh?"

"Yes, laugh, because laughter will always overcome the mistakes of the day. Laughter always resets your mind for another day. Laughter feeds your soul and allows you to let it all go. Without laughter—"

"I'd be Georgia," Sophie said

"Little girl," Angela said. "You do realize that under all of the complex layers is a woman who loves you?"

"Yeah, right. She gushes love out of her black heart."

"She knew you'd need a friend. She knew I needed a home because although they're good at quilts and plant holders, Gorgons are kind of awkward mothers. She put the two of us together."

For a second, Sophie chewed on what Angela said. "You know, I was going to ask you how you came to this Vasilikós."

"Georgia, that's how. Now, don't get me wrong. With Georgia, there's always a motive behind her generosity. Whether she brought me here because she was sorry for me, or she was in a generous mood, or she knew her granddaughter needed a friend, or even if she knew having a powerful witch with Gorgon abilities would be a big plus for the battle to come, who knows. But I'm here. Think of it this way. Thanks to Georgia, you've a whole household of powerful entities available to you. And if anything goes wrong, you'll have eight other Vasilikós to stand behind you. Compared to Joan of Arc, I think you're in pretty good shape."

Sophie knew Angela was right and nodded in agreement. Wiping her tears away, she touched the beautiful quilt her friend was still holding.

"Are you sure you want to give this to me? It's incredibly beautiful."

~ ☾ ~

"Yes, I think I'm covered in the quilt department. Besides, I have a duplicate of this hanging on the wall in my sitting room over the fireplace. But, let me make this one a little extra special for you."

Angela closed her eyes and mumbled some words Sophie couldn't hear. A sudden burst of air took the Muse by surprise. Angela gave the quilt a shake and opened her eyes.

Sophie broke out into a wide smile. "How did you do that?"

The quilt was still the same, but now each of the squares had come alive. In the spring square, snow melted away, tulips bloomed and bare trees became green and lush. For summer, the tree remained green, but stalks in the right hand corner grew taller and produced ears of corn. A child swinging on a rope jumped into a lake with a big splash. The square for fall had the tree's leaves turn vibrant red and orange. The same child jumped into a leaf pile. Sophie noticed the little girl had dreads like Angela. The dreads had tiny smiling snakeheads. Winter was a classic New England holiday scene, complete with a sleigh and a young woman in a white muff and red bonnet. A man climbed into the sleigh and shook the reins. The candlelight from a Christmas tree flickered inside a small cottage.

"I love it," Sophie said. "I will always treasure it."

"The scenes should continue to run, but if they stop, shake the quilt. The spell kind of makes it like a snow globe."

There was a small tap on the door and Angela yelled for the person to come in.

In walked a girl Sophie didn't recognize.

"I am so sorry to interrupt." Her southern drawl dripped like honey. "But Georgia sent me to find you. My name is Miranda and I'm assigned as your personal assistant."

"Miranda?" Sophie said, searching her mind, wondering why it sounded familiar. Suddenly she remembered and panicked.

It couldn't be. What are the chances Bennett's ex-girlfriend would end up here?

"Which Vasilikós are you from, Miranda?" Sophie asked.

"Well, I originally was stationed out of this Vasilikós, but an opportunity opened up in our Italy branch and I took it."

~ ☾ ~

She leaned over and touched the gold coin necklace that lay against her collarbone. "A bit of boyfriend trouble made it necessary for a change. Being pretty as you are, I'm sure you understand." Miranda said.

Sophie's heart sank. It was bad enough the last interaction hadn't gone well with Bennett. And now, she had to deal with Bennett's ex-girlfriend as her personal assistant for the event preparations?

Is this one of my grandmother's tricks? It's probably my incredibly good luck. My life continues to be one big crap pie.

"Sophia?" Miranda said.

"Oh, sorry," Sophie said, flustered. "Yes, boyfriend troubles can be a bit awkward."

"Well, I'll get through this. Bennett is just the sweetest boy and as hard as it was for him to deal with our breakup, I'm sure he's completely over me. I felt so awful about breaking his heart. It wasn't a good match. The whole Minotaur thing kind of freaked me out."

"Minotaur?"

"Soph," Angela said, jumping off the bed. "Let's go take the quilt to your room."

"Wait," Miranda said, pulling out her note pad. "We have several things to do today. We have a dress fitting to take care of. Angela's mother has arrived and then—."

"Wait," Angela said, holding out her hand. "My mother is here?"

"Yes she is and what a lovely woman. Just looking at you tells me you most definitely take after your father."

Sophie walked out of the room, carrying the quilt.

"Don't forget. I have to take you to your fitting in about an hour," Miranda called after her.

~ ☾ ~

Chapter 27

The quilt lay on the chair of Sophie's desk. Several stacks of interior design magazines, material swatch books and wallpaper samples were in piles all over the floor. As Angela walked in, Sophie put down a back issue of *Cottage-centric magazine* with several pages of bright florescent sticky notes sticking out of them.

This whole place is crazy. I can't even have a single space I can call my own.

"Eupheme heard I was in the mood for a change," Sophie said. "As I was walking in, the last of these books floated by me. She introduced herself and shook my hand. I must have been a ball of emotions because she literally evaporated, practically exploding in front of me."

Angela nodded. "She'll be drunk on your emotions for a while. You're probably like 110% proof to her."

Sophie didn't know what to do and hated the awkward silence she was sharing with her friend.

"I'm sorry if you feel I did something wrong by not telling you about Bennett, but it isn't for anyone, even Miranda, to 'out' a Demigod's power," Angela said. "You understand, right?"

"I do. It's still a lot to get used to. I mean, what does it mean that he's a Minotaur? Is that the thing that is half-horse?"

Angela remembered the Whatsit application and typed the word Minotaur.

"It means this," Angela said.

Sophie glanced down at the tablet's screen where there was a picture of a ferocious beast with long horns, sharp teeth and a muscular body made for attacking and tearing its foes apart. Its claw-like hands were huge, and its body was covered in fur from head to toe. It didn't have feet, but had

~ ☾ ~

hooves attached to muscular, trunk-like legs and thighs. The creature was frightening.

"It's horrible and I think I have feelings for it. I mean him," she whispered.

Angela sighed. "Sophie, you're being overly dramatic. Look at the picture and realize the person makes the power, not the other way around. If the person is evil then the power is evil, but if the person is good, the power is good. I've seen Bennett in Minotaur form and I will admit it is frightening at first. But for all of the power and ferociousness of his exterior, you can still see Bennett in the creature's eyes and you know it's Bennett. He's just in an incredibly hairy and even taller package."

Sophie shook her head in understanding, still staring at the image.

"Sophie, look at me," Angela said.

For the first time she saw her friend in Gorgon form. It was still Angela, but her dreads were now writhing black snakes and her skin had taken on an olive green tint. Veins appeared more prominent all over her, but particularly around her eyes and face. Her straight teeth had the addition of two exposed fangs.

"This is my power," Angela said. "I am in full control of it, because if I wasn't you would have passed out by now, and then your joints, muscles and bones would have all petrified." She gritted her teeth and her fangs came into full view. "Am I terrifying?"

"Yes and no," Sophie said. "If I didn't know you and ran into you in a dark alley, it would be terrifying. But—" She stopped for a moment to gather her thoughts. "It's still you and I know you wouldn't hurt me."

"Well," Angela said with a half smile. "Take one of my favorite hair combs without asking and my hair might think differently." A few of Angela's snakes hissed and snapped to emphasize her point.

Angela closed her eyes and took a few deep breaths, and the snakes retreated, the fangs withdrew, the veins and green tinge to her skin faded. When she opened her eyes, they had turned back to their normal deep brown. "And please don't start feeling left out. I'm sure you look at me and think I'm

~ ☾ ~

totally cool with the hair and eyes, and I'm so *The Vampire Diaries* with my fangs. After some training, you'll start to think you're hot stuff too."

"You know me so well," Sophie said. "So, where should my new quilt hang?"

There was a knock at the door and Angela cringed, mouthing the name "Miranda." Sophie put her finger to her lips for Angela to be quiet, but the door swung open and in Miranda walked.

"I knew you were here. Let's go, it is time for your fitting," Miranda said, glancing around the room. "My, your room is a bit sloppy. Should I have housekeeping take care of it?"

Sophie sighed. "Why bother, I'll make it sloppy all over again."

"Angela, your mother asked that you join us." Miranda said.

"Well, I'm beside myself with joy," Angela said, imitating Miranda's southern drawl.

Miranda laughed. "Well, aren't you just a clever little thang," she said, clearly putting her southern drawl into overdrive.

They walked down the hall in silence and made their way towards a sitting room, directly off of Georgia's formal offices. Standing at the entrance were Georgia and Bennett.

"Have Winnie assign a few Hobs to help you. It should all be straightforward," Georgia said.

"I'll do my best, Georgia," Bennett said.

"I know you will. You never cease to amaze me, Bennett. If you need to take a break tonight, because of the positioning of the stars, do so."

"Thanks, Georgia," he said and walked toward Sophie. "Hi."

"Hi," she said back.

"I'm sorry," they both said at the same time and Sophie laughed.

"The whole rule thing is silly. I need to let the past go. And I was wondering..."

"You were wondering about what type of fertilizer to use on the lawn?" Sophie said.

"Umm, yes. I mean no." Bennett laughed nervously. "I was

~ ☽ ~

wondering if we could grab a coffee in the village. I know this great place where they serve incredible chocolate pastries."

"Sounds wonderful. When?"

"Bennett." Georgia called to him. "That list isn't getting any shorter while you chat up my granddaughter."

He grimaced. "Tomorrow morning. Meet me in the village square by the fountain."

"Bennett." Georgia shouted.

"You better go. I'll see you tomorrow morning," Sophie said.

"Bye," Bennett said, smiling, rushing down the hall and weaving in and out of people.

"You'll have to order the chocolate croissants," Miranda said, stepping out from behind a column and making Sophie jump. "They were our favorite."

Sophie couldn't help but wince inwardly at the "our" reference. "Thanks, Miranda. I'll make a note of it."

"Oh shoot, I'm double booked. Now how did that happen? You and Angela need to go into the room at the end of the hall, after you turn left at Georgia's office. I'll meet up with you later, once I take care of a few other items."

Miranda dashed off before either Sophie or Angela could react.

"Can I be honest?" Angela said, leading the way towards their destination. "I really don't like her. The term "skank" is the only word I can come up with to describe her. "

"I don't get her." Sophie replied. "She seems to go out of her way to make me feel miserable about Bennett."

They stood in front of the door Angela's mother was behind and for a second Sophie preferred not to open it. She knew Angela had an awkward relationship with her mother and it had been a long time since Angela had seen her. Then, there was the fact that Sophie wasn't sure what to expect of Angela's mother. A Demigod was one thing, but a full-blown Gorgon was another. Angela knocked and a voice called for them to enter.

The room was large and served as a conservatory. It was all glass and hung over a cliff, providing an incredible view of the ocean and the rocks below. Presently, the room was serving as a dressmaker's studio crammed with hundreds of

~ ☾ ~

reams of material thrown around the room in piles and an army of assistants fussing about the dressmaker dummies. There also were several long cutting tables, three sewing machines, a fluffy couch and an overstuffed chair. Callie stood speaking with a tall woman who stood with her back to Sophie and Angela.

"Euryale, we could go with the traditional white," Callie said to the woman. "But I'm liking this pale blue you have here."

Euryale, Angela's mother, was athletically fit and wore her hair in a fashionable yet severe wedge cut. The jacket of her tailored suit lay on the chair behind her. Her shirt was sleeveless and revealed toned arms decorated with warrior-like gold bands. She was wearing sunglasses indoors, which Sophie thought was strange but was pleasantly surprised at how lovely Euryale was.

"Honey, come over here," Callie said, impatiently gesturing for her daughter to come forward. "Don't keep Euryale waiting. We have limited time with her."

"Lovely." Euryale exclaimed, getting a look at Sophie. "She is everything I expected." The Gorgon extended her hand for Sophie to shake and Sophie took it.

"Hi, I'm—" Sophie began.

"I know exactly who you are. You look just like your mother, except for your smile. Her father's?" Euryale asked Callie.

"Yes, definitely her father's," Callie responded.

Euryale held out her arms for her daughter to accept a hug and Angela ran to her.

"Hello, mother," the girl said.

"Angela, how are you doing? Is Georgia treating you well?"

"Yes, mother. I'm treated very well."

"Good. I brought you a gift. Several boxes are on the loading docks and will be brought to your room."

Angela gave Sophie a look, and Sophie knew Angela was getting more quilts and toilet paper dolls.

"Now, let's get to work," Euryale said. Grabbing several fabrics, she laid them against Sophie's skin.

~ ☾ ~

Chapter 28

The next morning couldn't have come any quicker for Sophie. She woke up hours early to take care of the items on her Georgia To-Do List and fussed over outfits in her attempt to look perfect for her date with Bennett.

She raced downstairs and met with Euryale for another fitting. The Gorgon had managed to put the main pieces of her dress together, and as Sophie stood there while Euryale put pins here and there, Euryale reminded Sophie that gaining weight was not an option with this dress. Sophie glanced to her right and saw the dresses her mother and grandmother would wear displayed on their dummies.

"Euryale, those are beautiful. Mom and Georgia are going to be knockouts in them."

"Of course they will. Lovely women in lovely dresses look lovely. However, you will be stunning."

Euryale's sunglasses slipped and Sophie saw a flash of green eyes similar to Angela's Gorgonian eyes, but Euryale's eyes were different. The colored center wasn't round, but more egg shaped and they glowed continuously.

"Euryale, you don't have to hide your eyes. It doesn't freak me out."

Euryale sighed and slipped off her glasses. "Thank you, Sophia. Some are a bit unnerved by them. Some can't get beyond ancient history. You're not going to fall over dead, made of stone, to be placed in Georgia's garden. You see, there was a time when we were hunted. We were misunderstood and some of the other gods thought it would be fun to include the killing of one of our sisters as part of an overall quest. Poor Medusa. She was so kind, but she was headstrong, and when you are not immortal like us...well, it was a long time ago. So that's the reason for the sunglasses." Euryale folded them up and threw them onto the overstuffed chair. "I think we're done for today.

~ ☾ ~

Go and have fun. Angela told me you have a special date after this. How exciting, young love."

After helping Sophie carefully take off the pinned dress, Sophie ran out of the room and up to her bedroom to jump into the shower.

Much to Sophie's dismay, on her way out she ran into Miranda, who invited herself to join Sophie on her trip to town. She tried to figure out a way to get out of spending more time with Miranda and hoped by suggesting they walk Miranda might decide otherwise.

I just think that's a wonderful magnolia blossom idea... Blah blah blah. Of course you would, you miserable...

The walk was almost painless, with Miranda managing to only mention Bennett once or twice. Sophie was sure her own quick pace, which was practically a run, contributed to Miranda's lack of speech.

The path they took went by a small roadside shrine. Miranda explained one of the villagers must have created it for someone who had tragically died. Sophie barely heard what Miranda was saying. A black cloud of flies was buzzing around the shrine, which was coated in a dripping liquid.

"Is that blood?" Sophie mumbled.

At the foot of the shrine weren't flowers, but a pile of rotting carcasses.

"Sophie, don't look," Miranda said, trying to pull Sophie away from the horrific scene. "They're probably wild dogs that were getting into someone's livestock."

Sophie couldn't take her eyes away from the rotting pile of dogs.

"Wild dogs don't have collars," Sophie said, pointing to where the broken stone cross was located. At least a dozen dog collars were looped around the cross.

I think I'm going to be sick.

"Those poor animals," Miranda said. "Let's go. There's nothing we can do for them."

Sophie allowed Miranda to pull her away, but not before she saw, written in blood, the word *Nothos* on the side of the shrine.

They arrived at the town square sooner than Sophie expected.

~ ☾ ~

"Guess I'll hang out for a while."

"I hate to leave you, but you know Georgia and her lists," Miranda said reaching into her shoulder bag and pulling out several folded papers from the yellow legal pad Georgia favored.

"No, I'll be fine," Sophie said.

Go away and let me have a moment to myself. All I want is just one, brief moment to think without people dissecting me.

"All right. Well, you be a good Muse and don't do anything I wouldn't do," Miranda said over her shoulder.

"I'm guessing you've left me with a long list of nasty things to do." Sophie mumbled to herself. As she walked along the shop-lined streets she couldn't stop thinking of the poor animals lying dead at the shrine. She eyed a café and thought a cup of coffee was in order.

In spite of the horrible beginning of her day in town, Sophie admitted it was a beautiful morning. She sat by herself, reveling in the quiet, watching a group of old men play chess in the shaded area of the square's park. A small boy wandered in front of her table, walking the family dog with the help of his mother, and Sophie's knotted neck and shoulder muscles relaxed a little and she smiled, enjoying the peaceful moment.

A young woman walked by, so preoccupied with the tall stack of magazines she was carrying she didn't notice the gap in the sidewalk. Her high stiletto heel caught in the crack sending the woman falling face forward and her magazines flying everywhere.

Sophie immediately jumped up to help the woman.

"Are you okay?" Sophie asked, helping her back to her feet and retrieving her magazines. The woman had a cut on her leg that started to bleed and Sophie offered a napkin.

"Thank you. I am so sorry to burst into your morning. I am such a klutz," the woman said, brushing herself off. A piece of gum from the sidewalk was now stuck to her hair and Sophie pointed it out.

"That is just great," the woman said. "I can't think of a better beginning to my day. I can only imagine what tonight will bring."

~ ☾ ~

"Would you like to sit down with me? I'm waiting for someone, but I've got plenty of time."

"You know, I really could use a break. You are the sweetest. Thank you so much."

Sophie handed back the woman's Restoration Beautiful and Pottery Farm catalogs. They settled into their seats and Sophie ordered the woman a cup of coffee.

"Decaffeinated, please," the woman said. "Doctor says I have to lay off the caffeine. Apparently, it makes me a bit crazy."

After the waiter brought their coffee, Sophie took a sip and noticed the many catalogs the stranger had been carrying.

"It looks like you are buying some beautiful furniture," Sophie said.

"You like Pottery Farm?" the woman asked, wide-eyed.

"They have some great stuff. We could never afford it, but I used to look through their catalog and cut pictures out, as a kind of wish list."

"I do the same thing, except I don't cut them out. I use little sticky notes. Red is for the stuff I have to have. Blue is for the stuff I have to have but only after I get all of my red items. Yellow is the stuff I really like but it won't kill me if I have to wait. And green are the items that, well, I really, really, really want."

"You *really* like Pottery Farm."

"I do. So, you said you were waiting for someone. Is it a boy?"

"Yes."

"A boy you like? Someone you have a crush on?" the woman egged her on.

"We'll see," Sophie said. "My name is..."

"Oh, please, I know who you are, Sophie."

Alert lights went off in Sophie's head. "Do I know you? Have we met before?"

"No, I rarely make it up to topside. I know your father?"

Major alert lights were now flashing.

Get away, get away from her.

"I'm sorry, I should go," Sophie said, throwing some money down on the table. She got up to leave when the woman grabbed her arm. The petite woman was stronger

~ ☾ ~

than Sophie would have guessed and she winced at the pressure of her grip.

"You're hurting me," Sophie said, pulling on her arm in an attempt to wrench it away.

The woman let go. "I'm sorry. I didn't mean it. I'm such a klutz and I don't know my own strength half the time. Please sit down. I'm not going to harm you. I just want to talk."

Sophie knew she had a chance to leave, but something in the woman's manner told her she should remain.

"You said you know my father. That's impossible, my father is dead," Sophie said.

"Well, of course he's dead. That's why you're here in Greece, at least that and your recent change." She motioned for Sophie to lean closer and with caution the girl did so. "But when your husband is Hades, you get to meet some of the most interesting people. Just the other day, I had the most wonderful chat with Mary Todd Lincoln. Now I've met crazy before – but she was too far gone to be an interesting guest at my dinner parties…"

"Oh wait… I know who you are. Don't tell me, umm, you're Persephone? You have dinner parties for the dead?"

"Call me Saphie. All my friends do. And who else would come to a dinner party thrown by Hades? People aren't exactly lining up for an invitation to the Underworld."

I can't resist. I have to know.

"What do you serve at your parties?" Sophie asked.

"Barbecue. Strangely enough, the dead can't get enough of barbecue. But let's not talk shop. Let's talk about your father."

"How… is he?"

"He misses you very much. I have seen love in many forms. Married couples that have been married eighty years dying within hours of each other. So touching. And the love a parent has for a child. You do understand just because someone has passed onto the Underworld it doesn't mean they lose the capacity to love or that they forget their past loves? Your father is such a handsome man and he is so kind and so much in love with you. He begged me to give him a moment to see you as you are now and I didn't have the heart to say no. So, I allowed him to appear to you."

"You mean *it was* him in the garden?"

~ ☾ ~

"Yes. Well, it was just a shade of him." Persephone took a sip of her coffee.

"A shade?"

"Yes, a shade. A shade is what the dead turn into when they are traveling through the Underworld. He was able to remain for a few seconds and then he had to return. I wonder if they have any of those sweet Greek cookies I love," Persephone said, picking up the menu to scan it.

"You said you allowed him. Does that mean you could do it again, for a longer visit?"

"I'm not supposed to. Hades would have an absolute fit if he knew. My husband in a bad mood makes a complete hell of the Underworld." She called the waiter over and ordered a dish of cookies and more coffee.

"Oh," Sophie said, disappointed.

"Oh, sweetie, I'm sorry. I wish there were something I could do. I mean, I could make it happen, but the risk comes with a price tag I'm not willing to entertain. And you must understand that everything has its price... Unless—"

"Unless, what?" Sophie said, dabbing her eyes with her napkin.

"I would have to be there. You see, my power is so limited and he would have to be in contact with me or else the connection would be broken and he would sink back into the Underworld. It would have to happen at the right time...like...well, I'm almost embarrassed to suggest this like during the night of the Mid-Summer Wine Ceremony. The stars are lined up perfectly on that night."

"It won't work," Sophie said, disappointed. "I've got a big event, a ball, happening that night and I'm pretty much the guest of honor, so sneaking off isn't an option."

"Oh!" Persephone cried with joy. "A party? I love a party. I never get the chance to attend a ball. The dead have the worst time deciding what to wear and they can't dance to save their lives. But, how can we make this work? We can't parade your dead father in the middle of the ball. It would be too shocking."

"Unless he wore a disguise," Sophie said.

"A masquerade? Oh, what fun." Persephone clapped her hands. "A masquerade ball with ladies carrying masks on sticks. You have to suggest it. That way, I can get your father

~ ☾ ~

there and you can have a long visit with him."

"Well, I could suggest it to Georgia."

"Yes, please do. I am so excited. What will I wear, oh, what will I wear?" Persephone paused. "Then, it's a deal?"

Sophie thought for a moment and remembered what Angela had said. She had a whole army of people behind her.

"Sure," Sophie said. "It's a deal." Persephone extended her hand to Sophie and Sophie shook it.

Why do I feel like I just made a deal with the devil? Stop it, Sophie. She's too focused on catalog shopping to be a danger to anyone.

"Okay, here is the catch. No one can know about this. People in our circles are such gossips."

Sophie nodded her head in agreement.

"Is your boy really tall and...part Minotaur?"

Sophie saw Bennett standing by the fountain looking at his watch. "Hey, over here." She called out to him and then turned to say something to Persephone, but she and her catalogs were gone.

Bennett jogged over to where Sophie was sitting. "No fair. You started without me."

"I was just talking—" Sophie stopped, remembering what Persephone had said, and decided to keep her end of the bargain. "—with the waiter and he was rude and pushy. Let's go somewhere else."

"Good, because this wasn't the place I was talking about. They have the crappiest pastries. Total tourist trap."

They walked along the shops, stopping here and there along the way to glance at various storefronts that caught Sophie's eye. It was the first time since she arrived in Greece that she was starting to feel like herself again. Sophie was enjoying each and every moment. She dreaded reaching the restaurant, knowing it would mean they were closer to the moment their time together would end, so she walked even slower and stopped at every storefront she came close to.

"How do you like Greece?" Bennett asked.

"It's nice. I haven't had the opportunity to explore the island, with everything that's been going on." Her mind drifted to the shrine and she pushed the image out of her head. "Were you born here?"

~ ☾ ~

"Me? No, although I have lived on the island since I was twelve. My mother, Caronwyn, was a Scotswoman who one day decided she wanted to leave the wee village of Blair Athol and find adventure. But, fortunate for me, she found a bit too much adventure. Or, as I like to often say, adventure found her in the guise of my father. I'm embarrassed to admit I was the tragic result of a drunken evening and a short courtship. My mother lived on a neighboring island and was seduced by a Demigod who, once he found out my mother was preggers, promptly left her. When it became apparent I was different, my mother had met Georgia a few years prior, Georgia thought it was best I come and live here. Georgia was in the right place at the right time and she saved me."

"What gave your mother the clue you were different?" Sophie asked.

"Well, for one, on certain nights, depending on the alignment of the stars, my pajamas would be torn to shreds. When most boys were terrified about the boogieman, I was terrified of waking up, butt naked in my mother's garden with a dead possum clutched in my hands like a teddy bear."

"Ewwww."

"You know I'm a—"

"A Minotaur. Yeah." She was about to say Miranda told her, but decided otherwise. "I have an app on my tablet that scans a person and says what they are. I'm sorry. I didn't realize a person's Demigod status was a sensitive topic."

"Hey. It's okay. It's taken me a long time to come to terms with who I am. Some of us have the ability to inspire, throw the occasional energy ball, and blush whenever I'm around her."

Sophie blushed.

"Then, there are some who turn into big, hairy, strong Minotaurs who can throw a bus."

"You can throw a bus?"

"Well, maybe a small one. I need to workout some more. But understand I would never hurt you, no matter what form I was in."

"I think you should be worried *I* would hurt *you*," Sophie said, with a smirk.

"I think you both should be worried about Georgia hurting

~ ☾ ~

both of you," Callie said, appearing in front of them. "I have been looking all over for you, Sophie. I'm all for whatever this is, but it needs to be put on hold until we get through the next few weeks. Okay?"

Bennett and Sophie nodded to show their agreement. Sophie didn't know when they began holding hands, but was surprised when she looked down and saw her hand in his.

"Can you give me a minute?" Sophie asked.

"*Sophie*, you've got *fifteen seconds*. Make it count," Callie replied.

Callie walked away and waited near the old men playing chess.

"She's right," Bennett said.

"I know," Sophie said. "Now we just need to figure out how to make it through the next few weeks. I guess you being my date for the ball would be a start."

Bennett leaned down to where his face was only a few inches from her.

Oh my God, Oh my God, Oh my God... He's going to kiss me. Remember, go slow. Not too much tongue.

He angled his head, clearly moving in for a kiss on the cheek.

Oh, to hell with that. Sophie twisted her head and their lips met.

His lips were soft, warm and she felt a hunger coming from him that overwhelmed her.

She tingled all over and the sparks jumping inside of her chest made her heart ache and beg for more.

He pulled away and gave her hand a squeeze before letting it go. The look on his face told Sophie he was feeling the same thing.

"See you around, Muse," Bennett said, backing away, smiling.

"Catch you later, Beast," Sophie said before turning to run towards her mother. She caught up with her and together they walked back to the Vasilikós.

Callie waved goodbye to Bennett and then roughly grabbed Sophie's arm.

"You can't wander around this island, by yourself. It isn't safe."

~ ☾ ~

"I saw the shrine, mom."

"Then you understand. No more wandering off." Callie let go of her arm. "Okay, he's cute and a really nice kid. You do realize Georgia will give you a hard time."

"Well, I guess I'm my mother's daughter after all," Sophie said, putting her arm around her mother's waist. "Mom, I was wondering. Do you think we could make one change to the party? I want it to be a masquerade ball."

"Jeez, Sophie. Are you kidding? Don't even attempt to suggest it to Georgia."

"You and Georgia are always saying I need to stand-up for what I want. This is my party. This is my introduction into Demigod society and if I want it to be a masquerade, then it should be a masquerade. Considering what is being asked of me, it is the least Georgia can do."

"I'm not saying you don't have a point," Callie said. "But let me approach Georgia about it. If she explodes again at least I'll make sure Winnie is around to pick up the pieces."

"Do you think she'll agree to it?"

"I'll do my best, but I think I have a few favors to bring up that will make it impossible for her to say no."

~ ☾ ~

Chapter 29

A week had passed and all the Gorgon-sewn dresses were completed. Sophie watched from the staircase as Euryale stood with Angela in front of a large mirror in the Entry Hall.

"I've enjoyed our time together, Angela," Euryale said, tucking a stray dreadlock behind Angela's ear.

"Me too, mother."

"Did you like the dresses I made for you? I thought you looked incredibly beautiful in them. Your Aunt will be so disappointed she couldn't be here for the ball."

"You took a million pictures and then there was the video."

"Well, you can't blame me for being so proud of you. Living here in the Vasilikós, being a close friend to Georgia's granddaughter and becoming such a strong Gorgonian woman. Well, let me say we both are so proud of you."

"Thanks, Mom," Angela said and hugged her mother.

"Okay, I've got to run. Your Aunt is capable of creating some more garden statuary and I can't stomach another stone bunny."

Euryale gave her daughter a kiss on the cheek and waved goodbye to Sophie.

"Goodbye, Euryale. Thank you so much for the beautiful dress. I love it."

"Any time, Sophie. Please say goodbye to your mother and grandmother." Euryale took a last look at her daughter and stepped through the mirror.

"Where have you been?" Sophie asked Angela.

"Sorry. Things have been kind of crazy. My mother wanted me to assist her with the dresses."

"How did that go?"

"Let's just say I take after my Aunt. So I ended up doing a lot of the running around and various menial tasks. She told me to remind you, no dessert until after the ball. She said the built-in corset can only do so much. How was your date, Soph?"

~ ☾ ~

Sophie laughed.

"That good? Did he kiss you? Oh my God, you kissed him? Details woman, I must have details."

Sophie slugged Angela's arm. "It was a sweet kiss."

"One kiss?" Angela asked.

"Well, it couldn't be anything more, with my mother showing up. I could have died."

"Yeah, I'm guessing it killed the moment. So where's your BFF, Miranda?" Angela asked.

"I'm guessing running around, her heart all aflutter as she fans herself and says "fiddle-de-dee" while looking for a piece of shoofly pie."

"You had me at "all aflutter." I heard about your idea to change the ball. A masquerade? How did you get Georgia to agree to it?"

"My mother did. She and Georgia had a huge fight and my mother threatened that neither of us would attend the ball unless Georgia gave in. Georgia threw a fit and smashed the huge table in the morning room and threw two chandeliers against a wall. When she saw my mother wouldn't budge, she relented."

"Girls!" Winnie yelled from across the room. "It's time to harvest the grapes and Georgia is waiting for you. Now, go get changed and get out to the vineyards before she skins both of you and has me doing catacomb duty." A crash from behind Winnie caught her attention and she closed the door, screaming. "Neville, did you drop those platters? I swear on all that is holy. If you weren't my cousin's second cousin twice removed, I would have gotten rid of you. Well, don't just stand there."

Sophie and Angela arrived in the vineyard dressed in ritual, pure white cotton dresses. They wore loose sandals and wreaths of heather and sage on their heads.

"I feel ridiculous," Sophie whispered as they moved forward and joined Georgia and Callie. A crowd gathered outside of the ornate iron gates that protected the vines.

"So glad you could find the time to join us," Georgia said. "Now please stand behind me and Callie, so we can begin."

In the center of the crowd there were two large grape stomping barrels for the harvest to be poured into. Several

~ ☾ ~

other Muses, who had done this ritual before, also wore the traditional costumes and waited for Georgia's signal.

Georgia walked forward and stepped onto a raised platform and up to a carved wood podium. The crowd applauded and cheered. Georgia beamed and acknowledged the warm welcome.

"How kind. Thank you. Thank you so much. Thank you." The crowd grew silent and Georgia began. "What a glorious day. May God continue to shine down upon this Vasilikós and keep each and every one of you in his grace. Amen. For more years than I care to remember, or am willing to admit to—"

The crowd chuckled.

"—I have been the keeper of these vines. Together, as a Vasilikós united, we have ushered in year after year of plentiful harvests, thereby keeping the balance of this world and providing the Fates with their much-needed libation. While the rest of the world goes on with their daily business, we of the Demigod community continue our dutiful watch over those entrusted in our care. My role, as harvester, continues to be one I'm incredibly proud of and one I've sacrificed so—" Georgia paused, looking down at her speech. "— and I have sacrificed a lot...and...I..."

Callie went to her mother and stood next to her on the platform, clasping her mother's hand.

"I never lost faith that my humble prayers would be answered, and my dearest friends, they have."

Angela gestured for Sophie to go up and stand by her grandmother. Sophie walked up and stood next to Georgia, clasping her grandmother's other hand. "For you see, for this harvest, things are different. My daughter Callista and my granddaughter Sophia have joined us for this harvest. They have returned to stay in this Vasilikós. My heart and soul have returned to me and I am a humbled woman for it. So, without going on and on about how happy I am, please give me the honor of shouting: Blessed be this wine, for it is the nectar of the gods. And blessed be each of you. Let the harvest begin."

The crowd burst into shouts and yells as they clapped and cheered.

The gates behind Georgia opened and everyone rushed

~ ☾ ~

past carrying wicker baskets to collect the grapes. Georgia reached down and picked up three baskets, giving Callie and Sophie a basket each.

"Well, don't just stand there," Georgia said with a laugh. "It's harvest time. Go harvest."

The Muses of the Vasilikós were joined by Hobs, Nymphs and a whole host of Demigods that either lived in the Vasilikós or nearby. Bennett walked up to Sophie wearing pale khaki pants, sandals and a long sleeved white shirt with the sleeves rolled up. He carried a large, deep basket balanced against his hip. He gestured for Sophie to pour her grapes into his basket and placed his basket on the ground. As she bent at the waist to transfer her grapes, he squatted and took her face into his hands and kissed her tenderly on the lips. Her mind was swimming as she lost herself for a moment, until Angela grabbed her arm through the vines.

"Watch it. Georgia is walking the rows," Angela warned and returned back to her picking.

Sophie smiled and after rolling her eyes, pushed his face away from hers.

The combination of the right temperature mixed with the perfect breeze made what would have been hard work pleasant enough to be enjoyable. Everyone chattered with the person next to them and Georgia's pleased expression told everyone it was an excellent harvest. The grapes were taken from the fields and poured into the vat.

Walking with Sophie, Bennett and Angela, Callie explained the next part of the harvest.

"The stomping of the grapes is an important part of the harvest and has its very own ceremony. For hygienic reasons, feet are washed thoroughly. The leader of the Vasilikós selects a person of honor, someone close to their heart, to be the first person to begin the stomping of the grapes. Georgia will not participate in the actual stomping. She'll most probably choose you, my sweet daughter."

A hush fell over the crowd, as they watched Georgia walk towards Sophie and Callie.

"I choose you, most beloved daughter."

Callie burst into tears, reached over and hugged her mother. Tears rushed forth from both women. Georgia led

~ ☾ ~

Callie to several stools with small tables with neatly folded cloths and towels, and large bars of roughly cut homemade soap. Callie sat down on the stool and slid off her sandals, placing her feet into the water. Georgia began the process of washing her daughter's feet by kneeling on the ground. She grabbed a bar of soap, a piece of cloth and threw a towel over her right shoulder. Dipping the cloth in the water, and then rubbing it on the large bar of soap, Georgia began cleaning Callie's feet.

"I remember washing you as a baby in the old tub just outside this very orchard and how I promised to be a good mother and to always be there for you. I know I failed. I am so sorry, daughter. So sorry." Georgia wept.

"Oh, Momma," Callie said. "It's okay. I know."

The crowd fell silent and Sophie was lost in the emotion of the moment. Knowing Bennett stood behind her, Sophie reached back and took his hand.

After Georgia finished drying her daughter's feet, she kissed each one on the instep. Callie stood up and then helped her mother to her feet. They gave each other a kiss on both cheeks and Callie climbed the ladder and stepped into the first vat of grapes. The crowd roared and Georgia walked over to her Sophie.

As her grandmother approached her, she saw Georgia's eyes glance down to see Sophie holding Bennett's hand.

Georgia sighed. She kissed Sophie on the cheek and whispered, "Go ahead. Wash the boy's feet. I won't put up a fuss."

Sophie pulled her grandmother into a quick hug, kissing her on the cheek. Others chose their partners and began the washing process.

"Thanks, Yiayia. Thank you."

Sophie pulled Bennett towards the benches and followed what Georgia had done. Sophie laughed at how Bennett's feet barely fit the basin and he jumped several times as Sophie tickled his feet.

"I didn't know Minotaurs were so ticklish."

He flicked some water out of his basin and she squealed in protest. She dried his feet and kissed the tops of them. He repeated the process and washed, dried and kissed Sophie's

~ ☾ ~

feet, but instead of allowing her to walk and climb into the vat, Bennett carried Sophie on his back and she playfully shrieked as he climbed the ladder. In a moment of panic, Sophie placed her hands over Bennett's eyes and in his disorientation he missed the last wrung of the ladder, falling face first into the grapes, with a laughing Sophie still clinging to his back. Bennett rolled over and trapped Sophie against the smashed grapes and she laughed until tears ran down her face.

Callie and Angela, who were busy crushing grapes and laughing at the two, helped them both to their feet. Both of their clothes were stained with burgundy splotches and Bennett pulled out handkerchief dripping with grape juice and used it to wipe Sophie's face.

Angela grabbed Sophie's hand and the girls ran, enjoying the feeling of the pulp squishing through their toes. Callie and Bennett waltzed around them, nearly falling several times.

"Hobs," Georgia called thirty minutes later. "It is time to begin turning on the taps to capture the juice and begin straining and cooking."

Sophie glanced towards the Vasilikós and saw Miranda watching the festivities from the terrace. She panicked, attempting to grab Bennett's attention, hoping he had not seen his ex-girlfriend. She turned back looking over his shoulder, relieved to see Miranda had disappeared.

~ ☾ ~

Chapter 30

Sophie couldn't believe she actually had a moment to herself. The hot bubble bath was exactly what she needed to relax and attempt to scrub the sticky grape juice off of her skin. Her mother had dropped off a special bubble bath that seemed to be doing the job, and Sophie stuck her head below the water to get the rest of the pulp and seeds out of her hair and ears.

"Sophie," Angela's voice came from the bedroom. "You can soak for another fifteen minutes."

Miranda's voice interrupted Angela's. "You have a dance lesson and ceremony rehearsal in twenty-five minutes. Which means unless you want to have wet hair you'll need to get out right about now," Miranda said, reaching down into Sophie's tub and pulling the plug out of the drain.

"Hey!" Sophie protested.

"My dear, hey or no hey, you are only two weeks away from the ball and you must stick to your schedule. Angela, if you aren't able to help Sophia keep her many obligations, I'm sure we can find another Vasilikós staffer, like a maid, to do so."

Light flickered in Sophie's bath water as the anger seeped out of her hands.

"Sophie," Angela warned. "I'll get her down to the ballroom on time, Miranda."

"Good," Miranda said, turning to leave the room. "I always knew Angela would be such a big help to me. So useful."

While Miranda's back was turned Angela raised her fist like she was going to punch her. "Well, at least we are in agreement on that."

"Get the door," Miranda said. Angela waved her hand and made the door swing shut. Sophie laughed as she walked out of her bathroom wearing a robe and using a towel to dry her hair.

"So you can slam a door, but when I create one minor

~ ☾ ~

energy burst, you get all concerned. You know, now that I get to know her, Miranda isn't half bad."

"I was just thinking the same thing. She grows on you, like a light case of leprosy."

Sophie threw her towel onto her latest addition to her room—a mission-style desk and matching heavy wooden chair. She hadn't decided if she liked it or not, but she was told it was an original Stickley, whatever that meant, and it was growing on her. She grabbed the wet towel, afraid it would ruin the desk's finish, and walked back into her bathroom.

"What am I supposed to wear for this thing?" she asked.

"Well, if you review the sweet little sticky note Miranda left you, you have to wear something with a long skirt and dancing shoes."

Sophie walked out wearing a mismatched white short-sleeved shirt and a long flowing, multi-colored skirt.

"Well," Angela said, eyeing the outfit. "It isn't red carpet, but it'll do."

"Let's get this over with," Sophie said, and after Angela took the hex off the door they were able to make it down to the ballroom with five minutes to spare. Callie, Georgia and Winnie appeared to be discussing plans for the event. A staircase Sophie didn't remember was attached to the second floor balcony where the orchestra would be, along with additional seating for those wanting to view the entire dance floor. She knew from her exploration of the Vasilikós that there was also a whole set of dressing rooms, including a large sitting room Angela referred to as a Green Room, off of the orchestra area.

"Girls. Over here." Georgia waved.

Sophie saw Bennett had arrived, dressed in a tunic. It was made for a much shorter person and Bennett appeared mortified as he attempted to stretch the material to cover anything that shouldn't be showing.

"Oh, that will not do. Not at all. Callista, just look at this. It's hopeless," Georgia said.

"Let me try," Angela said, stepping around Bennett and shaking her head. "The shortness of the front is nothing compared to the shortness of the back. Nice boxers, Bennett."

~ ☾ ~

"Ha ha ha," Bennett said. "Nice try, Angela, but I'm not wearing boxers today."

"Oh my, my, my," Angela teased. "Hey, Soph, would you like to guess whether Bennett is wearing any underwear at all?"

"Okay, I give," Bennett said, backing up until his back pressed against the wall. "Can you fix it?"

Angela eyed it and grabbed a front part of the tunic. "Don't get too excited or you'll make the hem even shorter," she said to him with a grin. "See, there's plenty of material here, but the material is so old I'm concerned it might tear when we try to alter it."

"Well," Georgia said. "Bennett can wear his traditional Scotsmen's kilt and dress jacket. I won't say I'm not disappointed, but it's a minor detail we can do away with."

Bennett slipped into a pair of cargo shorts and lifted the tunic over his head, leaving himself bare-chested.

All five women stared at him as he grabbed the undershirt hanging from his front pocket.

"What?" Bennett said, as the awkward silence continued.

"Okay," Georgia began. "This is pretty standard protocol. Sophia, you and Angela will enter from the Green Room and descend the staircase. Sophie you'll be in front and Angela will follow you. Bennett, you will stand at the bottom of the stairs waiting for Sophia to meet you. She will take your arm and you will escort her to meet the representatives of each of the Vasilikós."

What the heck are we talking about? Why is everyone acting like we're planning a high school dance?

"Sophia," Georgia said. "Please pay attention. This part is important. Bennett will present you to each of the Leaders of the Vasilikós. You will curtsy all the way down and stay down until the Leader of the Vasilikós gives you permission to rise. Now, some of the Vasilikós will test you because they can and will make you curtsy a lot longer than the others."

"Wait one sec," Sophie interrupted. "We have a real threat of some sort of Olympian out to get me...heck, all of Olympus is out to get everyone in this Vasilikós. You have been branded to spend your afterlife in Hell—"

"The Underworld—" Georgia corrected.

~ ☾ ~

"Unless I'm mistaken," Sophie arched her eyebrow, "the Underworld isn't a spa or a bed-and-breakfast, so I'm guessing Hell is pretty close. So everyone I love, everyone important to me, this entire Vasilikós are in danger and yet we're focusing on whether or not I can hold a curtsy? I've got dancing shoes on when I should be wearing combat boots. Are you all insane? Am I the only one who sees this?"

"But you aren't ready." Callie said.

"Ready for what?" Sophie asked, no longer bothering to hide her frustration, as her voice became louder in volume. "I'm ready to put my life on the line. I'm ready to walk into a stupid dance with a great big target on my back. What are all of you waiting for? Train me. Teach me how to use my powers. I need to be able to defend myself."

"Sophia, enough of this." Georgia said, throwing her hands up in the air. "We don't have time for this nonsense. Your powers are volatile, unpredictable."

"Do you want to know what is unpre—"

"Sophie, don't." Callie warns.

"Don't what? Are you kidding me, mom? I saw a pile of dead dogs, branded with Nothos, not even three miles away from here. Something rounded up those poor dogs and slaughtered them. I got their message."

"I know...I know," Callie said. "Look, you have to understand what we are stressing about your powers. A new Muse's powers are developed with time and you haven't been a Muse long enough to be able to benefit from any sort of training. Your powers have to mature, plus we're not sure enough of their extent. You are more powerful than you think, and right now, your powers are controlled by your emotions. It isn't wise to mess around with something like this unless you know what to expect—"

"Then teach me how to trigger them. Does it work if I'm scared, pissed, in love? Something. Anything."

Georgia walked up to Sophie. "Listen to me, girl. You will do what I say. I don't have time to explain each and every detail, but understand you will be safe. I will lay down my own life before I let anything happen to you. But for now, you're going to have to trust me."

Sophie didn't know what to do. She wanted to admit the

~ ☾ ~

deal she had made with Persephone. She had literally invited
the enemy into her home

Wasn't there something about inviting a god into your
home... no, that's vampires. Wait, I never gave her the
invitation. If she doesn't have an invitation, she can't get in.
But, what about daddy? I have to see him. Shoot, shoot,
shoo—

Georgia gripped each side of Sophie's head. A burst of light
was followed by blinding pain and nausea. Sophie yelled out
in pain and fell to her knees, unable to catch her breath.
When Sophie could breathe again, she wiped the spit from
her lips and chin, and looked up at her grandmother. "What
have you done to me?"

"I did what was necessary. I always do what is necessary.
Your powers are bound, so the issue is no longer about
training you to use them. Now, control that mouth of yours,
do what is expected of you and leave the rest to us. Is that
really too much to ask, *child*?"

Sophie shook her head and glared at Georgia. "You had
no—"

"Sophie, that's enough." Callie said.

Georgia laughed and forced Sophie onto her feet. She
turned Sophie to face the center of the room. "*After* you've
made it through the other eight Vasilikós, you will come
forward and curtsy to me. No need to wait for me to tell you
to rise. I will come forward..."

Sophie stopped listening to her grandmother. She
concentrated on trying to boil up enough emotions to cause
some sort of power burst.

Just a flicker. That's all I need. A spark and I can work on
the rest. Please...just a twinkle.

But the buzzing in her head almost made her feel like
vomiting. It was like a mesh wall was separating her from her
powers, stopping her from connecting with her core. Instead
of retreating from the buzzing, she focused on it, sweat
dripped from her forehead and the tip of her nose.

I won't let her do this to me. I won't let her control me. I
won't be helpless.

Sophie felt a small hole in the layers of mind fabric holding
back her powers. The buzzing was mind splitting. The hole

~ ☾ ~

was tiny, the size of the point of a needle. She grew excited. She had done it. She had forced the hole to become bigger.

Boy, Georgia would be so pissed. I am in control. I can do this. I can.

She focused on the hole, while pretending to seem interested in Georgia's speech. She wedged her will into that small, pinpoint-size hole and could feel the magical weave give way a little, forcing it to widen ever so slightly. Her head pounded so hard, she was sure it was going to explode, but she pushed on, the hole becoming larger, now the size of a tiny piece of candy. Her powers were behind a wall, trying in desperation to reach her. She closed her eyes for a second and opened the hole even wider, now the size of a dime, and much to Sophie's relief, a spark shot from her right pinky. Exhausted and unable to keep the hole open, it closed up and she opened her eyes.

"Sophia? Are you listening?" Georgia demanded.

"Sounds pretty straight forward," Sophie said, wiping her face and neck on the towel Angela handed her.

"So relieved to hear," Georgia said. "Now, let's start from the top."

"Let's," Sophie said, dropping the towel onto a chair.

My risk. My life. My Vasilikós.

It hit Sophie.

For once, Georgia told the truth. They don't know how strong my powers will be. She's underestimated me, like everyone has for all my life. Her spell wasn't powerful enough to bind me. This will be my Vasilikós, not Georgia's. Mine. Georgia is going to have to get used to me knowing what is best and for now, what Georgia doesn't know, won't hurt her. God, it feels so good to have control of something.

After the twenty-fifth time through the process of descending the staircase, curtsying in front of the pretend foreign Vasilikós, including the one that would force her to perform the lethal three-minute curtsy, Sophie was exhausted, but relieved when Georgia said they were done for the evening. Her head was still throbbing, as she continued to sneak moments to force her way through Georgia's spell and make the tiny spark flicker for a few seconds before snuffing it out. She glanced at her watch, groaning at the time. It was one a.m.

~ ☾ ~

"Now girls and Bennett, rehearsal will begin promptly at nine a.m. I have several other items I need to take care of, so Tammy the librarian will take over for me. Review over and over again the details we have gone over tonight because Tammy has been with our Vasilikós for over two hundred years and she is a stickler for details." Georgia exited with Callie, party plans in hand.

"Great," Sophie said, collapsing onto the side benches. She wished the cushions were still there, but Winnie had removed them earlier.

"If you weren't my great, great cousin twice removed's best friend's sister's brother's cousin, I would have gotten rid of you years ago," Sophie mocked, sending an exhausted Bennett and Angela into rolls of laughter. Sophie rested her head on Bennett's shoulder and after a few moments of listening to his breathing in and out, and almost falling asleep, she gave him a playful shove, stood up and said goodnight. She walked up the stairs to the orchestra balcony, having been shown a shortcut to her room through the Green Room.

"Come to my room at eight a.m.?" Sophie shouted over her shoulder at Angela.

"Okay," Angela said.

"Goodnight, Beast," Sophie called.

"Goodnight, Muse," Bennett replied.

"Angie, before you go, can you go through the waltz with me for a few minutes," Bennett asked.

"Sure," Angela said. She snapped her fingers and the CD player came to life. Bennett walked up to her, and they bowed and began waltzing.

Every muscle in Sophie's body was screaming as she made her way up the stairs, carrying her heels in one hand. When she reached the top, she looked back at Bennett and Angela dancing and couldn't help smiling at them. Something caught her eye and she glanced towards the open French doors on the other side of the dance floor. Her father stood there, looking up at her. She almost burst into tears, the ache of seeing her father being too much for her to bear, but she swallowed it down, as the hole in the magical weave grew bigger and an even bigger spark flickered from the center of her hand. Once again, the hole closed up again, leaving her helpless.

~ ☾ ~

"It can wait, Daddy, until the ball," Sophie mumbled. She knew she would have to somehow get an invitation to Persephone. She *had to* have another moment with her father.

I miss you so much, Daddy. Then she remembered Persephone.

How does someone contact a goddess in the Underworld?

Knowing that with some work she could work her way past Georgia's binding spell made her feel safe, capable and strong.

I can handle Persephone. It's one ditzy goddess. How bad could she be? She's too busy ordering catalog crap to think about destroying the world.

"Hey Muse, you're supposed to be in bed," Bennett called up to her.

"I was going to say the same to you, Beast," she said.

Bennett excused himself from Angela and raced up the stairs, taking three at a time.

"You okay?" he asked.

"Yeah, I'm fine," Sophie said, preoccupied. She saw the concerned look on Bennett's face. *I'm such a bad girlfriend for making him worry about me. I wish I could tell him about daddy, but I can't and he'll figure it out if I'm not more careful.*

He took her into his arms and kissed the top of her head. "Sorry, I know I'm sweaty enough for the both of us. I got to get to bed. In about five hours I have to get up and do some planting."

"Okay," she said, squeezing her arms around him tighter.

He still looked worried. "You sure you're okay? Muse, if something were wrong, you'd tell me, right? After all, you are my Muse, aren't you?"

"I guess I am, considering how sweaty and smelly you are. You reek."

"Come on. You know my musk is one big slice of sexy. Smell my armpits," he teased her and she laughed. "Just one whiff. If you smell my armpits, I know you'll love me forever."

And there it is...the word every girl wants to hear from a boy and now he's said it.

Even though it wasn't the way she had imagined it and

~ ☾ ~

wasn't a one-hundred percent real declaration of love, he still had said it and she stood there awkwardly, wondering who would be the first one to flinch?

He kissed her on the lips and while he backed away lifted his armpit, pointing at it. Sophie backed away and shaking her head "no". He was wearing a stretched out tank top that gave Sophie an occasional glance at his muscular torso and his broad chest.

As armpits go, that's one sexy armpit.

She wasn't shocked at the thoughts running through her mind, having gotten used to the way Bennett made her feel and think. But she was sure Georgia wouldn't approve and smiled at the thought.

***

The last week leading up to the ball was even more crazed than the previous three. Sophie, Bennett and Angela continued with their rehearsal schedule. Sophie was exhausted.

Every moment she had alone, she continued her attack on Georgia's binding spell, managing to make the dime size hole into a quarter, then into a silver dollar.

It isn't enough.

She worked into the early morning hours, lucky to catch two hours of sleep each night. She didn't like keeping Angela in the dark about what she was doing, but she couldn't take the chance of her friend getting in trouble for what Sophie was trying to accomplish.

Then, there was the added security. After several bodies of villagers were found mangled, with the brand Nothos on them, Sophie locked herself in her room, refusing to eat and see anyone. From that day forward, all newspapers and talk of any news outside of the Vasilikós was hidden from her.

Added to Sophie's frustration about not knowing what was going on outside of the Vasilikós, were the measures Georgia took to keep Sophie safe. Safe came in the embodiment of Sarah, Christine, and Bonnie—the three Furies. On loan from some of the worst dungeons of the Underworld, these vengeful goddesses were the embodiment of curses against those who went unpunished for crimes against the mortal race. An Olympian didn't exist who would dare challenge the

~ ☾ ~

Furies. Sophie wasn't thrilled to be forced to have the three women with her every moment of the day. The only time they left her alone was when Sophie returned to her private rooms or if she was with her mother or grandmother. The three women, dressed in black from head to toe, resembled high fashion models with their long hair slicked back into severe ponytails.

Additionally, the Furies had the annoying habit of considering every action a slight on the honor of Sophie, which caused them to argue with anyone who dared to cross Sophie's path, along with their habit of crying tears of blood whenever Sophie would become frustrated with them. Each imaginary slight was followed by the same question, 'May we pursue them, until death?' Sophie stopped answering 'no', after the fiftieth time the question had been asked of her.

Winnie's shouting orders throughout the Vasilikós started at five a.m. and continued until midnight as she readied the guest rooms and main congregating areas. She seemed to be a whirlwind of crazy as she conducted inventory for the event.

After another rigorous rehearsal, Sophie and Angela took a break and wandered into the kitchen for a snack of cold roast beef and a glass of iced tea. Apparently the sight of Sophie, Angela and the three Furies was too much for the Hob.

"What do you think you're doing?" Winnie demanded.

The two girls stood there, frozen to the spot. The Furies glared at Winnie.

"The day my kitchen turns into Grand Central Station is the day this Hob turns in her apron."

"I'm sorry, Winnie," Sophie said, feeling both shocked and pissed off at Winnie's tone. Winnie had never spoken to her that way before. The buzzing in Sophie's head began to become deafening. Like she had been practicing numerous times, Sophie focused on the weakest point of the binding spell's mesh. The mesh gave a little, exposing yet another quarter size opening. Warmth in the center of Sophie's hand began to build, but instead of allowing the spark to appear, Sophie channeled the energy back towards the hole. The pain was horrible, almost sickening, but she continued to focus on the opening.

The magical mesh tore. Sophie couldn't be sure, but it felt

~ ☾ ~

like it tore. Even though the mesh remained in place, the buzzing had stopped and as the spark of energy died away, the hole Sophie created in the mind mesh didn't close.

This is new.

"Don't you ignore me, Sophia Drago." Winnie yelled. "Lunch is served promptly at noon each day. Breakfast at nine. Dinner is served at five-thirty. Until this event is done, you will avoid the bloody kitchen at all other times. If you need a beverage, find the nearest garden hose and turn the water on and knock yourself out. Now, if you'll excuse me, I have a dessert meeting to continue with." Winnie turned away.

Christine, the Fury turned to Sophie, "How dare she talk to you like that. May we..."

"No! For the love of God, leave me alone," Sophie yelled and then apologized over and over again when the pretty, strawberry blond Fury began to cry tears of blood, all over her vintage black cocktail dress.

Sophie made a mental note to avoid the kitchen at all costs, along with deciding to fake a headache so she could ditch Angela and the Furies, and return to her room to continue her fight against Georgia's spell.

Today's small tear means freedom tomorrow. Georgia can suck it.

~ ☾ ~

Chapter 31

Persephone was having a good day. Out of the many things she loved, two of her favorites were warm cookies and catalog shopping. While she sat outside the little café where she had met Sophie, she enjoyed both, along with a cup of hot chocolate into which she had deposited ten teaspoons of sugar. The goddess had received a shipment of Pottery Farm dishes and a Restoration Beautiful patio table.

She dipped a cookie into her hot chocolate and popped it into her mouth while she flipped the pages of a new Wallaby Road catalog. She was a bit frustrated that the little Muse brat had forgotten a minor detail that was going to become major if Persephone was going to get entrance into the ball. Sophie had forgotten to get the goddess an invitation. But Persephone was in a forgiving mood and, besides, she had her own methods of correcting Sophie's mistake.

A woman approached Persephone and sat down.

"I am assuming you were careful. Nobody saw you sneak out of the Vasilikos?" Persephone said, swatting the woman's hand away as she attempted to take one of the goddess' cookies for herself.

"Well, let's not waste time. Do you have what I asked you to get? None of this will work unless I get an official invitation. With a gathering of this size, plus the Fate sisters being there, there will be heightened security. I won't get in without an invitation and I would hate to be discovered by blasting my way in. If I'm going to make a big splash at this party, it will be on my terms."

The woman grabbed her purse and pulled out several invitations, handing them to the goddess.

"Good. This should take care of me and my large entourage."

"But won't they recognize you? A mask can only do so

~ ☾ ~

much. Meaning no offense, but having lived in the Underworld for such a long time, I can smell the sulfur and your pure Olympian blood flowing through your veins," the woman said.

Persephone paused. "Trust me, I have it covered. My mother once gave me a long scarf, a wrap of sorts, created from sylph wings. It has the ability to heighten a supernatural's ability to Glamour. Whatever supernatural creature Georgia has on security detail will be eating out of the palm of my hand. And as for my special entourage, nobody will recognize them because as of a few days ago they didn't exist. . But enough of this. You had better get back to the Vasilikós before anyone notices you are gone." Persephone glanced up at the woman and handed her a small box of paints. "You had better fix your face. You've smeared it."

The woman took out a compact, grabbed the paints and excused herself to the bathroom. She returned and walked past Persephone, giving the goddess a chance to review the overall effect. Persephone nodded in approval.

"It's always such a pleasure seeing you," Persephone said as she watched the woman smile and walk away. She gulped down her hot cocoa and threw some money down on the table before grabbing her catalogs and the gold coin on a chain around her neck. She had to twist Penny's arm off to get her to realize she needed to use one of the five coins Penny had hidden from Charon. She loved the incredible power of the Aphrodite coins. They allowed the owner to travel a certain number of times between the Underworld and the mortal realm virtually undetected. She knew she needed to get back to the Underworld because she was waiting for another delivery of table linens that hadn't come in her last shipment. She had a feeling Charon will be delivering it any moment and she had to sign for the package.

~ ☾ ~

Chapter 32

Much to Sophie's dismay, Miranda was waiting back at her room with one of Georgia's lists. Half of the items were scratched out, but the remaining items were for her to complete.

Miranda hadn't even given the Furies a chance to enter the room by slamming the door in their faces. Sophie winced when she heard Bonnie argue with Christine, as Sarah's muffled cries told Sophie another outfit was ruined with bloodstains. "We have some important activities today," Miranda said, sitting down at Sophie's new desk.

"As you know, we have one day before the event. Today, we have the arrival of the other Vasilikós. They'll be here around one p.m. We will gather in Georgia's office for a pre-arrival meeting at eleven-thirty. Do not, and I stress this, do *not* be late."

"Got it," she said, sitting up.

"Are you writing any of this down?"

"Don't need to," Sophie said, pointing to her head.

"I thought so. I've made you a copy of my notes." Miranda handed Sophie a copy.

"You dot your i's with hearts?"

Miranda frowned, but continued. "So, at nine a.m., you have breakfast. At ten, you have a quick rehearsal in the ballroom. That lasts until eleven, which will give you about twenty minutes to get back to your room for a quick shower and back downstairs for Georgia's meeting at eleven-thirty. The meeting is expected to last thirty minutes. You will then have forty-five minutes to race back to your room, where several Muses and your attendant, Angela, will help you dress for the arrival event."

"Umm, not necessary and kind of strange," Sophie said.

"As a new Muse, that is the tradition and you know Georgia is a stickler for tradition."

"But…"

~ ☾ ~

Miranda stopped and glared at Sophie. "Sophie, look, I know it's kind of strange, the whole thing with you dating my boyfriend."

"Ex-boyfriend," Angela said as she walked into the room.

"Yes, sorry, ex-boyfriend. And I know I've been a real pain."

"I second that," Angela offered, climbing onto Sophie's new bed. The room was almost finished and Sophie loved it, especially her new king-size box springs and mattress.

"Do you mind?" Miranda responded. "What I'm trying to say is I'm sorry. I could say I've been under a lot of pressure and that's the reason why I've been out of sorts."

"And been a total nasty piece of work," Angela said.

"*But*, if I'm being *completely* honest, seeing Bennett so happy has been a bit of a blow to my ego and the kiss I shared with him yesterday meant nothing. I'm being serious. It wasn't anything. So just put it out of your mind. It was passionate, but truly, nothing to worry about."

Did she just say, 'kiss'? Did that witch just say she kissed my boyfriend? That little—

"Whew, I feel so much better. Well, I've got a few items to work on," Miranda continued. "So I'll be off. I'm so glad we had this talk. By the way, Angela, Georgia wants to see you in her office. " Miranda walked towards the open door. "Don't worry, I'll get the door."

Sophie looked at Angela.

"Come one, Soph. It's right out of the playbook of every bad chick flick. Don't you dare let that miserable little Harpy—"

"Don't insult Tammy. Miranda is worse than a Harpy. Get the Furies in here, I have a job for them," Sophie said, throwing on her sandals.

"What are you going to do?" Angela said.

"As per the skank, we have breakfast in ten minutes. Can't be late for breakfast."

"I meant about Bennett," Angela said. "You know he didn't do it. She's playing mind games."

"Let me say this," Sophie began. "I find it strange that out of all of the Muses, literally thousands that Georgia could pick, she picks Miranda."

~ ☾ ~

"That would be just like her."

"My mother warned me about Georgia's motives a long time ago. I'm sure she has some sort of plan on who she thinks I should be *mated* with." Sophie grabbed her hairbrush off her dresser and brushed out her hair. As her emotions rushed through her mind and heart, Sophie could feel an even larger tear in Georgia's spell.

I can't think about it now. Now I'm pissed.

"And Bennett?"

"I'll give him every opportunity to mention kissing the Gone with the Wind slut. If the Minotaur thinks I'm a fool, he's got a surprise coming to him."

"Why don't you just ask him?" Angela asked. "If you ask him about it—"

"And have me look like the desperate girlfriend? So *not* going to happen. I am, after all, my mother's daughter."

Sophie's bedroom door crashed open as the three Furies walked in with some eagerness.

"May we?" Bonnie asked, but frowned knowing the answer already as the three woman followed Angela and Sophie down the hall.

~ ☾ ~

Chapter 33

Sophie walked into the ballroom, grateful to be Fury-less, to find Callie smiling at her.

"Want to skip rehearsal and have some quality time with your mother?"

"I love you." Sophie exclaimed. "If I have to curtsy one more time, I'll scream."

The two women returned to Sophie's room and sat next to each other on her bed.

"I'm sorry I haven't had a lot of time to spend with you."

"It's okay, Mom. Angela and I kept ourselves from going crazy."

"I like her," Callie said. "You know, I used to have a good friend. We were about as close as you and Angela are. She even served as my second for my introduction ceremony, just like Angela will do for you. The fun we had. So many nights of long conversations. It was a shame."

"What happened to her?"

"Well," Callie said, standing up and examining the dress Sophie planned on wearing. "Your father happened. I fell in love and all of my attentions were focused on him. It didn't sit well with her. I also began to suspect there was more to her than meets the eye. Nasty accidents were happening and I suspected she might be behind it."

"Kind of like what is happening in the village, the things no one will talk about?"

"No, they weren't that bad. Even though someone got hurt, the accidents were childish pranks and I kept pushing the thought out of my mind that my friend was responsible. I loved her like a sister and I felt sorry for her because she wasn't a Muse. She had a diluted Demigod family heritage. I believed she was some sort of Siren. The only thing she had was the whole social status of being the best friend to the daughter of the Vasilikós leader. But then, the incident happened."

~ ☾ ~

"Incident?" Sophie asked.

"Winnie's husband died under mysterious circumstances and an investigation was launched. It involved all Nine Vasilikós and a body of independent Demigods. All facts pointed to my friend and she was exiled to the edge of the Underworld. It became clear she was insane and not what she'd always appeared to be. She was a goddess in Demigod clothing. Her real name was Pandora."

"Pandora?"

"Remember the myth I told you about the girl made out of clay? This kind of demonstrates how vicious the gods were. They created this girl out of clay and made her so beautiful nobody could resist her. But inside she was ugly. She was a liar, a manipulator and I'm guessing today they would have called her a sociopath. She was to be the ultimate mortal punishment. They gave her a beautiful box but told her she could never open it. Well, telling Pandora not to do something was like telling a two year old not to touch a hot stove. So, she opened the box and let out creatures that continue to plague Man to this very day. What she didn't realize was that she also damned herself to being chained to the horrors she unleashed. But what I'm talking about is ancient history and we've got to get you ready."

"But, I thought—"

"Yeah, I've decided to break with tradition. I've always thought it was kind of creepy standing around in your bra and panties while a group of Muses dressed you. I've already told Georgia not to expect us for her meeting, so we can take a little longer to prepare," Callie said, walking into Sophie's dressing room and returning with her own outfit for the occasion and Sophie's own dress.

Angela joined Callie and Sophie and the three women walked down the main staircase in the Entry Hall fifteen minutes early. Most of the welcoming committee already had assembled and Georgia was speaking with Winnie, who was dressed in her tweed suit jacket and a long, tartan print skirt that pooled slightly on the ground. Her frizzy mop of hair was now arranged into flattering curls and Sophie made it a point of telling her how pretty she looked today.

~ ☾ ~

"Well, you can only do so much with what the Lord has given you to work with. But, thank you, dear. Very kind of you to say so," Winnie replied.

The front door opened and Bennett walked in, accompanied by two other men who Sophie knew were his Honor Guard and would be available to Sophie, Bennett and Angela if help was needed. Bennett was dressed in a dark charcoal pinstriped suit.

Sophie wanted to walk over and kiss him, but then remembered what Miranda said and her blood boiled. Her hands grew warm and tingled. After a few deep breaths, Sophie managed to keep her blood at a low simmer.

Neville the Hob walked in with a tall staff, which he handed to Bennett. Bennett in turn handed it to one member of his Honor Guard. This man took his place on the first landing of the grand staircase.

When he got the signal, Bennett walked over to Sophie. His remaining Honor Guard offered his hand to Angela, which she accepted with a smile.

The man paired with Angela was a Demigod who was part Merman. Angela had mentioned to Sophie that she had always been attracted to him and made it a point to attend all of his home swim meets, but never had the nerve to talk to him. After admitting her crush to Sophie, Sophie made a special request for him to be part of Bennett's Honor Guard and Callie made sure it was granted.

Sophie almost laughed when she saw her normally confident friend become nervous and tongue-tied. She imagined it was because even though the Merman wore a suit, Angela couldn't stop picturing him in his tight bathing suit.

Bennett reached Sophie and couldn't stop smiling. "You...look," he said.

Sophie's eyes watered a bit. She looked up into his eyes and then down to his lips, the image of Miranda kissing him flashing across her mind. "Kissable?" she said.

"Very, but I was going to say...breathtaking."

Damn, you would say that. He's so beautiful. How could I doubt him? He couldn't have kissed her. Maybe Angela was right. Maybe it was all made up.

~ ☾ ~

She took his hand as he led the way to their positions. It was two minutes before one p.m.

The Honor Guard on the stairs banged his staff down three times. Angela had mentioned to Sophie his name was Stavros and he was a rare male Siren.

"Attention!" His voice drew the attention of the gathered welcoming committee. "Attention."

The clock struck one and everyone was silent as the first of the eight mirrors began to glow and then ripple.

"The Vasilikós of Europe," the Siren said. "Helena, Grand Duchess to the Vasilikós of Europe and Member of the Order of Helios."

A large entourage exited from the mirror, led by a beautiful, tall blond woman with delicate features. Her mouth was pressed with a disapproving air and she carried a walking stick with a golden sun on its handle. She and Georgia exchanged a few clearly forced niceties.

Sophie and Bennett walked forward and Bennett bowed while Sophie curtsied low. After she told Sophie to rise, Helena and her group exited the room.

Angela leaned over to Sophie. "One down, seven more to go."

"Attention!" The Siren called again. "Attention! The Vasilikós of Russia. Elena, Grand Duchess to the Vasilikós of Russia and Member of the Order of Boreas."

A large group exited the second mirror, led by a woman wearing a long velvet coat with fur cuffs and lapels. The train of her coat seemed endless.

Elena approached Sophie, but appeared to be more interested in Bennett, who kept his eyes forward, appearing to ignore Elena's stare.

"Charming," Elena remarked to Sophie as the Russian's group exited the room. Sophie wasn't sure if she meant her or Bennett.

"Attention!" Stavros shouted. "Attention! The Inspirational Assembly of the United States. Rhonda, Representative for The Inspirational Assembly of the United States of America and Member of the Order of Hermes."

Rhonda stepped out with several members of her group walking along with her.

~ ☾ ~

"She walks with her group to signal equality," Angela commented to Sophie under her breath.

Rhonda was an attractive woman and looked like she was either a Congresswoman or the First Lady of the United States.

"Representative," Georgia said, shaking Rhonda's hand. "So glad you could join us."

"Georgia, I wouldn't have missed this for the world. Callie, it has been ages, though I must say we were pleased to have you living stateside."

"It was my pleasure, Representative. Thank you for taking care of the necessary immigration paperwork."

"No thanks necessary. You are family and it is the least I could do." She addressed Sophie. "Oh, my, just look at this little one. She is a precious and welcome addition." Rhonda glanced at Bennett.

"And what is your name, son?" Rhonda asked Bennett.

"Bennett, Representative," Bennett answered.

"Fine, strapping boy. Were you raised on a farm?"

Georgia interrupted. "Sorry, Rhonda, if you would have your group make their way to the Dining Hall where luncheon will be served shortly."

"Oops, I'm holding up the line," Rhonda said.

"Attention." Stavros shouted. "Attention. The Vasilikós of Asia. Qiaohui, Grand Duchess to the Vasilikós of Asia and Member of the Order of Hesychia."

Qiaohui and her group stepped out of the mirror, Georgia rushed forward and the women warmly embraced. Qiaohui was an older woman, her hair was down, snowy white and straight, a single black blossom adorned it.

Sophie stepped forward and was surprised when Qiaohui presented her with the black flower and without saying a word to Sophie, exited the room.

As she passed Winnie, Qiaohui asked her if she was still making those delicious Celtic Spiral Cookies.

Winnie curtsied several times, stumbling a little. "My pleasure, Your Grace. You will find a tin of them in your room. The tin will be replenished for Your Grace's entire stay."

"As always, dearest Winnie, you never cease to amaze

~ ☾ ~

me with your dedication to this Vasilikós and attention to detail."

"Thank you, Your Grace. I am humbled by your....gracious comments, Your Grace."

Sophie was grateful that meeting the Vasilikós of Africa, the Middle East, the Northern Territories and Australia went without issue. Her legs were screaming and she wanted to get something in her stomach.

Georgia dismissed the staff to join those already prepping for the luncheon. She walked towards Callie, Sophie, Bennett and Angela.

"That went adequately," Georgia said. "Now we have the marathon luncheon. Remember, Sophie with Bennett and Angela, myself with Callie. We need to circulate and give equal attention to everyone. Do not expect to eat. You can do your eating later."

They all groaned.

***

Sophie woke up the next morning feeling trapped. As tradition dictated, like a bride before her wedding, no one could see her, except her Lady in Waiting and her mother and grandmother. The Furies had been sent back to the Underworld, to handle some sort of situation that wasn't explained to Sophie. Sophie was enjoying not having to be babysat. Callie and Angela stopped in for breakfast and the three women went through the breakdown of the evening then moved onto more important items like the fried eggs, bacon, biscuits, sausage gravy, and pancakes Callie had somehow smuggled in.

"Don't stuff yourself," Callie said. "Taking your dress out is not an option."

"My dress, my dress, my dress. I haven't gained a pound since I got here." Sophie glanced behind her mother, got up and walked toward her dressing room. "Mom, where is my dress?" Sophie said, walking out of her closet chomping on a piece of bacon.

"Well, it was right..." Callie got up and went through her daughter's closet. "Hmmm. Maybe it's over..."

"Maybe nothing. And that isn't the breakfast I sent up," Georgia said, walking in with two huge garment bags and

~ ☾ ~

motioning for the Hob behind her to remove the breakfast immediately. Two Hobs followed behind pushing a dress dummy. "There's been a change of plans. I didn't like the first dress. You will be wearing the dress I wore when I became a member of this Vasilikós."

Georgia and the Hobs walked into the sitting room area. The Hobs laid down their loads and closed the dividing drapes to the sitting room, cutting off any view of what they were doing.

"Did you know about this?" Sophie asked.

"Do you see the expression on my face?" Callie said, and all three sat down to wait for the unveiling.

After about fifteen minutes, Sophie was worried and nudged her mom to do something.

"Georgia?" Callie said.

The air became still and Sophie could feel the electricity building in the air. Right before she was ready to rush the curtains out of concern they opened and a burst of tiny twinkling sparks drifted down from the ceiling, leaving everyone in the room speechless. The strapless white organdy gown had a tight, close-fitting bodice. White elbow-length gloves with crystal buttons hung from the dress form. A white and silver beaded mask with delicate chinchilla coque feathers lay on the nearest table.

"Yiayia," Sophie said, placing both hands on her heart. "That's not a dress. It's a ball gown. I..." Sophie didn't know what to say.

Why does she always do this? Every time I have her figured out, Georgia pulls something so incredibly sweet. I don't think I'll ever figure her out.

"You don't like it?" Georgia said in shock. "I'll have you know this dress was created by Angela's mother Euryale. There are plenty of young girls who would be honored to wear such a dress."

"No, Yiayia, you don't understand. I love it."

"Will it fit?" Callie asked.

"It has been altered by Euryale, to Sophia's specific measurements. I was more *blessed* in the figure area, but it should fit her like a glove."

And there's the Georgia I know. Nothing like a

~ ☾ ~

backhanded compliment to get the day started on the right foot.

Georgia walked over and took a velvet box from the Hob closest to her.

"This was given to me a long time ago, as a gift to celebrate my induction into our world. Hades himself gave them to me. The stones were mined from the Underworld, which is why they sparkle so when the light hits them. When he gave them to me he said, 'For your daughter.' Callista had not been born yet, but he intended for me to give them to her when she was of age. I'm giving these to you, Callista, after the ball, but for tonight they are yours, Sophia."

Callie gasped. "No, Mama."

"It had been my intention to give them to you on your wedding day, but things didn't work out the way I thought they should," Georgia said. "Apparently, you can't control everything. You can always try, but Fate always seems to get in the way. I blame Rose, Callista, for the road she created for you."

Sophie opened up the box. Inside of it was a diamond choker with hanging diamond teardrops that swayed with each movement, catching the light. A matching bracelet, large hair comb and two large studs completed the collection.

"I don't know what to say," Sophie said as she handed the box back to the Hob.

"Maybe words aren't necessary," Georgia said. Sophie rushed forward and gave Georgia a hug. Georgia began to pull away, but Sophie held her and for the briefest of moments she felt Georgia tighten her arms around her.

"Practice your curtseys," Georgia said, stepping away. "They were a bit sloppy yesterday morning." She exited with the Hobs.

"She's trying, Sophie," Callie said.

"I know, mom," Sophie said.

"I've got a few final things to check on. Are you going to be okay for a while?"

"Yeah," Sophie said. "I've got *my curtsies* to practice." Sophie heard the door close and rushed to her new dress. She loved it.

I feel like Cinderella.

~ ☾ ~

She squeaked out in excitement, as she glanced at the mask and elbow length gloves. Sophie unpinned the dress from the dummy and held it out in front of her, glancing at her reflection in the floor length mirror. There was no doubt about it; this was the most beautiful dress she had ever seen.

I am Cinderella. I have a prince, whom I'm in love with. It's all so wonderful.

Several raised voices and the sound of a group of people running past her door made her almost open the door into the hallway. She stopped when she heard Georgia's commanding voice drift in through her open terrace door.

Still carrying the dress, Sophie walked out to her balcony. Impaled on the many sharp spikes of the vineyard's gate was an object. Sophie couldn't make it out, but from the way it hung, it wasn't any sort of decoration. She judged by Georgia's reaction it wasn't meant to be there. There were several black birds picking at it and Sophie remembered her biology class and how it discussed in detail the concept of the food chain. Those birds ate dead things. Sophie took a few steps back and hid herself behind a pillar where she could still get a decent view without anyone seeing her.

Georgia rushed towards the gate.

"Somebody do something!" Georgia shouted. "Get that thing down before our guests see it."

Sophie focused on the gate and as if she were standing in front of it, the object became visible. She let out a small, high-pitched sound, but caught it before it became anything more. Hung on the top of the gate was the lifeless body of a male Hob, its tiny body crumbled and broken, dripping blood down the massive gate and onto the ground. Winnie appeared out of nowhere, as Bennett ran toward the gate carrying the large extension ladder.

"Neville? Oh, dear sweet Jesus! Neville!" Winnie wailed as she rushed the gate and attempted to climb it. The old Hob's hands became coated with Neville's blood and Winnie screamed in horror. Georgia rushed towards her and wrapped her arms around her friend, as Winnie cried hysterically, trying to reach her cousin's second cousin.

"It's too late, Winnie. It's too late, my love. He's gone." Georgia said, trying to hide the sight from Winnie's view.

~ ☾ ~

"There's nothing we can do for him."

"No!" Winnie cried out, crumbling to the ground, taking Georgia with her.

Bennett sobbed, wiping his tears away with his forearm, as he climbed down the ladder with Neville's body in his arms. He held Neville close to him.

"I'm so sorry." He said, shaking, standing in front of Winnie. "I'm so sorry."

Winnie screamed as she took Neville's body into her arms.

"They branded him. Those miserable, filthy Olympians branded him a Nothos. Just like they did to my poor Aaron. Oh, God! Why? Oh sweet Jesus, please help us."

Sophie shook with sobs she managed to muffle in the folds of her dress.

This isn't a fairytale. It's a nightmare. Please, daddy, I want to go home. I just want to go home.

She dropped the dress. A surge of emotion raged through her. She tried to control it, but couldn't. A horrible ripping sound filled her ears and assuming the sound was caused by Georgia's spell giving way, Sophie ignored the intense pain in her head as whatever small hold Georgia's spell had on her slipped away and disappeared. Without realizing what she was doing, Sophie threw an energy ball large enough to shatter her new desk into a million little pieces. She stood there, her breath coming in gasps, sobbing, trying to calm herself. She ignored the smoldering pieces of her desk and put her dress back on the dummy. She then began to pick up what remained of her desk, shoving them in the back of her closet where she hoped no one would find them.

~ ☾ ~

Chapter 34

Hades knew Persephone was up to something, but he didn't know what. As he unpacked yet another box of catalog crap, he chastised himself for being so ignorant about what was happening under his nose, in his own kingdom, and he wondered what the hell he was doing.

I love her, so much. Am I doing the right thing with Saphie? I never know what she is thinking or if she's truly happy. How long do I have before everything falls apart again like it has done so many times over the centuries?

If he were to list his one and only weakness—and being the god of the Underworld made it difficult for him to admit he even had a weakness—he would list Persephone as his Achilles heel. He admitted to himself his love was blind. There were moments he loved her so much the very sight of her made his heart pump faster and his desire to have her a ravenous aching that he had to satisfy. Then there were the moments, usually when Persephone was throwing one of her tirades, he wished he could throw her into one of the rivers.

He pulled out the directions on how to assemble the new CD rack, saw how complicated it was and threw the fifteen page document back in the box. He would get one of the shades to take care of this. He figured any shade that could put together this junk would earn a direct ticket into the afterlife.

He walked out to the porch and stepped off it, making his way to his campfire. He found the flickering flames comforting, and in the Underworld comfort wasn't easily found.

Hades acknowledged his marriage wasn't perfect and in part he believed the troubles in it might have been his fault. However, he would not take the full blame for his mess of a marriage.

~ ☾ ~

He glanced at the empty spaces on the opposite side of the campfire and snapped his fingers. Three shades appeared in front of him.

"Okay," Hades said to the three. "I'm so glad you could make the time to meet with me. Sorry for the short notice."

One of the shades put down its book. "Is this our book club night? I'm still a few chapters behind."

"No," said the second shade. "It's bridge night."

"It's not bridge night," Hades said. "That's tomorrow."

"Then it *is* book club. Shoot. Let's keep our discussion focused on chapters two through four."

"It isn't book club night, either," Hades said, already losing his patience.

"Oh, now I get it," said the third shade. "It's a 'how do I deal with Persephone' session."

"Oh, for the love of God. You got me out of the river for this?" said the second shade.

"Look, I admit I may have built my marriage on a weak foundation, but there are moments when I think it could work. Unfortunately, right now isn't one of them," Hades said. "I don't trust her. Can she be happy with a person who kind of forced her into marriage?"

"Dear lord, this is going to be a painful session. Can we do book club instead?" the first shade said. "I'd like to reach the end of the Harry Potter series before I cross over."

"I could cross you over right now and you'd never know how it ended," Hades growled.

The first shade sulked a bit and put away the book. "You were saying you built your marriage on a weak foundation."

"Why you are asking marriage advice from me, I'll never know," the second shade said, violet eyes flashed and a phantom of a diamond necklace twinkled in the firelight. "I've been married so many times I've lost count. If it had a pulse, I considered it fair game."

"You think you had it bad?" said the first shade. "I was married several times and I think two of them were gay. Now, don't get me wrong, I love the gays, *love them*. They always bought my records, came to my concerts, and all the drag queens imitated me. *Fabulous*. It was so flattering, but gays in my marriage bed, not a good thing."

~ ☾ ~

"Can we get back to my issue?" Hades said.

"If I may, Haddie. May I call you Haddie?" said the third shade.

"No, you may not call me Haddie."

"You're asking me for marriage advice and I'm getting too personal?"

Hades paused a moment and nodded.

The third shade began, "Haddie, you kidnapped your goddess wife. You then added a stipulation that as long as she didn't eat anything during her brief stay with you, you would let her go. You then tricked her into eating some orange seeds."

"They were pomegranate seeds," Hades replied.

"Doesn't matter. You tricked her into eating some pomegranate seeds, which I have always thought to be too tart and a very *messy* fruit, but anyway, she eats the seeds and ends up having to spend half her life down here with you, which she was able to deal with, but since Olympus has been locked away, she's stuck down here twenty-four seven, three hundred sixty-five days a year. Do I have this correct?"

"It was her choice to eat the seeds," Hades said, but after a few seconds, he gave in. "Yes, you have it correct."

"Well, I am sorry to say this, but you got what you wished for and if there was one thing my mother told me it was to be careful what you wish for because you may just get it."

"Tell me about it," the second shade said. "I married the same man twice. What a boozer he was, but oh how I loved that man of mine. I don't mind a little rough around the edges, if you know what I mean." The shade winked and took a sip of its cocktail before throwing the phantom glass into the fire.

Hades ignored the comment and concentrated his attention on the third shade.

"So what you're saying is my marriage is doomed to fail?"

"If you want to save your marriage, maybe you need to start with a new foundation, because the one you have is built on quicksand. But then, maybe you aren't looking for an honest answer. Maybe you're only looking for the answers you want to hear?"

Hades thought about it for a few moments.

~ ☾ ~

"I'll see everyone tomorrow for bridge," he said, snapping his fingers and sending the three back into the river.

"I thought so," the third shade said, before it was gone.

"Honey?" Persephone called from the house. "Were you talking with someone?"

"You're back," he said. "Where'd you go?"

"Nowhere, silly. I decided to walk along the river and skip stones. You know how I love to tease the dead. I see the CD rack came in. Let's put it together."

"Be careful what you wish for," Hades mumbled.

"What?"

"Coming," he said and walked back into the house.

~ ☾ ~

Chapter 35

Later that evening, Sophie made her way through the back hall leading to the green room. Overwhelmed by everything that had taken place in the last few hours, she was finding it hard to breathe. The green room's walls were closing around her and she snuck out to clear her head. She was relieved to find the hallway quiet and not surprised to find it empty, considering how everyone was avoiding her. She was sure they didn't know she knew about poor Neville and she tried her best to play the part of a naïve Muse. She jumped into a room off the hallway and hid behind the door when she saw Georgia coming down the hall with Bennett. When they stopped directly in front of her doorway, she held her breath and peeked through the door crack.

Even though she felt miserable at the mere thought of poor Neville, her heart still raced when she got a peek of Bennett in his native Scotsman's kilt and tuxedo dress coat. Bennett's mask sat high on his cheekbones, making him look like a Scottish superhero.

I wonder if he's wearing anything under his kilt? Oh my God, what kind of horrible person am I to get hot and bothered so soon after Neville's death? Poor Neville. I hate myself.

"Georgia, you look lovely this evening."

Well, she does look lovely.

"Thank you, Bennett. It's a shame about the tunic," Georgia said. "Remember, you are never to leave her side."

Sophie frowned and stuck her tongue out at Georgia.

Bennett nodded and left.

Qiaohui walked up to Georgia.

"I love your dress, Georgia."

Am I never going to get out of this room?

"Thank you, Qiaohui. You look beautiful, as always."

Qiaohui didn't wear a mask, but had one painted on her face. She lifted her fan and opened it so she could talk to Georgia behind it.

~ ☾ ~

"The other Vasilikós suspect," Qiaohui said.

Suspect what? What are they talking about? Her damn fan must be made of lead. It's muffling their voices. Sophie shifted closer to hear better.

"And you said?" Georgia asked.

"Nothing, as agreed. But, I don't know how long we will be able to keep this secret. Her power becomes more and more evident."

"After tonight, it won't matter."

"As you wish, Georgia," Qiaohui replied. "You will always have the backing of the Vasilikós of Asia, as long as you stay true to our agreement."

"You have my word, Qiaohui. As the Vasilikós of Greece and Italy rise in power, so will the Vasilikós of Asia. With Sophie's rise as ruler, and my guiding hand and advice, your Vasilikós will replace Europe as number two."

What is she up to? What does she mean by ruler? Nobody said anything about being a ruler.

Qiaohui closed her fan and walked away. Georgia took a deep breath, checked her hair in the mirror on the wall and made her way towards the green room.

She doesn't care about poor little Neville. Mom was right. All Georgia love is power. Why do I allow myself to believe she has any sort of heart? Shoot. Shoot. Shoot. She's going to catch me out of the green room. Think... She needs a distraction.

Sophie glanced at the end of the hallway and concentrated on a chair flanking a door. She shot an energy spark from her hand, which bounced off the wall and collided with the chair. The sound of the chair smashing against the wall made Georgia stop and change direction. Sophie hoped it gave her enough time to make it back to the green room.

Not bad. I guess I'm a natural at this Muse stuff.

***

While Callie circled around her, adjusting the dress here and there and fluffing the skirt, Sophie stood in front of a floor length mirror looking at herself.

Not bad. Can this really be me? Am I this person and is this now my life?

Angela handed Sophie her mask and stood smoothing out

~ ☾ ~

her own dress. She leaned over and checked out her hair, which like Sophie's hair, was pulled back into a French twist.

Sophie playfully pushed her out of the way and Angela shoved back.

"Girls," I swear, if you two mess up your hair or make-up, I will kill you."

"Way to go, Mom. Debbie Downer."

Callie frowned. "I'm serious. Grab the velvet boxes and let's get your jewelry on, Sophie."

"About that, Mom, let me make a suggestion." Sophie took the choker out of the box. She walked behind Callie and placed it around her mother's throat. Sophie closed the clasp and stood back to look at her mother.

"I can't," Callie said, but Sophie had moved onto the bracelet, which she placed on Angela's wrist. "I couldn't have made it this far without you."

Angela hugged Sophie and said, "Thanks for the loaner." Sophie put on the earrings and comb, checked the mirror again. She pulled out of her dressing table a single strand of pearls and asked Angela to help her put them on. They weren't real, but her father had given them to her for her sixteenth birthday and the necklace was priceless to her. Once she had it secured around her neck, Sophie told everyone she was ready.

Georgia walked in and saw her diamond collection dispersed among the women and shook her head.

"It isn't worth me arguing about it. It is time. Remember, you are representing this Vasilikós. Do not, I repeat, do not disappoint me."

"I'll do my best, Georgia," Sophie said.

"You'll have to do better than your best," Georgia said. She glanced at the group of three women. "Very nice. Oh, Sophia, knowing you didn't have the opportunity to practice in this dress, Bennett will be waiting for you at the top of the stairs instead of the bottom. Now, let's get this over with so we can get our lives back to normalcy."

"Whatever normal is," Callie mumbled to the girls.

Georgia and Callie were about to leave when Sophie called her mother back. She grabbed her mother's hand.

"Mom?" She was desperate to tell her mother that her dad

~ ☾ ~

would be at the ball, but couldn't get the words out.

Maybe this moment with Dad should be mine and mine alone.

Callie started first. "Listen honey, I know I've told you a million times how lovely you look, but I also wanted to say how proud I am." Callie clasped Sophie's hand in her own and kissed it.

"Thanks Mom, but..." She didn't know what to do. She was on the verge of jumping into her new life and on top of everything she was going to see her father, for however long an invitation to this ball gave her. Sophie had left two invitations at the restaurant she had seen Persephone at, hoping she would retrieve them. She addressed them to 'Saphie'.

"My only regret is that...," Callie said, tearing up.

"Mom, please, don't."

"I wish your father were here. Angelo would have, well, he might have cried a little," Callie said with a chuckle. "But, he would have been so proud, so very proud, sweetie. But, in his own way, he'll always be with us."

"In his own way," Sophie said, touching her pearls, and deciding this wasn't the right time.

"Okay, I have to run. Georgia is giving me the evil eye. Remember to lean on Bennett and don't trip on your skirt."

"I won't and Mom..."

"Don't say it or we'll both start to cry. I know. Me too."

Angela came up from behind and patted Sophie's shoulder with her gloved hand.

"Ready, Soph?"

"Ready, Ang."

"I'm thinking my nickname needs reworked."

~ ☾ ~

Chapter 36

Persephone arrived without pomp and circumstance, followed closely by her entourage. She nervously clutched her invitation and the magical sylph scarf. She had almost left the scarf at home, thinking she didn't need it. She had dipped her mask into the River Styx, which gave it the power to make a person unrecognizable. However, once she had her mask secured to her head, she second-guessed herself and brought her scarf as a precaution. Looking at the extensive security Georgia had created, Persephone was relieved she had. The security was impressive, and had she been a Demigod or a lesser goddess, it would have proven impenetrable. However, she stopped for a moment before entering the first of five checkpoints and covered her head with the sylph wrap.

The first security detail, which included several herculean-sized men, a few powerful witches and numerous Olympian-sensitive beasts almost made her turn away, but she reminded herself she was Persephone, daughter of Zeus and Demeter, Queen of the Underworld, and failure was not an option. A unicorn approached and she stood frozen as the beast sniffed her curiously. She pulled the scarf tighter around her head and watched the creature's eyes glaze over. In its hypnotic trance, the beast bowed down to her, offering the top of its head for her to touch. She reached over and patted it wishing she had a knife to slit its throat, but her hunt didn't involve this lowly creature, and she moved on to the next checkpoint. Once in the interior of the ballroom, she told herself tonight was a night that must begin with subtlety.

"Take your positions," she said to the group escorting her and off they went, weaving into the crowd and disappearing. She scanned the room and found an alcove that would serve her purposes and placed herself behind a group of people in it. She remembered how things used to be. She had been the

~ ☾ ~

goddess of spring, responsible for creating new growth during the season of rebirth. But now, damned to permanent residence in the Underworld, surrounded by soil so dead nothing grew in it, her powers were diminished and the only flowers she saw were the ones she painted in her studio. Thankfully, Penny's revenge project was just what she needed and her recent visits to the mortal realm quickly restored her powers to a decent level.

Persephone believed chaos required light brush strokes because creating a masterpiece of carnage required careful consideration of each and every detail. She took in the room and was nauseous at seeing so many Demigods enjoying themselves.

How had the unwanted mistakes of Olympus risen to power while the Olympians suffered horribly? It's disgusting. It's taking every ounce of control not to begin killing each and every one of them. They were the abominations, not me. I was part of Zeus' plan, not them. And yet, they walk around like they were gods, protecting mortals—of all things.

The idea of inflicting enough pain on those who for their sake she was damned to a year-round existence with her miserable husband made all of her suffering so worthwhile and satisfying. She was relieved admitting her marriage was miserable. It wasn't about whether or not she hated Hades because she didn't completely dislike him. Sure, to a certain degree she had a love/more hate relationship with him, but he did have some positives. But she was willing to admit she hated their life together. She hated the Underworld, but most of all, she hated Demigods and mortals, and if she was successful tonight she would doom the mortal race to an unending Hell of waste while also making her husband even more miserable. That was a win-win for her. The man, posing as her plus-one, remained with her and she glanced up at him.

"You know what to do," she said.

"Yes," he replied.

Persephone saw Penny in the balcony. She waved at her and Penny waved back.

"Dear me, Penny has the worst taste in clothing."

~ ☾ ~

Persephone commented. "I will have to introduce her to Versace because she looks like a two-Drachma hooker."

Persephone noticed a male Siren taking his place with the orchestra. He signaled for them to end the waltz they were playing. She watched the tall Minotaur she remembered seeing in the village square reach the top of the stairs.

The Siren banged the tall staff three times. "Attention, attention, Vasilikós and guests...it is my privilege to announce the arrival of Rose, Agatha and Cleo, the Fates."

Persephone applauded as the three sisters entered. They were near the end of their three-hundred-sixty-five days of power and looked frail. They were seated in wheelchairs at the center of the cheering crowd, and the three Fates waved and thanked everyone for their warm welcome. The Fates' escorts moved them to an area that was corded off, where they could easily receive any additional well wishes from attendees.

Persephone turned her attention away from the Fates as the Siren banged the staff again.

"Attention, attention, Vasilikós and guests, it is my pleasure to announce Sophia, Muse to the Vasilikós of Greece and Italy, granddaughter to Grand Duchess Georgia of the Vasilikós of Greece and Italy, and daughter to Callista, Lady in Waiting to Grand Duchess Georgia and Muse to the Vasilikós of Greece and Italy."

The door opened and Sophie stepped out. For a second, Persephone held her breath because the young Muse was breathtaking.

"Too bad you'll be dead before the end of this evening," the goddess said with a smirk. "Maybe I can do it without much bloodshed. I would hate to ruin her lovely dress." Persephone focused her attention on the young couple, as the loud cheering died away and willed herself to hear the exchange between them.

"Hello, Beast," the Muse said.

He beamed. "I don't have words."

The Muse smiled back at him and slipped her arm into his. "Sometimes, words aren't necessary."

"I love you," he said.

"I love you, too," the Muse replied.

~ ☾ ~

Had she not been so intent on chaos, Persephone would have wept with joy. *It was too sweet. Such a shame. Well, such a shame that after I rip it off of her dead body, Sophie's dress will have to be taken in. That Muse is kind of pudgy. And just look at that miserable Gorgon mutt. It makes me sick.*

"Disgusting. I can smell the Gorgon from all the way over here."

Persephone caught Sophie's eye and blew a kiss to her. The goddess nudged the man standing next to her. He wore a black bird-beak mask that covered most of his face. He waved and Persephone could see the Muse fighting back tears.

"Enjoy it, while you can," Persephone said.

~ ☾ ~

Chapter 37

Much to Sophie's relief, she had made it through the curtsy marathon without a single Vasilikós leaving her for dead in that low, miserable position. With her final curtsy done, Bennett helped her kneel and she took her oath.

She watched Georgia making her way towards her and her heart leapt into her throat.

There's no turning back. Oh, God, what am I doing? Do I really want to do this?

Georgia took her place and began. "Sophia, Muse to the Vasilikós of Greece and Italy, do you pledge to serve this Vasilikós and its leader?"

It's your fate. Accept it. Sophie replied, "I do."

"Sophia, Muse to the Vasilikós of Greece and Italy, do you pledge to protect the Olympic Portal, thereby preserving the safety of Demigods and Humankind?"

"I do."

Georgia asked the final question. "Sophia, Muse to the Vasilikós of Greece and Italy, do you pledge to protect the mortals of this world without whom we would have no purpose, and do you also pledge to guide those mortals onto the right path, giving them free will to do what they will do?"

Sophie replied, "I do."

The crowd froze as it waited for Bennett to help Sophie to her feet and Angela to straighten Sophie's train.

"Everyone, I am blessed and proud to present my granddaughter, Sophia. May Zeus continue to smile upon us." Georgia shouted the words for all to hear.

Angela raised her arms, "Let the heavens rain down on us." Glitter and confetti fell from the ceiling onto the crowd. The entire room erupted into a roar as everyone rushed forward to congratulate Sophie, Callie and Georgia.

Thirty minutes of well wishes had passed when Georgia

~ ☾ ~

signaled the orchestra. Sophie, with the help of Bennett and Angela, took her place on the dance floor. Her train had been removed to allow her to dance.

"I could get used to this," Bennett said smiling, taking Sophie's hand and placing his as close to her waist as his height would allow.

In-between her second and third waltz, Sophie saw Georgia signal for the Fates' wine to be brought forward and placed into Georgia's hands.

After the third waltz, Sophie knew it was tradition for the newly inducted Muse to select another partner to dance with for at least one waltz. She scanned the crowd and decided now was the time. She could see her father and walked to him. He stepped forward, bowed and while smiling, extended his hand for her to accept. Without hesitation, Sophie took it. They faced each other and before they began to dance, he bestowed a single kiss unto Sophie's forehead. His lips were ice cold and left a painful burning sensation on her skin.

That's strange. My father never kissed me on my forehead. He always kissed me on my cheek.

Sophie didn't feel well. Her skin was on fire and the burning sensation was at its worst where her father had kissed her. She tried to walk away, tried to signal someone to help her, but before she could, he pulled her closer and whispered in her ear.

"We're in grave danger. Don't let anyone know you know. Unless you listen to me, we will all die."

"What are you talking about? Daddy, I'm not feeling so well. I need to stop."

"Listen to me," he said, beginning to waltz. "This ball isn't what you think it is. Persephone has tricked you. She's tricked us all. We aren't at the ball. We aren't even in the Vasilikós. Persephone has dragged you down into the Underworld. All of this is an illusion. We've got to get out of here."

He pulled her closer and Sophie was sure she was going to vomit. A wave of sickness fell over her and with feverous eyes she looked up at her father.

What is that awful stench? Is it coming from my father?

"Look around," he said. "This isn't a ballroom. It's the clearing in front of the River Styx. These aren't your friends.

~ ☾ ~

They aren't even Muses. They're demons. Hades has sent his demons to kill us."

She couldn't move her head. The pain shooting through her body was unbearable. She didn't know why she felt so awful. The ballroom was hazy, like asphalt on a hot Ohio highway. Things began to change around her. The polished wooden floors seeped with a foul-smelling muck and piles of the dead, their white bodies glowing, were scattered throughout the room.

Daddy's right, but I'm not in the Underworld. I'm in Hell.

To her right was a couple dancing beside them who smiled and nodded. The woman's face melted away, her skin bubbling and dripping, exposing a blistering, horrific face with burning red eyes. She laughed at Sophie. Her partner leered at her, causing his face to slice open in various spots, leaving the man's once handsome face into bloody shreds. They twirled around Sophie and her father, before disappearing. Every couple around her was changing into hideous creatures. A couple with reptilian skin and intertwined horns danced by them, while two half-decomposed corpses seemed to float by, their lifeless feet a few inches above the ground. Sophie stifled a scream as her father yanked her face back, forcing her to look up at him.

"Don't scream," he whispered. "Stay calm and we'll get out of this."

"Daddy, you're hurting me." She said, pushing his hand away from her chin. His nail scratched her chin and chills began to wrack her body.

She took her eyes away from him and looked to her right and then to her left. Every person around her was more horrific than the person next to them. A tall, monstrous creature dressed in what she knew was Bennett's kilt, swooshed by her, with a horrific Gorgon in his arms. The Gorgon had two heads fused into one. It screeched at her as its long, eel-like snakes whipped around, trying to bite anyone who was close. Several of the snakes ripped off pieces of flesh from several couples and they swallowed the chucks whole. Sophie covered her mouth and retched into her glove.

"You have to do it. You have to attack them. Focus. They're trying to stop me from helping you and I fear—I

~ ☾ ~

can't hold on much longer."

"I don't know how." Sophie began to weep. "Get me out of here, Daddy. I want to go home."

"Concentrate. Close your eyes and focus on my voice."

Sophie did as she was told. The sounds of the creatures around here began to die away. She heard her heart and her breaths calming as her father soothed her with his words. Suddenly his words changed and she was frightened.

"They killed me, Sophie. They murdered me as I drove home to be with you and Mommy. They took me away. How does that make you feel?"

The burning sensation associated with her powers began to build in Sophie's core and she fought the instinct to cry out in pain. Her blood was boiling and it scalded her veins as it coursed toward her heart and out toward her hands.

"Sad, angry.... furious," Sophie said, lost in her father's voice.

"What do they deserve for killing me, Sophie? What do they deserve for taking me away from you and ruining your life?

"I don't..."

"They ruined any chance for you to be happy."

"I used to be happy, back in Ohio."

"And now, where are you? You're surrounded by all of these freaks. These mutts with their filthy, Demigod ways are beneath you. You're pure, a true Olympian. That's why you feel so sick. That's why you have pain."

"Daddy, I feel so bad. I want it all to stop." Sophie whimpered.

"You have to wipe them off the face of the Earth. You have to do what is right. They killed me, Sophie. They, the Demigods killed me. They tortured me for hours, threw my body into our car and smashed it against a tree. They killed me. They're filthy mutts, aren't they?"

"They're all filthy mutts."

"What do they deserve?"

"They deserve pain."

"But why stop at that? What do they truly deserve?"

"They deserve to die. They all deserve to die."

"Then kill them. Kill them all, baby."

~ ☾ ~

Chapter 38

Callie stood next to Bennett and listened to the mindless chatter around her.

She was frustrated. The ballroom was hot and sticky, packed shoulder-to-shoulder with people. Even if she could ignore the deafening noise from all the conversations taking place, her gut told her something wasn't right.

Dread. Something is about to break and it isn't good. My gut is never wrong.

She couldn't concentrate with all of the distractions. She turned and watched Sophie dance with a man she didn't recognize.

No, that's not correct. He does look familiar. Who the hell is he?

The man's mask hid his face, expect for his jaw line and lips. He was whispering something in Sophie's ear. Her thoughts were interrupted.

"May I be so bold as to say you look beautiful tonight?" Bennett said to Angela.

"You may," Angela said. "Not that my many admirers haven't already told me many times over."

"I see," he said. "Would that include my Honor Guard who you keep undressing with your eyes?"

"I have not." Angela said and Bennett snorted.

Callie dug her fingernails into her palm, as she tried to focus. *Dear lord, give me the strength not to tell these two to shut up.*

"Okay, listen. He was asking me about you and I *was* going to tell him you were interested, but if you would rather me tell him otherwise." Bennett said

"Bennett, I would not be opposed to you mentioning I admire his swimming abilities."

"You admire his six-pack abs," Bennett muttered.

~ ☾ ~

"Yours didn't hurt your case for winning Sophie," Angela commented.

"Well, it took me a while, but she came around." Bennett said.

I think I'm going to be sick. Was I this vapid when I was their age? Probably.

"You almost lost her with your Miranda crap." Angela said.

"Miranda crap? What are you talking about?" Bennett asked.

"It's not my place."

"Oh, no you don't. You opened it up; now spit it out, Pandora."

"She knows you kissed Miranda."

"Yeah, over a year ago." Bennett glanced at Callie and shook his head no.

"You kissed someone else, other than my daughter?" Callie said, reluctantly turning her attention away from Sophie. When Bennett didn't have a quick answer for her, she went back to watching her daughter.

Sophie looks ill. Maybe I should go to her. No, I'll wait for her to signal. If she's sick, she'll signal for me to help her.

"I haven't seen Miranda for a long time. I haven't kissed anyone but your daughter," Bennett said to Callie. "What have I got to be forgiven for?"

"For kissing Miranda," Angela said. "You have to have known for the past several weeks Miranda has been serving as Sophie's personal assistant."

"Are you joking?" Bennett said. "Miranda isn't here. There is no way she could be."

"Isn't that her, over there?" Angela pointed across the dance floor and Bennett shook his head no.

"Angela, who is that?" Bennett asked.

"Who the hell is Miranda?" Callie asked, wanting to bring the conversation to an end.

"I have no idea who that is, but I can say it isn't Miranda. Even without the mask, Miranda was a redhead and several inches taller than that woman. I've seen her in the Vasilikós, but I have not kissed her. I don't know what bloody game she's playing, but it isn't funny."

Georgia walked up and grabbed Callie's arm.

~ ☾ ~

"What is wrong with you? Pay attention to the cues I'm giving you. We need to start the wine ceremony."

"Before you go, can we have a second?" Angela asked Callie.

"Not a good time. We're about to start the wine ceremony for the Fates." Callie said.

"Did you and Georgia assign a girl by the name of Miranda to serve as Sophie's personal assistant?"

"What are you two talking about?" Georgia said, overhearing part of the conversation. "Angela is Sophia's Lady in Waiting for this event and serves as her assistant. The only Miranda I know of was a young Muse who transferred to the Italy Vasilikós, but she's not here. She's on a special assignment in Milan."

"Out of all of the Muses to select from, why would we choose a girl who dated my daughter's boyfriend?" Callie said, but as the words left her mouth, they all turned towards Georgia.

"Do not even think it, Callista. If that girl is here, it has nothing to do with me," Georgia said.

"Georgia, look at me."

Georgia looked directly into Callie's eyes. "By all I hold dear, my position in our society, by my family, which you seem to believe I don't care about, I swear the only girl I assigned to Sophia was Angela. If you can't trust a *Gorgon* to keep your granddaughter safe, who else can you trust?"

Angela winced.

"Which girl are you talking about?" Callie asked. Angela scanned the ballroom and spotted her.

"There." Angela pointed.

Callie focused on the girl. "Well, she kind of looks familiar. Wait, very familiar, but I can't make her out because her mask is hiding her face."

Miranda waved to Callie. Digging her fingers into her face, she tore it off and threw it to the ground. The clay mask shattered when it hit the floor.

"Oh my God. Oh my God. No, no, *no.*" Callie said in a loud whisper and pulled Georgia closer. "It's Penny."

"What are you talking about?" Georgia said.

"Georgia, listen to me carefully," Callie said. "It's Penny. She's older, but it's Penny."

~ ☾ ~

Georgia looked confused.

"Penny? Pandora? Made of clay, Pandora?"

"It can't be. She was banished to the wastelands of the Underworld. There's no way she could have gotten free."

Callie was panicking. "I don't care where they put her. I'm telling you right now she is here."

"Dear lord. All the Vasilikós. This will not do."

"You listen to me," Callie said. "I don't care about any of that. My daughter is out there unprotected. *That* is what will not do."

A growl escaped Bennett's lips as his body strained against his clothing. "I remember the stories you told me about her. I'll kill her if she lays a hand on Sophie."

Georgia reached over and shot a burst of energy from her hand and shocked Bennett. "You will do no such thing. We will do this without making a scene. Everyone break up and search for her. I have the wine ceremony to perform."

Callie protested, but Georgia held out her hand. "We will not have an international incident to clean up. Do you hear me, Callista?"

Callie had tears in her eyes. "Okay."

Georgia gestured for everyone to get closer. "Now, the two of you spread out. Angela, you might want to let your hair down in case your talents are needed. Callista, you stay here. We can't let on something is wrong and too many people are watching you."

Angela reached over and pulled out the pins holding her hair in place. Her eyes flashed green and a single snake snuck its head out for a second and retreated.

"Okay, let's go," Angela said to Bennett, leaving Callie behind.

The music stopped and Stavros, the male Siren banged his staff three times.

"Attention! Attention!" the Siren shouted.

Georgia stepped forward, carrying the ancient decanter full of the harvested wine. The decanter was a gift to the Muses, from Dionysus and Amphityonis, god and goddess of wine. The decanter was compact but could hold a whole harvest's wine. This served the Fates perfectly, since their villa had limited storage space.

~ ☾ ~

Georgia began her introduction, and Rose grimaced. "She's such a blowhard," Callie overheard Rose comment to Agatha and Callie agreed. Agatha shushed Rose and told her to pay attention.

"As we have done so, for thousands of years, and as we will continue to do for thousands more, we bless our relationship with the Fates through the gift of wine. I remember my first wine harvest and ceremony..."

Callie watched Bennett working his way through the crowd.

Damn it, Penny. Where the hell did you go?

Bennett caught Callie's eye and pointed in the direction of the balcony. She saw Penny signal to a group of several men a few yards away from Bennett. They were looking directly at the goddess and gathered in a semi-circle. At the center of the semi-circle was Sophie, standing with her dance partner.

"It's a trap," Callie said, frantically signaling to Georgia. Not knowing what to do, Callie watched as a woman approached Georgia from behind.

Dear God, it's Persephone. But how is she out of the Underworld?

"Without further words, I present this year's harvest to—" Georgia said and turned to find Persephone smiling at her.

Georgia raised her hand to send an energy burst towards her, but Persephone was too quick and punched Georgia so hard the sickening crunch told everyone in close proximity Georgia's jaw was broken. The blow threw Georgia through the air and she landed in front of the wheelchair-bound Fates. The decanter had fallen out of Georgia's hands and Persephone grabbed it before it struck the ground.

"That's one way to shut the woman up," Rose shouted as she lifted her foot and gave Georgia as much of a kick as the elderly Fate could manage. "You should have held onto the decanter, idiot."

A huge burst of energy erupted in the center of the crowd and several people were thrown in all directions. Chaos broke out as several people screamed; trying to escape, but all the doors slammed shut. Some of them caught guests who thought they had escaped, their bodies shaking in pain as their bones splintered and broke.

~ ☾ ~

In the center of the fallen guests stood Sophie and the stranger she had been dancing with.

"They all deserve to die," Sophie said. "I want you all to die!" Sophie shouted, sending another burst of energy at a group of guests who attempted to defend themselves but were too weak against Sophie's power. She was drawing the energy from the room. She was drawing her energy from the guests she was murdering.

Oh, lord. The binding spell didn't hold. How could it not have held?

"Sophie!" Callie yelled. "Stop, Sophie!"

She saw her daughter turn her head and look at her.

She's seeing something, but it isn't me. He's controlling her.

Callie jumped out of the way before a burst of energy hit her. It struck Rhonda, the United States' Representative, in the center of her chest and the woman slumped over, lifeless. Callie cried out but knew she was too late to help her.

"Sophie...look at me. It's Mommy. You have to stop. I don't know what it is you are seeing, but you have to stop."

Another burst erupted from her daughter, except this time it struck the guest trying to escape through the jammed French doors. The explosion sent wood and glass shattering throughout the room.

Callie struggled to reach Sophie. She saw Bennett and Angela working their way through the panicking crowd, also trying to get to her. Callie was a few yards away, but the crowd trying to escape was pushing her in the opposite direction. She looked at the man standing next to Sophie and knew she had to break his hold on her. She watched as the man threw off his mask.

Angelo?

The air around the man shimmered and Callie knew right away it wasn't her husband.

My husband is dead. Who the hell is that?

Sophie shot several more energy bursts into the room and grazed Callie in the arm, making her bleed. Elena, the Russian leader, wasn't as lucky. She screamed, clutching her face, and fell onto the ground writhing in pain. Standing close to her was Helena, who was missing part of her right leg,

~ ☾ ~

from the knee down. Blood gushed from her wound, as one of her aides tore off a piece of her dress to tie a tourniquet around her leg and stop the bleeding.

Sophie's attacks were coming quicker and quicker, and no one seemed to have a chance to mount a counterattack. Callie saw Qiaohui crouching low and as Sophie had turned her attention to another group, the leader threw a burst of energy at the man standing next to Sophie. It struck him in the head and his head cracked open, exposing a hideous face.

It's clay. Callie realized.

Qiaohui threw another energy burst, but a burst from Sophie collided with it, and the Asian leader was thrown into several guests and knocked unconscious.

Sophie raised her hands to her head and held it. Callie was sure Sophie was going to pass out.

"Mom?" Sophie said before collapsing.

Callie was within a few feet from reaching Sophie when the twelve men, who had received the signal from Pandora, stretched out their arms and promptly exploded into shards of pottery, the blast and debris knocking a larger portion of the ballroom guests unconscious. The guests who managed to avoid the blast fled in terror through the broken French doors, as the creatures that were hidden in the clay shells took flight and began attacking them.

Callie tried to stand again, but threw herself to the ground, nearly colliding with one of the flying demons. The sound of tearing flesh and screams made Callie terrified for the wounded and dying around her. She could see some had already begun to heal, while others were too far gone to be helped. Right now, she had to stop Pandora and Persephone. She had to make sure Bennett and Angela were okay. She had to save Sophie.

Callie stood up and saw Sophie unconscious at the feet of her dance partner. Before Callie could react, the man picked up Sophie.

Pandora raised her hand toward the man and with a flick of her wrist liquefied his exterior shell, exposing yet another one of the hideous creatures.

Pestilence. My daughter is being held by one of the evils Pandora let out of her damn box. Callie didn't know what to

~ ☾ ~

do. She couldn't risk attacking the creature holding her daughter for fear of hurting Sophie, so she focused on Persephone as the electricity crackled around her.

~ ☾ ~

Chapter 39

Out of the corner of her eye, Pandora saw Sophie's tall mutt regain consciousness. She could smell the rage and fear building inside the boy, knowing full well it wouldn't be too long before he wouldn't be able to control himself.

"Finally, it's going to get interesting," she said.

She watched as the boy's muscles underneath his skin grow, expand and stretch. A low, guttural sound of pain came from his throat. She enjoyed the sounds of his pain, as he stretched and grew, and even winced as the sickening sound of bones breaking, growing, and fusing together filled her ears. Blood seeped out of his mouth as his jaw expanded and teeth pushed out of his gums to form fangs.

"Now that has got to hurt," she said, taking in the energy caused by his pain. It had been so long since she had experienced such horrific agony. It was delicious to her.

She was surprised how the extensive transformation only took a few seconds. Transformed, the boy was a ten-foot-tall Minotaur. Pandora knew now was the time to take care of the girl and she turned as the Minotaur roared at her and charged.

She laughed at him and raised both of her arms, levitating the shards of Persephone's former escorts off the floor. She knew the creature was going too fast to stop and she smacked her hands together, sending the jagged-pieces of pottery shooting towards him. They struck him in the head, pierced his limbs and torso, and with each impact he roared in pain, but he didn't stop.

She closed her eyes for a second and called her legacy to her defense. She didn't have to open her eyes to know they were there, her demons in all of their hellish glory, with their gnashing jaws and their leathery wings flapping with excitement. She reached over to the demon closest to her and

~ ☾ ~

her hand gently caressed its black flesh, which was covered in oozing sulfuric slime. Its yellow eyes glowed in ecstasy.

With her mind she commanded them to concentrate their powers on the Minotaur, bringing him to his knees.

"It's amazing how far concentrated evil can go," Pandora said, walking down the staircase, towards Bennett. "These creatures, the evils of the world, are my legacy. I carry them with me always. The gods thought they were cursing me for opening up the box, but little did they know they were giving me ultimate power."

Pandora raised her hand and used her will to pull Bennett toward her. She licked her lips as she watched pieces of debris slice into his flesh.

"I can only imagine the horrific visions you are seeing, paralyzing you with all of the human suffering and agony my evils cause in the world," Pandora said. She knelt to look him in the face. "For all of your strength and ability, you still aren't anything more than a disgusting Demigod born of inferior stock. You're nothing but a mutt." She kicked Bennett, sending him skidding several yards away from her. "Let me give you the honor of being the first I kill tonight. But first, I need to leave my mark on you."

She wondered if she'd made a mistake and walked towards the boy. He was too far away from her demons and she needed to make sure he continued to remain frozen so he could watch her kill his love. She reached him and noticed his eyes were shut and chuckled.

I'm being foolish. He's not going anywhere.

She began to gather her energy to brand the Minotaur mutt with the word Nothos. She saw him turn over and heard his roar before she sensed she was flying through the air.

That little bastard punched me. How dare—

She grunted as part of her torso caught the balcony railing and her exterior clay shell cracked. A piece of the wooden orchestra screen smashed against her face and she was sure her flight took her through the middle of the piano, cutting it in half. She blacked out, as she tasted the back balcony wall and saw a huge chunk of her face break away and crash to the floor.

~ ☾ ~

Chapter 40

Callie was attacking Persephone. She glanced over and saw Bennett's attack on Pandora. He clearly had used the last of his strength and lay unconscious as his body changed back into his human form, leaving the boy naked and bleeding. She thrust her hands forward and walked towards the goddess, hurling one energy burst after another, hoping she would catch the goddess off guard. But Persephone managed to deflect each of the bursts, sending them careening around the room.

Callie was exhausted. One energy burst struck a chandelier that crashed to the ground near Sophie. Not thinking clearly, Callie allowed her attention to be drawn away from Persephone as she made sure the chandelier hadn't hurt her daughter. Callie's pause allowed Persephone to send a powerful burst of energy that struck Callie with such force she was slammed into the wood floors, shattering them and breaking her ankle.

I can't fail. I have to keep them talking, delay them until I can heal, come up with another plan, do something. It can't end like this. I refuse to let Sophie die like this. Please God, take me, not my daughter.

"Why?" Callie demanded in anguish, somehow managing to get back to her feet. She limped towards Persephone. She wiped away the blood dripping from her mouth and nose with the back of her hand.

"Do you *really* need to know why?" Persephone said. "How about you start, Penny?"

"With pleasure," Pandora said as she made her way from the balcony. Bennett had hit the goddess so hard Pandora's exterior casing cracked in several places. She now had large chunks missing from her face and other parts of her body. With each step she took, large chunks of her shell fell off,

~ ☾ ~

exposing a wet, bubbling center of hot molten clay.

"Excuse my appearance, but in a few short moments the damage the mutt caused will be fixed. The molten clay you see allows me to regenerate body parts. It has also allowed me to take on the painful process of slicing off portions of myself to create the living clay figures that were part of Persephone's entourage. Thanks to Persephone's painting talents, my evils were able to pass for mortal."

Pandora smoothed out her hair. "Callie, for me, it's all about who I am. Don't get me wrong, revenge is part of it and I know that sounds so unoriginal, but it's all about what I was born to do. I was placed on this Earth by the gods to inflict pain into this world. I was the punishment of Mankind. But allow me to correct one historic mistake about myself. I wasn't torn up about whether or not to open the box. I *wanted* to open it because the sounds of sorrow and grief are music to my ears."

Callie saw a brief flash of Angela's dress and tried to get Persephone's attention.

Oh, thank God. I have to give Angela a chance.

"I'm sorry, Pandora. I don't mean to interrupt, but your babbling was boring me," Callie said. "Where exactly do you fit in this, Persephone? Is this really your style?" Callie asked.

"I have an adaptable nature, but I'm always up for a good time. Take this wine for example. No wine, no Fates. No Fates, no mortal future. No mortal future, no souls for Hades. And if there is one thing Hades still takes pride in it's his work. I know it's dysfunctional, but I'm not the one who cursed me to an eternity in the Underworld. My mother still weeps at my loss."

"Your mother has long since forgotten about you. In case you don't remember, she's locked away in Olympus and has other things to worry about."

"How dare you! Shut your filthy Nothos mouth. " Persephone shouted, shooting another energy burst at Callie. It struck her in the legs and her knees slammed onto wood floors again. But the pain didn't deter Callie from struggling back to her feet.

"You've lost your sense of style, Persephone. I'm sure you can do better than that," Callie said, throwing a burst back at

~ ☾ ~

the goddess, which almost brought Persephone to her knees. Persephone pointed to the decanter and gave a look to Callie, warning her if she tried that again, she would smash it.

Callie saw Angela had removed her shoes and was a few steps away from Pandora. Pandora faced the Gorgon, with Angela's snakes hissing and her green eyes burning with intensity.

"Now that is hysterical? A Gorgon? You disgusting, ignorant, filthy Nothos, I'm made of clay," Pandora said. She grabbed Angela by the throat, burning the Nothos brand on her neck. Angela screamed in pain and the goddess laughed as she threw her against the wall, instantly knocking the Gorgon out, the snakes in her hair retreating.

Callie's heart sank. She raised her hand, hoping she would be able to stage an attack. Persephone shot a bolt of energy that struck a few inches from Callie's feet. Callie put her hand down and stifled the energy building inside of her.

"Be a smart Muse and behave," Persephone warned.

"Persephone, can we cut to the chase?" Without waiting for an answer, Pandora walked towards the unconscious Sophie.

"What we have here is a choice?" Pandora said. "Your Sophia or your harvest?"

"Well, that's an easy answer," Rose said, "Muses are a dime a dozen. Screw the girl. Give us the wine."

Pandora leaned over and touched Sophie's face. "Pick, Callie. If it's the wine, then all we need to do is decide how Sophie dies. Pestilence could give her the plague or we can watch her suffer from an awful skin-rotting disease. With her being so close to him, I promise you it will be a quick death."

"So pick, Callie," Persephone said. "Your daughter or the lives of millions of unborn mortals and the destruction of the Fates?"

"You are a nasty piece of work," Agatha cried.

"Agatha, control yourself. We mustn't interfere," Rose said.

"Hurry, Callie, Sophie is running out of time," said Pandora.

Callie began to cry.

Georgia had regained consciousness and got to her feet. "Take me. Pandora, your fight is with me. Take me instead of my granddaughter."

~ ☾ ~

"Not an option," Pandora replied.

Persephone forced the older Muse to her knees with a mere glance.

Sophie coughed up blood and jerked awake with a gasp. With feverish eyes she looked at her mother. Callie saw Sophie was trying to talk and she knew her daughter would be dead unless she did something, but she didn't know what to do. She had to stall.

"I will hunt both of you down," Callie said, limping towards Pandora. "And when I'm done with you..."

Sophie said, "No, mama." Grabbing the creature holding her, she lifted her head and kissed its blackened cheek tenderly. Callie screamed in anguish, as she watched her daughter mount a final attack. Sophie shot a burst of energy through the back of the creature's head. Pestilence exploded and Sophie also hit by the energy burst was thrown roughly to the ground, her body lifeless. As quickly as it had disappeared, Pestilence reappeared and joined his fellow evils as they disappeared back into Pandora.

"Bottoms up," Persephone said. She tilted the wine decanter and began to drink.

Callie rushed towards Sophie, screaming, as Persephone threw the decanter down, smashing it.

"What the hell?" Rose said.

Pandora laughed and turned to run. She took only two steps when an Olympian in armor and tunic crashed through the ceiling, landing on top of her and crushing her into hundreds of pieces. Several pieces of Pandora continued to move on their own. Her left and right legs flopped on the floor and her right hand crawled towards her attacker. The god raised his right hand and clenched it into a fist, causing the moving pieces of Pandora to shatter. Pandora continued to scream until he located and crushed the shard of pottery that was her moving mouth.

The god looked around at the many Demigods lying either unconscious or dead. He lowered his head, clearly saddened by what he saw and grimly walked over to Sophie's lifeless body and knelt down, cradling her head in his hands. He wept.

"My poor little soldier. You were so brave," the Olympian said.

~ ☾ ~

A hysterical Callie tried to push the god out of the way. Tears and screams of sorrow came from deep inside her. He stood up, allowing Callie the chance to hold Sophie.

Persephone tried to look for an exit, but stopped as the ground shook violently and cracked open. Hades broke through the orchestra's staircase, sending debris shooting into the air as his chariot and horses rode past Callie and Sophie. Hades, still wearing jeans and an Ohio State University sweatshirt, jumped off of the chariot and walked barefoot toward his wife. "I think, my dear Saphie, you have caused enough trouble for today. It's time to return to me."

"Just when things were getting interesting," Persephone said, pouting. "You always have to ruin my fun."

"You've attempted to ruin the balance of this mortal world. It is a balance I have pledged to uphold."

"Why are you so serious? You know that's your problem. You can't kick back and...wait...what did you mean by attempted? I *have* ruined the balance. The Fates will cease to be. This world will wither and rot. And you, my dear, won't have any more new shades for your stupid book club and your ridiculous bridge night. You think I didn't know about that? You think I didn't know about your marriage counseling sessions?"

"Do you believe I didn't know what you were up to?" he asked her. "I'm the god of the Underworld. I know everything that happens in my realm. Had you drunk the real wine—"

"Real wine? You changed the wine?"

Hades glanced over at the other Olympian standing near Callie. "Perseus. It's been ages. Who let you out of Olympus?" Hades motioned towards Persephone. "This woman will be the death of me, Perseus."

Hades walked towards Persephone. "I've always been torn about the whole pomegranate seeds thing. It was a trick not worthy of the King of the Underworld. But you see, a shade, whom I have since allowed to cross over once, asked me if I wanted to hear the truth, and I'm surprised to find out that I do. Thanks to your need for chaos, I now have removed the one block that kept me from seeing who you really are. You aren't a victim damned to the Underworld anymore. You're a flawed, spoiled goddess with major mommy issues. With time

~ ☾ ~

and counseling I'm sure we can get you cured of your
obsession with death and destruction. This is the new
foundation our marriage will be built on. Oh, and by the way,
the wine you drank wasn't pressed from Georgia's vines. They
were pressed from the grapevine gripping the stone entrance
to the ferryman."

"Well, I wondered why the wine didn't finish as nice as....
Wait...You tricked me again. You made me think—"

"I did no such thing. You did it to yourself." Hades walked
to where his wife stood and threw her over his shoulders
while she kicked and protested.

"I will make you wish you never were born, Haddie. I hate
you. You will wish I never ate those damn seeds."

"Don't worry, Saphie," he said. "I'll bring you some
company." Hades snapped his fingers and the crushed pieces
of Pandora fell into a black box strapped to the back of the
chariot. Once the last piece flew into it, the box slammed
shut. Hades tugged on his reins and the horses charged,
taking the chariot back into the dark hole they had come
from, the rubble filling in.

Aletheria appeared in a cloud of ink and stood before the
remaining Olympian who watched Callie cradle Sophie.

"You must do it, Perseus," Aletheria said to the man. "It is
the only reason bringing you from Mount Olympus was worth
the risk. It isn't her time."

"I know," he said.

"Don't you do it, Perseus." Rose shouted from across the
room. "I just got finished cutting her thread. I hate
exceptions! Damn it, Cleo. Measure out another thread."

Callie had been so distraught at the sight of her lifeless
daughter; she didn't have a chance to look at the god who'd
defeated Pandora, but now watched as he took Sophie into
his arms and brought her cheek to his lips, kissing it lightly. A
burst of light shot from him, consuming Sophie.

Sophie screamed and writhed, gasping for air, and
coughing out the remaining blood from her windpipe. She
opened her eyes.

"Hi, Daddy," she said.

"Hi, baby," Perseus, formerly known as Angelo Drago,
replied.

~ ☾ ~

Acknowledgments

The journey from idea to finished work has been over five years for *Muse, Unexpected* and I would be remiss if I didn't acknowledge all of those individuals who supported me along the way.

To my publishers, Stephanie Murray and Marlene Castricato with Crescent Moon Press. Thank you for believing in Sophie's story and the crazy world I've created.

To the Crescent Moon Press family of authors. Your advice and friendship has been invaluable to me.

To my editor, Kerri Nelson. Thank you for your patience and for leaving me only slightly bloodied.

To Grace and Christine Day. Two Muses who never cease to inspire me.

To Reverend and Mrs. Charles Frederick. You've given me so much. I would need several lifetimes to thank you correctly.

Uncle Steven, for the last time, Olive will not do Spider-pig. Now stop asking.

Special thanks to the first person who ever said, "I love it"— Paula Friedrich, your love and support has meant the world to me.

You supported and pushed me. I love you, Aunt Maryann.

To my two youngest tween test readers, Sarah Thieken and Abigail Neibert, thank you, now go do your homework.

To the many supporters, whose continued belief and support were greatly appreciated. Thank you: Alice Patterson, Angie and Troy Halstead, Bev and Howard Hickman, Carolyn and Bob Hayzlett, Charley and Michelle Maghes, Chris and Milissa Ettrich, Colleen and Steve Andrasko, Dan and Melissa Parker, Danny and Marybeth Pierce, Deb Corder, Estelle Wallace, Frances Gagne, James Meyer, Jane Gilbert, Jean Herr, Jeannie Andrews, Jill Cottone, Karen and Steve McDaniel, Kelley Bright, Kirk & Jan Hilliard, Laura Dutton, Laura Gunn, Laurie Barr, Layne Ogden, Mark and Dennis Velco, Matt, Lorena, Max and Sophia Ritchey, Michael Casey, Michael Box, Michelle Umali, Rhonda, Joe, Josh and Rachel Weithman, and Susan Van Kley.

V.C. Birlidis

V.C. Birlidis grew up in Miami, Florida, but now calls Columbus, Ohio and its many seasons home. He earned degrees at Capital University and North Central State College. When he's not dabbling in the world of Muses, he works for the award-winning agency, SBC Advertising, as the Director of Marketing. This is his first novel. Visit him on the web at: www.vcbirlidis.com or on Facebook at www.facebook.com/vcbirlidis.